Choose your Lane to love!
Readers love
AMY LANE

More praise for
AMY LANE

Christmas Kitsch

"I've heard so many people talk about the virtues of this book and I'm glad to have the chance to finally read it myself and recommend it to everyone that hasn't been to the world of Rusty & Oliver."

—Love Bytes

"The story is written perfectly, the characters come to life and it is a storyline that happens all too often in real life. You get behind these two young men cheering for them as they build their lives…"

—MM Good Book Reviews

A Few Good Fish

"…this book is the perfect combination of romance and suspense, and pulls together the storylines that have been building up over the past two books just perfectly."

—Joyfully Jay

"*A Few Good Fish* is a riveting page-turner with high-stakes action scenes, an intriguing plot and two compelling, incredibly likeable central characters."

—All About Romance

A Fool and His Manny

"Reading this novel is like being enveloped is large, welcoming mommy arms or walking in the door home and getting the welcome you always dreamed about from the family you always wanted."

—Scattered Thoughts and Rogue Words

By Amy Lane

An Amy Lane Christmas
Behind the Curtain
Beneath the Stain
Bewitched by Bella's Brother
Bolt-hole
Christmas Kitsch
Christmas with Danny Fit
Clear Water
Do-over
Food for Thought
Freckles
Gambling Men
Going Up
Hammer & Air
Homebird
If I Must
Immortal
It's Not Shakespeare
Left on St. Truth-be-Well
The Locker Room
Mourning Heaven
Phonebook
Puppy, Car, and Snow
Racing for the Sun • Hiding the Moon
Raising the Stakes
Regret Me Not
Shiny!
Shirt
Sidecar
String Boys
A Solid Core of Alpha
Tales of the Curious Cookbook Anthology
Three Fates
Truth in the Dark
Turkey in the Snow
Under the Rushes
Wishing on a Blue Star

BONFIRES
Bonfires • Crocus

CANDY MAN
Candy Man • Bitter Taffy
Lollipop • Tart and Sweet

DREAMSPUN DESIRES
THE MANNIES
#25 – The Virgin Manny
#37 – Manny Get Your Guy
#57 – Stand by Your Manny
#62 – A Fool and His Manny

FAMILIAR LOVE
Familiar Angel • Familiar Demon

FISH OUT OF WATER
Fish Out of Water
Red Fish, Dead Fish
A Few Good Fish • Hiding the Moon

KEEPING PROMISE ROCK
Keeping Promise Rock
Making Promises
Living Promises • Forever Promised

JOHNNIES
Chase in Shadow • Dex in Blue
Ethan in Gold • Black John
Bobby Green
Super Sock Man

Published by DREAMSPINNER PRESS
www.dreamspinnerpress.com

Published by Dreamspinner Press
www.dreamspinnerpress.com

AMY LANE
STRING BOYS

REAMSPINNER PRESS

Published by
DREAMSPINNER PRESS

5032 Capital Circle SW, Suite 2, PMB# 279, Tallahassee, FL 32305-7886 USA
www.dreamspinnerpress.com

Cover Art
© 2019 Reese Dante
http://www.reesedante.com
Cover content is for illustrative purposes only and any person depicted on the cover is a model.

Trade Paperback ISBN: 978-1-64405-340-9
Digital ISBN: 978-1-64405-339-3
Library of Congress Control Number: 2018914539
Trade Paperback published May 2019
v. 1.0

Printed in the United States of America

This paper meets the requirements of
ANSI/NISO Z39.48-1992 (Permanence of Paper).

Mate and Mary—you guys had to live with it before I wrote it, while I was writing it, and now that it's done, I'll be mourning it for another year. Rayna, Karen, you guys put up with my inarticulate hand-waving and half-coherent plot summaries with good grace. Thank you, everyone, for being kind when I'm being ridden by the beast. Giving birth to a thing like this ain't easy.

Now

THE WIND hit Seth solid in the chest as he emerged from the back entrance of David Geffen Hall. Oh my God, the Hudson was unmerciful! Temperatures tonight threatened to sink to the thirties, with a healthy dose of sleet to seal the ice in any unwary traveler's veins. It wasn't even December yet—not even Thanksgiving.

It was Seth's first winter in New York, and his heart felt as cold as the wind.

"Hey! Seth! Come on! You said I could crash on your couch!"

Seth looked up and smiled gamely. "Yeah. Sorry. Just not used to the winters, you know?"

"You look sad," Caleb said perceptively. "You know, the offer still stands. I, uh, don't have to sleep on the couch."

Seth's heart felt too heavy for Caleb's usual flirting to even elicit a smile. "Definitely the couch," he said, pulling the solid wool of his coat up to his chin and making sure the violin case he was cradling against his chest under the coat was secure.

"Your performance was good," Caleb said earnestly, his pale face shining in the light from a nearby streetlamp. Together they were walking toward the 66th Street Subway Station. Seth's agent had managed to find an apartment on the Lower East Side—tiny, cramped, and stifling, even in April when he'd moved. It still boasted just enough living space for one person.

Of course, in New York that meant Seth had a bunk bed that he shared with his friend Amara, who was alternate flute when they needed one. Caleb could sleep on the couch.

Amara was home in Sacramento, where Seth yearned to be, visiting her boyfriend and her family. But Seth had two more weeks of performances on his contract.

He had tickets to Sacramento in December. *You've got to try*, he told himself. *Maybe if he sees you, he'll remember we're stronger together. It doesn't matter if he told you it was done.* Then, as he always did, he heard, *You'll never stop trying.* The insidious little voice gave him hope, and he warmed up some.

"Thank you," he said absently to Caleb. "That's kind."

Seth was a soloist, which was something he wasn't supposed to be in his twenties—everybody had said that as he was coming up. You had to be *really* good to play solo, to be first chair, to get a job in an orchestra, to play in New York at all. Seth had lived his life assuming he wasn't the guy who got to do those things special. It was always a shock to realize that every other violinist in the world didn't get the same opportunities he had.

Kelly had always said Seth was meant to walk among the stars… but that had only seemed possible when Kelly was there.

"It's not kindness," Caleb argued. "It's pure envy! My God—it's like the only part of you engaged is the part that connects with your violin!"

Seth shrugged. Old news. His family all knew what was in his heart, and that had always been good enough for him. Without Kelly there to understand the things Seth didn't say, it was like the good parts of Seth weren't there at all.

As though summoned, Seth's phone buzzed. He stiffened, there on the sidewalk as they approached the stairway to the subway station, because he knew. When it was Kelly texting, he *always* knew.

He pulled it out and read the message, biting his lip.

He's got maybe a week. Please, Seth, for Matty. Please come home.

Seth stopped and shuddered, his heart finally converted to ice.

But that didn't stop him from writing the message. Didn't stop him from pressing Send.

Not for Matty. For you, Kelly. All you had to do was ask.

"What is it?" Caleb asked, sounding worried. It didn't take a genius to see Seth was upset.

"I should pack," he mumbled, trying not to lose his head. "And I have to trade in my ticket for one on standby. I need to go home."

"Home?" Caleb sounded incredulous. "Seth, I don't even know where you come from!"

Seth shook his head, trying to keep his breathing even. Always, always, that amorphous threat, the long arm of the law reaching for a moment Seth couldn't remember—but it had never been enough to keep him away for this long.

"I come from a shitty school in a cow town," he said, knowing his voice was sharp and not sure how to fix it. There was more to his home than that; there must have been. He'd risked so much to return, time and time again. The last time, though, the time Kelly had frozen his heart, had been the time he'd risked and lost it all.

"I never fucking left."

Then

THE OLD school multipurpose room let in the most terrific draft, and the parents in the audience shivered. Wrapped in coats, mittens, and scarves, the collective assembly of the inner-city school tried to exude as much goodwill as humanly possible, while the babies in the many carriages in the aisles all whimpered or grizzled from cold or tiredness, and the younger children fidgeted, anxious to get their little hands on the free cookies lined up on the folding table in the corner of the cafeteria.

The program had started with the choir and progressed to the band, and the little ones had endured quite enough of hesitant voices and shrieking flutes, thank you very much.

Then Mrs. Joyce, sainted woman that she was, stood up and beamed at the mothers and fathers—some of them young enough to remember when she was *their* principal—and everything settled down as it should. Mrs. Joyce was a bosomy woman with skin of rich dark teak, who wore her tightly kinked graying hair back in the same bun she'd worn for the last thirty years. *Nobody* wanted to feel the weight of her disappointment fall upon their heads.

"So our next performance is entirely unexpected," she said warmly. "Mrs. Sheridan, our retired orchestra teacher, was given a donation of nine violins last year. She asked a friend to restore them, restring them, and tune them as a donation to the school, and then she picked nine volunteers—volunteers, mind you—who wanted to play the fiddle. The first hands that shot up were all young men, and we call them our string boys. Everybody, please give it up for Mrs. Sheridan and our string boys!"

BEFORE THE introduction, Seth Arnold peeped through the dusty scarlet curtain surrounding the stage and surveyed the crowd with a cynical eye. His best friend, Matty Cruz, shouldered his way underneath Seth's chin and did the same thing.

"Our mom's here," Matty muttered, trying to sound bored. "She had to bring the twins, but still…."

"Dad's here too," Matty's little brother, Kelly, chimed in, making the curtain gap wider. "See? Leaning against the back wall?"

Matty's shoulders relaxed. Their parents were separated, like a lot of parents, but their father was still trying.

Seth nodded at his best friend soberly. "That's good," he said, letting a little smile grace his lips. Matty and Kelly still believed parents could be kind. Seth was relieved his father wasn't in the crowd. He'd gone to great lengths not to let Craig Arnold know where he'd been after school for the past ten weeks.

When Mrs. Joyce got to the part about the boys being volunteers, everybody behind the curtain let out a silent groan.

Volunteers, Seth's scrawny ass.

They weren't volunteers. They were *sacrifices*, that's what they were! Mrs. Applegate, the new teacher, fresh and shiny and straight out of teacher school, was having such a heinous time with Seth and Matty's fourth-grade class—the class with twenty-seven boys and eight girls— that when old Mrs. Sheridan had come piping into the principal's office about wanting to teach *somebody* the violin, Mrs. Joyce had grabbed the first boys she could find, to give Mrs. Applegate a break.

Matty's little brother got stuck on the end because the musicians needed after-school practices as well. Since the boys walked to and from school together, period the end, Kelly got to pick up a violin too, even though he was only in third grade.

The main reason—the *only* reason, really—they'd all been so eager to keep up with the violin was that it saved them from having to deal with Mrs. Applegate's sorry attempts to teach long division. Mrs. Joyce had taken the boys into the computer room after their rehearsal and let them participate in online math tutorials. Even though the computers were dinosaurs and the room was freakin' hot, even in the wintertime, the math tutorials were still better than knowing Castor Durant was beating up three kids a day just because Mrs. Applegate couldn't keep track of the chaos.

Or it *had* been the only reason.

Last week, Mrs. Sheridan had dismissed the other boys to math tutorial and kept Seth in the multipurpose room for a moment.

Mrs. Sheridan was an old white lady. She had gray hair in braids around her head, like white ladies in the movies, and wore antique white blouses with ruffles. She might have ended up an unfortunate victim, just like Mrs. Applegate, but she was just so danged… nice. Consistently kind. Not stupid, just… nice.

And she'd politely asked Seth to stay in the room, and asked him to hold the violin under his chin like they'd been practicing for the last ten weeks.

"Now, Seth," she said gently. "You've done everything I've asked. Everything. I'm so proud of you. But I want you to do me a favor here—just a small one. Could you pull the bow across for the first note in 'Twinkle, Twinkle, Little Star' for me? Just once. Slowly. And I want you to close your eyes and hear the note as you make it."

She'd asked them to do this many times, and Seth fought off the temptation to roll his eyes before he closed them.

It was such a small request, and she always got so happy when they did what she asked.

How hard would it be to do what she asked now?

He held the bow loosely in his hand, making sure his fingers didn't brush the string, and kept the violin firmly under his chin. Then he let out his breath, and on the inhale, he dragged the bow slowly and surely across the string.

And almost forgot to breathe entirely.

For the first time since he'd come to the cafeteria, happy to be let loose from the everyday routine, he got to hear the noise he had the potential to make.

And it was lovely. Pure and perfect, beautiful in a way the music his dad played on their boom box at home had never been, the note wavered in the ancient multipurpose room with its cracked linoleum and missing ceiling tiles. And even though his eyes were closed, he suddenly saw his battered surroundings with an air of faded grace.

His bow finished its journey, and he let out his breath again and opened his eyes, stunned and in awe.

Mrs. Sheridan was beaming gently at him. "That was exquisite, Seth. Would you like to practice a little more, to see if you can get that sound again?"

Seth nodded at her, his eyes enormous. What the hell? He already knew how to do long division anyway.

So this night, the night of the winter concert, Seth was not particularly concerned that his father wasn't in the audience. He just wanted to make that noise—the pure one—the best he could.

"You ready?" Kelly asked, pulling his attention away from the audience for a moment. "You have to do that solo thing."

At eight, Kelly Cruz was about the cutest thing Seth would ever see. He was missing two teeth and had dimples on his little round clay-tinted cheeks. His mom had combed his loose curls tightly back, and only a few springlike strands sprang across his forehead, making him look impish. Adorable but capable of great mischief, Kelly was the one who spent hours occupying his twin sisters so his mom could talk on the phone, which was her job and helped them make the rent.

Like most of the students at Three Oaks Elementary School, Kelly and Matty weren't just one thing. Seth had shown up in the second grade with his speech all prepared. His father had gotten a job in California, and they'd moved up from Arizona, where he'd needed to say, "My mom's dad and mom are mostly black, and my dad's mom and dad are white. And my mom was mostly black. That's why I'm pale brown." Everybody in his old school had asked. But when he'd shown up at Three Oaks, nine out of ten kids had a complexion between his own pale tan and Mrs. Joyce's dark teak, while the few all-white kids showed up like a freakish neon pink. Nobody had seemed to care, and Seth had been grateful.

Kelly and Matty's dad was half Mexican and half white, and their mom was half black and half white, but they'd only told him that while they'd been playing cars at their house, because it was something to say. Not because they expected Seth to ask them so they could rank themselves by who was the most white.

And unlike in Arizona, where everyone had expected his dad to leave him with his mom's parents when his mom died, nobody in California asked about that either.

Seth liked Sacramento.

He could disappear.

Except he wasn't disappearing on the stage this night. Or if he did, it was the best magic trick ever, where he could play that violin and it would speak for him. Nobody had to see the boy attached.

All they would notice was that sound—that pure string sound, like the violin was crying—that he could make when his body was loose and his soul was dreamy and everything in the world was made of light.

Kelly's charming smile, his perpetual goodwill, told Seth that was possible.

"Yeah," Seth told him, smiling back quietly. "I'm ready to make that sound."

LATER, THE boys walked home with Matty and Kelly's mom. Matty took stroller duty because he wanted to be the man of the house, and while he talked to his mom about the concert, Kelly kept pace with Seth behind them.

"You were really wonderful tonight," he said, and Seth managed a smile for him. Seth didn't smile a lot. Matty often said he was mysterious, but the truth was, smiles attracted attention. Seth was just as glad to be invisible in his house.

But for Matty and Kelly, he'd smile.

"Thank you," he said, feeling shy. "So were you."

But Kelly shook his head, almost shaking off his red knit hat—a hand-me-down from Matty and a little too big around the ears. "No!" he protested, then winced when his voice carried. "No," he said a little more quietly. "I don't mean 'You're great!' and you say 'No, you're great!' This isn't a… a tradeoff, where I'm saying you're good 'cause I want to hear it back—"

"Don't you want to hear it?" Seth asked. He did. He'd been given a solo, and the audience had applauded wildly. For him. No, he hadn't grinned or preened or strutted—he'd given his usual small smile and bowed slightly, like Mrs. Sheridan had taught him.

"Only if I'm good," Kelly whispered, his words so honest, Seth's heart broke a little. "And you're… you were like a different animal. All of us were cats, and you were a lion. I want to hear you play again."

Seth's cheeks tingled, because he was blushing against the winter wind that had become colder close to the river. "I practice every day," he admitted softly. "I go home and practice before my dad gets home. You… you could listen to me sometimes."

"You practice at *home*?" Obviously, the ultimate sacrifice.

And Seth lowered his voice and admitted something to Kelly that he hadn't even admitted to Matty. "I like it when people say I'm good."

Kelly's brown eyes practically glowed. "You're good," he said reverently. "You're real good. You practice all you need to, okay?"

Seth looked away, even from Kelly, who only recently turned eight, and nodded. "Deal," he said softly.

Matty's mom asked Seth in for hot chocolate after he helped Matty get the stroller up the stairs to the top of the fourplex. Seth and his dad lived in the two-bedroom apartment downstairs, but Matty and Kelly needed a room, and the twins—Lily and Lulu—needed one too, and Matty and Kelly's mom, Linda, had one as well.

Seth sipped his hot chocolate and stared at the small Christmas tree that stood in front of the landing window in a haze of colored lights, and listened as Matty proclaimed his relief to be done with all stringed instruments, at least for a while.

"But Mrs. Joyce says we may have to practice for the spring concert too," he finished, deflating.

"We need to practice," Kelly said pragmatically, "so we can walk Seth home."

Matty got the same look on his face that he got when Seth was trying to help him with his math. "Why does Seth have to do it too?"

"Because Seth's really good," his mom said, laughing a little. When Seth got old enough to appreciate grown-ups being pretty, he would always think Matty and Kelly's mother was the gold standard to pretty people. She had glossy brown hair that she pulled into a thick ponytail, lush lips that often curved into a smile, skin the color of pale clay—darker than white but light enough to show blushes on her cheeks easily when she was pleased, and the biggest, brownest eyes Seth would ever see in anybody other than her son, Kelly.

She was lovely, and her smiles always made Seth feel warm.

"Thank you," he mumbled, embarrassed and pleased.

"No," she said seriously. "Thank *you*. I know you three had to work hard to be string boys this year, but I think you should keep going. Matty, Seth doesn't have a mom or an older brother. He needs you to keep him going to practice. Kelly, you're the best cheerleader in the world—I know you'll help him out." She bit her lip and looked a little sad. "Boys, I know your father tells you that you need to play sports to be men, but sometimes all you need is to do something really super good, and work to do it better. That's what it takes to be men." She eyed Seth thoughtfully. "Seth, sweetheart, I think being a string boy is your thing."

Seth nodded soberly and took a sip of his chocolate. He didn't want to argue with her. He loved this idea. But he didn't like being the center of attention either.

"Fine," Matty said, sounding bored. "Fine. We'll be string boys one more year. But after that, we'll just walk him home from practice. Playing the violin isn't anything I want to do any more than soccer!"

"Understood, Little Man," Linda said, her face completely straight.

Seth wondered at first if he was the only one who could tell she was laughing kindly at her son's machismo. Then he caught Kelly rolling his eyes, and he smiled back.

For once he was in on the joke.

There was a knock at the door then—not scary. An asking knock.

Seth jumped to his feet, and Linda gave him an understanding look.

"It's okay," she said softly. "You won't get in trouble for being here. Besides, I don't think it's him." She frowned as she moved from the tiny kitchen to the door. "Javi?"

Matty and Kelly's dad stood outside, an obviously newly purchased bouquet of flowers in his fist and a small bag of toys dangling from his other hand.

"Hi." Xavier Cruz was a barrel-chested man with a blocky head who wore giant denim cargo shorts and oversized sports shirts all year round. Tonight he wore a thick navy peacoat over the ensemble and a shy, tentative look on his face. "I… I wanted to tell the boys congratulations. And say hi. And see the girls. I should have called, I know, but I didn't know if I could get the second job off, and—"

Seth never knew why they had split up in the first place. He was a child, and they were grown-ups, and he wouldn't have asked anyway. But for the rest of his life, he would remember what forgiveness looked like.

"Come in, Javi," Linda said, smiling shyly back. "We were celebrating."

Xavier ducked his head. "That's awesome. Is that hot chocolate?" His look held a terrible hope.

"Sit down—I'll get you some."

Matty and Kelly's dad walked inside, laughing when Lulu, the more adventurous of the twins, who had a head full of fine black curls like Seth's except his were yellow, ran headfirst into his legs. "Lulu-bear! Come here!"

And that was the signal. All of the children, Matty included, ran to embrace their father, and it was time to leave.

Seth set his chocolate down quietly and walked through the kitchen toward the door, but Linda stopped him. "Sit down, honey. I'm breaking out the cookies, and you don't want to miss that."

Seth gaped at her, but then Matty and Kelly's dad stuck his head into the kitchen. "Come on out, Seth. I got you a present too—you played real nice."

Seth's face heated. "Thank you," he stammered.

Xavier winked and walked to the sink, the grocery store flowers still clutched in his fist. "Wanted to make sure they got water," he said, looking shyly at Linda again. She glanced away, biting her lip, and Seth wouldn't have made it to the door anyway without getting between them. He turned around just as Xavier touched her shoulder and she murmured something about a vase, and they probably kissed after that, but Seth was already in the living room again.

"Look!" Matty said, waving three Hot Wheels triumphantly in front of him. "Dad brought presents, and Christmas isn't until next week!"

He thrust a small rectangular fire truck into Seth's hands, and Seth turned it around delightedly. "That was really nice," he said softly. "I have to remember to say thank—"

At that moment, they all heard the slam of the door to the apartment below them.

Seth's skin went cold. "I have to go," he said simply. He looked to the table where his violin case sat, and thought of the consequences of his father coming home so late and what they might mean for the fragile instrument he'd come to love. He'd gotten all of his practice in well before Craig Arnold had any idea what he was doing. "Watch my violin for me?" he asked, not wanting to know what Kelly and Matty's sober nods might mean. He swallowed. "And the car," he whispered, pushing it into Matty's hand. "I'll get them tomorrow."

They could all hear Seth's dad knocking about in the apartment below. "Mrs. Cruz, Mr. Cruz, I gotta go!" he hollered, and then, bypassing the kitchen, he ran around the living room to the landing, grabbing his coat from the peg before he hit the door.

His father was still kicking off his boots and hollering his name by the time he slid inside.

"Seth!"

"Right here." Seth kept his voice even, because the consequences of shouting back were terrifying.

Craig Arnold turned around, displeasure written large on his once-handsome face. Seth had seen his parents' wedding photo. His mother had been beautiful, golden-eyed, with skin of pale bronze, black curly hair. His father had been just as pretty—narrow peach-toned face, blond hair even as an adult, and eyes about three shades darker than his new wife's.

He'd smiled in all of Seth's baby pictures.

But once Kesha Arnold passed away in a car wreck, all smiles stopped. "Where were you?"

"There was a school assembly. I went with the neighbors. They walked me home."

Craig nodded. "Get ready for bed," he said gruffly, and Seth gave a sigh of relief. Not tonight, maybe.

He was pulling on his pajamas—they were tight, showing his wrists and ankles, but that was the only size he had—when he heard his father's heavy tread down the hall.

"What kind of school assembly?"

"Christmas," Seth said and then wished he'd lied. Their apartment was painfully bare. None of his projects on the wall. He kept them all in a folder under his bed. No family pictures—no pictures, period.

And no tree, no lights, no decorations.

"Christmas?" Craig scowled. "Since fucking *when*?"

"It's next week. There were people singing and a band and…." He swallowed. "Violins."

"Aw, man."

Seth's heart dropped for a moment.

"Pretty? Was it pretty?"

"Yeah."

"Sorry about Christmas," Craig slurred. He must have had another swallow or two while Seth was dressing. "This was a good thing?"

"It was pretty," Seth told him. "Fun."

Seth could hear his father's uneven temper spike. "Like I'm not?"

"I was part of it." He hadn't wanted to tell him, but… but Craig was his *father.* Once upon a time, he'd smiled at Seth. He'd held him gently. This—this hadn't happened overnight. They'd moved to Sacramento, and they'd been all alone.

"You didn't think I'd want to go?"

"I didn't want to bother you," Seth said, hating where this seemed to be going. It had only happened once before, but it was enough to make him walk on eggshells.

"You fucking embarrassed of me?"

A spark of anger shot up Seth's spine. "I thought you'd be too busy at the bar," he replied baldly, retreating to the corner of his room.

He made it two steps before his father's heavy hand caught him across the face. Then another blow hit across his chest, and he went flying into the coffee table, catching it painfully across the thighs.

It hurt, but he tuned out the pain. He was good at that. It was like tuning out the lack of a Christmas tree or the way his once smiling father had become this terrible alien, a thing to be afraid of. In his head, he heard the lone, pure note of the violin.

He finally dragged himself to bed, where he pulled the covers over his head to hide from his father's broken sobbing.

"I'm sorry… I'm sorry… I'm sorry…."

Now Seth cried. He'd been sorry the last time. Sorry enough to quit drinking for a week, to be home on time, to try to make up for the bruise on Seth's face.

But was there a way to be sorry enough to make that stick?

Daddies

HAVING THEIR father back was really the best part of Christmas, Kelly thought.

After Seth ran out of the house and their mother got the girls to bed, Matty and Kelly climbed up onto Daddy's lap, even though Matty was a little too big, and Kelly probably was too.

But they hadn't seen him in a week, and he was there, in the apartment. And he'd brought their mother flowers, and she was smiling softly at him.

Oh, they'd missed him.

He'd been there for their soccer banquet and wanted to know all about indoor soccer and if they were going to play again this year.

"Only if we can still walk Seth home after violin practice," Kelly said staunchly.

"He can't walk home by himself?" Daddy asked.

"He needs us," Matty told him, and Kelly let out a little sigh of relief. Matty was the leader. "Other kids will beat him up."

There was a thump below them, and Kelly and Matty both jumped and hunched their shoulders. "Or maybe not kids," Matty muttered.

They'd seen Seth's bruises that one time.

Another thump sounded, and Mom walked back into the living room, wincing. "Oh no," she said. "Not again."

She went back into the kitchen and picked up her phone from the charger.

"Wait!" Dad said, standing up. "What are you—"

"Calling the cops," Mom said, voice low. "He swore the last time it would never happen again, but Seth's been terrified. He's obviously drunk again. Maybe they'll bring CPS in and Craig will stop for good. Or Seth will get put somewhere else. It sucks, but it's all I can think of!"

"Why don't you—"

And for the first time since Dad walked in, Mom got that scrunched-up look on her face. "What? Go down and knock on the door so he can belt me too? Not when I'm the only adult home, Xavier!"

Dad looked stricken, then nodded. "Yeah," he said. "I hear you. I'll go down. I… I might not be back soon. I'll text you to go down and get the boy if this goes how I think."

Mom tilted her head. "Where do you think it's going?" she asked.

"Same place I went," he replied with a crooked smile. "I was gone for a month, Linda. With a couple of half days off because I asked permission and signed myself out. Twenty-eight days to be exact." He looked away. "I was going to tell you—"

She stopped him with a kiss. "You really mean it," she murmured. "You mean it about changing. You never did that before."

"I mean it. Let me go talk to Seth's dad, okay?"

She nodded and let him go.

Kelly would wonder later why they weren't scared when he walked out the door. He texted Mom an hour later and told her to go down and get Seth, that he'd be staying with them for a couple of weeks, and that he'd be back by morning.

But when Kelly's life had fallen apart again and again, he'd remember his father walking into a potentially dangerous situation, just assuming he'd be back. Because that's what people who loved you did, right? They came back.

Well, they did that night.

AND WHEN they woke up, Seth was asleep on the couch. He spent that Christmas with them and helped bake cookies and decorate, helped watch the twins. He didn't go back to his own place until after they started school again, after he started playing the violin again.

After school, Matty and Kelly would join him for practice and then walk him home. Sometimes they'd go to indoor soccer practice, and Seth would play the violin alone in his apartment until it was time to come upstairs for dinner.

And sometimes, Kelly would have to watch the twins with Matty, because Mom needed to work.

But sometimes, Kelly would sneak downstairs, just to listen to Seth. When they played together as string boys, Seth was still a lion and Kelly still played like a goat.

But Kelly loved to see Seth being a lion.

He loved the way Seth's green eyes glowed when he was playing something hard, something no boy his age should be able to practice, and he was doing it right.

He loved the way Seth's lips curved into a smile when a piece was long and slow, and he had to concentrate on just the pure sound of the string.

He loved the way Seth's tightly kinked blond hair fell loose out of its gel by the end of the night, clustering over his brow.

He loved the way Seth smiled shyly at him when practice was done, as though coming out of a dream and Kelly was the face he needed to see when he woke up.

Kelly especially loved that last part.

Even after Seth's daddy came home and started working again, Kelly would still listen to Seth play. His mom had quietly told him to mention if any bruises showed up on Seth's face after that, or if he seemed scared any more than usual.

Kelly wasn't sure what words to say to open up the tightly locked box of Seth Arnold. Even at his most animated, Seth spoke quietly, in as few words as he could.

But when he came out of that moment, out of that practice, when he smiled at Kelly and offered him something to drink from what was often an empty refrigerator, *then* he would talk.

"I like that piece," he said one day in March. "It reminds me of spring."

"Me too. What are you doing for Easter?" Easter was one of the three days a year Kelly's family went to church, the big Catholic one in downtown Sacramento. Kelly and Matty privately agreed that doing it every Sunday would be the worst, but dressing up on holidays wasn't so bad. It seemed to make that day seem more special.

Seth frowned. "I don't know." He looked at the table uncertainly, where a bag of decorations sat. "I was supposed to decorate the apartment before he got home."

"I'll help you!" Kelly bounced on his toes a little. He loved art things.

"Sure. But, you know, once my dad gets here, you gotta go."

Oh yeah. He remembered all those crashing noises and Seth's black-and-blue face on the night Kelly's dad came home.

"Has he…?" Kelly pulled out a package of brightly colored paper eggs and some tape. "Has he… you know…?"

Seth shrugged. "Naw. He said he was sorry for all that." But Seth still grabbed the stuff out of the package tentatively, like he was afraid to rip it.

"Sorry?" Did that work? Did adults say sorry for things and it just went away?

"He hasn't done it since," Seth defended. "He gets home on time, right after work." He gave Kelly one of his guarded smiles. "I just don't want to bother him, you know, with the violin."

Yeah, well, Kelly would have been walking on tiptoes too if his daddy beat his face up. But Kelly wasn't going to say anything to make Seth feel less safe.

"Then we'll go really fast," Kelly said. "So he thinks you did it right after school."

Seth nodded, and they strung the Easter banner up in the window and carefully taped the colored eggs there too. There were spangles that they taped over the couch, and plastic eggs that were supposed to go in a bowl on the small table. Kelly made Seth laugh by pretending he pooped them out himself and plopped them on the rug, which was totally gross. But Kelly didn't care.

He got Seth to laugh.

It was a perfect gift.

They were so involved laughing, they didn't even notice when Seth's dad came in—quiet, this time, and smiling.

He and Seth had the same smile.

Seth saw him first and started picking up the eggs super quick. "Sorry, Dad. We were just messing around, but see? We got everything else done, right? See?"

"Yeah, Seth," his father said, voice sounding gruff but not mad. "It looks good. Kelly, you don't have the right equipment to lay eggs. You're going to have to buy them from the supermarket like everybody else."

Kelly laughed, because it was a good joke.

"Okay, Mr. Arnold," Kelly said, grinning and showing off his lost teeth. Third grade was the year of nobody having any teeth. Kelly liked it very much because all the smiles were equally ugly, and he could show his off, just like everybody else. "I'll put these in a bowl, then, howzat?"

"Good job," Mr. Arnold said. "What are you doing here, Kelly? I thought you had to watch your sisters today."

"Yeah, usually, but Mom wasn't feeling good, so she took a nap with them, and Matty had homework. I came down to listen—" *Oh no! No!* He wasn't supposed to listen. God, he was bad at lying. "—help. I came down to help Seth put up the Easter decorations. They look real good, Mr. Arnold. Way better than at Christmas. I helped put the eggs in the window. Don't they look good?"

"Looks great, Kelly," Craig said, like he was humoring Kelly, but since Kelly was babbling, that was okay. "What were you listening to again?"

Kelly looked at Seth unhappily, but Seth didn't get mad or anything that Kelly spilled the beans. "I was practicing for the spring assembly," Seth said, putting a handful of plastic eggs in the bowl with Kelly's before going to find the others on the floor. He was acting like there wouldn't be a follow-up question to that, but Kelly was pretty sure adults weren't that stupid.

"Singing?" Seth's dad sounded genuinely interested, so Kelly looked at Seth, pleading with his eyes.

"No," Seth said, but whether to Kelly or to his father, Kelly couldn't be certain.

"Poetry?" Mr. Arnold said, and for the first time ever, Kelly looked at him and realized he was pretty too, like Seth. His skin was paler, and his hair wasn't super curly, but he was very much Seth's daddy. He even had the quiet smile that made Kelly want to make Seth laugh so much more.

"No," Seth told him, arranging the eggs carefully in the bowl.

"Seth!" Mr. Arnold laughed. "What are you doing for the spring assembly? I'm curious. I'd like to go see you!"

And the look on Seth's face was a terrible mixture of hope and fear. Oh! Seth wanted his daddy to be proud of him, but who was proud of the violin? Matty and Kelly's dad *said* he was proud of them, but that didn't stop him from swooping them up on Wednesdays and taking them to indoor soccer.

"He plays the violin!" Kelly burst out, the pressure so bad that he felt like he had to pee.

Nobody said anything, so he kept going. "Me and Matty play too, but Seth plays it best of all of us. He plays best of all the string boys. That's what Mrs. Sheridan calls us. String boys. I sort of want a T-shirt that says *string boys*, but Mrs. Sheridan says we can barely afford the violins."

Still, there was no response.

"Not that my violin's so great—there's a big chip off the bottom, and I'm pretty sure that's why it sounds so whiny, but Seth got the good one. His violin always sounds perfect. He can make it sing, sad, like on the radio. Someday his bow will get faster and he'll make it funny, like 'Turkey in the Straw.'"

Mr. Arnold was looking at Kelly in surprise, and, well, that was a lot of information in one go. Kelly knew that, but Seth was staring at them both, stricken, and Kelly didn't know what else to do but babble.

"Have you heard 'Turkey in the Straw,' Mr. Arnold? It goes really fast, and it's like all the ice cream truck songs. It goes dee-dee-dee-dee-da-dee-dee-dee-dee—"

Mr. Arnold was holding up his hand and laughing. "I know what 'Turkey in the Straw' sounds like, Kelly. I did *not* know that Seth could play it."

"I can't!" Seth said, sounding panicked. "We're learning that for the big assembly in June. It's not ready for spring assembly. Spring assembly is scales in rounds. And parts. But not—"

"Seth," Mr. Arnold said, his expression deepening to worry. "I'm not angry. I...." He looked away, and Kelly thought he looked sad and maybe ashamed. "I understand why you wouldn't have told me earlier. But how long have you been playing the violin?"

Seth looked at Kelly, who shrugged.

"October? Right, Seth? We started the beginning of October, and then practiced through Thanksgiving, and then we did the Christmas concert. You remember the Christmas concert, right? It's the night my daddy came home and...." Kelly trailed off and looked at Mr. Arnold's face. "You might remember that night."

Mr. Arnold nodded. "I do. Seth, don't be afraid to practice violin in front of me, okay?"

Seth's expression was... hurt. And angry. "I don't know if you'll feel like that all the time," he said, his eyes shiny. "What if you come home one day and hate it and break the violin? It's the school's, and it's expensive, and I love it, and—"

Mr. Arnold held up his hand. "And I haven't earned your trust yet," he said sadly. "I... I'm lucky I'm here to do it at all." He nodded to the kitchen. "I'm going to make some spaghetti for dinner. You boys can go play in your room, okay?"

Seth nodded angrily and ran into his room, and Kelly followed.

"I'm sorry!" he said as soon as the door was closed. "I'm sorry. I didn't mean to tell him everything. I just—"

Seth shook his head. "It's not your fault," he muttered. "I just... I'm so confused. If I knew he was going to hit me, I'd know what to expect. But now he's... he's nice. And I don't remember him being nice in so long. And I'm so afraid, because what if he gets mean after he's been nice—it's so damned scary when you don't know!"

Seth curled up on his bed then, miserable and tense, and Kelly patted his arm gently, like he did when the twins were crying. He didn't say anything about Seth using the grown-up word. He figured fourth graders got to do lots of stuff he didn't get to do in the third grade.

"Maybe… I don't know," he whispered. "Maybe just hope? We kept hoping our daddy would come back, and he did. Maybe you just keep hoping that this is the real daddy and not the mad one. And maybe it will be true, you think?"

Seth nodded, but he didn't look any less tense. Kelly just crouched there, patting his arm, until there was a knock on the door.

"Seth? Kelly?" It was Kelly's dad, and Seth scrambled up so quickly, Kelly fell on his ass.

"Daddy?" Kelly ran to the door. "Daddy, what are you doing here? Seth's daddy was making spaghetti. Is it done?"

Daddy shook his head. "No, son. We turned off the spaghetti. I think Seth's going upstairs to eat with us tonight. We need to go to a meeting."

Kelly knew his eyes got huge. "You and Seth's daddy work in the same place?" *How marvelous!*

His dad laughed. "No. We have some of the same friends. Seth's daddy got sad tonight—"

"Because Seth plays the violin?" Oh, he did not understand why this was such a big deal!

"No." Daddy crouched down and looked Kelly in the eye, and Kelly knew it was important. "Because he did bad things, and it's hard when you do bad things and hurt the people you love. He knows it's going to take a while before Seth can forgive him. He needs some help dealing with that so he doesn't drink some more."

Oh. Kelly nodded, only a little confused. "Seth is afraid he's going to hit again."

"Yeah, I know. Seth gets to feel like that. His daddy is the one who's got to work at making him believe he won't. Tonight's a hard night, so you take Seth upstairs and get some food. And did you guys decorate the apartment? It looks really good."

Kelly grinned. "I put the paper eggs up on the window."

Daddy nodded. "Nicely done. Seth?"

Seth just looked at him. "Sir?"

"We'll be home before bedtime. Don't worry. Your daddy wants to keep coming home and being your daddy. Is that okay?"

Seth nodded, his expression unreadable.

Kelly's dad sighed. "Sure, it is. Come on, boys. Let's get moving. Mom needs to know we've got one more for dinner."

And that was that.

SETH'S DADDY and Kelly's daddy went to lots more meetings together, but fewer and fewer over time. Soon it was down to once a week, but they never missed that once a week, and Kelly's mom said that was a good thing. Pleasing Kelly's mom was a big deal to Kelly's dad—her belly was getting *big*. By the time the end of the year concert rolled around, one of the girls could sit on that belly and dangle her legs.

But the end of the year concert was *wonderful*. Seth's daddy bought Seth a new shirt, made sure he did his hair, and bought him new shoes.

They all dressed up pretty and walked to the school together, and Seth played "Turkey in the Straw" and a slow song, something in C, which Kelly didn't understand because C was a note they played all the time and having a whole song in it didn't seem that big a deal, but Seth played the song like… like… like angels and starlight and the purest song of God and church and Christmas all wrapped into one.

It *was* a big deal, and both of their fathers were in the audience, listening to them.

Seth's daddy cried.

Kelly hadn't seen a daddy cry since his mom kicked his own daddy out of the house and told him not to come back until he got his shit together. And now he had his shit together, and Seth's daddy did too, and they were all playing music and getting ice cream afterward and that was the best thing.

No.

Scratch that.

Kelly got to see Seth's face, beaming and lovely, as he finished something in C.

He was the most beautiful thing Kelly had ever seen, and if Kelly had been a grown-up and Seth had been a grown-up, Kelly would have kissed him. It was so beautiful, and Kelly wanted all that beauty just gobbled up in his heart.

It wasn't until he was a little older that he realized this moment—this moment of seeing Seth happy, on stage, showing his beautiful soul to the world—was the moment he fell irrevocably, implacably, forever in love.

Baby Steps from Home

"OH NO!" Seth whispered harshly, peering out from behind the curtain.

"What? Didn't they make it?"

Seth glanced affectionately at Kelly, who was still hanging on to the violin, mostly, Seth was beginning to suspect, to keep Seth company. Matty, God love him, had quit after the fifth grade, but Seth and Kelly had been playing for two years.

"No, they made it," Seth muttered, seeing his father in the audience. He closed his eyes, hating the awkwardness. Two and a half years—it had been two and a half years since his dad had gone to rehab and come back a changed man.

And he *had* changed.

All of the promises he'd made—no more hitting, dinner every night, activities on the weekends, *being* there—Craig Arnold had taken that shit seriously. Seth had to give him that.

And Seth was grateful. So grateful. Not just for not being used as a punching bag, but because the world was starting to feel… solid again. It was like those dark times, right after they'd moved to Sacramento, were just a bad dream, and the better times now were what was real.

Now, when he didn't tell his father things, it wasn't because he was afraid he'd make him angry. It was because he was afraid of… changing things. They'd made a big change in second grade, coming from Arizona to here. For a while, that change had meant… bad things. Bad things all the time.

But he was keeping his grades up, and he was practicing the violin all the time, and… and he was getting promoted to the seventh grade, which meant a different school and different teachers and….

And it was all going to shift again.

And that change would be even worse if he couldn't keep Mrs. Sheridan away from his father.

"They're there, right?" Kelly said, peering through the curtain. Then he groaned. "No… no. Mom brought everybody!"

Everybody was the twins, now almost ready for kindergarten themselves, and Agnes, who was almost two. Seth had a special fondness for Agnes—he'd seen Linda and Xavier bring her home brand-new. When she'd been tiny, he'd held the bottle of expressed milk for her while Kelly and Matty had chased Lulu and Lily around the house so Linda could get a little bit of work done. He'd held Agnes's hands as she'd learned to walk and read her stories while Matty was getting the other two girls their baths.

All of the girls were special—they were like his little sisters too. But Agnes was… *his*. His dad had teased him gently about picking out a little sister just for himself, and he'd actually smiled.

"I don't mind your little sisters," he said to Kelly.

"But Agnes is gonna go nuts when she sees you on stage," Kelly muttered. "And when you and Matty are up there for the promotion thing, we'll be lucky if Mom and Dad can keep them from swarming you guys."

"My dad's there too," Seth offered, then bit his lip. Well, his father really *had* changed, right? He'd watched all the kids once every other week or so, so Kelly and Matty's parents could go to the movies.

Seth wondered if his dad ever wanted to go out with a girl himself, but he never asked.

It was one of those changing things he didn't want to do.

"Crap!" Seth muttered. "It's time to go out there!"

The choir had finished, and the band too. Mrs. Sheridan stood up and asked her string boys to come up on stage.

Then she did something that blew Seth's mind.

"Now, before we have the boys play," she said in her sweet, high-pitched voice, "I want to introduce you to someone very special. Dr. Barnard Boyle has taught music at CSU Northridge for the past ten years, and has had some very prominent students go on to play in the LA Symphony. He's now working at UC Davis, and as part of an outreach program, he's coming to Joseph Crocker Junior High to teach music to our newly promoted string boys. He's been working with our students—one in particular—to perform this next piece. Now, I haven't talked to every parent, but for those of you who haven't heard from me, please find me after the ceremony today. I have the paperwork to get your child enrolled and on the bus to Joseph Crocker. Don't let me forget to hand it to you in person."

Seth grimaced and looked down at his toes so he could avoid his father's irritated glower. Joseph Crocker was a charter school known for its art program—and *not* the neighborhood junior high.

He was surprised by a punch on his arm. "You knew?" Kelly whispered harshly. "That she wanted you to go to Crocker?" Kelly had known Dr. Boyle was there, of course. But he hadn't known it might mean Seth would go to a magnet school instead of the scary neighborhood junior high.

"I was trying to avoid it!" he whispered back, and before he could explain that he didn't *want* to go to a special school that would split him up from Matty, the auditorium grew hushed as Dr. Boyle stood up.

A handsome man in his late thirties, Dr. Boyle had skin the color of faded ebony—just enough brown to give him warmth. He'd shaved his head and kept a neatly trimmed goatee.

He stood in front of the students and winked, partially raising his hands with the baton in them.

"Hi, boys. You ready for what comes next?"

They all nodded, and Kelly sighed unhappily and pulled his violin up.

"Bows ready?" Dr. Boyle prompted.

Seth straightened his spine and positioned his violin, taking in a deep breath. Abruptly his concern about going to a different school faded away, as well as his father's possible irritation because Seth hadn't told him it was even a possibility. Even Kelly's hurt over Seth keeping secrets diminished, although it burned brightly as a presence next to him for the entire rest of the night.

All that remained was the music.

He'd progressed past "Turkey in the Straw" and moved on to "Running Dry." Dr. Boyle had written an adaptation of the violin classic so Seth played a slightly simplified solo part, and the rest of the boys played the other melody line.

The result was stunningly haunting.

They wrapped up the song, and Seth closed his eyes during the breathless pause that followed, holding those last notes close to his heart.

When the applause erupted, he opened them again, and was ready to face the consequences of his silence.

"WE'LL MEET you at the ice cream place," Seth's dad called to Kelly's dad. "Kelly, buck up. I promise, we'll be there."

Kelly nodded weakly, and Matty scowled. Nobody was happy with Mrs. Sheridan's announcement, and Seth knew they were holding back from going to the local Baskin-Robbins for one reason only.

They needed to talk.

Please don't get mad, please don't get mad, please don't get mad.

"Seth?" Craig Arnold said after the Cruz family had walked about fifty feet ahead. "Are you still afraid I'll hit you?" He asked it gently, but Seth knew if he answered this one wrong, his dad would be hurt. So hurt that maybe he'd have to have another meeting, and Seth always felt bad when that happened.

"No," Seth answered, voice a little rusty. "It's... it's not that."

"Okay." His father's relief was palpable. "Then why? Why would you keep an opportunity like this a secret?"

Seth shifted uncomfortably, still clutching his violin case to his chest. He was outgrowing this one; he knew it. There were notes he wanted to get from it, but no matter how well he tuned it, how carefully he drew his bow, it still sounded tinny and flat sometimes. But he loved it. It had been his first instrument, his first love.

"Matty can't come," he muttered. "And Kelly's only playing because I play. By the time he gets to junior high, I'll be on to high school—"

"A different one than they'll go to," Dad said, as though he understood. "And you don't want the change."

Seth looked at his father miserably. "Things just got good," he pleaded, hoping his dad would understand.

"And you don't want to change the balance," Dad said softly. "Got it." He sighed. "Seth, we're not moving. You'll still be home often enough to practice where Kelly can hear you, and help Matty with the girls. I promise. I wouldn't take that away from you."

Seth swallowed. "But high school—"

"Well, maybe they can go to the high school with the orchestra," his dad said hopefully. "I'll talk to their parents. It's a better school than the one in walking distance, and I'm home in the mornings. I can take everybody, maybe, if Linda can get you home. And you're getting old enough to take the city bus. But that's two years away, son. In the meantime...." Craig sighed. "I saw your face light up when Dr. Boyle stood up. You really like him, don't you?"

"He looks like Grandpa," Seth mumbled.

"And like you." Craig's voice sounded funny, like a violin string pulled too tight. "I think you should go. Mrs. Sheridan thought of everything— even the bus for Joseph Crocker. Don't worry. I'm not leaving my job at the warehouse. Xavier and Linda aren't winning the lottery. I think you're safe if you go to this junior high. It's a challenge you can meet."

Seth swallowed tightly. "Dad?"

"Yeah?"

"You're so good at this. Why'd it get so hard?"

His father's arm over his shoulders was one of the best things he'd ever felt. "Because I was weak. And alone. And I failed you. I'm sorry about that, Seth. I'm sorry you're still paying for it. I… I hurt you in ways that aren't going to heal soon. I… I don't know how to fix that."

"This is good," Seth muttered, leaning his head against his dad as they walked. "Let's just do this now."

His father's arm tightened, and they made plans for the future.

THE BEST part of junior high was orchestra with Dr. Boyle. Seth practiced during lunch, before school, and after he got home. He played with Matty when he didn't have soccer, but missed him sometimes and played with Kelly instead.

Kelly still came downstairs after his family ate to listen to Seth practice.

"Where's your brother?" Seth asked in early December.

"Out hanging with stupid Castor Durant. Stupid asshole. I hate him."

"Kelly!" Seth was so surprised he lowered his instrument. The school had given him a better one at the beginning of the year, and he'd been persuaded to return his first instrument to his grade school, where Mrs. Sheridan could find another young man or woman who would be moved by music.

"He's mean," Kelly insisted. "And my stupid brother is mean when he's done playing—I mean, *hanging out*—with him. And he smells like cigarettes after school. Mom and Dad got his report card and almost suspended *everybody* because they were so mad. And Matty said it was all your fault because you left. Who was he supposed to be friends with? And if he did his homework, Castor Durant and his stupid friends would beat him up anyway."

Seth stared. "Matty never said…." But Matty had smelled like cigarettes—Seth remembered that. He thought it was just junior high. Seth had avoided the bathrooms that smelled like that, but sometimes you couldn't. He didn't realize Matty had started to act like those boys, the ones who went to the school because it was closest and not because it was special, the ones who didn't care about their grades.

Kelly looked down. "He slugged me in the face last week. I told Mom I fell down playing."

Seth had to put the violin down because he had trouble breathing.

"Nobody hits you," he said, remembering those terrible days when his father had hit *him.* "Nobody." Kelly frowned, and Seth saw the fading bruise now. He'd assumed a playground accident. Kelly had always been the kid who jumped off the swings when they were at their highest point, or did cherry drops off the bars when he wasn't supposed to.

"You can't say anything," Kelly whispered. "Seth, he'll—"

Seth had put the violin away. "He'll what? Hit you again?"

He strode out of his apartment, Kelly dogging his heals. "Seth, no—"

"Nobody hurts you," he muttered, pounding up the stairs.

"Seth, he'll only make it worse—"

Seth stopped then, remembering how he hadn't said a word to anybody either. Matty and Kelly had known about the bruises, but unless someone knocked on the door when the hitting was happening, nobody else had known. "That's a lie they tell," he said, hoping his father would forgive him. "That it will only get worse if you tell the world. Your dad told my dad it had to stop. Your dad won't let him hurt you again."

Seth had great faith in Kelly and Matty's dad.

"Seth—"

But Seth was already up the stairs, bursting into the Cruz's living room like he and Kelly often did, without warning.

It seemed he was a bit late.

Matty was standing in the middle of the living room, staring at the carpet while his mother, holding baby Agnes on her hip, and his father, gesturing with his baseball hat like it was a weapon, were telling Matty he had made some bad choices.

"These grades?" his mother snapped. "These grades are what you bring home to us? Are you high—" She stopped. "*Are* you high?"

Matty stared some more holes in the carpet. "No."

"Have you been *getting* high?"

He bit his lip, and that was enough.

His father was front and center, dominating his son with his size until Matty backed up against the front room window. "What have you taken," he growled.

"Just some weed…."

The sound that came out of Xavier Cruz's mouth right then didn't sound human, but apparently Matty spoke just fine.

"And some booze," he muttered.

"Who?" Xavier grated. "Who are you doing this with? You don't do this shit alone—not in the seventh grade. Who?"

Seth looked at Kelly, who had his hand clapped over his mouth, and jumped into the breach.

"Castor Durant," he said, glaring at Matty. "He hit his little brother in the face too."

For a moment, he was afraid Xavier would hit Matty, but Xavier was a good man, the best. Kelly had told him that he hadn't been the kind of drunk that hit. Instead, he'd laughed and cried too much.

It was Linda who stepped in, and even though her son was almost as tall as she was in the seventh grade, he didn't try to dodge her hand as she reached out and grabbed his ear.

"Ouch! Mama!"

"Into your room. Kelly, you can sleep at Seth's this week. Xavier, you go get him his stuff."

"Linda?" Xavier asked, shocked.

"Oh yes. He's not going to school. We'll get his assignments. He's going to stay home with me for two weeks. He's going to take care of his sisters and help me with the groceries and go to work with you—"

"Go to work with me?" Xavier asked, still sounding surprised.

"Oh yes. You won't let a woman walk alone in your parking lot, Javi. There are people in that neighborhood who have done all the drugs and all the drinking and Matty is going to see them up close and personal. He's going to see what his life is going to be like if he has no job skills and no schooling. All he has to do is keep going like he's going. And then he's going to dedicate his life to leaving boys like this Castor Durant in his rearview mirror!"

"Mom! It's just a little—"

Linda gave a vicious yank on his ear. "It's just a little nothing. I am *not* letting you go down this path, Mateo Cruz. I am *not* letting you throw your life away because of someone named Castor Durant. What in the hell kind of name is that anyway?"

"It's a white boy name," Kelly whispered, but so loud that Seth saw even Xavier smirk.

"A mean boy," Seth corrected, and Kelly nodded.

"Not all white boys are mean," Kelly conceded. "But this one is bad."

"I'll go get your clothes," Xavier said to Kelly. "Seth, do you think this will be okay with your father?"

Seth swallowed. "Dad... Dad'll just be proud you trust him," he said, and Xavier stopped short.

"Do you trust him?"

Seth nodded—not automatically, but thinking. "He really wants me not to be afraid," he said.

Xavier's mouth pulled up, like he'd smile if everything else wasn't in such chaos. "Good. Did you come up here to tell us about Kelly?"

"Nobody hits Kelly," Seth said, angry about it all over again.

"No, son. You're right there. I'll be back."

When he came back, he had Kelly's violin, because Kelly was still a string boy, and Seth's heart squeezed a little in his chest. "You can practice with me," he said proudly.

Kelly shook his head and took the violin from his dad carefully, allowing Seth to grab the suitcase full of clothes his father had brought out to the living room.

"I'm not good like you," he said. "I don't want you to laugh."

"I'd never laugh at you, Kelly. I promise."

But Kelly just shrugged. Matty was still yelling at his mother, and Xavier was in the girls' room, calming them down. It was time to go.

Together they trudged downstairs, but Seth was a little happy.

Kelly was still one of his favorite people, even if he was younger and hadn't started growing yet. Still, for a week, he and his dad got to give Kelly's family back a little of what they'd given him.

He was still angry at Matty, and worried that his parents wouldn't fix what had gone wrong once Seth had started going to the other school, but those other things made him happy, and he'd hold them close to his heart.

Like Seth thought, his dad was so excited about giving back to the Cruz family a little that he went out of his way to be nice. He gave Kelly a key to the apartment so he could go there after school while he was waiting for Seth's bus to drop him off, and made sure to stock the kitchen with lots of snacks—potato chips and soda—so it was almost like a birthday.

Kelly had never turned down potato chips or pizza bites. So Seth would get home and Kelly would be on the couch, doing his homework in front of the television, a plate of pizza bites on the coffee table next to him. Sometimes he wasn't even doing his homework—he was just sketching what was on TV, and Seth had taken to pinning his drawings to his bedroom wall, because Kelly was just so good at drawing little cartoons that were as happy and as bouncy as he was.

Seth *really* liked having someone there when he got home from school.

For the next two weeks, unless Kelly's dad was taking him to soccer, Seth got to pretend that's the way it always was.

If Matty hadn't been having such a hard time, Seth would have been truly happy.

One night, he was taking the garbage out before his father got home and he met Matty as he was coming back from the dumpster.

"Hi," he said, hoping Matty wouldn't yell. For a moment, it looked like he was going to, but then his lower lip started to wobble.

"Castor Durant's an asshole," he blurted, as if he'd been dying to say it this whole time. "He told me he'd beat my brother up if I didn't make him go away."

"What's going to happen when you go back?" Seth asked. Matty's parents were trying, but… but the bad kid never just went away.

Matty shook his head. "My folks called the school, the school called Castor's parents, and they called some social workers. His dad is big in the church, so he's just going somewhere else for the rest of junior high. We won't have to see him again until high school."

Seth frowned. "He could be an even bigger asshole then," he said, and Matty nodded with feeling.

"I don't even want to know how bad it's going to be," he confided unhappily.

"Maybe you could come to my school," Seth offered shyly. "At least in high school."

"With what?" Matty demanded. "Kelly has art, and you have music. I don't got nothing! I don't got grades because I'm not smart, and I don't got—"

"You don't work," Seth said brutally. "You're plenty smart. You copied off me when your mom was pregnant because your family was busy. Only you got used to it. You've got a year to pull your grades up, Matty. I'll help you study. Your *folks* will help you study, but you're right. Castor Durant is going to be gunning for you, and you have got to get out of that school!"

They both shivered. Seth had forgotten to put a coat on when he went outside. Matty just didn't wear one that often.

"Missed you," he mumbled, his face crumpling. From Matty, it was a huge admission. "Everybody else wants to be all grown-up and shit." He looked both ways, like this was a terrible thing. "You still like to play with action figures. I miss that."

Seth looked down, embarrassed. "I thought you thought I was a baby."

Matty shook his head. "No. I don't know how to be when you're not at school with me. I… I hit my little brother. I can't ever do that again."

"Be smart," Seth said soberly. "Just… be smart."

Matty nodded. "Throw your trash away." The bag handle was starting to leave a mark on Seth's hand. "I'll ask my mom if you and Kelly can come eat dinner." He looked away unhappily. "I miss my brother too. He… he talks to you, right?"

Seth shoved the bag in the dumpster, and together they turned back to the fourplex, taking baby steps through the graveled parking lot. "When we're going to sleep." Every night, Kelly would just talk and talk until he drifted off. Seth had learned to cling to every word. "He misses your sisters." Lily and Lulu and Agnes—every night he remembered one funny thing about each kid.

"They miss him too." Matty shook his head. "The people where Dad works scare me. And not just the homeless guys. Dad works with guys who smoke, and they're rough, and they get in fights, and… and every day Dad drives me home and says, 'Jesus, Mateo, I want so much better for you.' But I don't know how!"

"School," Seth said. "Bring a notebook. Write down what the teacher says at the beginning of every class. That's the key. They have everything on the board."

Matty laughed a little. "Everybody knows that," he said gruffly.

"Please?" Seth begged, his stomach suddenly cramping. He realized he could have lived without Matty in his life, but he needed Kelly.

And Kelly needed Matty.

"For your little brother? For your sisters? Don't be like Cormorant Dural—"

Matty cackled. "Castor Durant! Oh my God! Seth, are other people real to you?"

"I've never met him!" Seth defended, feeling stupid.

"Well, I hope you never do," Matty said with feeling. "Guy's a psycho!"

They had reached the landing now, and Seth looked at Matty unhappily. "You know, your suspension ends at Christmas vacation," he said, and Matty looked surprised.

"It's like they did that on purpose."

"We can play a lot then," Seth said.

"When you're not practicing." Matty's expression got suddenly adult. "You… I got sort of mad at you when you went to that other school, but, Seth, you gotta stay there. That place'll get you out. You and Kelly can get through school and never deal with guys like Castor Durant—I'd kill for that, you know?"

Seth nodded. "There's bullies everywhere," he said, thinking of Joey Jefferson, who said mean things about Seth's pants, which were too small, and his shirts, which were getting too tight. "But sometimes they're meaner than others."

"Yeah. Well, I don't wish my bullies on you or Kelly for anything. I'm off suspension Friday night. Maybe… maybe you and Kelly can come over for dinner. Maybe we can have ice cream." Matty's smile was hesitant. Hopeful.

"Yeah," Seth said. Then, because his father had been so happy to have Kelly over these last two weeks, he added, "Maybe my dad can come for ice cream."

"Mateo!" Linda called, coming out on the landing at the top of the stairs. "Oh! There you are."

"Sorry, Mom," Matty said humbly. "Talking to Seth."

Linda nodded. "Well, you can talk to him more Friday night. How's that?"

Matty gave a quick smile, all eye sparkles and dimples like his brother. "I'd really like that," he said and then winked. Seth grinned as Matty's footfalls resounded on the metal-and-concrete staircase, and he went into his own apartment with a smile on his face.

"What?" Kelly asked. "Why was Mom yelling?"

Seth shook his head. "Matty and I were talking outside. I don't think he'll go on suspension again."

Kelly's habitual smile disappeared, and he looked so nakedly hopeful, Seth's chest hurt. "Really? Like… I'll have my brother back?"

"Yeah," Seth said. He'd do anything for Kelly.

Kelly's grin game back, blinding. "Yay! I'm starting to miss my sisters, you know?"

"Me too," Seth said, meaning it.

He wanted nothing more than for things to go back to the way they were before, when the three of them were string boys and his dad had just quit drinking and it was all going to be okay.

Only time never marched backward like that. It always pushed forward, inexorably, a glacier feeding ice into a vast and treacherous sea.

Even if you were on the glacier, and it felt like you were still, things were still changing. Trees were splintering; rocks were getting ground to powder.

Time was sanding your hopes and dreams smooth so they'd fit into the shape of the world, even as you saw them, beautiful, with bright and shiny edges, still in your mind.

MATTY FINISHED his suspension and pulled his grades up. Way up. Up enough to transfer to Seth's high school. Seth was taking orchestra and music classes—even extra ones, after school—and they both caught the city bus so their parents didn't have to worry about them. When Kelly graduated from eighth grade, he made it too, through his art, which had graduated from big line drawings, like cartoons, to more delicate, dancing drawings that looked like real life through a beautiful lens. He never stopped the habit of coming to Seth's house after school when he didn't have soccer or chores, and he would sit on the battered denim couch and draw, pages and pages of anything that caught his fancy, while Seth would practice, the two of them lost in their dreams of the things they could do with the raw talent given to them.

After Kelly transferred to the school where Seth and Matty went, they got to ride the bus together, eat lunch together, and usually Kelly would stay after school with Seth—even on the days Matty went home for soccer—to listen to him practice, or just to finish his homework.

Seeing Kelly was so much a part of Seth's life by then, *not* seeing him would have seemed odd.

One day in November, Kelly's sophomore year, they were riding the bus together, late because Seth was practicing for the winter holiday performance, when Kelly gave a little yawn and slumped sideways against him.

Seth wrapped his arm around Kelly's shoulders and let him rest his head on Seth's chest, and he had a small revelation.

Kelly's face wasn't round anymore.

It wasn't rectangular like Matty's, though. He still had dimples in the corners of his cheeks, and a little cleft in the center of his pointed chin. His eyes were round, with long, dark, thick lashes, and he had a tiny black mole on his cheek, back by his ear.

And he smelled good.

It was the same soap Matty used—Seth could smell it on Matty when they had gym class together. Seth knew the fresh smell of Matty's soap.

But it wasn't the same on Kelly.

On Kelly, it seemed sweeter and sharper. Like cedar shavings. More real.

His lips were a pink shade of the pale bronze of his skin.

And soft. And pillowy.

Seth stared at Kelly for the rest of the bus ride, trying to fit this new Kelly into his mind and wishing he didn't have to.

This was Matty's kid brother. Seth's life would be… incomplete if he wasn't there, all hours of the day, insinuating himself into Seth's blood.

He couldn't be seeing Kelly any different than he had since they were little kids, could he? Kelly. Who still talked the ears off a chipmunk if you let him. Who could prattle on about his English teacher and how she looked old but she was going to go out and start a revolution single-handedly if it killed her, and about the young math teacher who had just had her third kid and looked like death all the time, and how Kelly was going to ask his mom if she could make poor Mrs. Hennessy some hot chocolate for Christmas because that woman needed a mommy like nobody else and his mommy was the best.

Kelly.

Who sat in Seth's living room and listened to Seth play and drew random pictures and smiled just at the sound of scales.

Seth must have made a sound or something—something different about his breathing, maybe—because Kelly's eyes flew open, sparkling brown, lively, and definitely not stupid.

"What?" Kelly asked, wiping a self-conscious hand across his lips, looking for drool. "I totally got spit all over you, right?" He made to pull away, and for a moment, Seth's arms tightened.

No. Kelly was warm in his arms, and again, his *smell* heated Seth's blood.

Kelly stopped for a moment, and a little red-bronze crescent appeared on his cheekbones. "Keeping me warm?" he whispered.

Seth gaped at him, unable to find a good reason for holding him so close. The moment suspended there, as the two of them stared at each other, breathless, until Kelly suddenly bounded up. "Hey, that's our stop!"

"Sorry, kid," the bus driver responded. "I'll let you off on the next block."

"Dammit," Kelly muttered. "It's raining outside."

"I'm sorry," Seth whispered, feeling stupid about being caught completely unawares. "I'm sorry. I just... zoned out—"

Kelly met his eyes and shook his head, reminding Seth so much of Kelly's father that Seth's tongue stopped trying to apologize. "I know what happened," Kelly told him, his voice surprisingly mild.

And then he winked.

Seth swallowed and stood, waiting for the bus to come to a stop.

They got out just as the rain kicked in harder, and the two of them hustled to the nearest shelter. This stop used to open up into a small strip mall, little storefronts close together with alleyways between them and overhangs. The stores had all closed down, and the windows had been broken and boarded up and broken and boarded up and broken again. It wasn't a safe place, no—they had to dodge needles and condoms and trash to get to the place between the buildings where the overhang offered shelter. The good news was, the back opened up to a small field. If they could cross that field, they'd be in the back porch of the first fourplex of their block, and they'd be safe.

But for the moment, they'd walked to the back of the tiny alleyway and were looking out from the overhang, waiting for the rain to stop pounding as if it was trying to drill a hole in their heads.

"Sorry about the bus stop," Seth muttered. "This place is pretty gross."

Kelly nodded. "Yeah. Matty says Castor Durant hangs out in the old laundromat—but not when it's raining. The roof's no good. It floods."

Seth grunted. They'd all kept an ear to the ground for Castor Durant. He was back in the high school Matty had been headed for before he got his grades up. The rumors about that kid were unsettling—he'd been suspended once for hitting a teacher with a balled-up roll of tape. The only reason he hadn't been expelled was that she hadn't *seen* him do it, but everybody knew.

And what he did to students unwary enough to fall in his sway was worse.

"So we're lucky it's raining?" Seth wrinkled his nose, and Kelly laughed at him. They'd both grown, but where Seth probably had two or so more inches to go, Kelly had stopped about two inches from where Seth was now. He was going to be five-six, maybe five-seven, for the rest of his life, and his childhood plumpness had washed away, leaving him slender and tightly built. But his small size never seemed to stop him. He always stared up at the world with that same laughing-eyed joy that Seth saw now.

Seth stared back at him, just as entranced as he had been on the bus, but now it was worse, somehow.

Kelly was biting his lip, his eyes wise.

"You just saw it, didn't you?" he asked, his dimples popping out.

"Saw what?" Seth asked, helpless. He wanted to touch Kelly's cheeks, feel the little dent in skin.

"Saw my face and thought, 'Oh, it's *Kelly*,' and not 'Oh, it's Matty's little brother.'"

Seth shook his head. "You've always been Kelly," he replied with confidence. And then, shaken. "What's different?"

Kelly let out a soft chuff of air. They were standing so close, it brushed Seth's chin, and he moved his finger to his own face, trying to still the tingle.

"Two years ago, in the eighth grade, I went to dances," he whispered. "Remember?"

Seth nodded. "Yeah. Your mom got mad because she couldn't chaperone."

"Thank *God*," Kelly returned with feeling. "So I made out with two girls at those dances. 'Cause they were funny and they wanted to dance, and making out seemed like what you were supposed to do."

Seth's stomach went cold. "Awesome," he muttered. He hadn't made out with *anyone*. It was just… just… getting home and practicing his next piece always held more fascination to him. Being there to walk Kelly home, to have their own quiet after-school club, just the two of them, seemed so much more important.

"No," Kelly said, shaking his head sadly. "I mean, pleasant, but not awesome. And then Jimmy—you remember him? We used to sit at lunch together because the grades couldn't mix?"

"Jimmy Durreson?" Seth remembered. He was a white kid, which wasn't that common. Dark blond hair, a big dent in his chin. Green eyes.

A wave of panic crashed into Seth, like it had just been waiting to douse him as he stood on the shore of oblivion.

Cute.

Jimmy Durreson was damned cute.

Kelly nodded, mischief in his smile. "Yeah. Jimmy frickin' Durreson. We were at the dance together, and we got bored, and we went outside to use the bathrooms and didn't come in right away. And it was spring and just us, and he stops me and says, 'Wanna make out?' And I *did.* And it was *awesome.* And he wanted to do it again. Wanted to be boyfriends."

Oh God. "You have a boyfriend?" Panic in his voice.

Kelly patted his cheek gently. "You're so pretty, but oh my God. There's shit you don't see. No, I don't have a boyfriend. Not yet."

Seth nodded, trying to still the surge of jealousy that had followed the panic. "But if you thought it was awesome—"

Then Kelly kissed him.

Oh dear heavens, Kelly *kissed* him.

His plush little mouth was soft on Seth's, and that amazing smell Seth had just discovered filled his senses. Kelly's warmth blocked out the chill of the November rain.

Seth gasped, and Kelly pushed his tongue in, just enough to taste, and Seth closed his lips and sucked lightly.

Kelly pulled away and smiled, biting his lip.

"Jimmy wasn't *that* awesome," he whispered. "It was good. Jimmy Durreson is a good kisser. But he doesn't taste like you."

Seth kissed him back, licking along the seam of his lips, sighing when Kelly let him in. Kelly opened his mouth fully, and Seth thrust his tongue inside, wanting to taste him. Kelly's tongue met him halfway, and they stroked each other, stunningly intimate, terrifying.

Not scary enough to make him stop.

Seth groaned, wanting more… more… more what?

The question pulled him back, and he leaned his forehead against Kelly's.

"We're kissing," he gasped.

"You noticed!" Kelly teased, nuzzling Seth's cheek. "You want to do it some more?"

Seth's whole body tingled, so many parts he wasn't sure if he could inventory them all. He swallowed and nodded. "Yeah, but…." He pulled away and looked around them. The dank little alley, the rain that had finally let up. "Not here," he said. "We... we have tomorrow. It's your day to sit and draw while I practice—"

Kelly nodded excitedly. "Think maybe you can practice a little less?" he urged. "Just a little? 'Cause I gotta tell you, I've been waiting since eighth grade for that, and it was awesome, but I want to do more." He wrinkled his nose, which was still on the small side, and nodded. "Not here, 'cause you're right. It's gross. But... back then, in eighth grade, Jimmy Durreson said, 'You wanna do it more?' and I said, 'Yeah, but not with you.'" Kelly's face fell. "I coulda said that better. He was hurt. He didn't sit with me for a week until I explained that I just really had it bad for you and I wanted *you* to kiss me. And then he said that was okay, he was glad we got to make out just once, and it was ok—"

Seth kissed him again. Partly because he didn't want to hear one more damned word about Jimmy Durreson, but mostly because it was their last time before the next day.

He hated that he had to wait an entire day before he tasted Kelly again.

It was almost unbearable.

But Kelly kissed him back, and Seth got a little better at it. He understood that it was about being slow, and about taste, and that somehow all the things happening with their mouths were spreading to other parts of their bodies. Kelly raised his hand to Seth's stomach, encountering his jacket, and Seth pulled away.

"Tomorrow," he promised. "We won't have jackets on."

Kelly grinned. "Nope. It'll be good. It was so worth telling Jimmy no." His grin faded. "I... I'm not sure how long I knew in my heart I wanted it to be you I kissed, but it feels like my whole life. Like when Matty talks about his girlfriends, all I can picture is you."

Seth closed his eyes and tried analyze. "You always made me so happy," he said, shrugging. "I just didn't think about girls at all."

Kelly pretended to ponder for a moment. "I'll take it," he said with an impish little hop. "Now are you ready? We gotta run fast because it's fixing to pour again."

Seth looked out at the sky, which was, as Kelly said, growing darker.

But if they ran now, they could go inside.

And if they went inside, they could go to school tomorrow.

And after school tomorrow, they would be in Seth's house.

Alone.

With this newfound exciting activity.

Seth was so happy he ducked his head and planted a little kiss on Kelly's cheek.

"One, two—"

"Three!" Kelly cried. And together they charged out into the rain.

WATCHING KELLY walk up the steps to his apartment was unexpectedly hard. Seth swept inside his own door thoroughly preoccupied, barely remembering to pull his instrument case out of its special vinyl carrier that he used in the rain. He set it by the door and stripped off his sopping wet jacket—and only then registered that his father was already home.

He was in by the tiny dining room table, setting up takeout.

Seth stared at him blankly. Chinese food. His favorite.

"Dad?"

His father turned and smiled warmly, as though he knew Seth had been distracted. "You noticed. Go wash your hands."

"You're home early."

"Well, I figured we had something important to talk about."

Seth wasn't sure what his expression was, but all he could think about was that kiss, that wonderful shining kiss, and how he wanted to do more of it, and how that meant… oh God. What did it mean? Gay? He was gay? And he hadn't told his father?

His dad laughed gently. "Seth, in a million years, I can't imagine you doing something that would make your eyes look like that. Now move it!"

Seth nodded and tried to still his breathing. If his dad knew about Kelly and being gay and all the things Seth hadn't even thought of until just… just… ten minutes ago, it wasn't bad. And if he *didn't* know about all that other stuff, what else could it be? Oh God. Seth knew he wasn't always grounded, that his head was often somewhere else. What had he missed? He tried to connect with the people around him, tried to avoid being lured by the next note, the next chord, the next piece, all the music whirling in his head.

"What?" Dad asked as Seth sat down.

"Are you seeing anyone?" Seth blurted. Because that could be a thing. Seth wasn't sure how he'd feel about having a stepmom. He guessed seeing his dad be happy in theory was a good thing, but—

"No!" Dad was staring at him in surprise. "No. What would make you say—"

"I don't understand Chinese food."

Dad laughed a little. "Well, son, I think we've established that you eat it."

Seth blinked at him and smiled self-consciously. He had to calm down. If he didn't relax just a smidge and at least try to appear human, he might scream, "I think I'm gay, and I kissed Kelly, and I want to do it again!" at the top of his lungs before running out into the dark and stormy night.

"I mean why are we having it?" he said, enunciating every word. "I haven't done anything bad. Did you get a promotion?" And then, oh horror! "We're not moving, are we?"

"No," his dad said slowly. "At least, *I'm* not." He set down his box of orange chicken—his favorite—and looked Seth full-on in the eyes. "Son, were you even going to *tell* me about Bridgford?"

Seth jerked back. "What about it? The rich kids are going there next year."

Mr. Boyle had told them all about applying to Bridgford two months ago. Seth had listened with half an ear and figured he was talking about the other kids, not the kids who took the city bus from Seth's neighborhood.

"Dr. Boyle called me to ask if you'd considered a scholarship. So I applied online, Seth. You're good for a full ride. That could be room and board for the rest of this year, next year, and your first two years of college if you wanted it—and a fast track to your next two years at one of their feeder colleges. Aren't you even interested?"

Seth gaped at him. "You want me to leave?" he asked, wounded to the center of his mass. "I… I thought I didn't have to go anywhere until graduation."

His father blinked. "No. I don't want you to go. I'm not trying to get rid of you, Seth. I want you to fly." He picked up a forkful of orange chicken and chewed thoughtfully. "I was supposed to go to college," he said with a sigh. "I was in junior college, my parents had money saved. But…." He smiled—a faded version of the one Seth had only seen in pictures.

"I fell in love with your mother. And they weren't happy about that. And then we had you. I thought you were a miracle, but they weren't happy about having a grandson either. So, no college for me. And then your mom died and…." He swallowed, and Seth felt the pain all over again.

"Your grandparents were nice to me, Seth. I don't want you to think they weren't. But they thought I'd just give you to them when she died. And you were all I had left of her. So when I got the chance to work out here, I took it."

He shook his head, all pretense at eating Chinese food completely gone. "There's no excuse for me, when I started drinking. None. I think about...."

His voice grew rough, and Seth's body chilled to zero. Oh, he hated thinking about that time, and obviously, so did Dad. "I remember those days, and the planet isn't big enough for my shame. But I think it started when I took the job out here. It was just me and you. And I missed... everybody. My parents were.... I won't let them near you. Ever. And Kesha's parents weren't speaking to me either. You and me were so alone. There's no excuse for me, for what I did, but I'll tell you now... that time had its roots in being so lost in my own heart because I had no people around me to guide me. If it hadn't been for the Cruz family, we would have been lost, and I think you know that."

Seth did know that, and that's why he had wanted to stay. But he didn't know how to say that. It seemed his father had all the words anyway.

"But you, Seth, you have opportunities. You can go out in the world and know I'm right here to come back to. You can move to Almond Lakes and go to Bridgford, and come here for long weekends and holidays. It's right by San Francisco—we'll see each other. You... you can have the life my parents wanted for me, but without all the... the *strings* that went with it, you know? You can have it all, free and clear."

Seth bit his lip, his eyes burning. He didn't want to go. He knew, objectively, that college was coming and that he'd have to be making decisions soon. He'd been planning to take the PSATs in the spring. But this... this was so soon. *Kelly! That's a whole four years without Kelly!*

His father shook his head and sighed. "Well, you know, I didn't really expect you to leave in the middle of the year. You have until June. At least until the summer program starts. Then there's the scholarship for next year. You know that, right?"

Seth squinted at him. "No. Dr. Boyle said Christmas."

"That was for everybody else, Seth. Have you, I don't know, noticed anybody sitting through your practices in the last month?"

Seth shrugged. "We had a guest conductor. He audited the advanced orchestra class and then conducted a song or two. I guess he was going to be doing '1812 Overture' over Christmas."

Dad grimaced, and in light of his story—and remembering that Seth had been afraid he'd be getting a stepmom—Seth had a terrible, terrible realization.

His father wasn't old.

His father was… was *young.* Thirty-five? That was old for a kid but not old for a grown-up, was it?

And Seth was all he had.

"Do you remember where the guest conductor was *from*, Seth?" Dad was asking patiently.

Seth searched his memory and came up with studying the complicated first violin part for "The Devil Went Down to Georgia," which they were doing with the choir and Dr. Boyle assured them would be a fan favorite.

"No?"

Dad made that now-familiar, "I don't believe this!" face that Seth always associated particularly with himself. "Well, he came from Bridgford. Seth, he's been in that class for a month *scouting you.*"

"Mr. Pantalone? No." Mr. Pantalone was young for a grown-up—about ten years younger than Seth's dad. He had shoulder-length curly hair, fuzzy sideburns, and wicked gray eyes. Seth had always found him appealing in an absent sort of way. Oh wow, maybe Seth could have had a crush on his teacher if he hadn't had a raging heart-on for his best friend's brother.

"Mr. Pantalone, *yes.* He's spent a month at your school to see if he can convince you to come to Bridgford. They extended the deadline for *you* until June, just in case."

Seth scrubbed his hands through his hair, which had grown long enough to form tiny ringlets after the rain had hit the oil he used daily. His dad was good at buying him things—Shea butter for his skin, oil for his hair—that most white people wouldn't know black people used. He had a moment of remembering his mother, right before she'd died, telling both of them, him and his dad, about the oil and the butter and how his dad had to make sure he had butter on his shoulders and lower back.

His dad had never forgotten.

Even when he'd been drinking, and Seth had worried, every day, about his father yelling, or sometimes hitting, his father had never forgotten that he had a son. Had never forgotten his wife telling him how to care for his son.

"You'll forget me," he blurted. "You'll forget to eat. To bring food. You'll forget to go to your meetings and drink. You'll forget me!"

His dad looked like Seth had shot him in the heart. "Never," he croaked, eyes squeezed shut. "I swear, Seth. I'll never forget you. I'll *never* go back to drinking. I promise, if you go away, I'll always be right here when you need me, okay? I won't disappear like... like everybody did on me. I swear."

"No," Seth whispered, not wanting Chinese food or ice cream or any other bribe. "I have another year and a half. We... we can go for ice cream after performances. We can go to the movies on Saturdays like we always do. Kelly can come listen to me practice." Oh, he hadn't meant to say that. "I can play funny songs for his sisters on their birthdays."

Seth's Dad nodded and bit his lip, his eyes too bright and rimmed with red.

"Okay," he said quietly. "That's our plan for now." He took a deep breath. "I... I gotta say, Seth, I'm glad I made home safe for you. But I'm so sorry I didn't do that soon enough for you to trust it would always be here."

Seth rubbed the back of his hand across his eyes. "I just don't want to go," he said. "Not now."

"I hear you." Dad let out a sigh. "I.... C'mere, kid. I really need a hug."

Seth did, feeling too tall and too awkward, his hands and feet seeming too big. But his dad stood, and Seth was only two inches shorter than he was, and his shoulders used to seem so big, but Seth's were almost as wide, and Seth was on the slender side.

Dad was younger. He was smaller. And he was more afraid than Seth had ever dreamed.

Yet somehow this all made him harder to leave.

MR. PANTALONE kept Seth after school for half an hour. Seth was practically dancing in his need to get away, even though Kelly was sitting quietly in the room, doing his homework, apparently not hearing a word.

"Seth, are you sure?"

Oh, Mr. Pantalone was pretty. His name was really weird—he said it was Italian—but his face was narrow and sort of fox-shaped. He had gray eyes with black lashes, and his mouth was even plusher than Kelly's.

But Seth couldn't look at him as the man tried to get Seth to leave his home. He could only see Kelly.

Kelly stuck his tongue out the side of his mouth when he was working.

In the third grade, it had been really adorable.

In the sixth grade, it had still been cute.

Now that Kelly was in high school, Seth wanted to kiss his tongue and suck on it, and suck on Kelly's chin, and his cheeks and—

"Seth!" Mr. Pantalone snapped in exasperation. "Stop mooncalfing over your friend and pay attention! This is your chance to get out of your neighborhood! To get out of this town!"

"I like Sacramento," Seth said, confused. "Have you ever swam in the river—"

"Kids die in that river!" Mr. Pantalone argued.

"Only sometimes," Kelly said, without even looking up. "It's not bad."

Seth smiled at him, and Kelly looked up and grinned.

"What does it mean?" Kelly asked. "That word you just used. The one about the cow?"

Mr. Pantalone looked confused. "Mooncalfing?"

"Yeah. I've never heard that before."

"It means to sort of space out over, to get distracted by."

Kelly's grin lit up the room. "Were you really?" he asked Seth. "Were you really just spacing out on me?"

Seth's face heated, and he studied the frets on his violin. "I… uh…."

"I'm pretty, right?" Kelly pressed. "Like, like I'm whatwuzit? Mooncalfable."

"You *are* pretty," Seth blurted, and then looked at Mr. Pantalone in horror.

Mr. Pantalone was rubbing the back of his neck like he was in pain. "It's like herding fish," he mumbled. "You want them to go one way, and then you're riding a mooncalf in the river."

Kelly chortled. "He's funny! And pretty!" Then he gave Mr. Pantalone a scowl. "Now, if he'd stop trying to get you to leave Sacramento, I might be able to stand him."

Mr. Pantalone eyed Kelly speculatively. "You could visit him," he said pleasantly. "It's a fine arts school—sort of an experiment. A bridge for fine and performing arts students. There's an art department. And galleries. And field trips. You might even qualify yourself."

Kelly cocked his head. "Pretty *and* smart," he observed. "I have sisters to take care of. No fancy schools for me. But you want him to go, why?"

"Because he's insanely talented," Mr. Pantalone told him, dead serious. Seth's mouth dropped open. People just didn't *say* that about kids, did they? "He's insanely talented, and I want him to go somewhere where he'll find a way to make a difference. I want that thing he does, where he makes the instrument in his hands cry and laugh and sing? I want him to share that with the world. And he can't do that if he goes to American River College. I mean, he *could*, and then he could transfer to Northridge, and he might still have a career, but I want him to have it now. I want him to have the best teachers and the best opportunities. I want the world to hear him."

Kelly's lips parted slightly, and he licked the upper one in thought. "You want him to be important," he said, nodding.

"Yes."

"I think that's a good thing. What do you think, Seth?"

Seth had to shake himself. He'd been concentrating on Kelly's lips. "I don't know," he said helplessly. "I... I just want to play."

Mr. Pantalone looked at him in resignation. "You think about it, okay? The offer's open until June."

"So after my parents take us camping!" Kelly said, nodding like Seth knew about that already. Which he didn't. "And then I could visit you next year!"

Seth opened his mouth and closed it. "You want me to go?" Oh God. He said that. He said that in front of a *teacher.*

And Kelly—Kelly's happy, excited, shining expression dimmed suddenly, like a cloud in front of the sun. "I don't want you to go," he said, completely sober. "I want you to be important. You've been playing for me for years. I want you to play for the world."

I just want to play for you. "I—"

And at that moment Matty stalked in. "You done yet?" he asked, rolling his eyes. "Oh my God—Seth! We're going to miss the bus!"

Kelly's eyes got intense for a moment, and Seth could practically hear him thinking, *Not my brother. Not now.* Seth looked away and started packing up. "I'm sorry, Mr. Pantalone. This is the day Matty has soccer. We've got to hurry!"

Mr. Pantalone gave Seth the same steely-eyed, resolved look that Dr. Boyle had given him when he insisted that Seth could *too* play that concerto, even if it killed him. "I'll talk to you tomorrow, Seth. You too, Mooncalf. This isn't over yet!"

Kelly rolled his eyes. "I don't even have this class. What makes you think—"

But Mr. Pantalone cut him off with a quick shake of the head. "Tomorrow, Mooncalf. Not now."

"Whatever. Let's hurry. Matty'll be foul if he misses his damned game!"

Together they hustled through the school and toward the bus stop, catching up with Matty as he stood in front of the bench.

"What was that all about?" he asked, only mildly interested. His soccer team had made it to the District Cup this year. The indoor game they had that night was to practice for the outdoor game right before Christmas vacation.

"They're offering Seth a scholarship to a fancy school," Kelly said excitedly. "It's like, a bridge between high school and college, and it's made for performers, like Seth."

"And artists," Seth said loyally. To his dismay, Kelly's mouth twisted.

"I'm good, Seth, but I'm not 'here's the world on a silver platter' good. He was using me as bait. 'Here, come see your friend, he can come too.'"

Seth grunted. "That's low." Mr. Pantalone didn't look so pretty anymore.

"Yeah, well, he's getting desperate. You're not hearing him, and you need to."

"My dad and I talked about it last night," Seth told him reluctantly. He didn't mention his dad much still, mostly out of habit, but partly because even though his dad was eight years sober, Seth didn't want to jinx it. "I told him I didn't want to go."

"And how'd he take that?" Matty asked, stepping back from the curb as the bus approached.

Seth sighed. "I think it made him sad," he mumbled. The bus hissed to a halt and lowered, doors opening, and Seth followed Kelly and Matty on board. Matty found one seat toward the back, and Kelly and Seth took the two together in the middle.

Kelly looked back and waved at his brother, and then the bus started, noisy and chaotic, and he lowered his head to talk in Seth's ear.

"No telling my brother about us for a while, right?"

Seth nodded. "Right. Would he be mad?"

Kelly grimaced. "He's been going to church with his girlfriend—"

"Isela?" Last month it had been Miranda. He seemed to like tiny floaty girls who could make V-neck T-shirts look like lingerie.

"Yeah. Isela. She's a 'good girl,' which is Matty code for he hasn't got past second base. Anyway, it's not our church. They don't seem to like gay people very much." Kelly sighed and slumped forward. "Or, you know, I would have gone home and told the whole world that we finally kissed. And it was awesome. And I want to do it again."

Seth's heart ached. "I want to do it again too," he whispered.

Kelly's spine straightened, and his smile popped back in place, like the dimples were a lock. "I'll run up and drop my stuff like always," he said. "And that way, I don't have to go watch Mr. Righteous Asshole play ball and be a jock and shit."

"You...." Seth swallowed. "I thought you liked your brother."

Kelly just shook his head. "Not when... not when every word out of his mouth is about why you and me shouldn't kiss," he said sharply.

They were quiet then, and Seth opened his eyes to the damage this could do to Kelly's life. Kelly's family. The happy little enclave of people upstairs who had provided Seth with the security his father hadn't.

"I don't want you to hate your brother," he rasped after a few moments of the bus filling their senses.

Kelly looked sideways at him. "That's between my brother and me," he said firmly. Then he perked up. "Oh! Weren't you even curious about camping?"

Seth let out a little grunt of frustration. "There's a lot going on here!"

Kelly's burble told him he'd been unintentionally charming, and he'd take that as a win. "Yeah, there is. My folks reserved a campsite near one of those lakes near Tahoe over spring break. They were going to ask your dad if you could come. I think it's so they have a grown-up kid with each little kid. Personally, I think it's so they can hold hands in the woods and moon about, but I don't care. We get to swim in the lake and see bears."

"I'd settle for deer," Seth said practically. "Why bears?"

"I wanna see it *all*. I wanna see bears and deer and elk and birds and eagles and hawks and fish. I wanna see a hawk catch a fish while dive-bombing a deer. I wanna feed one of my little sisters to something bigger'n me. It's gonna be like frickin' Christmas, and I want you to be there."

Seth could only see one downside. "We won't be able to kiss," he said softly.

Kelly grunted. "Well, maybe Matty will calm down by then about God hating gay people. And even if he doesn't, this is… you know. Us. Like we are, without the kissing. That's still good."

Well, of course. Anything with Kelly was good. Seth's stomach tingled, and he could barely stay still in his seat.

"Excited?" Kelly whispered in his ear.

"Yes," he whispered back.

"Me too. I want to kiss all the parts of you."

Seth let out a little moan, and knew his groin, which had stayed rather quiet through several years of awkward sex ed videos, was swollen.

His *balls* hurt.

He'd never wanted something so bad his balls hurt.

How delicious.

They saw their stop coming up, and Kelly leaned over and said, "Now remember, I have to go say hi to everyone. Get your practice out of the way then!"

Seth nodded and they stood, Matty behind Seth as they walked toward the front and waited for the bus to stop.

That moment—that moment in his life, he knew exactly what he wanted.

Wingman

KELLY GRIMACED as they lined up to get off the bus. "Shit," he muttered, seeing the faces at the bus stop as they pulled near. "What's he doing there?"

Matty sucked in a breath. "I'll deal with him. You guys go home. I don't even want him to see you."

Seth pulled his attention away from, well, hopefully Kelly's lips, because Kelly had been looking forward to that *all day*, and finally noticed the skinny, narrow-eyed white boy with brown dreads standing a few feet back from the bus stop.

"Who's that?" he asked with distaste.

Yeah, well, the kid hadn't done well after his two-year expulsion from his home district. Wherever his parents had put him had apparently been thug-training, because Castor Durant had come back a certified "weapon-toting drug-abusing dirt-under-his-fingernails dyed-in-the-shitty-dreadlocked" criminal.

"Castor Durant," Matty muttered. "Heard he's been hanging around the junior high, passing out free samples."

"Free samples of what?" Seth asked fuzzily, and Kelly grimaced. He loved the guy—oh God, he loved him with his heart and his hormones and everything, but holy crap! Whatever planet Seth spent most of his mind on, it must have been awesome because he didn't come to Earth for anything but Kelly and his goddamned violin.

"Of meth!" Kelly growled. "Bad shit too. They had to take two kids to the hospital because it was cut with drain cleaner."

Matty gave him a hard look. "Where'd you hear that?"

"A kid in my art class has a little sister at the junior high. Parents are transferring her to the one Seth went to. Castor Durant is bad news."

The bus slowed to a halt and swerved to the curb. "Okay, we're gonna get off this bus talking loudly about my damned soccer game, okay? And we're gonna breeze right by him like he's a ghost. You hear that, Seth? No wandering brain like you get. Talk about my soccer team like it's the frickin' Bible, you understand?"

Kelly double-checked Seth's nod to make sure he was with them. He was, but he was also scared shitless—his big eyes made that clear. Kelly winked at him, and then the doors opened and Kelly started down the stairs, chattering for all he was worth.

"So tell me that idiot who kicked the ball in your face isn't playing again," he called over his shoulder. "Because that was supposed to be a pass and you almost lost all your teeth!"

"That was bad," Seth said seriously. "Next time, he needs to hit the basket."

Kelly's eyes got really wide—he could feel it. So he hopped down the step and laughed, because that's what he'd do if this was a real conversation. "In the basket! Good one, man! D'you hear that, Matty? Make sure the ball hits the basket!" He was a couple of feet down the curb now, and Castor Durant was still waiting to get on the bus. Kelly turned toward his brother, hoping the moron would see it was his turn to talk loudly and without meaning.

"Yeah," Matty said stiffly. "That's hilarious. You should tell that to the guys on the team and see how they like it."

Seth ducked his head. "Sorry. It's been a while since I played." And the hell of it is, he was sincere. Here they were, bantering for their life, and the guy was genuinely sorry he didn't know a basket from a goal.

"Yeah, well, you do plenty good in track," Matty said, his voice softening like it often did when they talked to Seth. "You gonna join again in the sp—"

Then… oh no!

Castor Durant had stopped, one hand on the pole just inside the door of the bus, one hand on Matty's arm. "Matty," he said, his voice a flinty smack to the nads. "Good to see you around. You don't go to Oak River?"

"Nope," Matty said, like this guy wasn't the whole reason he was taking the bus to a school half the city away. "Got my grades up. Going somewhere else. Gonna go to college."

"Didn't know you turned into an asshole while I was gone." Castor let go of Matty's arm so fast, Matty stumbled forward. "See you fags later."

Matty whirled, his fists balled up and ready to fly, but Castor was already on the bus and the doors were closing behind him.

"Asshole," he muttered. "I'll shut his filthy mouth and break his filthy teeth—"

"Matty!" Kelly said harshly, stomach cold. Oh God. Look at his brother, all mad. Because nothing pissed him off more than that fucking f-word. "You're gonna be late. C'mon!"

Together they all hustled the two blocks to their fourplex, moving fast enough to leave them breathless. Seth was fumbling with his key as Matty pounded up the stairs, and Kelly paused long enough to put a hand on his wrist.

"Calm down," he said softly. "Don't worry about that guy. He doesn't even go to school, okay?"

Seth nodded, then took a deep breath and smiled shakily. "I don't like that word," he said, and the expression on his face told Kelly that it had just occurred to him that *that* word actually applied to both him and Kelly.

Well, welcome to Kelly's big gay world. He'd been living with this knowledge for a year.

"Not my favorite either," he admitted. "But...." He bit his lip and winked. "It might have its perks."

Seth smiled shyly, and Kelly pulled away. "Start practicing your music," he instructed, backing toward the stairs. "I'll be down after I do the family thing."

Kelly ran upstairs, crashing in through the front door like always, only to practically run over a guy wearing a pastor's coat in their front room.

The guy—Mexican like Kelly's grandma, but leaner, like a basketball coach, and with white mixed in his hair—was standing next to his daughter, a pretty, sloe-eyed girl with a coal black ponytail that had a big curl in the back and a face like a porcelain oval, with an impish twist to her lips.

Matty was standing next to her, a stiff smile on his face, and Kelly groaned inwardly.

"You must be Kelly," Isela's father said, smiling with too many white teeth. "So nice to meet you. I'm sorry—your father tells me that your family was about to leave. I won't take much of your time."

"Yes," Mom said, her eyes squashed flat and her mouth pursed. "We are busy—Matty and the girls have games, and Kelly and the neighbor boy do their homework. What can we do for you?"

Kelly kept his face bland, but he wanted to raise his eyebrows. Do their homework? His mother knew very well that it was his drawing time, but she wasn't telling this asshole nothing!

"I was just coming to extend an invitation," he said congenially. "You called because you seemed to have concerns with the church and—"

"Our son has learned some very peculiar things from your church," Dad said, his eyes as narrow as Mom's.

"Well, yes, if you don't understand our beliefs—"

"I believe people who hate other people need to go," Mom said distinctly, and Matty let out a whine.

"Mom!"

She took a deep breath. "Your stand on the gay population is crystal clear," she said, pulling back her teeth.

"We don't even *know* any gay people—"

But Kelly's mom wasn't having any of that. "How do you know? You don't know that. I know people are all worked up about not liking gay people or not liking brown people—how much fun is not liking brown people, Matty? Are you excited about going to a church that says brown people aren't welcome?"

They'd all watched the news in horror over the last couple of years, waiting for the men in the big uniforms to come and drag them out of school because they looked like someone who shouldn't be there.

"No," Matty said, his defiance melting. "That sucks."

"Yeah, well, this is the same thing—"

"Except Leviticus said—" Matty protested.

"Yeah, well, Leviticus said it was okay to sell your daughter into slavery. You try to touch my daughters, and I will cut your balls off."

The family stared at Linda Cruz, mouths open.

"Mom?" Kelly squeaked.

"I'm sorry," Isela's father said, drawing himself up like he'd have magic powers if he was taller. "I thought you were people of good character—"

"My sons are of the best character," Dad interjected. "And Matty is free to go to your church with your daughter because that's his decision. But I'd rather my kids not be exposed to that sort of hate, frankly."

Isela's dad cast a not-too-subtle look at Kelly, and Kelly wondered if he had *twink* written on his ass or if the guy was just guessing. He didn't care. Good for Mom and Dad for not putting up with this asshole.

"Are you sure your other son wouldn't benefit—"

"No." Both parents yelled, in stereo, staring at the guy like he was ICE.

And then the guy turned to Kelly, and Kelly cocked his head, waiting for it. "Son, are you sure you wouldn't—"

"St. Mary's, downtown, three times a year," Kelly responded promptly. "Got a picture from my first communion and everything. And no. I don't think it's good to shit on LGBTQ people either. Or bite the heads off snakes. Or whip people in secret ceremonies or whatever you people do. Did you know tattoos get you sent to hell too? I swear. It's in Leviticus and everything."

Isela's dad was still staring, mouth open, so Kelly did what he did. "So, you know, my Dad's got our names on his arm. If you want to get picky about it, you can send him to hell, but I don't want him to go to hell 'cause he's a good dad. And I'm with Mom. Stay away from my little sisters. We don't want them sold into slavery. And I like my cotton polyester shirts too. Wasn't that in there? I forget, but you know, there's a club on campus, and they tell us all sorts of things that are way worse than being gay. And they're nice and they bring cookies. Anyway. No. I'll be Catholic until I find something that has better cookies after church. Do you guys do music? Because the music is pretty in the Catholic church—"

"I'll just take my leave, then," Isela's father said, sounding dazed. "Isela—"

"Daddy, you said I could go to Matty's game! You were going to pick me up afterward! When was that, Mrs. Cruz?"

Oh, that would be a treat, having that girl inside their family, pretending to be all friendly but really looking for a way to send the lot of them to hell. Maybe he was being unfair, but Kelly didn't really give a shit. He had Seth—*finally* had Seth—down here, on this planet, actually *looking at Kelly's lips* and Kelly was upstairs dealing with this bullshit?

As though conjured by thought, the strains of Seth's practice scales floated up through the heating vents like it did sometimes when the neighbors were home and had their heaters on too.

Everyone in the living room stopped, including Isela's father.

"That's… that's lovely," he said, surprised.

"That's my friend's homework," Kelly said sharply. "And I'm missing it." He kept his backpack on, although normally he'd take the art supplies out and leave the backpack there by the door. But his mother had told a lie for him and he'd be damned if he exposed her now.

"Your friend plays the violin?"

Well, duh! "He's transferring to a special school next year," Kelly said boldly, because he was going to work on Seth about that. He didn't want Seth to go any more than Seth wanted to leave, but the things that teacher had said—those things were important. So important. That sound wafting up from out of Seth's apartment was magic. This bozo in his living room could talk about what God wanted all he wanted, but the only thing Kelly knew for sure was that God wanted Seth's music to be bigger than this little fourplex in Sacramento.

"That's…." For a moment, it almost worked. For a moment, Isela Cortez's father looked like he was about to fall under the same magic spell that everybody fell under when they heard Seth play.

But apparently his God didn't like music. And right there was a reason for Kelly to ignore this idiot who wanted to make sure the Cruz family was good enough for his little girl.

Mr. Cortez shook himself, like he was waking up from a particularly good dream.

"Is he like you?" he asked. "Of 'good character'?"

Kelly looked him in the eyes like an adult. "He's the best," he said passionately. Then, without looking away, he said, "Mom. I'm going now."

"Fine, honey," his mother said calmly. "We'll wave as we leave."

And Kelly heard that loud and clear.

"Okay, text me when you stop for dinner." Because this was his mother's night not to cook.

"We'll bring you something," she said, and still, Kelly kept his eyes locked with Isela's father, as if he was hypnotizing a snake.

Kelly whirled around and headed back toward the door, but not before he caught his brother's glare.

Well, let him glare all he frickin' wanted. Kelly was done.

He clattered down the stairs and through Seth's front door like he always did, pausing to pull the curtains back so anybody who felt like it could look into the front room.

Seth blinked at the winter afternoon light making its way feebly into his apartment, and frowned. "Why—"

Kelly shook his head and unzipped his backpack with grim purpose. "My family is going to come downstairs and get into the car and wave, and we gotta wave back. And we gotta make sure Matty's girlfriend's useless fucking father sees us, being all chill and making music and doing homework and shit, so he doesn't tell his little girl that she can't date Matty because we're gay. And as soon as all that's over and done with, you gotta hold me for a little bit with no kissing because I'm so mad—so fucking angry—I need to fucking scream."

"Oh," Seth murmured, and he was so quiet that Kelly turned to see what he was doing. Scowling, Seth put the violin under his chin and, quicker than thought, started playing "The Devil Went Down to Georgia."

Kelly heard it then, Seth's anger and frustration, all in the scream of the violin.

Kelly nodded his head, caught the tempo, and started singing the words, 'cause he'd learned them when Seth had first played this song. When his mother knocked on the window and waved, Kelly was standing next to Seth singing cacophonously because he had no talent, and Seth was just about to start the super hard and fast part that beat the devil hands down.

Kelly's mom laughed and nodded, and his sisters waved happily before they all turned toward the car—Isela included, dammit.

Seth kept playing—because if he knew a song and didn't make mistakes, he always played through—and had just wrapped up the lightning quick ending when Isela's father strode by, looking furious.

"Round two," Kelly said under his breath. Seth nodded, and they started all over again, Seth playing so hard, the strings were fraying under his bow. Mr. Cortez stopped his stride across the parking lot as they stared at him, and Kelly strode over to the curtains. He'd been watching Seth for years; he understood drama. As the violin hit its final crashing chords, Kelly started to pull.

The curtains snapped almost shut just as the final chord hit and the third string on the instrument broke with a burst of sound. A two-inch space stayed open in the middle, and Kelly yanked on that, because it was a little bit broken and never shut by itself.

Seth and Kelly stood for a moment, panting, staring at each other in exultation, and then the quiet cool of the room sank into them. Seth set down his instrument just as Kelly started walking and they met at the couch, hesitating for a breathless moment before Seth cupped Kelly's cheeks and kissed him hard.

Kelly moaned. Oh, yes. This is what kissing was supposed to be. Seth's mouth moved over his repeatedly, tasting, licking, sucking on his lower lip, stroking Kelly's tongue with his own. Kelly slid his hands around Seth's waist, slipping behind his back and under his shirt, feeling the thrill of bare skin.

Seth whimpered and sank down onto the couch, Kelly joining him, mouths fused. Seth pulled away just enough to kiss the corner of Kelly's mouth, and then his jaw and ear. He paused for a moment, his breath a magical torment.

"Nibble," Kelly urged. Feeling Seth's lips on his earlobe made him sweat.

Seth tugged, then sucked the lobe into his mouth and nipped, and the thing in Kelly's pants gave a giant throb.

Seth did it again and it exploded.

"Nunghah!" Kelly gasped, pulling away and burying his face in Seth's neck. "Oh God. Oh God. That's no fair. No fair, no fair, no fair."

"What's no fair?" Seth breathed, moving to Kelly's neck.

"I came, dammit!" The wetness in the front of his pants was spreading, and Kelly wanted to cry. "I wanted to kiss you some—mmmff...."

Seth took his mouth again, and Kelly's groin began to swell again. Oh! Dang! Those things were magic, weren't they? Seth's whole body was shaking, though, and Kelly needed to help him out. He managed to pull away, and like Seth had, he moved his lips to Seth's earlobe. He sucked gently, then again, and to his surprise, Seth shook his head no. Instead, he issued a little whine and moved Kelly's hand to his chest. Kelly pulled away and shoved it under Seth's hoodie, rubbing his bare skin, cupping to feel the slight mounds of pectorals, developed nicely from holding the violin. Seth made a sound in his mouth, and Kelly found flat nipples and began to gently pinch, making them not so flat, making them hard and sensitive and—

Oh! Seth groaned loudly and arched his hips and Kelly gave a long, firm pinch—

Seth groaned again and bucked up against Kelly's thigh, shaking hard, like a violin string about to snap.

And then he broke.

The two of them collapsed onto the couch, Seth prone, Kelly on top, trembling in the coolness of the shaded living room.

Kelly didn't want to get up, but the wetness in his shorts was getting cold and clammy and urgent.

"Seth," he mumbled. "Seth, I've got come in my pants."

"Yeah," Seth said, sounding shocked. "So do I. I didn't know I could do that."

Kelly pulled back and squinted. "You never had a wet dream? A fantasy? Rubbed one out after dark?"

Seth's face, which had gone blotchy under the faded clay-brown of his skin, was suddenly suffused with a rosy undertone.

"No," he said, sounding lost. "I… I didn't know I liked boys."

"Then what did you dream about?" He was such a mystery, this boy Kelly had loved forever.

"Music," Seth said simply. "And sometimes your eyes."

Kelly giggled, burying his face against Seth's throat. "You're such a faraway boy," he said, rubbing his cheek against Seth's. "But you dreamed about me."

"Your eyes make me happy," Seth said, kissing his hair.

"You make me happy," Kelly told him, closing his eyes. His heart was so big, it hurt.

THEY WASHED.

Kelly went upstairs and started a load of laundry and put on clean sweats and new underwear. When he got back downstairs, Seth was in clean clothes, and his hair had droplets of water in it.

Seth was standing in his practice corner, tuning his newly strung violin, and he startled self-consciously when Kelly opened the door. Kelly laughed. "This is gonna be complicated," he said, because it had finally dawned on him. "We're gonna be jumping like rabbits at every sound in the building! How we gonna live? I mean—"

Seth scrubbed his face with his hand and set his violin down. "Calm down," he said, walking over to shut the door behind Kelly. "Look at the clock."

Kelly looked over his shoulder at the microwave. "Six o'clock."

"Dad gets home at seven thirty. So we've got time. Here." He pulled out his phone and set it for seven fifteen. "Let's do it this way. You and me, we'll be boyfriends until seven fifteen."

Kelly kissed him quick. "That's not long enough. I want to be boyfriends forever."

Seth's cheeks washed pink some more. "I mean, we can act like boyfriends," he mumbled. Then he frowned. "Why can't we tell people?"

Kelly put his hands over his eyes. "Because my brother's girlfriend's father's an asshole, and my brother's starting to smell like the same kind of asshole. And because we don't know what your dad will do. And because if we go walking down *this* street holding hands, we'll get the crap beat out of us. And…." This one was really selfish and personal, and he was almost embarrassed. "And because my parents don't let Matty and Isela stay in his room with the door shut. If they find out we do what we just did, they're going to make me go watch everybody play soccer and keep the curtains open forever. I might not ever find out what made that big wet spot on your jeans."

Seth smirked, looking like a normal sixteen-year-old boy. He would be seventeen in February, and for this tiny bit of time, after Kelly's birthday in late November, they were only one year apart.

Kelly loved it when he looked young and not a thousand miles away.

"You know what made that wet spot on my jeans," Seth said, biting his lip wickedly. "I'm pretty sure you have one too."

Kelly's earthy chuckle surprised them both, and he covered his mouth with his hand. "Think, you know, we'll see those things someday?"

His face burned, and the tips of Seth's ears were almost purple.

"Yeah," Seth mumbled, looking down at his music as if he was reading the words there. "Pretty sure."

Oh good. "Not now, though," Kelly told him, not even regretful. The afternoon had gone *much* better than he'd planned.

"I already started laundry," Seth said. And then, unaccountably, things were awkward between them, when they'd never been awkward before.

Kelly saw the music stand all set up, and his heart fell. "Did you want to, uh, practice—"

"No," Seth said, meeting his eyes. "You… you know. Sometimes, we watch TV. Think maybe we could watch some TV? Then when my alarm goes off, I can practice again."

Watch TV? "Okay…."

"I have one in my room," Seth said, his eyes darting away like fish or squirrels. "We could… you know. Just, lie on the bed and, uh…."

Oh! Kelly got it now. "Cuddle?" he asked, suddenly excited again. This was Seth, making Kelly important.

"Yeah," Seth said, nodding. "That." He swallowed. "Your body's so warm."

Kelly's heart suddenly throbbed in his throat, and he wanted to feel Seth behind him, the big spoon, as they watched something funny on TV.

He wanted that more than anything.

"Okay," he whispered. "Make sure your phone's set, okay?"

Seth nodded.

Seth led the way, holding his hand unselfconsciously, almost as if they were children. His bedroom was simple. He had a plain blue comforter on the bed and a TV on the sturdy wooden dresser next to it. A laptop sat on a small desk in the corner, next to a framed picture Seth's dad had taken of the boys the day Seth had graduated from junior high. The whole Cruz family had gone, even though it was a different school, because Seth had presented Matty's parents with a hand-written invitation two weeks before. Of course, he'd tagged along with them when Matty had *his* graduation, but this had been special.

And the picture had them all eating ice cream, with one of Seth's smiles making a rare appearance.

There were posters of Disney's *Fantasia* and *Fantasia 2000* on the other walls, and Kelly knew—because he'd asked—that it was because Seth loved to listen to the music and imagine the cartoons. He'd told Kelly that he did this with almost all his music after seeing those movies. He'd close his eyes and wait for stories to unfold.

But not tonight.

Tonight they watched Cartoon Network, which played old shows like *Danny Phantom*. The feeling of having Seth's long body behind his was everything he'd ever imagined, and having his hand splayed on the bare skin of Kelly's stomach was even better. Seth fell asleep for a little bit, probably because he stayed up late doing his homework a lot, and for a blissful moment, Kelly closed his eyes and imagined what being in Seth's arms would feel like forever.

It was warm here. And safe. And the world didn't revolve around Kelly's chatter. Things were real here, and the important thing—the only thing—was that they were together, and they were touching, and nobody could take that away from them.

When Seth's phone went off, Kelly almost cried. He rolled over in Seth's arms and kissed him, and the kisses were still new, and still special. Seth kissed him back, less urgently than when they'd been on the couch, but less awkwardly too. Finally they pulled back and regarded each other with grave eyes.

"We're still boyfriends," Kelly said, making this a law. "Even when we're not kissing or holding hands."

"Of course." Seth nodded. "But when we're alone, we can kiss."

"And hold hands," Kelly said hoarsely.

"And we don't have to tell anyone until we're ready."

Kelly let out a sigh. "Do you *want* to tell anyone?"

Seth bit his lip like he was trying to trap the shine of his smile behind his teeth, but Kelly was still almost blinded by it. "Of course! Look at you! You're… you're *beautiful*. And you're funny. And you like me. You're like the best thing I've ever done."

Kelly gave him another quick, hard kiss on the mouth before pulling back and rolling off the bed. "I think you're crazy, you know. You're a musical genius. I'm just—"

But Seth came and wrapped his arms around Kelly's shoulders, holding him tight. Into Kelly's ear, he said, "You're everything. Today was the best thing ever. I've never been this happy. You're always my best thing."

Kelly nodded, touching his lips to Seth's callused fingertips. "You're my best thing too," he whispered. He didn't want to mention Seth leaving for Bridgford in the summer, and how that would be the best thing for him. He didn't want to say that even if Seth didn't take *this* opportunity, there were bound to be others. He didn't even want to say that Seth wouldn't be able to sneak away from practices that often, because he needed to spend time with his violin, so he could go on to be great and bright and glittery and famous.

He just knew—deep in his heart, he knew—that Seth was going to have to leave him. Leave this neighborhood. Leave Kelly's family. Even leave his father, who he thought Seth really loved.

Because Seth was like a giant, with his head in the sky, touching the sun and the moon. He was too great for this place. That's why he always had his head in the clouds—because even his head knew that's where he belonged.

But his heart was still here, and Kelly was a selfish boy and knew it. He'd keep Seth right there, in his arms, for as long as he could have him.

When Your Feet Touch the Stars

MR. PANTALONE left Lone Oak High School at Christmas break, but he left Dr. Boyle with an entire list of things Seth needed to learn so he could be up with the kids at Bridgford.

Seth did them because they were fun, and because he wanted to make Dr. Boyle proud… and because his father had taken to leaving pamphlets and fliers for Bridgford out on their kitchen table.

He kept thinking that the decision about Bridgford could be made "later." Much, much "later."

Later, after those stolen moments with Kelly became less important. Became less intoxicating. Became anything, everything that could drive Seth out of bed in the morning and outside to meet Kelly and Matty on the landing.

Matty greeted him with a thermos of coffee most mornings. The Cruzes had given him the thermos for Christmas, and Kelly took it up every morning to wash, and Matty brought it down with coffee in the mornings. It was sort of their way to get behind all the practicing he had to do. He was often up until midnight, finishing homework for the honors classes, and Matty's efforts touched him.

He didn't have time to spend with the girls anymore, and he missed them. Lily and Lulu were in fourth grade now, and talking about their homework and history and English, subjects Seth enjoyed. He'd liked helping them, listening to them analyze things—Matty and Kelly's sisters were really smart. Agnes, the baby, was in second grade. Linda walked all three girls to school and picked them up in the afternoon, and Seth was glad.

They saw Castor Durant almost every other day.

Hanging with his buddies, all of them skinny, hyper, sped up by whatever they were taking. All of them dirty, pig-eyed, and mean.

He gave Seth the willies.

Seth had become better at keeping his head out of the clouds when he and Kelly and Matty were in transit. He and Kelly sat next to each other when they could, without being obvious, but never again would they be caught unawares by getting off at the wrong bus stop, or finding the wrong guy waiting at the bottom of the one they were leaving.

Castor had taken to bumping into the three of them when they got off the bus, hard enough to leave bruises.

But Matty didn't take the bait, and Kelly and Seth knew better than to do it if Matty didn't.

Kelly and Seth never held hands walking down the street.

Matty and Isela were getting serious. Kelly said he'd seen Matty get home from "study sessions" with his sweatshirt on inside out a couple of times. Kelly would shake his head.

"He'd better not be getting that girl pregnant. Because then we're stuck with her and her righteous stick up her ass about queer people and shit. Mom and Dad won't let her or Matty talk about it at the dinner table, but I keep asking them where else they're gonna hate next."

He'd scowl when he said this. "They gonna start hating people browner than us? How's that work? How about girls? We gonna make girls walk one step behind us? Only marry them when they prove they can squish out a puppy? I don't get it. They don't even like science. Matty tried to get out of his science unit because they were teaching evolution, but Mom and Dad said the only thing they had against evolution was that it seemed to make Matty stupider than his ancestors instead of smarter, and they thought he should go to school to figure out how in the hell that happened!"

Seth had guffawed at that—and then kissed Kelly stupid, until they were both panting and breathless with their hands up each other's shirts, because this had been during a soccer day when Kelly and Seth got uninterrupted time together to just be them.

Apparently, just being them involved kissing a lot and feeling each other up a lot, and sometimes licking each other's chests a lot.

Seth liked that part, because Kelly had found his nipples and liked to nibble, and that alone could bring Seth off like a bottle rocket most days. But that didn't mean they hadn't shoved their hands down the back of each other's pants already, kneading and squishing and spreading and teasing.

They hadn't yet ventured to the front, but it was only February, and they'd been doing this for two months, but not enough, not every day, not nearly enough for them to be familiar enough for Seth's comfort.

He was starting to look things up on his computer, though, to see what maybe came next.

He was starting to think about Kelly before falling asleep at night, his hand drifting below the waistband of his shorts to see what that thing did when he took it out for a ride.

It could go zero to orgasm in about ten seconds when he imagined it was Kelly's hand instead of his own.

Five if he thought about Kelly's wide, smiling, swollen mouth.

He started maybe wondering what it would be like to put his mouth on Kelly's... uh... oh. He couldn't even think the word "dick" without getting an erection.

The only time he wasn't thinking about sex with Kelly—and all the things they could do between touching lips and the other delicious stuff he'd learned on the internet—he was thinking about music.

It didn't really leave room for thoughts about changing schools and becoming a part of a statewide orchestra and leaving everything he'd ever known behind.

In February, Valentine's Day was on Soccer Wednesday—because sometimes God was kind. It was four days before Seth's birthday, but he wasn't really aware of that. His dad would take him and the Cruz family out for ice cream; that was the way of things.

It was Valentine's Day that made him crazy.

All day long, girls from student government ran in and out of classrooms, delivering little white and red carnations. Boys and girls proudly flaunted the flower from their sweetheart, from their crush, or even from their bestie.

Seth had wanted Kelly to have a flower so bad.

But if he did, he'd have to buy it. He thought about lying, saying he was buying it for... for... and that was the problem.

Seth spoke to Matty and Kelly and the kids from the orchestra and that was it.

He couldn't even think of a girl he could lie about and say, "This girl has a crush on my friend so I'm buying a flower."

The thought of Bridgford suddenly intruded—of being somewhere without Matty and Kelly. Junior high had been a vortex of loneliness. If the Cruz boys hadn't started going to the same high school, his entire life would be a vast echo chamber of all the dumb things running around his own head.

In fifth period, a girl from the student council ran into his Pre-Calculus class, a lone flower in her hand. She squinted at the name on the flower, looked around the class, and then read the name out loud, like she'd never heard of this person before, even though they'd both gone to Three Oaks Elementary School together.

"Seth Arnold?"

He raised his hand, and she ran the flower over to him. He took it shyly and stroked the petals, wondering if Kelly had found a girl to send it to him.

But when he opened the envelope, the name said "Amara," and he blinked in surprise.

Amara? She was a flutist in the orchestra. They were both first chair players and had to come in for practices on solo work a lot. She was a dreamy, red-haired, moon-pale girl with wide green eyes and a soft pillowy body.

He stared at the flower and hoped it was just a friend thing, not a crush thing. *Oh, please, let it not be a crush thing!*

He contemplated throwing it away but didn't. That would be hurtful. Kelly would understand if a girl had a crush. Amara wouldn't understand if he trashed her thoughtfulness.

He pinned the flower to his shoulder and smiled a little at the teacher.

"Someone has a special friend?" the teacher asked kindly. He was a big solid family man, with a sunburned face and red neck from coaching track. Seth was on his team, and Mr. Lipinski liked to give them high fives when they turned in their homework or bettered their time.

"Just a friend," Seth said. "But it was kind. Everybody likes to feel special."

Most of the class looked at him in surprise. "Seth, that's the most you've said all year," Mr. Lipinski said in awe. "I wonder what would happen if someone you really cared about gave you a flower."

Seth grinned, imagining Kelly's eyes over a single carnation. "I'd be speechless," he said before clapping his hand over his dorky little laugh.

Too late. The teacher laughed with him, and the class did too. Seth left fifth period in a happy daze and ran right into a very unhappy Kelly.

"You got a flower?" he asked, his voice pitching in outrage as he grabbed Seth's arm and hustled him to the spot behind a bank of lockers and next to a closed classroom.

"From a friend," Seth said, hoping that would calm him down. "She's shy too. I have to wear it or it would hurt her feelings."

Kelly scowled. "What about *my* feelings?"

Seth bit his lip. "Well, I have a…." Oh, he'd just planned to give Kelly this and not tell him about it first. "I have a card," he said, voice low. "For you. For your feelings."

Kelly perked up. "Really?"

Oh, how embarrassing. "I, uh, wanted to buy you flowers, but you'd have to explain them to people and…." He shrugged.

Kelly nodded and bit his lip. "Okay. You win. Feelings good. You can wear her flower so she doesn't get hurt none. It's okay."

The urge to kiss him was so strong, Seth's heart practically beat in his lips.

The locker next to them slammed, and Kelly jumped back, hustling down the hallway after giving Seth a long backward glance.

His heart was in his eyes, and Seth was suddenly glad he'd kept Amara's flower.

His eyes, his lips, his sleeve—having his heart anywhere but his chest left him with a tremendous ache.

"Seth?"

Amara was sitting in her customary chair as he walked into Advanced Orchestra, and her look at him was so hopeful, he hurt for her.

"Thank you," he said with a gentle smile. "This was thoughtful."

Her face bloomed—that was the only word for it. Suddenly she looked every inch a delicate pale rose.

"You're welcome. I was wondering… do you… you know? Have a date for the dance on Friday?"

Seth frowned. "There's a dance Friday night?"

She laughed. "Yes, Seth. Dance Friday. I guess that means you aren't going with anyone?"

Oh, how to do this…? "I… I wasn't, but…."

Her face fell, and he nodded her over to the band locker, where he was putting his backpack and pulling out his violin. "This was really nice," he said, his voice low. "But I have a… a friend already. We're not going to the dance, though."

She pursed her rather adorable pink mouth, and her eyebrows did a jumping thing that he usually only saw in the very intelligent giant dog that he and Kelly tried to pet when they were picking the girls up from school. "But… but why? Why wouldn't you go to the—" She stopped talking and her green eyes grew huge. "Uhm…."

"What?" he said. "Uhm what?"

"Is your friend not a girl?"

"I have no idea what you mean," he said, but his voice was all over the place, and he knew his lower lip quivered too.

"Shh…." She patted his hand. "It's okay, Seth. Calm down. You have a friend. You're not going to the dance. That's all I needed to know. I'm sorry I pried." She looked a little sad but not destroyed. And her hand on his was everything.

Suddenly he could breathe again. He caught her hand and squeezed it. "I really did like the flower," he said softly. "It was really sweet. I'm sorry I can't be… you know. That friend."

"But I *am* a friend, right?" she asked, and that it seemed that important to her meant the world to him.

"Of course."

"Can I…?" She looked away, embarrassed. "Can I sit with you at lunch, then? I know you sit with the Cruz boys, but I was eating lunch in the library, and the cheerleaders have sort of taken over there, and they're all talking about salads and how to lose weight and…." She gestured to her lush body and shrugged. "I just want to eat lunch with someone. Sorry. I'll go now. We're starting—"

"Of course," Seth said, hoping Matty and Kelly would forgive him. "But Matty's sort of an asshole. I need to apologize in advance for anything he says."

Amara's face lit up. "Really?"

He nodded, and she stood on tiptoe and kissed his cheek. "Thanks, Seth. You're a good friend."

They sat down and started tuning their instruments, and Seth thought wryly that if only she'd given him a flower last week, he might have had her give one to Kelly on Valentine's Day.

He'd really love to have given Kelly a flower in front of the world.

"REALLY?" MATTY asked as they all stood at the back of the full bus on the way home. "She has to sit with us at lunch?"

"She's smart," Seth said, because he had her in English class. "And funny. And she likes Kelly's drawings a lot."

Kelly grinned. "She stays!" he proclaimed. "I like this girl already."

Matty snorted. "Whatever. You morons eat lunch with the fat girl. Me and Isela can go eat our own lunch in the quad."

"She's not fat," Seth said, feeling a flash of anger. "She's sweet."

"Are you finally dating?" Matty asked, staring at him like he'd grown another head. "And *her*?"

"She's a *friend*!" Seth argued. "And don't call friends mean names!" God, it all sounded like those special programs they got in the fourth grade. "You and Isela can go sit anywhere you want, as long as you're not mean to my other friends!"

"Whoa, whoa—whatever, Seth. You guys give *me* a bad time about *my* girlfriend!"

"Your girlfriend hates half the band and most of the drama club," Kelly muttered. "And she doesn't even know them. Seth's girlfriend—"

"She's a friend!" Seth protested, only subsiding when Kelly gave him a bored look.

"Seth's *girl*friend is nice to everybody. Isn't she, Seth?"

Kelly continued the pointed glare, which felt more like a pointed question by now.

"She is," Seth said, nodding at Kelly slightly. "She likes all those people Isela's father tells you to hate. And she'd laugh her ass off if you tried to teach her there's no evolution. And if you tried to teach her that a woman was less than a man, she'd laugh *your* ass off. She's fierce."

Kelly gave a slight smile. "Good to know," he said, his voice mild. "Shit. Goddammit, Matty, can't you do something about him?"

They all looked up to see—who else?—Castor Durant and his buddies, smoking cigarettes and waiting for the bus.

Matty scowled, and for once, they were all in agreement. "Look, guys? Just don't mention the girls, okay? I hear he's going to the grade school and trying to get kids to follow him into his little shit pile in the store. He's got bad things in there. Keep him away from our sisters, okay?"

Seth and Kelly nodded. This was a common goal they could get behind.

They filed off the bus, not pretending they didn't see him, and not getting out of the way either. All the boys—and there were about five of them—lined up, as though making a soccer tunnel for Matty, Kelly, and Seth.

Seth gathered his violin case close to his chest, grateful for the thousandth time for its almost crush-proof construction. The boys smelled foul, unwashed and like cigarettes and some sort of oily smoke that clung to all of them. They crashed their shoulders against Matty,

Kelly, and then Seth as they streamed off the bus, muttering, "Fag. Faggot. Cocksucker," as well as other fun epithets.

The bus doors finally shut on them, and Matty gave a sigh of relief.

"Well, maybe it's a good thing you've got a girlfriend," he said to Seth as they set off for home at a trot. "I am damned tired of that word."

"If he's so damned tired of it," Kelly muttered in an undertone, "why does he always fuckin' use it?"

Seth grimaced, but neither of them had an answer.

Just a pressing need to get home.

Kelly always ran upstairs to say hi to his family before he came down to visit Seth. Today, this gave Seth a little time to set up. He hadn't lied about the flowers—flowers were so clearly a romantic thing, and something you had to display in your kitchen or on your shirt or something.

But a little stuffed animal, that was another thing. He chose a dog because Kelly had always wanted a dog, but the fourplexes didn't let you keep anything but cats. This one was purple and orange, because the colors were whimsical and reminded Seth of Kelly's boundless joy, and its brown eyes were enormous.

He set the card and the stuffed animal up on the coffee table behind him, so he was—*thank God*—standing in front of them when Matty burst in, Kelly at his heels.

"Seth! Tell my stupid brother not to overreact!" Matty snarled, glaring at Kelly with such fierceness Seth would have recoiled—if he hadn't been setting his violin on top of Kelly's card and gift, that is.

"Seth, please tell my brain-damaged idiot sibling that Castor Durant is a serious threat to my damned family and that my mom should know to keep the girls safe and not to let Lily and Lulu walk Agnes home like she did today. If she doesn't know what's out there, she doesn't know that's a bad move. And Dorkface here would rather our little sisters get kidnapped and beat up and hurt and shit, than admit some scumsucking slagdump called him a fag!"

Seth was used to waiting until Kelly paused for breath.

"Kelly's right," he said shortly. "Durant's dangerous. You were the one who was afraid he'd find out who your sisters were. Tell your mother, Matty. She needs to know."

Matty scowled, shaking his head. "And I say she doesn't."

Seth and Kelly exchanged glances. "And Kelly says she does," Seth said, stepping into the role of equal, since Kelly seemed forever locked into "little brother" position. "Kelly can tell her, and you can pretend it has nothing to do with you."

"You two are so stupid!" Matty burst out. "Don't you get it? Castor Durant's parents are fucking bigwigs in Isela's church! His father is co-pastor with her dad! We can't do *anything* about him! If we tell my mom—"

"You don't have to tell her his name, you big coward!" Seth snapped. "Just tell her there's some kids who like to mess with us and we've heard rumors. Jesus, Matty, your girlfriend's church is *not* more important than your family!"

Matty jerked back like Seth had slapped him hard in the face. Even Kelly was looking at him with some shock.

"That's a shitty thing to say!" he snapped with just enough defensiveness for Seth to know he'd hit home.

"Then tell your mother," Seth said, lowering his voice. "I'll tell my dad if you want. He'll pass it along. C'mon, Matty. I... I mean, I know I'm not... you know. Family. But they're your sisters. I.... Maybe you gotta be all alone in the house to know why that's important."

Because Seth had been.

Those moments playing with Matty and Kelly when they were younger had meant everything to him. Running around the house playing horsy, with a little girl on his back spurring him on—those had been some of his best moments.

Until he'd looked at Kelly sleeping, he'd thought ice cream with the Cruz family, his dad a sober, smiling presence by his side, was the best thing in the world.

Matty snorted. "You're so fucking pathetic. Get your own damned family. C'mon, Kelly—"

"Uh, no, moron," Kelly muttered. "It's my night to stay here with Seth. He *is* our family, and you're being an asshole. I'll tell Mom if you don't, and then she'll want to know why it was me."

"Whatever." Matty turned on his heel and stormed out, slamming the door behind him.

Kelly gave Seth a worried look and opened the drapes to the late afternoon sun before the windows stopped rattling.

Seth took a big shaky breath and swallowed. "I'm sorry—" he muttered just as Kelly said, "I'm so sor—"

They stopped and grimaced.

"I hate that he's my brother," Kelly said bitterly. He looked down at his feet and swallowed. "Jimmy Durreson gave Tevin Crane a fucking carnation in second period this morning. Kissed him on the cheek and asked him to the dance and everything. Dammit. I really wanted to give you a fucking flower."

Seth's hands were still shaking, but he turned around and made sure his instrument was okay, and then pulled out his gift.

"Me too," he said softly.

And like that, the sadness washed away. Kelly's eyes went bright, and he took the little stuffed dog and the card with a giant smile.

"This is the dumbest thing," he said, kissing it on the head and rubbing it against his cheek. Seth saw movement from outside and gestured with his chin. Kelly lowered his hand and looked out the window, waving merrily to his mom and dad. Agnes ran up to Seth's window, her customary black pigtails bobbing as she blew a bubble on the glass. Seth laughed and put his hand on Kelly's shoulder.

"I got something for them too," he said, and ran to the door, grabbing the candy necklaces from the end table as he did so. "Agnes!" She stuck her head inside cheekily.

"Did you get me candy hearts?" she lisped, her front teeth a second-grade casualty, like the teeth of every other kid in her class.

"Of course," he said. "Don't I always?"

She nodded like a bobble doll and took the necklaces from him. "Ooh… Lily and Lulu will be all excited. Their Valentine's Day sucked. Some stupid boy said he liked Lily, but he got them mixed up."

Seth grimaced. It didn't help that they both preferred jeans and flowered shirts and they traded all the time. Identical twins, except for the hair. "That's too bad," he said, figuring they'd put things together on their own. "Tell them I said happy Valentine's Day, okay?"

"Yeah. Thanks, Seth! I love you!"

Seth flicked one of her ponytails. "Love you back. Go kill someone in the arena, okay?"

She laughed. "I don't even know what that means! I'm playing soccer." And then she ran to where her mother waited patiently by the car.

"We have ice cream cake," Linda Cruz called. "Come up with Kelly. Bring your dad."

Seth nodded and waved and then closed the door. As he watched the car drive away, he started to close the curtains with the pulley and was unsurprised when Kelly's arms wrapped around his waist.

"Mm." Seth closed his eyes and savored Kelly's warmth at his back.

"Your card was cute," Kelly said softly, standing on tiptoe to whisper in Seth's ear. "And I'm keeping it forever."

Two kittens, draped over each other, surrounded with sparkling hearts and music notes that were superimposed on the picture. The inside had been blank, so Seth had written, "You're my favorite song."

"Good," Seth whispered, turning in his arms. He hadn't closed that final two-inch gap between the curtains, but he figured it was good enough.

"You lied to Matty, though," Kelly said, brushing their lips together softly.

"How?"

"You're our family. If Isela's gonna be family after Matty knocks her up, then you're our family already."

Seth's chuckle sounded strained as he remembered sex ed classes and all those surreptitiously watched videos. "You gonna knock me up?" he teased.

Kelly's eyes went to half-mast, and he raised his chin. Seth lowered his head so Kelly could whisper in his ear, "Only if that happens when I touch your dick."

Seth grunted, his words a touch on their own. His mouth crashed down on Kelly's with a hunger he'd never had for food, and Kelly responded just as hard.

It was like they'd been practicing dancing at slow speed for nearly three months, and now they were going at triple time.

But it was okay now, because they knew the steps.

Kelly's hands fumbled with Seth's shirt and sweatshirt, and he pulled them over Seth's head and dropped them on the floor while Seth fiddled with Kelly's jeans. His button fly was super stubborn, and after three or four tries, he gave a growl and yanked all the buttons open.

Kelly laughed softly and put his hand on Seth's. "It's full in there," he said, giving a geeky little laugh. "Careful."

Seth buried his face against Kelly's shoulder and groaned. "I want to touch all of your skin," he confessed raggedly. "How do we do that?"

Kelly stepped back and yanked off both his shirts, his shoulders and torso gleaming softly brown in the low light from the lamp. They were both shirtless then, and Kelly's jeans were halfway to his knees. He wore boxer briefs, Seth realized, licking his mouth and trying to get some moisture in there.

Tented boxer briefs.

They both locked eyes, and Kelly gave him a quick smile. "I want to kiss all your skin too, *mijo*," he said, and Seth recognized the endearment.

He didn't have a good one for Kelly, but he could be brave.

"On three?" He bit his lip, and Kelly nodded, counting first.

"One…." Kelly slid his thumbs under his waistband.

"Two…." Seth unbuttoned his fly.

"Three!" They both said in tandem, and Seth shucked everything, jeans, underwear, even his socks by mistake. For a moment, they were both too busy kicking their shoes off so their jeans wouldn't get stuck to see what they'd revealed.

He looked up in time to see Kelly, standing on one foot while he crossed the other over his knee and yanked on his socks, and for a moment, the comedy gave him room to breathe.

Then the socks were gone, and there were two boys, naked, in Seth's living room. Seth reached out to touch Kelly's bare arm, running his fingertips down the bicep carefully, and Kelly shuddered.

"C'mere," he ordered. "Let's just…."

Naked body to naked body, they held each other, and Kelly's skin felt like satin, but warm, living and perfect, and Seth nibbled under Kelly's jaw, near his earlobe, so he could taste Kelly's sweat.

Kelly didn't disappoint.

As Seth toyed with his earlobe and skated tender fingertips across his hip bones, Kelly moaned softly and pushed at Seth's shoulders until Seth turned and moved to the couch.

Kelly grinned at him. "You're too tall. Let me sit on your lap."

Naked.

Seth's knees buckled. The couch—still the worn denim from his childhood—felt nubbly under his bare ass.

"Grab a T-shirt," he muttered, and Kelly threw him the one on top— Kelly's, black with a retro band on the front. Seth sat up quickly and laid it out to sit on. When he was back, he saw Kelly's grin had only widened, showing off the dimples on his cheeks that Seth loved so much.

"What?"

Kelly shook his head, moving forward and putting one knee on the couch and then the other as he straddled Seth's thighs.

Oh God.

Kelly sat down, his bare flesh pressed against Seth's, and Seth was *right there, looking at it.*

"I want to touch," Seth rasped, even before he knew his brain could make words.

"It's all hard." Kelly rocked his hips forward, and his... his... *dick, cock, prick* thrust out, begging for Seth's touch.

He started gently. With his fingertips, he traced the length, the bell—Kelly wasn't circumcised, so pulling the hood back to reveal the head was like a magic trick.

Surprise!

A penis, with a purple head wet and shiny and waiting for Seth's fingers to skate over the sensitive face of the thing.

Kelly whimpered and Seth did it again, watching as fluid welled up out of the slit in the top. More magic. Curious, Seth touched his fingers to his mouth, then closed his eyes and sucked.

Kelly whimpered again.

"You want...?" Seth's voice caught. "You want me to do that to *you?*"

In response, Kelly rocked forward, and for a delirious moment, their *dicks, cocks, pricks* rubbed together, and Seth's eyes rolled back in his head.

The skin was so soft. So very, very soft.

Then he realized Kelly had put hands on Seth's shoulders and was pushing up on his knees.

And it got closer, sticking out starkly in its thatch of silky hair. Seth leaned his head forward just as Kelly thrust toward his lips. Seth opened his mouth, and it should have been a comedy of errors right there, Kelly's prick bobbing around, getting caught on his teeth, and then they'd laugh about it and go back to pushing at each other's groins through their jeans.

But it wasn't.

The head slid right past Seth's lips, and he covered his teeth and closed his mouth, making a tight seal, and sucked.

Kelly cried out, right there, and came.

For a moment, Seth panicked. *Come. He's coming in my mouth!* Then he remembered that he liked the taste, and there wasn't that much, and he swallowed and slurped and made sure his mouth was wet. Kelly was still hard, so Seth pressed forward until he could feel the head in the back of his throat, and Kelly convulsed completely, cradling Seth's head in his hands and crying out as Seth swallowed the last burst of come.

With a little sound of repletion, Kelly sank down, sitting in his lap for real and laying his head against Seth's shoulder.

The puddle of come Seth had shot when Kelly was in his mouth cooled on Seth's abdomen, and Kelly ran his finger through it fitfully.

"You came too," he murmured.

"I dreamed about doing that," Seth confessed.

"You enjoyed it?" Kelly sounded uncertain.

Seth smiled, closing his eyes. "I could do that all the time," he confessed.

Kelly lifted his fingers to his mouth and tasted, wrinkling his nose. "It's...."

"It's better hot," Seth told him, and Kelly laughed softly before taking his mouth.

No more words. Just kissing. Kissing and touching. Hands over skin again. They both grew hard, and for an amazing moment, all Seth could think about was stroking Kelly off in his palm. It fit! Fat and thick, it was made for Seth's strong, callused fingers wrapping around it and squeezing, but then... oh then... Kelly did the same to him.

He gave a moan of his own and threw his head back against the couch.

Kelly slid off his lap and to his knees, his head between Seth's thighs. This time Kelly wrapped his lips around Seth's cock—*cock! Yes, a cock! What a wonderful word*—and sucked gently.

"Harder," Seth begged. "But no teeth."

And harder.

And he used his fist at the base and his lips on the head.

And that's about as far as he got before Seth came again.

This time when Kelly sat on his lap, they just made out, soft and slow until Seth wondered when his phone would go off.

And then he sat up abruptly, dumping Kelly on his ass.

"What?" Kelly asked, sounding fuzzy.

"My alarm! Kelly, I didn't set my alarm! It's seven forty-five!"

"Oh shit!"

Kelly popped up, and the next few minutes were a mad scramble. Kelly's shirt was full of come and sweat and Seth threw it in his laundry and gave Kelly one of his own. Both of them needed a washcloth, and wiping off was hard because they were tender, and finally, at seven fifty-one, they were both done and sitting in the front room with the TV on, trying to look casual, when Seth's dad walked in.

"Hey, Seth," he said, his voice low and unusually quiet. "You have a good, uh, practice?"

Seth and Kelly looked at each other and tried not to smirk.

"Yeah. It was okay. Uh, Kelly's folks should be home in a few. They said to come up and eat ice cream cake when they got here."

Craig Arnold took a deep breath and looked at Seth. For no reason, his eyes seemed a little shiny in the lamplight, but he smiled anyway. "Did you even eat dinner?" he asked, sounding unaccountably plaintive.

Seth grimaced. "No." And as if to prove it, Kelly's stomach growled, punctuating the silence.

Dad laughed then, and some of the sadness left his voice. "Well, we've got frozen burritos. I'll put them in the microwave and come watch TV with you guys until Kelly's folks get home. How's that?"

"Sure, Dad. Uh, we were going to ask you something anyway." And it was funny, because when he looked at Kelly for confirmation, neither of them was thinking about sex, just like that.

"Yeah? What's on your mind?"

Seth and Kelly started talking about the kids by the bus stop, and how Castor Durant was the son of someone at Isela's church, and he was threatening without saying anything, and they were afraid.

Dad came back into the room with the burritos on plates and some apple slices with them, because he made sure Seth had vegetables or fruit with every meal.

He regarded the boys seriously and grabbed the remote to put the show they were watching on pause.

"Are *you* afraid of these boys?" he asked bluntly, taking his seat in the battered corduroy recliner. Seth used to sit there alone, doing his homework, before Kelly's dad had started taking Seth's dad to meetings.

"Yes," Seth replied without hesitation. He darted his eyes to Kelly, who was nodding quickly.

"They're nobody to mess with. They smell bad. Like they been lighting up. And they're dirty. And they bump into us all the time. And call us names. It's, like, if my brother just goes and decides to turn on us, we're toast, 'cause Seth can run, but neither of us can fight, and—"

"What sort of names?" Dad asked, looking them both in the eye in turn.

Seth's stomach grew cold. "Just… you know. Names." *Oh God. No. Not going there.* "Just… you know. They're not nice. And there's rumors about them and drugs and kids and the school and—could you just make sure Linda doesn't let the girls walk home alone anymore?"

Dad nodded and gave them both a weak smile, chewing thoughtfully. "I think that's a very good idea. And you know what? *I* don't have any ties to that church. Maybe I'll stop by and give Castor Durant's dad a happy hello."

"Yeah, just don't tell Isela's dad you like *my* happy ass," Kelly muttered. "That man does *not* like me."

"I'm starting to get that," Dad said grimly. "And he probably wouldn't like Seth either."

"I would imagine not."

Seth and Kelly exchanged glances again, and Seth's dad hit Play on the remote.

Later, Seth would remember that moment and think about how funny it was. Kids always thought they knew everything, when adults often saw through them from the start.

He'd also think about his father's lingering guilt about the bad times, the dark times, when there had been yelling and hitting, and about how his dad had worked so very hard to fix the thing he had broken when they'd both been young and sad.

And how this moment, right here, went a long way to putting paid to all that went on before.

A Dark Alley

"AGNES!" SETH called, treading water by where the rope swing let off. "I'm freezing! C'mon, baby girl, do it or let me come in!"

Kelly wrapped a towel around his shoulders and made himself comfortable on the camp chair.

"I think we should bring Seth on all our outings," Mom said next to him. "He's the best toy the girls have ever had."

Well, of course he was. While Kelly and his dad were busy helping Mom build the camp and help with the dishes and the food—and Matty was busy showing Isela that he didn't have to do anything but be freaking useless unless he was stepping and fetching for her—Seth was playing with the girls, inventing games, going swimming, and taking them out in the rented canoe. Matty sneeringly said he made a great little woman.

Kelly was done with his older brother.

But he was falling more and more in love with Seth every day.

Soccer Wednesdays had continued. Seth's birthday gift had been another blowjob, this one with Seth lying in bed and Kelly between his spread thighs.

Kelly had also given him a present—stickers to put on his violin case, because his father had given him his own violin for his birthday. It was used, because a new one, custom-made, would have cost more than Seth's dad made in a year, but Seth's face had lit up the moment he played it.

His father had put his heart and soul into finding that gift.

The stickers on the violin case were rainbow ones—LGBTQ if someone wanted to read that into them—but they also had a leprechaun on them, and Kelly was very aware his name could be construed as Irish.

He told Seth it was his way of sticking to Seth through thick and thin.

He also told Seth that meant he could go to Bridgford and not worry about losing Kelly, but Seth had sort of... tuned out of the rest of that discussion, the same way he'd done with his father for the past two months. Here it was, the beginning of April. They were on spring break, and Seth had *still* not made a decision.

It was driving his teachers batshit crazy.

It was driving *Amara* batshit crazy too, because she had the same opportunity, but she didn't want to go without a friend.

Kelly had finally taken her aside one day and told her point-blank. "Look. We both want him to do what's best for him, but he's really stupid right now. *You* should go. You have his cell number. You have his address. For that matter, you have *mine.* Write him. Call him. Text him. If nothing else, he might come in the middle of next year because you frickin' nagged him into it, okay?"

Amara had drawn her little cupid-bow mouth into a weird figure-eight shape, and she patted his cheek. "Kelly, has it occurred to you that *you're* the reason he's stupid right now?"

Kelly grimaced. They hadn't said anything about their relationship, but of the three of them, she was the least stupid. Seth had been right—she was funny and smart. The first day she'd come to sit down with them, Matty had given her a dirty look and said, "Just don't eat my dessert, okay?"

Before Seth and Kelly could tell him to go to hell, she'd said, "I'm a good girl. Everybody knows we don't eat pudding until we're married. You go ahead and have all the pudding you want."

And then she'd just stared at him, her eyes big and emerald green, and Seth and Kelly suddenly realized that she'd said something incredibly filthy.

They burst out laughing, and they could see when it hit Matty, because his ears turned practically purple. Instead of laughing—like any decent person would do when someone had just thrown that much awesome shade over their heads—Matty stood up and stalked to the trash, where he'd thrown his pudding away. Then he'd grabbed Isela from where she was having lunch with her friends and made her follow him to wherever. Probably a cave, so they could hang upside down like bats and eat pudding *that* way.

Kelly loved Amara so much for that moment, he gave her his dessert with a grin, and she thanked him.

"As long as this is the only pudding you expect me to eat," she said primly, licking the foil lid.

"Naw, I don't get that way with girls," Kelly said, and then he and Seth froze. He'd *meant* that to be, he didn't get crude with girls, but in that silence, they could all hear the truth.

"Well, that's too bad," Amara muttered, rolling her eyes. "And I'm so surprised. I could have a heart attack and die from that surprise. Next you'll tell me that pudding is bad for me and I should cut down on carbs."

"Pudding is the food of the gods," Kelly argued. "And you should eat anything you want. I swear. Girls and being skinny. You're great. If I liked girls even a little, I'd date you. But I don't. So sit with us all the time and keep being our friend and ignore my dumbass fuckin' brother, okay?"

And that had been that. Amara had been solid with them. She texted Seth, she texted Kelly, and both of them had one mutual project to work on.

Getting Seth off his ass to commit to Bridgford.

But Seth was being Seth about it. He'd play all the beautiful music in the world, but figuring out how to make that work for him, take him places, was just… outside his universe.

Especially now that he and Kelly were taking Soccer Wednesdays to some unprecedented levels.

They hadn't made it past the blowjob yet. Kelly kept hoping they'd manage to work a sixty-nine into their repertoire, but every time one of them touched the other with his mouth, there was come everywhere and it was game over.

It didn't matter.

They were in blowjob territory, giving and receiving, and Kelly couldn't decide which he liked better.

On the one hand, having Seth's mouth on him, as well as his rough, strong fingers—he was incredibly talented and enthusiastic. At one point, he asked Kelly if he should take up the trumpet so his mouth muscles could get tighter, and then he'd blown Kelly stupid. So Kelly told him to take a hard pass or he wouldn't be able to think because all his brains would be sucked out his dick, and as it was, it was a close call to make sure that didn't happen.

On the other hand, touching Seth's body was like the holiest part of church that no priest ever talked about. Making him shiver and make his noises and gasp and moan and come?

That was Kelly's best thing.

It's too bad he didn't get *graded* on that shit, because he sure did do a lot of studying and planning and thinking about it. He could practically write a paper on the best way to suck Seth's dick, starting with teasing the end and finishing up with a little tug on his balls and a hard, slow stroke inside Kelly's hot mouth.

But it had taken two months' worth of Wednesdays for them to get there, and Kelly was falling down in the make-Seth-not-be-stupid department. Now, on their long-awaited camping trip in the Sierra Foothills, he watched as Agnes finally committed to the rope swing, letting go with a shriek in the middle of the lake and practically drowning Seth in her scramble to hang on to someone after she surfaced.

Seth pushed up out of the water, though, and laughed with her. "You did great!" he sputtered. "You want to do it again?"

"Yes! Yes! Lily! Lulu! You have to try this thing!"

Kelly's mom laughed softly. "I'll have to make Seth get out in a minute. His lips are blue."

Kelly nodded and grunted, still thoughtful.

"What's wrong?" His mom was so very good about knowing when something was wrong. She hadn't said a word to him about Matty, or the way they'd stopped talking and barely acknowledged they were together when walking home. But she didn't let Matty or even Isela talk shit about gay people or poor people or *any* of the people Isela's church seemed to hate so much.

"He needs to commit to that school," he said.

"Bridgford?"

"Yeah. Mom, have you heard him play?"

"Yeah." She sighed. "That's... it's an amazing talent, you know that."

"He can go anywhere. He could have apartments in New York and Paris." Kelly had read about Paris and its art galleries and artists. Part of him wanted to go to LA, where the street artists were, but a whole other part wanted to see the *Mona Lisa*, even though he knew it was only the size of a postage stamp and fifty-thousand people saw it every day. "He could play for a million people who would all walk away thinking, 'That's the sound of God crying,' and it would make their hearts better."

He didn't realize *he* was so close to crying until his voice cracked.

"You would miss him," she said. Well, who couldn't see that?

"But what sort of"—*boyfriend*—"friend would I be if I didn't make him go? If I just kept him in our neighborhood. It's not fair, Mom, but it would be even less fair if he didn't do what he's supposed to do."

"Have you stopped to think about what Seth would want?" Linda asked gently. She seemed to know something Kelly didn't about that—but Kelly knew a lot of things *she* didn't know too. He knew that Seth didn't want to leave his father because he was afraid Craig would start drinking again. He knew Seth was also afraid that the peace they had, the peace where Seth was loved and cared for and wanted, would go away. He knew that Seth tried really hard to keep his head in the here and now so he could do things like get to school on time and do his homework on time. Kelly had seen his phone. It was full of reminders like "Get up early to write paper," and "Brush teeth every day," and "Scrub *all* the places *super good* Tuesday night." Kelly was especially fond of that last one.

He knew what Seth looked like right after he'd come, and he was vulnerable and dreamy and he said sweet things that no boy said if he wasn't in love.

And he knew that Seth wouldn't admit to wanting to go to Bridgford because it might hurt his dad or Kelly or even Agnes and Lily and Lulu— but Kelly didn't want to say that because it would mean saying too much about himself.

And that would hurt.

"I know he needs to go," Kelly said simply, for once not talking about all the thousands of things in his head all at the same time.

"Well, *mijo*, I think if he listens to anybody, he'll listen to you."

Kelly rolled his eyes at his own mother. "Sure," he said sullenly. "Here, watch this." He sat up straighter. "Get out of the water, dumbass! Your teeth are chattering!"

"L-let m-m-me c-c-atch the tw-twins first!" Seth chattered back, and Kelly looked at his mother pointedly.

His mother raised her eyebrows. "Javi, honey?" she said sweetly, and Kelly's dad looked up from the fishing pole he was trying to set up, because he promised Matty there would be fishing, even though Xavier Cruz had never fished a day in his life.

"Yeah?"

"Get Seth out of the water, would you? He's freezing."

Dad set the fishing pole down, made sure the hooks were in the tackle box and sealed it, then waded out into the late afternoon waters of Lake Sugarpine like he was marching to his doom. "Holy God, Seth. Get your ass in to shore and warm up before dinner. Jesus, kid, if we bring you home like a giant popsicle, your dad will never forgive us."

"Daddy!" Lily called, standing on the granite rock with her hands on the rope swing. "Daddy, Seth was gonna catch us!"

"No, he wasn't!" Xavier called back. "He was going to get you to dump your fuzzy butt out here and then try not to get dropped on. I can do that just as well. Now come on, you three. One last jump with the rope for all of you, and then go up on shore. Seth, go."

"Ok-k-k-k-k-ay." Seth chattered his way to shore, walking stiffly in his water shoes, probably because his joints had frozen up. Linda stood with a big brightly colored towel and wrapped it around his shoulders, and Kelly tried hard not to be mesmerized by the way Seth's dark brown nipples drew up into teeny little bullets in the cold.

"You, go sit in the sun next to Kelly," she ordered. "I'm going to go see if the chili's almost ready and start the hot dogs. When you can actually move again, you two can come up and set the table, since we can't trust you to have the good sense not to freeze to death." Then she stood and pitched her voice across the lake. "Javi! When you get the girls out of the water, come make a fire! It's going to be chilly tonight!"

"I hear you." Dad frowned. "Where's Matty and that gi—I mean Isela. He needs to help too!"

Kelly's mother rolled her eyes. "They're off taking a *nature walk*," she said, insinuation dripping from her voice.

"A nature walk? They went to go find out about the birds and the bees is more like it!" Dad laughed. "Augh! Lily! Warn me!"

Kelly's sister swung out of nowhere and dropped on his head. They went down in the water, floundering, and Kelly took the moment of privacy to make sure Seth was warming up.

"Your lips are blue, *mijo*," he said softly. "You need to get out of the water sooner, or your balls will disappear."

Seth made that dorky little laugh in his throat and bobbed his head, and Kelly wished they were alone so he could rub his thumb on Seth's blue lips and maybe put some color back in them.

"So," Seth said, his voice still an undertone, "you think your b-b-rother will still—"

"Sneak off to get laid?" Kelly finished. "I hope so. Best time of the trip!"

They didn't do anything, not really. Last night, Matty had waited until they both grew quiet and their breathing grew even, then had snuck out of the tent, mumbling something about the bathroom. But they'd both heard Isela getting out of the girls' tent at the same time. Mom and Dad were sleeping on an air mattress on the floor of the minivan, so they probably didn't hear. Either way, Matty and Isela snuck off to be alone at night, and Kelly and Seth kissed.

That's all. Kissed. Cuddled. Held hands.

Quietly acknowledged that they were there as a couple.

It was the first time Kelly wondered if it might be worth it to call a halt to Soccer Wednesdays. It would almost be worth it to work harder to find time for sex if they could kiss everywhere—or even just touch hands, or hips, or shoulders.

If only Kelly could rub his thumb over Seth's lips and make them pink again.

"Kelly!"

They both jerked, and Kelly wondered how long his dad had been calling his name. He was out of the water already, and Seth's lips *were* pink again, and they'd apparently been staring into each other's eyes like his totally disgusting brother and his bitchy girlfriend.

How gross.

But it was totally unavoidable, and he'd stare into Seth's eyes again and again if he could.

"What, Dad?" he asked, seeing Seth looking away at the lake with his secret Kelly-smile on his lips.

"If you two are dry, go put on some sweatshirts and help your mother like she asked. Geez, you guys, you were totally…."

Kelly's dad turned his head sideways and stared. His lips moved, and he looked hard at Seth and then back at Kelly, and Kelly kept his eyes big and round and innocent, like he had when he'd been little and had taken the last cookie, because the girls *always* got the last cookie, and sometimes Kelly just liked more than one, that was all.

Kelly stood up and tagged Seth on the shoulder. "C'mon, let's get dressed. The skeeters'll come out and eat us both if we don't."

Seth nodded and gave Kelly's dad an absent smile. "I hate mosquito bites," he said serenely, with so much space cowboy in his voice that even Kelly doubted he'd been mooncalfing at Kelly the way Kelly had been mooncalfing at him.

It worked, because Kelly's dad shook his head like he was shaking off a particularly new and scary idea, and Seth and Kelly ventured through the woods, using the path that cut from the campground to the lake.

"That was close," Kelly muttered.

"That wasn't close," Seth said, surprising him. "That actually happened. Kelly, I'm betting Soccer Wednesdays aren't gonna continue after this week."

As. If.

"What? They're gonna make me go with them? With all the other kids playing? I don't think so. What are they gonna say? 'Erm, Kelly, you have to do homework up in your room because, even though you're getting As and Bs, we think you need to be alone to get more As and Bs?'"

Seth let out a sigh. "They could just say it's inappropriate for two young people who are dating to have so much time alone together."

Kelly scowled and kicked a rock. "Like my brother?"

"Those were actually your mom's *exact* words to your brother last night when they went for a nature walk."

Kelly guffawed, worry forgotten. "Nature walk. Seriously. They probably mean walk au naturale!"

He heard Seth choke on a snort, and the topic was dropped as they negotiated the divots in the path and the logs lying on top of it. Suddenly Seth hissed, "Shh!" He put his hand on Kelly's shoulder and moved close enough that Kelly could still feel the chill of the lake water radiating from his skin. He leaned forward and whispered, "Look!" into Kelly's ear.

And besides the insta-boner, because Kelly's ears had *not* gotten any less sensitive, Kelly was also alerted to… "Ooooh…." Both of them took the moment to look at the mama deer and her half-grown fawn, moving through the woods at a leisurely pace, picking delicately at the grass growing between the trees and the rocks on the ground.

They stood, frozen, watching the tableaux, enchanted, when Seth's body behind Kelly's became an unbearable temptation.

He turned and captured Seth's mouth, shuddering at the taste, when a harsh gasp broke into their moment.

They both turned their heads toward the sound, and Kelly let out a bark of shocked laughter.

Off the path, about twenty yards away, hidden by the shadows and some trees, Isela was bent over a log, her hair hanging in her face, her palm jammed into her mouth. Matty was pumping behind her, both of them naked from the waist down.

At Kelly's sound, Matty and Isela both looked up, while Kelly was still in Seth's arms.

Kelly swallowed. "I think we need to go help Mom," he said loudly, then turned without looking at Seth and led the way down the path.

They were within sight of the campground before Seth spoke. "What now?"

Kelly shrugged. "Checkmate," he said. "You and I were kissing. He was *banging his girlfriend.* He squeals on me, I squeal on him."

Seth's hand, tugging on his, was hot now, like the exertion and the embarrassment had flooded under his skin. "But... but Matty won't like us anymore."

Kelly turned, feeling suddenly older than he was. "Yeah, Seth, but did he really like us anyway? I mean, we have to live in the same place because we're brothers, but his whole life is about Isela, and the two of them, they don't like anything we are."

Seth swallowed hard, and his eyes did that thing where it seemed like he was two hundred years away without even blinking.

"Okay," Seth said, his voice as remote as his eyes.

And Kelly got it then, so hard and so quickly his chest ached like he'd just caught a soccer ball with it. "Seth?"

"Yeah?"

"You're really hurt right now."

Seth blinked, and his eyes grew a little shiny. "I'm fine."

Oh God.

Kelly had always known Seth was his dreamy boy, that he seemed to float in from far away to visit planet Earth to make sure it was all doing okay.

Until this moment he'd never realized that Seth did that because being here on planet Earth hurt.

Oh Seth. All those times you were so dreamy—except when you were playing music. Or with me. Did the world hurt so very much?

He stood up on his tiptoes and kissed Seth, hard, like he didn't care who saw him, like he was proud Seth was his.

Seth responded eagerly, only pulling back when Kelly did.

"I'll be enough, right?" Kelly asked, surprised at his own hurt.

"All I need." He was right there, in the here and now, and Kelly's chest eased up a little.

Kelly caught enough breath to walk back to the campsite and find his mom. Chili that night, which probably meant Matty would fart up the tent right before he bailed to bang Isela again, but that was okay. As long as he left.

That night, Matty managed to completely avoid Seth and Kelly through dinner, through campfire songs, through marshmallows. Kelly pretended he didn't notice, and Seth was light-years away. For a brief moment, Kelly wished Seth could be there *with* Kelly, and then he caught Matty shoving up against Seth on their way to the tent. Seth hit a tree with a muffled grunt, and Kelly whirled to confront Matty.

Well, in a stage whisper. "What the fuck's your problem," he hissed. "You got something to say to us?"

"Do I got something to say to two little faggots who can't—"

"Can't what?" Kelly snarled. "Can't keep it in our pants? 'Cause our things were exactly where they were supposed to be, Matty. Where the fuck was yours?"

"You shut your filthy mouth!" Matty pulled back his arm, cocking to release a punch, and to Kelly's horror, Seth wandered in between them like this wasn't about to go WWF on them.

"Congratulations on you and Isela," Seth said, as though he meant it. "You must really care about her."

"Don't even say her name, faggot!"

And Seth just ignored him. "I mean, if we fight right now, we're gonna have to say why. And we're pretty sure your folks'll still love Kelly, you know, but what's Isela's dad gonna say when they tell him?"

"About what? You guys necking in the woods or what we were doing?"

And then Seth smiled, just a twist of the lips in the light from the still glowing campfire. "Either one, Matty. Either one."

Matty let out a furious breath, but his fist lowered. "You two, don't even bother to speak to me. I don't fucking know you. Not at school. Not on the bus. Not with Castor Durant. You hear me? You're both fucking abortions—you never should have been born."

He turned around and took off, not even bothering to get in the tent. Seth and Kelly took their shoes off at the entrance and then slid into their sleeping bags, wearing the sweats they'd put on before dinner.

"That was awful," Kelly said, breaking the silence first.

"I'm sorry he said that to you," Seth murmured, and Kelly saw his outstretched hand near the sleeping bag. Kelly took it, and then, because his brother could either tell their parents or not, he scooted his sleeping bag a little closer to Seth's on the foam pad they were sleeping on, and pulled his pillow closer too.

"He said that to you too," he reminded Seth gently.

"Mm. I hope he's not awful to you when you get home."

Kelly sighed and squeezed Seth's hand, glad when he squeezed back. He couldn't see his boy's eyes, but he bet they were a thousand miles away.

TRUE TO his word, Matty stayed his awful, pestilential self when they got home.

He tried to put an end to Kelly staying with Seth during Soccer Wednesdays, but his mom reminded him that if Kelly came, he'd have to sit in the same seat with Matty and Isela, since she was coming too. Matty's look of horror might have been a little funny, but the way he kept slamming Kelly into the wall as they walked down the hallway at home was getting damned old.

Kelly and Seth started taking more risks at school. There were other kids, girls and boys, who held hands with *their* same-sex crushes. Not all the time, but in a certain part of the quad, where they felt safe. Kelly and Seth—and Amara, because they loved her and didn't want to leave her behind—started eating there so they could sit together, at least, and not worry about Matty dumping Seth's tray.

Which he did twice before they wised up and left their table in the cafeteria.

And Kelly had to admit, the whole thing would have been easier to bear if Seth had been there for him in his head. But Seth and his dad were starting to talk about Bridgford *every day*, and Castor Durant had realized that Matty wasn't protecting them anymore. In fact, the fucking traitor had started sprinting to take the earlier bus, leaving them behind. Every day Kelly and Seth got off and had to fight their way through foul, smoky bodies, sharp elbows, hard shoulders, dirty teeth, and laughing demons, just to get home.

Dr. Boyle, whom Seth would do about anything for, had dumped so much extra practicing on Seth that Kelly was surprised he could even surface enough to know Kelly was there on Soccer Wednesdays.

But he was.

Kelly would fly through the door, and they'd close the drapes, and before Kelly could even walk across the room, Seth had set down the violin—Amara, he'd named it Amara, because he said it was a girl, and he'd never want to "play" Kelly—and walked across the room and was holding Kelly, holding him so tight that Kelly would wonder if he hadn't just saved all of his "being on Earth Seth" for Kelly and this moment right here, when Kelly was in his arms.

Kelly always thought it was sort of an honor when he did that.

And their moments together were painfully sweet, slow, almost like they were drawing out every touch because they knew things were changing.

Kelly hated himself for how much he wished that wouldn't happen.

ONE FRIDAY in late May, the family was huddling in the air-conditioning, hiding from the unseasonable heat that had hit Sacramento like a fucking hammer.

Kelly was listening to music on the iPhone his father had passed down to him for his birthday, since Matty had gotten a new one for Christmas.

That was it. Just music. Seth's music—modern pop hits adapted to violin, which was Seth's favorite. Seth had asked him to pick out some songs he liked best, because Seth had to learn something to audition with again, and he wanted to play a song for Kelly.

He was on his back, in bed, when Matty strode in, out of nowhere, and slugged him on the shoulder, then slapped his head.

"Get the fuck out of my room, faggot. I'm so fucking tired of looking at your face!"

And maybe because the attack came out of nowhere, Kelly's temper flared. He was tired of this shit.

He propelled himself up off the bed and threw his brother across the room.

"Say it again!" he snarled, as Matty was picking himself up. "Call me a fag again! Tell me why it's bad! Tell me why you can assfuck Isela in the fucking woods but I can't kiss my boyfriend? Say it!"

Matty stared at him, his eyes wide and darting to the door behind Kelly, but Kelly didn't care. He was done caring who heard him. He was going to lose Seth anyway. Seth and his father were downstairs talking about Bridgford—again—and this time, *this* time, Seth was right here on planet Earth, because Kelly could hear him yelling too.

"You said you wouldn't tell," Matty hissed.

"Well, you shouldn't have been an asshole," Kelly shouted, and that did it. He heard the door crash open behind him just as Matty launched himself at him. Xavier caught Kelly before he wrapped his hands around his brother's throat and beat his head against the floor.

"Whoa! Whoa! Whoa! Oh my God! Boys! What in the *hell*?"

"He started it!" Kelly struggled furiously against his father's grip. "I was lying here, listening to music, not touching nothing, and he comes in and starts beating on me. Him and his good Christian values—he can keep them!"

Kelly twisted away then, and hurtled through the house toward the door. His little sisters were in the kitchen, begging piteously for some soda or something, but of course it was all gone because of the ungodly heat.

"Kelly, where are you going?" his mother called.

"To get some ice!" Kelly snapped, slamming the door behind him. He clattered down the stairs in a huff, fully intent on running to the gas station two blocks away to get some ice and some sodas for his little sisters. Yeah, sure it was by Castor Durant's little crack house, but Castor and his buddies were usually off the streets by now, either in their homes or in the vacant stores, getting high.

He slowed, though, as he came to the bottom of the steps, and thought yearningly of Seth's company.

They were both having a sucky night at home. Maybe some time together would make up for it.

He knocked on the door to Seth's apartment tentatively, and then peered inside through the gap in the curtains, hoping for the best.

Not so much.

Seth was standing, arms crossed over his chest, near his practice corner, glaring at his father, who was standing by the kitchen table.

Shit. He stuck his head in anyway.

"Uh… Seth?"

They both startled, shaken out of their death-match stare, and Seth's dad struggled to remember words.

"I'm sorry, Kelly. Can I help you?"

Kelly tried to wipe his own glare away. He liked Seth's dad. He brought them dessert on Soccer Wednesdays, and always knocked on the door to his own house before he came in. Kelly wasn't sure why he did that, but it sure did predispose him to love the guy.

"Uh, yeah. I was going to the Ampm to get some sodas. You guys want something? Ice cream? Anything? It's hotter than *ass* out here!"

Seth's dad's mouth twisted on the sides. "That's, uh, a very attractive offer, Kelly. Seth, did you want anything?"

Seth shook his head and sent a "Please help me" look at Kelly. "Can I go with him?" he asked hopefully.

"No." Mr. Arnold sighed. "But Kelly, if you want to stop by afterward with some root beer and ice cream, we can watch movies or something. Seth and I need to finish our conversation."

Oh, thank God for Seth's dad.

"Thanks, Mr. Arnold. That sounds like the best. Like the greatest. I'll bring—"

"Here." Seth's dad dug in his pocket and came back with a ten. "My treat. Just ten more minutes, okay?"

Kelly was just so grateful. Sure, Seth's company would be nice, but God. To spend some time here with Seth, even on opposite ends of the couch, where it was cool, without his brother's toxic presence—it sounded like heaven.

"I'll be back in twenty," he said happily, taking the ten and winking at Seth. "After I bring my sisters some soda and some ice."

It would be a bitch to carry home, but hey, it would be worth it, right?

He closed the door behind him and went whistling into the humid darkness. For a moment, he contemplated cutting across the vacant field, but decided against it. There were no streetlights over that field, and even though the moon was big and yellow tonight, high overhead, there were lots of nasty things there—broken bottles, needles, pipes—and Kelly just wanted some goddamned ice. He ignored the shadows of weeds and abandoned shopping carts under the moon and strode quickly down the sidewalk, making it to the relative safety of the gas station with a sigh of relief.

He gathered his purchases, including the ice cream and the root beer and the ice, and then asked the bored sales clerk for a bag.

The sales clerk—a redneck guy with thinning gray hair, a wide ruddy face, and more tats than teeth—rolled his eyes, like this was a big deal, and found a big plastic bag for the food and soda.

"Gonna have to carry that bag of ice yerself," he cautioned, and Kelly shrugged.

"It's hot. Won't be too bad," he said with a smile.

There was a raucous burst of laughter from outside the gas station, and his smile died. The redneck guy glanced outside and grimaced.

"Shit. Them fuckers. Kid, I'm calling the cops. You want to stay here?"

Kelly looked outside and groaned. Castor Durant. Seriously? "I hate that guy," he muttered. He was here by himself, the ice cream melting, the ice dripping, and God....

All he wanted was Seth's battered denim couch.

And air-conditioning.

And his boy's dreamy smile.

"I'll deal," he said with a shrug. "What're they gonna do? Shoulder me to death?"

The guy already had the phone up to his ear, and he shook his head now, even as one of Castor's goons let out a cackle. But Kelly, he had home on his mind.

He squared his shoulders, because he was nobody's bait, and started outside.

Under the Yellow Moon

SETH WATCHED the door close behind Kelly and wished like anything he could go with him.

He didn't want to be there, arguing with his dad anymore.

"Dad—"

But his dad wasn't standing with his hands on hips, angry like he had been. He was looking at the door instead, his hand on the back of his neck like he had a headache.

"Dad?"

"Seth, you can't stay here for Kelly."

Seth swallowed, feeling betrayed. He thought his dad would…. Never mind. "You don't understand about Kelly!" he cried out. "I thought I'd have until June!"

"You have until *next week*!" his dad reiterated. "The bus leaves next week, and I promised them I'd get you on it. You get on that bus and start the tour, and end up in Bridgford and a whole new life."

"I don't want a new life!" Seth hated the thought. "I like it here. I like it with you." *And with Kelly.* The words hung between them, unsaid, unheard.

He thought.

His father sighed and dropped into the kitchen chair. "Seth. Son. Hear me out. All the way. This is important, because I want you to know. I *do* understand about Kelly. Do you think I haven't been there? I had college offered to me on a platter, and I chose your mother instead. And I don't regret that decision. I don't."

Seth was going to say, "Then why are we having this fight!" but then it hit him.

Sunk in.

His father was comparing Kelly to Seth's mother.

Oh.

"Then why…?" He couldn't say it, he was so stunned.

"I'm not asking you to make that decision, son." Craig looked up and smiled at him, the soft smile that Seth remembered from when his dad got back from rehab. From those moments getting ice cream. From birthdays, when his father surprised him with something important and music related.

From the times he brought takeout and sat in his recliner while Seth and Kelly sprawled on the couch and they all watched TV together.

The smile that said his father loved him.

Seth's breath caught.

There was something important going on here.

"I'm not asking you to choose," Dad said again, softly. "There's iPhones and texting and emails and Skype. There's me going down to visit you and bringing Kelly with me. There's you coming home for holidays and you and Kelly having time to yourselves. I love you, Seth. If Kelly's the person you want, I don't want to take him away from you. But I want you to have the world too. Is that so bad? This is a way for you to have the world at your feet, son. If you want to take Kelly on that ride with you, I'm fine with that. I'll help." He swallowed, his eyes growing red-rimmed. "I'd be proud to help you become the man you're growing into. Every minute you let me be your dad is a blessing I don't deserve. So think about it right now, and ask yourself. Can you do it with my help? If you know you're not leaving him for good? If you know you have support—at least my support—here at home? Is that something you think you can do?"

Seth stared at his father, his mouth open, trying to find something, *anything* to say.

What came out was stupid and obvious and painful.

"How did you know?"

Seth's dad let out a strangled half laugh and gestured to the plain brown curtains that came with the apartment and mostly sat there and gathered dust unless he or his dad remembered the vacuum attachment on odd cleaning days. They were open about two inches, because the pulley was broken and blocked, and they never seemed to shut on their own.

"Do you guys think you're invisible? Like, you *tried* to pull the curtains so I can't see what you're doing?"

Seth stared at the gap in the curtains in horror. "Uh… uh… I mean… uh…."

His father laughed softly. "You were young. And in love. I'm right? In love?"

Seth swallowed and nodded. "You saw the right thing if you saw that," he said.

His father's smile… gah! Seth would remember it forever. "Well, it was obvious, even if I didn't get the X-rated version," he said. "You two—the way you look at each other." He grinned then, like he was inviting Seth in on a joke. "It was so sweet, I totally needed insulin. You guys are like buttercream frosting. It's gross."

Seth laughed, embarrassed, and sank down on the arm of the couch, relief pulsing out his body.

"So gross," he agreed, remembering when Matty had used that word, and it wasn't funny at all. But this was his father, and his father had just given him... well, everything.

His father had told him it was okay.

That he was loved.

And that his father loved Kelly too.

"What if...?" Seth swallowed, and listened for the sound of Kelly's footsteps up the stairs. *Shouldn't he be back by now?* "What if Kelly and I... I mean, what if we don't make it?"

His dad stood and ventured toward him, arms out a little. Seth nodded, and Craig Arnold stepped into his space and held him, tight, like he had when Seth had been a little kid and his father had been safety and kindness and all the things they'd lost but found again.

"I can't say it'll last for sure," Dad whispered. "But I can do what I can to help you guys, okay? I know Kelly's been nagging you to do this too. Imagine how badly he wants an opportunity like this. He loves art more than anything, Seth. Except you. You'll hurt him if you don't take this chance. He knows it. I know it. Please. Sleep on it. Talk to him when he gets back...."

They both pulled apart.

"Shouldn't he be back already?"

Seth nodded, and worry slammed down on him like a jackhammer. "Want to walk to the store? We can just sort of... make sure he's okay."

Dad nodded, and they both grabbed their phones and keys and went off into the night.

They walked quickly, avoiding the vacant field for the same reasons Seth and Kelly avoided it in the daytime. Yuck! By the time they'd gotten to the gas station, they were jogging.

Seth saw it first—a bag full of sodas, lying by one of the gas pumps. There was a quart of ice cream in it, vanilla, lying on its side and melting onto the pavement, and a two-liter plastic bottle of root beer rolling fitfully nearby.

And a bag of ice, halfway to water, on the pavement right next to the pump.

"Oh God," Seth whispered. "Kelly. Dad?"

Dad already had his phone out and was calling Kelly's parents. Seth ran into the gas station, where a grizzled guy with a lot of tattoos was looking outside in alarm.

"Did you see him?" Seth asked. "Kid my age? Straight hair, bangs? Big brown eyes?"

The guy nodded. "Sweet smile? Yeah. I called the cops about ten minutes ago. He walked outside and that group of hooligans, they just surrounded him. I said it looked like assault, and then they just grabbed him and disappeared. The kid was hollering for help and the damned cops haven't gotten here, and—"

"Kelly Cruz," Seth told him, crying, not caring. "Tell the cops his name is Kelly Cruz and he's a good boy and—oh God!"

"Seth!" his father was calling him as he ran, but Seth couldn't think about that now, because Kelly, *his* Kelly, with the laughing brown eyes and the dimples in the corners of his cheeks, who could talk about blowjobs while he was drawing a picture of their friend that looked like an angel—he was out there… in the night. By the shitty vacant field with the terrible things that Seth didn't want touching his skin.

Seth ran straight to the vacant stores, and it wasn't that he didn't hear the ruckus inside—it was that he didn't care.

"The cops are coming! The cops are coming!" he shouted at the top of his lungs, not caring if it was true or not, just caring that whatever was going on stopped. He crashed through the boarded-up front door, surprised when it opened without a problem, and arrived just in time to watch the last of the gang disappear out the back door of the empty, vacant 7-Eleven.

"Kelly!" he called, his eyes adjusting to the total darkness. He pulled out his phone and fumbled, not finding the flashlight function because his fingers were shaking too hard. Instead he just used the light from it to look around, and that's how he saw him.

Lying on a filthy mattress in the corner, on his side. His pants down around his ankles. Blood on his backside. His face buried in the piss-sodden flocking spilling from the split seams while he sobbed.

"Oh… oh God. Baby."

Seth crouched down next to him, ignoring the filth, the smell of pee, the smell of shit.

"Go away," Kelly rasped, and Seth was crying too hard to take exception.

He wouldn't want Kelly to see him like this either, but he couldn't leave.

"Baby," he said instead, sinking to his knees. "C'mere."

"Don't let them see," Kelly begged. "My mommy and daddy… don't let them see…."

His voice rasped weakly, broken, and Seth would see the choke marks against his skin in his nightmares for years.

But he couldn't see them now.

He could just see his bright, beautiful boy, still alive. Still breathing. Bruised and broken, but still good.

"C'mere," Seth whispered again, pulling him into his arms.

"Don't go nowhere just yet," Kelly said. "Next week, okay? But not now."

And Seth broke down and sobbed, holding his boy in his arms, not escaping, not going anywhere else but here, because he'd never forgive himself if he left Kelly now.

SETH DIDN'T remember the call to his dad, but it must have been pretty bad, because there were ambulances and fire trucks and cop cars pulling up by the time his father crashed through the door to the vacant store, Xavier Cruz at his heels.

Seth had pulled up Kelly's pants by then, because Kelly had begged him to.

"Don't want them to see," he rasped. "Can't see. Dirty."

"You didn't do anything wrong," Seth told him. "You didn't do anything wrong. You're not dirty."

"Don't touch me. Dirty."

But Seth ignored him, settling Kelly into his arms, cradling him like he used to cradle Agnes when she was too tiny to even smile.

Their fathers burst through the door, and Seth just held him tighter and cried.

Xavier squatted by them. "Oh, *mijo*. My boy. What did they do to you?"

"Daddy…." Kelly's voice broke, and Seth was crying so hard by then he didn't remember anything else until the ambulance got there and they pried Kelly out of his arms. Seth tried to get in the back of the ambulance, but his own father stopped him.

"We'll go in the morning," his dad said, looking at Xavier, who was sitting by his son. "We'll be there in the morning," he said more clearly. "Call us if you need anything."

Xavier nodded, looking wrecked and hurt. "Tell Linda," he said. "Tell Linda—I'll call her when we know."

"Why not tonight?" Seth asked, his voice cracking. "Dad, why can't I go? Why not tonight?"

His father grunted. "Because the police want to talk to you first."

Seth didn't remember much about that. Far away, there was an ocean. He'd never been to the ocean, but he liked to dream about it. There was a violin playing such music, it could only mean salt air and the crashing of waves and heartbreak and struggle and triumph and joy.

Seth went there in his mind, listened to that music, and let his mouth move on its own.

HE WOKE up early the next morning, disoriented, only to realize that he'd fallen asleep next to his dad, on top of the covers of his dad's bed. His dad had managed to get him out of his wretched clothes and into a clean pair of sleep pants, and after that....

Seth remembered holding on to his father, as if holding on to the mast of a ship in a storm, and sobbing until he couldn't breathe.

Sometime in the middle of that, his dad's phone buzzed. "It's Linda. Xavier says Kelly's going to be okay, and we can visit in the morning."

It was probably the only thing that let him sleep at all.

He'd managed to get up and pee and brush his teeth when Linda banged on the door.

"I'm sorry," she said, as frazzled as he'd ever seen her. "I'm sorry. I'm so sorry. Agnes is sick—summer cold. She was whining for soda last night, and that's what Kelly was going to the store for and...." She took a deep breath. "I can't take her to the hospital like this. I can't. She'll pick up every bug known to man, and then she'll be in the hospital, and Kelly will be, and—"

Seth's dad came out of the bedroom wearing his jeans over his boxer shorts, his powerful chest bare. "Linda?" he mumbled, scrubbing at his dark blond hair. "What do you need from us?"

She almost started to cry. "I'll take Seth, Craig, but could you stay with Agnes? She's upstairs, asleep, and her fever just broke, and...." She wiped the back of her hand under her eyes, and Seth realized it was the first time he'd ever seen her without makeup. "I just want to see my son, but if you can't help, I have to stay here!"

"Yeah, of course. I'll be up in ten. Seth'll be waiting by the car. Don't worry about it. We can help."

She swallowed hard and wiped her eyes again. "You two.... Seth, did you really scare off the people attacking Kelly? Javi said you saved his life and—"

"I told them the cops were coming," Seth said, staring at her. "I was lucky. They could have turned on me."

"Oh God." Seth's dad had turned the color of old mashed potatoes. "Seth? Oh my God!"

"They were hurting him," Seth said, not seeing the problem.

"Of course," his dad whispered. "Of course you'd see it that way." He seemed to gather himself. "Linda, I'll be up in ten. Uhm, maybe you and I, after Kelly's feeling better, we can have a conversation, you know?"

The smile that twisted Linda Cruz's mouth was both comforting because it was familiar, and frightening, because it was out of place. "I think it's long overdue," she said, giving Seth the kind of glance she saved for Kelly when he'd shirked his chores. Again, familiar, but not frightening.

But Seth didn't care either way.

"Can we stop at a store?" he asked plaintively. "Like Target? I want to get him something. While he's in the hospital. I've got money saved. Is that okay?"

Linda hugged him.

No words, and no warning either. Just a solid, hard Mom hug when he seemed to need it most.

"Yeah," she said, voice broken again. "Of course."

And then she was gone, leaving Seth and his dad to get ready.

THE DRIVE to the hospital was made awkward only by Matty, who got mad because Seth was in the front, and because they had to stop, and apparently because Seth and Kelly had been kissing in the woods and Matty had been sitting on that information for a month and a half and something like that made a guy mean.

"Awesome," Matty sneered. "Another stuffed animal. That blue one he's got is falling apart. He's fifteen years old, and you're gonna keep him a baby, man—great. My brother can be street bait for the rest of his life!"

Seth ignored him, far away on an alien beach, until Linda spoke up.

"Seth is bringing him a gift, Matty. If he likes the gift, that's okay with me. Lay off. What happened to you two? You used to be friends."

"Seth knows what he did," Matty snarled. "It's his fault this happened. Once word hit the street, everybody knew my brother would bend over for anyone!"

Seth had to hold on to the praise Jesus bar then, because Linda cut across three lanes of traffic to screech to a halt in the parking lot of a Black Bear Diner.

"Matty! Not another word—"

"How did he know?" Seth asked, from the part of him still there. "How would word get out? How would anybody connected to Castor Durant's gang know anything about Kelly?"

"Because you two don't make no secret about being fucking faggots!" Matty snarled. "Everybody fucking knows—"

"Matty, get out!" Linda ordered, and Seth closed his mouth so fast, he almost bit his tongue.

"Mom?" Matty was shocked. Shocked and hurt, and Seth wasn't sorry at all.

"Your sisters are in the back of the car, and you can't use either one of those F words here. Not about your brother. Not about Seth. Not about anybody. You shut up, or you be nice about it, or you *get out of my fucking car*!" She finished off on a shriek, and Seth looked back and saw Matty huddled against the back of his seat.

"I don't know the neighborhood, Mommy," he said humbly. "I don't even know how to get home."

Seth did. Seth knew you took the 29 to midtown, and then took the 8 to the fourplexes off of Carro. But he wouldn't tell Matty that. Not now.

Matty had pretty much sicced Castor Durant on him and Kelly.

Matty, screaming terrible shit in the back of the car, had turned his brother over to the wolves.

In spite of everything that had happened, until that moment right there, Seth had thought they were still friends.

But now he knew. Now that he knew how much Matty hated them, he realized that part of their lives was over.

"Then you know how to stay in the car," Linda finished, and Seth, snapped back to the here and now, saw her hands shake.

Kelly's mother was not okay.

Matty had betrayed them, and Kelly's mother was not okay.

Seth had to live with that information. He had to close his eyes and live with it, counting the seconds until he could see Kelly.

Of course, the Cruz family went in first, but Matty came out after just a minute, scowling.

Seth just looked at him, too stunned to hide his hurt.

"He doesn't want me there," Matty spat. "I hope you're happy. My brother hates me."

"You betrayed him," Seth said quietly. "You turned them onto him. You'll have to live with that."

Matty took two steps forward, cocking his fist back, and Seth stood up and met him.

"Go ahead," Seth said. "Hit me and tell everybody why it's my fault. You're the one who's choosing to hate, Matty. Your mom didn't tell you to. They're fine with it. Hit me and tell everyone why I had it coming." He sighed and let himself wander away in his mind. A song was forming, swelling, something that had Kelly's smile in it, the way he slouched when he walked, like he knew it was sexy, the way he rambled like a stream in the spring.

Seth needed a song for Kelly so Kelly could remember himself.

Matty was frozen, his fist falling limply to his side, and Seth wandered away for real, until Kelly's dad stuck his head out. "Seth? He's been asking for you."

"Dad! You're just going to let him—"

"Shut up, Matty." Xavier Cruz looked exhausted. "I don't want to hear it. What you said to him last night? You think you're not responsible for this? Just sit down there and be glad it's not you in the hospital."

Seth didn't even look at Matty as he walked into the room, passing Linda and the girls as they left.

They were all crying, Lily and Lulu leaning painfully against Linda as she guided them out.

"He needs to hear good things," Linda said softly. "Make him happy, okay?"

Seth nodded and tried hard to pull himself from that place in his head. Kelly needed him.

"Ouch," he muttered, because who wouldn't? Kelly had a brace around his throat, and his left eye was brick red, the flesh around it puffy and swollen. Various tubes were coming from his arm, and one from under the covers.

"You think?" Kelly mouthed.

"I think your mom's not gonna let you leave the house for a year," Seth said, pulling a chair up next to the bed.

"No more Soccer Wednesday, anyway," Kelly sighed.

"Well, yeah, but in the fall—"

Kelly frowned. "You're going."

Seth frowned back. "You want me to leave?"

"To Bridgford."

Seth's stomach cramped. "No."

"Please—"

"Don't talk about it," Seth ordered. He reached into his pocket and pulled out the stuffed animal, this one an absurdly bright orange. "Here." He reached over to Kelly's hand, which was wrapped, but not in a cast, like it had been injured but not broken. "I brought this for you."

Kelly smiled a little, his eyes watering. "Seth, what he did to me… it hurt. It hurt so bad."

Seth stood and leaned over the bed then, dropping the rail on the side and kissing his forehead gently. "I'm sorry. I don't know how to make that better. All I want is for you to feel better. I'd do anything to fix that, fix that thing he did. But all I can do is wrap my arms around you forever. It's all I got."

"I'm afraid," Kelly whispered. "For me. For you. I'll be afraid forever. You need to go so I'm not afraid."

Seth shook his head. "I'll take care of it," he promised rashly. "I'll make sure you never have to be afraid again. I swear. He'll never touch you. I promise."

"No—"

But Seth was crying again, and so was Kelly, and they didn't have words.

It would take them years before they found words again.

This moment right here, Seth holding Kelly's hand around the little comfort object, them rubbing their salty cheeks together, crying, would be one big howl in their chests for long goddamned years.

SETH'S DAD was asleep next to little Agnes when they got back, and Seth slipped quietly out of the apartment. They'd stopped for food on the way home, but Seth wasn't hungry.

He slid in his own front door and went where he always went—to his music stand and his instrument.

He played angry scales, again and again, the rote memorization of the chords guiding his hands, his muscles, his talent—it was all he had.

He finally set the violin down, hands and shoulders shaking, T-shirt drenched in sweat. Before he could ask himself what he was doing, where he was going, he'd slammed the door behind him, forgetting his phone and barely remembering his keys.

He knew where he was going.

Night had barely fallen, a faint river breeze ruffling the beech trees lining the sidewalk as Seth strode into the purpling dark. He wondered where his dad had gone. He'd probably offered to watch Lily and Lulu and help with dinner or something, and Seth was glad.

His dad loved him. Loved Kelly. He thought Seth was a good boy. Seth didn't have the heart to tell his dad that he had inherited the same violence in his heart that his father had. Craig Arnold had worked so hard to protect Seth from that in the past years.

It wasn't Craig's fault it was roaring through Seth's soul tonight.

The vacant store was still marked by police tape, but as Seth moved through the night, he knew he wouldn't find Castor there.

The field, shadowed under the moon, backed up against a fence. Behind it was an apartment complex, one with a gate and some security, and trees. The trees cast absolute darkness over the fence, and even the field, with all its urban detritus, was brighter and better lit than that hollow of nothingness against the apartment fence.

Seth wasn't even aware of where his feet were carrying him until he tripped over a patch of grass.

Low, mocking laughter from the void under the trees told him he wasn't alone.

"You here for more?" Castor Durant rasped from the shadows. There was a glow as he inhaled from something—a joint, maybe, but one laced with a chemical smell, like cotton candy and drain cleaner, that made Seth want to puke.

Meth. He was smoking weed laced with meth.

The lone rational part of Seth's brain started to scream that this boy was dangerous.

Very, very dangerous.

"I'm here to warn you," Seth told him, not dreamy in the least. He was right here, right now, under the moon hanging low like rotting fruit. "You stay away from us. Don't touch us again. Not ever again."

"Or what?" Castor exhaled throatily. "What're you gonna do? Suck my dick off?"

Seth kicked him.

He didn't even know he was going to do it.

One minute he was standing—looming over Castor Durant as the boy got high and higher—and the next, he'd swung his foot back and landed a hard kick to his side.

Castor dropped his joint and yelped, and then propelled himself, crashing into Seth's midsection and throwing him to the ground.

Seth kicked hard and tried to roll, throwing his elbows back and catching Castor in the jaw. For a moment, Seth was almost standing on higher ground, where he could kick the bastard's face in, but Castor grabbed his foot before he got his balance, and he fell heavily, catching his weight on his elbow. He yelped, but his upper body was strong. Stronger than anybody suspected. He practiced for hours, until his back and chest ached and his biceps and triceps caught fire.

He rolled to one side on the ground that was littered with cigarette butts and worse and then rolled back, catching Castor Durant in the jaw with a hard elbow, leaving him stunned. With a heave, Seth pulled away, scrambling to his knees, and again, oh God, almost made it to his feet, almost made it to the point where he could kick the shit out of him, to where he could hurt him, make him afraid, make him never want a thing to do with Kelly Cruz or his family ever again.

But Castor was high, and desperate. With a snarl, he tackled Seth, trying to shove his face into the ground. But Seth was a runner. And tall. He used his leverage to roll his body over… only for Castor to straddle him. He hit Seth again and again, bloody and spitting and shouting obscenities, pinning Seth by the throat with one hand while he fumbled at his waist for something… something….

Seth's vision was fading, his air strangling in his windpipe, cut off by Castor's palm. *Oh God, Kelly. Was this how you felt? Was this the place they sent you before they raped you and beat you?* His struggles were weakening, his arms and hands heavy, the world growing dark… so dark… *Kelly… Dad….*

He was so far gone, he didn't even realize he'd started breathing again.

He still felt heavy. Something like slimy cement weighed him down. He took some more breaths, enough to struggle, and pushed it off.

Castor Durant rolled over, a gaping red smile where his throat used to be, white bone gleaming in the moonlight.

Seth stared, aghast.

Blood that had pumped all over Seth, all over Castor, had slowed to a trickle, and from the corner of Seth's mottled vision, he saw someone's foot as they disappeared around the corner.

But he couldn't make out whose it was.

The blood drenching him—had he done that?

Seth tried to remember, his head pounding, his throat bruised and aching.

Where had the knife come from?

Was that what Castor had been struggling for?

Oh God. Oh God. Seth couldn't remember. *He couldn't remember.* Castor Durant was dead. Not one breath gurgled from the gaping smile at his throat, and Seth couldn't remember if there had been a knife.

SETH MADE it to the apartment wall before he stopped and threw up bile, his throat burning more than ever. Another few steps and he was on the sidewalk, the moon hanging over his head like a rotten lemon.

His hands wouldn't stop shaking.

The laundry room he and his dad used sat in the space between two of the three apartments on the ground floor of the fourplex. Seth and his dad did laundry on Sundays, always, so he didn't often run into the other people there, and the Cruzes had their own unit upstairs.

Seth fumbled for his key, his mind blank. Not even thought of the ocean could make this better. All he could think of was the black night and the obscene moon.

The laundry room was vacant. *Oh, thank God.* An old beach towel nobody wanted to claim sat on the folding counter in the cramped space, and a washcloth hung from the soaking sink. Without thinking about it, Seth started to strip.

T-shirt, cargo shorts, underwear.

It was all soaked with blood. Saturated. He took off his tennis shoes and added those to the load, surprised when he found quarters—just enough for a wash—in his pocket.

His hands were bloody too. Bloody as he touched his clothes, took everything off. After he shoved it all in the washer, adding soap from the communal box on the floor, he started running water in the sink. Then he scrubbed his face. Scrubbed his hands. Used the washcloth to scrub his arms, scrub his legs. To scrub his feet.

Rinsed. Scrubbed himself again.

Scrubbed the things he'd touched. Scrubbed the concrete he'd walked on, even though there were no prints. There was no blood on his shoes. How weird was that? Blood everywhere, on his hands, in his hair—

He stuck his head under the sink and rinsed it off again.

And his body, again.

The washer lapsed into spin cycle and the change in the sound startled him—his shoes thumped warningly inside.

He needed to go upstairs and put on some clothes.

He needed to get quarters so he could dry everything.

Or maybe he should run it through again, using bleach this time.

He needed to move.

He grabbed his keys from the bottom of the sink where he'd washed them off, and wrapped the faded beach towel around his waist.

Not a soul saw him walk to his front door wearing only a towel and terror. That would puzzle him in the years to come.

How could he have done something so terrible, so huge, and not a soul could say they'd seen him do it?

Where was God when all this was happening?

Where in the fuck was God?

That sound haunted him. Beat at his brain. Pounded in his head as he jumped in the shower, scalding himself with hot water until it too ran cold.

He'd brought clothes into the bathroom, and he dressed carefully, slowly, everything in his body hurting—his joints, bones, muscles, heart. He felt like an old man.

His father was standing outside the bathroom, staring at him like he'd never seen him before.

"Seth?"

"Daddy?" His voice was hoarse, like Kelly's had been, and he'd looked in the mirror. He had marks on his face, his neck. His eyeball was blood red.

He looked like he'd been in a fight.

"Son…. Son, what happened?"

Seth swallowed, and it hurt too, and he had to fight not to look at his hands. "I…." But he couldn't. He slid against the wall of the hallway, too exhausted to sob, weak tears trickling down the sides of his nose.

His father sat next to him and slung an arm over his shoulder. "What do I need to know, son?"

Seth swallowed again. He thought of that body, lying under the nightmare sky.

"I should probably be on the bus to Bridgford next week," he said hoarsely. "Do you think Kelly will forgive me?"

"What happened?"

Seth just shook his head. "Oh, Daddy…."

And that's all he could make himself say for the rest of the night.

Kept in Cages

"KELLY!"

Kelly looked up from the tablet his father had bought him and smiled weakly at Seth. This was his third day in the hospital—the day the rape counselor had come in and talked to him about his injuries and how it was going to hurt to poop for a long time and how he needed to cry a lot before everything got better.

He was done with crying. He just wanted to stare at the stupid little game on the bright glowing screen and be someone else for a while.

But Seth was here, and that needed Kelly's attention.

Seth had come the first day and promised Kelly he'd be safe.

He'd come the second day and had just sat there, way across the room full of all Kelly's family, and turned his face to the wall while Matty glowered at them all.

Kelly was supposed to go home tomorrow, and all he could think about was sitting on Seth's couch and being somewhere he felt safe. Seth wouldn't treat him like he had the plague.

Seth had another one of those little stuffed animals in his hand. This made the third—Kelly was keeping them all lined up next to his pillow.

"Hey," he said, smiling, and to his dismay, Seth shook his head like he was shaking off the smile. His eyes looked hollow and red, and Kelly noticed he was wearing a shirt with a collar, even though it was still a bajillion degrees outside.

"Kelly, I have to go tomorrow," Seth said, his voice breaking. "I don't want to. But I have to go. Dad's putting me on the bus to Bridgford. I… I don't have everything I need, but he's sending it to me."

Kelly gasped, and it still hurt, dammit. But Seth's voice sounded like his—a sore croak—and Kelly wondered when that happened.

"You have to go?" he squeaked, the betrayal acute. *You told him to go. You told him.* And then, *But yeah, I didn't think it would be that quick.*

Seth nodded and wiped his face with the back of his hand. One of his eyes was red, like Kelly's, and he was wearing a sweater—an old man's sweater—over his arms.

Kelly squinted. "What happened?"

More of that terrible head shake. "I can't tell you," he whispered. "I don't know myself. But… but you're safe, okay? Whatever happened, you're safe. I'm not sure if I'm the one who made you safe, but you're safe. And that's all that matters."

"But I'm not safe!" Kelly cried. "Even if Castor Durant drops off the planet, there's still my brother, who's gonna fuckin' beat on me for bein' a fag and—"

Seth ventured all the way in the door then and grabbed his hand, putting the little stuffed animal in it before leaning over so they could touch foreheads.

"Your mom and dad won't let that happen," he promised. "I've heard them, Kelly. Even if they don't know for sure, your mom, she won't let your brother say shit to you. Trust her." He nodded, like just doing that could take away the hurt of it. "And…." Oh! Kelly's boy was crying. Crying so hard he couldn't breathe. Crying so hard he could barely talk! Kelly's arms were sprained at the shoulders, because two guys had held them behind him and he'd struggled, oh, he'd struggled so fucking hard. Carefully he raised his hand to cup Seth's cheek and saw the bruises, then felt his stomach go cold.

"Seth? Seth… *mijo*. What did you do?"

"Whatever it was, you're safe. But my dad… my dad will miss me." Seth reached into his pocket and shoved something else into Kelly's hand. "This is my key. My house key. Make a copy for me when you can, okay? But Soccer Wednesdays—go see my dad. He'll be expecting you. I told him."

"You told him?"

Seth took a deep, shuddery breath. "That night… right after you went to the store. He said… he said he'd do anything to help us. Just as long as I went and did this thing that everyone says only I can do. He said… he said he wouldn't ever try to keep us apart. So… so be his friend, okay? He's putting me on a bus, and he's going to be all alone, and you're going to be all alone, and I'll miss you both. Just… keep each other company, okay?"

Kelly nodded just a little, and dammit. Apparently being ready to be all cried out didn't mean there weren't any tears left. "You can't go…." Hell. That wasn't what he meant to say. "Don't leave me!" That wasn't it either. "I'm sorry! I'm sorry! I thought I could let you go, but I was wrong—"

Seth kissed him.

Kelly was so surprised he opened his mouth, and the kiss wasn't gentle. It was needy and scared, just like Kelly's, and it was salty and bloody like Kelly's, from the cuts on the inside of his lips.

Kelly gasped, and Seth pulled back and cupped his cheeks in his hands. "Your family's coming," Seth warned. "And I can't… I just…. Believe the best in me, okay?"

Kelly nodded, adrift and in pain. "Always."

"I'll write you. If you don't hear from me, it's because the world came to an end, okay? 'Cause you're the only thing keeping me on the planet, you understand? Otherwise, my head, it's a thousand miles away all the time. So I gotta think about you or I'll be in outer space."

Kelly squeezed his eyes tight. "I like you here," he said, thinking that on any other day, he could make that funny.

Seth's lips on his again was his only answer. Then all that was left was the chill of the hospital air and the sound of Seth's tennis shoes squeaking across the floor.

He opened his eyes and Seth had paused in the doorway, looking awful and sad and wrecked.

"I love you, Kelly Cruz," Seth said, nodding like that would make this all okay. "I love you more than… than my fucking violin. You're safe now. Get better. Write me back. I love you."

And then he was gone.

Kelly's parents came in about two minutes later, and Kelly wondered how Seth had known they were on their way.

They told him that Castor Durant was dead. His body had been found that morning in the nearby field. And they told him that Seth was leaving the next day.

But Kelly couldn't stop crying to hear anything else. Because his boy had bruises and a bloody eye and cuts on the inside of his mouth, and he'd known. He'd known and he'd wanted to tell Kelly goodbye before his parents could tell him what happened.

And Kelly knew what happened. Knew what he could never tell them. Knew what nobody else could ever put together.

His boy. His beautiful, faraway boy.

He'd made Kelly safe. He'd done his best to make Kelly safe.

But oh God—the cost.

They'd be paying for that safety for years and years to come.

THAT AFTERNOON, a police officer came into his room. Young, he was young and pretty hot, when it came to that. Blond, green-eyed, and out of uniform.

His father greeted the man suspiciously. Apparently, Xavier Cruz remembered the cops who arrived when Kelly was found, and they hadn't made a good impression.

"Officer Rivers," Dad said, his face stony. "You bothered to follow up?"

The officer had super-fair skin, pitted a little from old acne, and it turned rosy in embarrassment. "My partner's a dick," he said, his mouth twisting in a way that said it went much deeper than that. "I'm sorry he was one to talk to you. I was worried about the boy."

"And the boy you were supposed to find that attacked him got killed, so now you have a murder you want us to solve." No, Dad was not going to forgive this guy.

But Rivers surprised them all. "I'm not on that case," he said, shaking his head. "I wanted to be. But I picked up some info I thought you'd like to know."

Dad cocked his head a little, like he was ready to listen. "Linda? You want to take the girls and Matty to go get sodas?"

"Sure, Javi." Mom kissed Dad's cheek before she left, and an ache bloomed in Kelly's chest. His parents were still in love. They'd met right out of high school, and they were still in love. He could believe in them. Believe in love. Seth had done a bad thing and needed to leave. But he could come back, right?

His family filtered out—Agnes too, looking tired but apparently not feverish anymore—and Matty took the rear, glaring at the cop and at Kelly as he went.

Asshole.

Kelly had never thought a day would come when he'd trust a cop over his own brother, but Kelly was not interested in anything Matty had to say right now.

"So," Dad said, sitting down in the comfy chair and gesturing for the cop to take the not-so-comfy one. "You got something important to say?"

Rivers nodded. "Two things. One, Castor Durant's DNA matched the person who assaulted you, Kelly."

"They said it would take months," Kelly croaked, but Rivers shook his head.

"I know people." And then he shrugged self-consciously. "I thought it would help to know that the guy who attacked you couldn't do it again."

"He wasn't alone," Dad said. "He and his gang of goons—"

Rivers nodded. "We've picked them up. Apparently, Durant's murder spooked them all into running home. It wasn't hard to find them. There were confessions all the way around. They'll go to juvie, and Kelly won't have to testify. That's one of the things I wanted you to know."

Kelly closed his eyes, letting relief wash over him. Talking about it in public? Oh, that would be a fucking treat. Yeah. He didn't want to relive those moments when he'd been helpless, violated, the smell coating his skin like grime....

"Breathe, Kelly," his dad said softly, and Kelly inhaled as spots danced in front of his eyes.

"Thanks," he said, because Rivers didn't have to come here on his time off and tell him this. It was nice.

"I'm sorry," Rivers said, instead of "You're welcome." "It was a sucktastic time for you. I wish we could have found you sooner." He sighed. "I can't honestly say the same for Castor Durant."

Dad made a face like he would have spat if they hadn't been somewhere clean. "Yeah, well, that kid had it coming."

"Kelly's was not the only match that came up on the DNA," Rivers agreed. "Mostly girls, but maybe that's because the boys weren't reported. He... he was bad news. And from the looks of things, it took more than one person to take him down."

Kelly turned his head so quickly, he hurt his entire body. When his vision cleared, he found himself on the receiving end of a speculative look from pretty-as-cake Officer Rivers.

"What makes you say that?" Dad asked, which was good, because Kelly didn't have to.

"There were two different things going on at the crime scene," Rivers said, his eyes on Kelly. "One person was under Durant, getting the crap beat out of him, and someone else got Durant from behind. Do you know who those people could be, Kelly?"

"No," Kelly lied. Seth had obviously been the one getting the crap beat out of him. His eye, the marks on his throat he'd been trying to hide. His voice. *Oh God.*

But Seth thought he'd done it.

Kelly could put that much together from how quickly he'd left. How he'd avoided Kelly's family.

From the way he evaded Kelly's eyes until Kelly had needed him most.

Rivers nodded and glanced away. Then he looked back. "Durant was bad news. Murder, cold-blooded murder, that's not right. Killing for revenge, that's not right. But maybe someone had just gone to, say, warn Durant to stay away from you. And shit went down. That could be… not terrible. A few months in juvie maybe, at the most. You know. In case you have any ideas."

Seth? In juvenile hall? When he should be making music? Making his violin weep? When he was on Mars half the time because he heard music in his head and all the music was somewhere else far away?

Seth?

In jail? With the same guys who'd held Kelly's arms while Castor Durant… did what he did?

His Seth?

"I got no idea," he croaked. "I've been here. Nothing to see here, right?"

Rivers tightened his lips. "Still. We'd like to talk to your buddy. The one who found you in the abandoned store. For one thing, he's a hero. Did you know that?"

"Because he found Kelly?" Dad asked. "He led the police to him?"

Officer Rivers raised an eyebrow. "We weren't on the scene yet. Your buddy kicked the door in and yelled, 'It's the cops!' and scared those assholes away. Didn't he tell you that?"

"Oh God…," Kelly whispered. *Seth.*

"He's a good boy," Dad rasped, grabbing Kelly's hand. "We won't forget that, will we, Kelly?"

"No."

Seth. So brave. Who would have guessed he only came to Earth to be a superhero?

"He *is* a good boy," Officer Rivers agreed. "Do you know where he might be? We've been knocking on his door, but neither he nor his father are home."

Well, Seth's Dad had been at Kelly's house, helping the girls while his parents had been busy at the hospital.

"No idea." Kelly let his voice go weaker, like he was getting tired, which wasn't a stretch.

Officer Rivers wasn't buying it, but he wasn't pressing either. "Well, let him know that if he wants to talk, he needs to talk to me. Not my partner. Deal?"

Yeah. Neither of them. Seth wasn't talking to either of these bozos.

"Will do," Dad said earnestly, and if Kelly hadn't been getting tired, he would have smirked.

As it was, he closed his eyes as his father stood up and saw Rivers out. He kept his eyes closed, even when his dad came back and sat next to his bed, letting out a sigh that almost shook the hospital bed.

"We won't tell your mom about that, okay, *mijo*?"

"Okay," Kelly whispered. And he wouldn't. For many years.

KELLY WENT home two days later, with a standing appointment to talk to a rape counselor that he had every intention of missing. He'd managed to get out of all his finals at school, which was great. His teachers had all sent emails telling him that his standing grade would suffice, and he was getting As and Bs anyway. Not super-awesome grades—not scholarship grades—but nothing to be ashamed of either.

He checked the tablet dispiritedly, though, thanking his teachers and then hitting refresh on his email. No word from Seth yet. It had been three days since he'd gotten out of the hospital—and still no word. He could poop okay on his own, the red had cleared from his vision, and with some painkillers, he could lift the tablet, but not much else.

Recovery was fucking slow was what it was, and not having Seth at home to talk to made it slower.

"Kelly, please?" Lily was looking at him and biting her lip. "I know you had stuff to check, but I've got a project due!"

"What about Mom's laptop?"

"Lulu has that one for her own project. I'm sorry. I wouldn't ask, but it's important and—"

Kelly sighed and handed it over. "Yeah, sorry, Easter flower. I just… you know. Thought Seth would email." He could still talk about Seth, right? Nobody had charged him with anything. Nobody had said it out loud.

There were two things happening at that crime scene.

"Why would Seth want to talk to you?" Matty sneered, walking right out of Kelly's blind spot, past the kitchen table, and shattering his peace and his train of thought. "Think he wants you now? He *left*, remember?"

And Kelly got a cold feeling in his stomach.

They *all* used the tablet.

Matty too. They'd known each other's passwords since middle school.

"You deleted the emails, didn't you?" Kelly asked flatly, anger pulling him to his feet when he'd mostly been one with the couch in the past days.

"What's it to you, fa—"

Kelly didn't wait around to hear the rest. He could walk. He could make it down the stairs. He wasn't an invalid, trapped in this apartment with his sisters and his mother and his horrible fucking brother.

He touched his pocket, where he'd put Seth's key on a plain chrome key ring, and started for the door.

"Kelly!"

His mother launched herself from her small desk in the corner by the kitchen and went trailing after him. "Where are you going?"

"Seth's dad is home in an hour," Kelly told her. "I'll be downstairs when he gets home."

"But, Kelly—"

Kelly shook his head—slowly, because fucking ouch, everything hurt!—but with meaning. "I can't, Mom. Not with him. Not with that word. Not with him *deleting my fucking emails*!" Kelly yelled, making sure Matty knew he'd told Mom. "You want me to stay in here and be happy? You make sure your other son can't be an asshole. In the meantime, I'm going to Seth's."

He got winded going down the stairs, but still, he made it in the front door.

Ah!

Air-conditioning!

Seth used to tell him that his dad put it on a timer, so if people were gone for the day, it got cooler an hour before they got home.

Not something his dad would think of, but then, his mom stayed home and did books for a local restaurant now so she could pick everybody up and drop everybody off and make sure everybody was okay.

But this was cool—coolness not breathed in by six other human beings all day.

With a grateful little whimper, Kelly wandered inside, making himself comfortable in front of the television, like he always did. There was a pile of mail on the end table, and he moved it slightly so he could lean some of his weight on the arm of the couch.

And his own name caught his attention, written in Seth's spidery, erratic handwriting.

Kelly Cruz, C/O Craig Arnold.

It was a mailer—a big envelope with squishy bubbles inside to keep things safe. Kelly picked it up and squeezed it, and could feel the tiny stuffed animal inside and the little metallic weight.

A key chain.

He'd sent Kelly a key chain.

Kelly didn't open it. He'd ask Seth's dad's permission later.

He just held it, close to his chest, and turned on the stupid TV.

That's where he was forty-five minutes later when Seth's dad walked in.

Craig wasn't even surprised. First thing out of his mouth was "Can I get you a soda?"

"Yeah," Kelly said, smiling. "Something light. The caffeine is supposed to irritate my throat."

"Ah. Got it."

He had his uniform shirt for the warehouse over his arm, and he blew by the couch on his way to go drop it in his bedroom. Then he went to the kitchen and came back with some Sprite and some of that presliced fruit you got at the grocery store, all cold and ready-made.

Kelly ate and drank happily and then remembered his manners.

"This is really human of you," he said at the commercial break. "Thank you."

Seth's dad shrugged. "Thank you for being here. I…." He let out a sigh. "I knew it would be lonely once he left, but I didn't count on… on…."

"On your heart being so sad," Kelly said, because that's how he felt.

"Yeah. That. Did you find your packages?"

Packages? "Only one." Kelly sat up, but Craig was already heading for the main table.

"No, no—here. He's been sending you a letter or something for the last three days. I was going to take them up tomorrow."

"My stupid brother," Kelly grunted, taking the other two big mailers from him. "He deleted my emails. I got no idea how long Seth's been trying to get hold of me."

"Fuck."

Kelly blinked, because Seth's dad didn't usually let out expletives. "Sir?"

"I was trying to give your family some space. Goddammit. I didn't count on Matty being—"

"Such a flaming asshole?" Kelly felt this wound, even as he inflicted it. "I guess that's just who he is now, sir. I'll have to get used to it."

"Well, that's a shame. You three used to be so tight."

"Yeah, well, then Seth and I wanted to get tighter, and Matty wanted to get religious. It's okay. I picked Seth over Matty, and Matty picked Isela over human fucking decency. I guess it evens out."

Craig snorted. "Alrighty, then. I'll just not count on you being able to get Seth's emails. Or…." He stopped and chewed his lower lip. "You know? I've got an idea. Can you come by tomorrow? Same time?"

"No, sir, I'm afraid my social calendar is full this summer. Everybody wants to hang out with the kid who's injured and has an incurable disease."

This time Craig slapped his hand over his mouth. "You do *not* have an incurable disease!" he protested.

"No, but I might as well have! I'm the kid who was raped. It's like everybody knows what's been in my butt and nobody wants to call and talk to my face."

Seth's dad abruptly sobered. "I'm here," he said. "I'll talk to your face. I'm sure Seth will, once we find a way for you guys to Skype. You don't have the plague. You're not dying. But you were hurt. You just need to tell us how you want to be treated so we know, that's all."

Kelly gave him a suddenly tearful smile and nodded. "I like being treated like this," he said after a moment. "Like I got a friend to watch TV with. And I can say something that's not going to piss you off or hurt your feelings or scare my little sisters. Is that okay?"

"Yeah." Seth's dad sank into the couch and held out his arm. "Are you feeling seven today? Agnes let me hold her in my lap."

"I'm feeling twelve," Kelly said after a moment's thought. "I wouldn't mind an arm over my shoulder."

Maybe he should have been afraid. But it hadn't been an adult who'd attacked him. A kid had. A mob of them. Kelly had been around kind adult men all his life. It would be like being afraid of a housecat because he'd been captured by jackals.

He sidled up to Seth's dad and leaned, and that arm came around his shoulders, like one of those safety bars in a roller coaster ride.

Not to trap him.

Just to keep him safe.

He leaned against Seth's dad's chest and handed him the remote control.

"Don't you want to open your presents?" Craig asked softly.

"Later." Kelly took his first deep breath in six days. "Right now, I know he loves me. It's enough."

But he kept the mailers on his other side so he could open them as soon as he woke up. He could feel the damned nap coming on, and he was so grateful for Seth's dad right then, he didn't want to miss it.

> *Heya, Seth!*
>
> *Your dad bought me a tablet and let me hook it up to his printer. I'm sending you this right now because I'm pretty sure you'll get it, and there's nothing Matty can do about it, so there. Your dad also got me a new phone, because my other one was smashed. I'll put the number at the end of this email so we can text and stuff.*
>
> *I miss you.*
>
> *I mean, I wasn't sure whether to tell you or not. But then I thought, I hope you are missing the SHIT out of me, so I figured it would be better to say it and get it out of the way.*
>
> *You were right. I came over to your place last night for Soccer Wednesday, and your dad and I sat on the couch and watched detective shows. I know this is stupid, but I sort of like detective shows. All you do is turn off the part of your brain that worries about today or tomorrow and turn on the part that wonders who did it. I never figure it out, but your dad is pretty good at it. I came downstairs again tonight, and he got home with a bag full of electronics.*
>
> *On the one hand, I feel bad—I just sucked up a bunch of his money. But he said he doesn't have to feed you anymore and shrugged like that wasn't hard on him at all when I know it is. So I figure it's a tradeoff. I sit and watch detective shows with him, and he gives me a way to talk to you.*
>
> *Except it's better than that, because we both like the thing we're doing for the other person, right?*
>
> *I'm fine.*
>
> *I thought you'd want to know.*
>
> *I mean, my body's still banged up, and there's nightmares. I keep waking up thinking I can smell that*

place. And my temper is, like, short. Like, shorter than recess when we were little kids. Like, I'll rip the face off of anyone in my grill, short—and part of that is because I'm still banged up and because pooping is still a world-class event and you don't get a gold medal in it, you just get a reminder that somebody got to touch you some way you didn't want them to.

And that sucks.

Lulu tried to give me a hug from behind today, and I screamed bloody murder, and she cried. Then I had to hug her and sit with her for an hour and I felt like shit.

Okay. So that sucks too.

But I got your key chain and your card and the stuffed flamingo. Why a flamingo? I don't care. I loved it. And I want to say partly... don't keep buying me things, but I love them so much. I guess I'm still a little kid. Presents, man. They do it for me.

Anyway, you can send me emails again, and don't forget to text and shit. I'm on your dad's data plan. He says it's unlimited, and you know something?

Your dad bought me a phone so I could talk to his son, my boyfriend.

I'm still wrapping my head around that.

I need to tell my folks. I mean, they know. They figured shit out. They keep telling Matty to shut up, and Matty deleted all your emails and got suspended from the computer. Mom made him stay after school in the computer lab to work on his finals.

I can't even gloat, man.

I don't know what the hell happened to my brother, but that's not even him anymore.

By the way, tell Amara to text me at the new number too. I didn't realize how much I'd miss her until she was gone. I mean, I won't even notice Jimmy Durreson is gone for summer vacation, but I think you, me, and Amara need to watch scary movies on the computer and text together, you know?

Somebody told me they did that.

I'm hoping it helps me get over being scared.

I keep remembering all you did to keep me safe, mijo. And when I try to feel better, feel safer, I just get scared for you.

So text me asap.

Email me when you can.

Your dad says you're traveling around a lot right now on the big bus, and he's worried because your clothes were old and your shoes were old, and he didn't have a chance to set up a bank account for you, so he's doing all of that.

And I keep thinking it's a good thing you have him to worry about all of that, because you probably haven't noticed your toes hanging out of your shoes and your shirt rotting off your neck and the shorts that your waist is too small for and your legs are too long for.

I notice those things.

They make up my dreamy boy, right there.

But your dad's right.

You still need to dress better.

Nobody needs to know you're my dreamy boy but me.

I love you. That didn't change. I mean, the whole world flopped on its head and died like that fish my dad caught camping, but the loving you didn't change even a little.

Isn't that weird?

Yeah, that's weird.

But it's true.

So know that all those moments we had that were quiet and perfect, even though you're in a whole other place, those things are still in my heart.

I'll try not to freak out so much when Lulu startles me. I'm afraid I'm gonna turn around and backhand Agnes if she does the same jumping thing, and that would feel awful.

Take care of my dreamy boy.

Kelly

Long Beginnings

SETH STARED at his laptop as he sat in his college dorm, his heart pounding in his chest.

Oh God. Oh God oh God oh God.... Kelly *wrote him.*

And Matty had deleted his emails, like Seth's dad had texted the night before.

And Kelly was getting better—but not all fine like he said. And he hurt, but he was trying. And he was spending time with Seth's dad. And he missed Amara—Seth pulled out his phone and patiently sent Kelly's new contact info to Amara before he could forget.

She'd asked him about Kelly, and then she'd asked him about the bruises on his throat, and then she'd stopped asking when he'd just looked at her helplessly before disappearing into his head.

Amara really was smart.

The day he bought the flamingo, he hadn't had enough allowance to eat. They were rehearsing at a college campus, doing a special workshop for the new students of Bridgford, which paired them up with a senior in the music program at a prominent UC. They rehearsed together, played together, performed together, and the idea probably went, the incoming student would be inspired and reassured—oh, hey, this person got through school, *they* could too!

But Seth's "buddy" was a super-competitive blonde girl who seemed constantly irritated that Seth knew his material so well.

So when it was lunchtime, she went to go bitch to her friends and her teacher, probably, and Seth ate lunch with Amara, so grateful that she was on this trip too that he could almost cry.

Even more so because he had no money for lunch. He'd already spent his allowance on the key chain and the cards and the flamingo and the mailers. This was day four since he'd left home, and they were fed one meal a day while on the trip.

He'd have to wait for dinner, and while that didn't usually bother him—Kelly and Matty had kept him fed through his first three years of high school anyway—it was apparently pissing Amara the hell off.

"Why aren't you eating?" she whispered, looking sideways at her *own* buddy. Apparently they made college-aged flutists insanely hot here, and Seth's heart had hurt a little for his friend, who got awkward around cute guys in the worst way.

"Not hungry," he lied, and she handed him an apple off her plate.

He bit into it ravenously and then smiled like he hadn't been that easy to catch.

"Try again," she muttered. "The truth this time."

"You are not my mother," he said through a full mouth, and she gave him a look that Kelly's mother would have been proud of. "Fine. I have no money. Happy?"

She frowned. "Your dad gave you money before you got on the bus. I saw that. Did you lose it?"

He shrugged. "Spent it."

"Don't make me come over there and beat you," she said with a perfectly straight face.

But she was trying, so he gave in. "I bought Kelly some stuff. He's... he got hurt. And he needed something reassuring. Because, you know, I left before he got out of the hospital."

She stared at him and handed him her pudding without blinking. "Four days? It took you four days to bring this up? No wonder you were out to lunch. Oh my God, *Seth.* That must have sucked. Did you get hurt in the same fight?"

"No," Seth said.

She waited for him to say something else, cocking her head.

He smiled back, faraway. "Can I use your spoon?"

She handed him the spoon and waited some more. "I ignored it when you got on the bus," she said.

"I appreciate that."

"I was grateful because I wanted a friend."

"I appreciate that too."

"You left your boyfriend in the hospital and looked like you should have been with him."

Seth thought of Kelly, the way he'd been brutalized in that dank shithole of a room, and something must have shown on his face.

"He was hurt worse," she said softly.

"Way worse," Seth told her. "But he'll be okay. He should be home by now. I just...." He grimaced. "I wanted him to know I love him."

"I don't think he could doubt that, even for a minute."

"Amara, I left. My mom left when I was five years old. She died in a car accident that I'm pretty sure wasn't her idea, but my dad and I were pissed at her for the next four years. Because even if it's not their fault, you still get mad that they're gone."

Amara looked at her plate disconsolately. She'd eaten her sandwich and given Seth her fruit and her dessert, and she was eyeballing her chips, he could tell.

He reached out and put her hand on her chips. "I'll save some bread at dinner for tomorrow," he told her, untroubled. "It was worth it."

She shook her head. "I'll buy you lunch tomorrow, you dingus. And for the rest of the week. And if you ask me nice and don't be too much of a moron, I can show you how to buy stuffed animals for way cheaper at the campus store. Wait until your dad sets up your bank account and card. You'll be able to eat *and* spoil Kelly, I swear."

Seth smiled at her then, as bright as he'd been able to summon since Kelly had disappeared. *Oh God. Had it really been a week ago?*

"Thanks," he said softly. He peeled the lid off the pudding and began to eat. Yeah. He'd been hungry. He could admit it now.

So getting back to his dorm room to "rest," as the counselors called it, had been his chance to check his laptop and see if maybe, maybe this time, Kelly had been able to answer.

Getting Kelly's email had been even better than the apple and the pudding.

It had fed his soul.

And he couldn't wait to send an email back.

Heya, Kelly.

I hated leaving you. I need you to take a selfie if you can, so I can imagine you in my dad's apartment and not in the hospital.

That would be good.

I'm not sure if I told you, but we're doing an internship this summer before we start actual school at Bridgford. It's like permanent summer camp for band nerds.

I'm supposed to be partnered with someone who can teach me, but after lunch, the teacher pulled me aside and said I was the best violinist here and then gave me a bunch of first-chair work to practice instead of the second chair I'd learned all semester.

I wish they'd find someone who wasn't here during the summer to play first chair, because this shit is really hard, and I only had the practice room for an hour today.

I wish you were in the practice room listening to me play.

Anyway, I'm glad you got the presents. I'll probably only be able to send you cards for a little while, but you deserve presents every day.

Maybe have your little sisters warn you. Tell them it has to be a Kelly rule now. They have to say they're there.

You can write me anytime about healing. And about being scared. And about what it takes to feel better.

I won't tell anyone.

And I'll try to remember to tell you about my day.

Amara gave me lunch today. Even her pudding. She was sorry you were hurt too, but I didn't tell her how bad.

That's private. And yours.

Anyway, it's embarrassing how long this letter took me. I'm going to take pictures of my dorm room and the campus now so I can text them to you.

That way you won't feel cheated.

I love you
Get better.
Seth

KELLY RESPONDED the next day. And the next. And the next. It became a rhythm. Wake up and text Kelly. Lunchtime, check his phone. Right after class, check his email. If Kelly hadn't written him back, he'd write him something anyway.

It got Seth through the summer, and a performance in which he knew there would be no friendly faces in the theater because his dad was working overtime, and Kelly…. Kelly didn't say anything, but Seth hadn't seen a lot of pictures outside his apartment.

He'd asked Kelly for pictures of his art, but Kelly had replied *Nothing good to draw. It's all horror movies here.*

And Seth hadn't known what to do about that.

He had his own horror movies. He understood. But he needed Kelly to not be living there anymore, and he wasn't sure what to do from a hundred miles away.

His hands started to shake every time he checked the email, because he wasn't sure what minefield of Kelly's pain would be laid out in an email for Seth to stumble through.

He wasn't sure what made him break. But in early September, something about Kelly's last email did the trick.

Dear Seth—

So I watched that video you sent me a thousand times. Your performance was amazing, and I know you told me that the music was really hard and you didn't have any time to learn it, but that's not what I heard. I heard you make God cry with your violin, and I was so proud of you.

I think it's funny that you have to work so hard to find words for all your letters. I wonder what you hear in your head when you're going about your day. I hear words, all the time, telling me what I have to do and how I have to act and how I can not be weird and how I can not choke the crap out of my stupid brother.

And you hear emotions but no words. And all the emotions are in your instrument. I'm thinking you need to tape your practices more often, so it's like I am there.

I liked watching that freaky movie with you and Amara. With the little video windows, I could watch you jump when you got scared, even though you were really quiet about it. I might have missed that little jump if we were together, unless we were touching.

I forget that you have reasons to be startled too.

Your dad came home sad again last night, and before he could turn on the TV, I texted my dad and suggested maybe a meeting. Lulu came down and watched our detective show with me while they were gone, and when our dads came back, your dad had ice cream.

I stayed the night on the couch, and he told me in the morning that I could crash in your bed anytime I wanted to.

I tell you, mijo, it was like I could smell you on the sheets.

I miss your touch. I miss seeing you smile. I send you pictures and we Skype, but it's not the same as having you hug me and make it all better.

I was trying to tell the stupid rape counselor this the other day, and she got mad and said that I was supposed to be talking about my FEELINGS about being touched. And I told her that I WAS telling her about my feelings, because I WANTED to be touched.

By you. I wanted your hug so bad, I cried.

I can't talk no more, mijo. Your dad is about to come home, and I know you've left the college and are trying to settle into the new place now. And I'll be honest—I just can't. If I was your violin, I'd be making all the oceans cry today, and you don't need that.

I'll write you again tomorrow, Seth.
Today is just too hard.

Kelly

SETH STARED at his computer on a Friday afternoon and felt his heart thump in his throat. Kelly needed him.

So he went to the one person he knew could help.

"Sure," Amara said, not even flinching when he went charging into her dorm room. The boys and girls were supposed to be off-limits from each other, but everybody knew they were besties and Seth didn't try to grope or leer. He just came in to talk, so they treated him like a pet.

Nobody cared if your dog saw you take your bra off under your T-shirt. He didn't either.

"Sure what?" Seth asked, almost frantic.

"Well, it's Friday," she said. "How much money do you have in your account?"

He grimaced. "I've been trying to save," he said, because he knew where this was going. "I don't have enough for a train ticket—"

"That's no problem," she said, looking at her computer. "Remember, I get a decent allowance. I got you a ticket from the nearby Amtrak in two hours. If you can get an Uber there, when should I get you a return trip?"

Seth thought about it, thought about the risk of someone finding out he was there. Thought about getting there late Friday night and coming back late Sunday. "Sunday night," he said promptly. "Last train running. I'll be on it."

"We have curfew," she argued. "I'll get you back Sunday afternoon. Dammit, Seth, you can't get yourself kicked out by going home."

"He needs me," Seth said simply. "I don't have words. If I had words, I could write him a symphony in email and text him all the best things. But I don't have words. He needs me."

She sighed and tilted her head back. "Three o'clock train. It will get you here at six. Curfew's at eight. I want to hear everything, okay? You need to tell me why you're so worried. But not now. So go pack."

What was there to pack? His violin and two changes of underwear? Seth looked at his backpack again and decided on jeans and some shirts. And his hoodie, the new one with the school's logo.

And then the car was there, pulling up through the long drive to the small private dorm, and he was in it. He tried to take pictures on his way out so he could show Kelly what his life looked like now.

He'd never felt so ill-equipped, so inadequate, to be loved by somebody at that moment.

Kelly needed him, and all he could manage was a weekend.

Instead of joy at going to see him, all Seth wanted to do was cry.

That changed, though, when the Uber got him to the train station. Once the train pulled into the station, it wasn't very far afterward—a five-dollar ride—and Seth was driving through the familiar tree-shaded parts of Sacramento he loved best. It was weird, he'd seen two other cities since he'd left, San Francisco and Oakland, and even though he lived in a sort of poor neighborhood in Sacramento, he'd never appreciated that there were trees everywhere until he saw the good neighborhoods in other places.

He really liked the trees, even if they crumpled the sidewalks sometimes with their roots.

There was a big tree root under the blacktop in the complex of fourplexes he and Kelly lived in—it was so big it felt like a speed bump as the car went over it, and Seth remembered watching Agnes go sprawling over it more than once when she was a baby. As Seth grabbed his instrument and his backpack and went walking up to the chipped stucco of his home, he had a thought that someday they'd have to rip that out and take down the tree. The thought made him sad. Everybody said you learned things and you got better as time went on, but sometimes you just had to rip shit down and start from the beginning.

He tipped the driver—a rather harried-looking girl who had talked about her college classes during the entire trip, making Seth so self-conscious about his free ride at Bridgford and a possible college afterward that he didn't even want to talk to her—and then turned, wondering which door he should go through first. His dad's car, a gracefully aging Cadillac that his mom had loved with all her heart, wasn't in the carport, so he wasn't home.

Seth realized he didn't even have his key.

With a dry swallow, he pulled out his phone and texted Kelly. *Where are you?*

Watching TV at your dad's place. Why?

Don't be startled. I'm going to knock on the door.

He'd taken two steps when the door flew open and Kelly launched himself into his arms.

His eyes were all puffy and red and—oh! God!—he was even skinnier than Seth. Seth just gathered him close and held on, like soothing a wriggling puppy, except this puppy was wriggling with tears.

He wasn't sure how long they stood there, but before he could even think of what to do next, Kelly was tugging him to the open door of his apartment.

"Inside," he said. "C'mon. Before my brother sees you. Or the neighbors."

It dawned on Seth that the thing he'd gone running from in the first place hadn't gone away. He allowed himself to be hustled into his apartment, which looked exactly the same as it had when he left.

Seth took in the curtains, which were still open with the two-inch gap in between, and grimaced.

You'd think that, at least, would change, right?

With a sigh he walked over and shortened the gap by hand, and Kelly snorted.

"You think so?" he asked skeptically, and it took Seth a minute to figure out what he meant by that.

"No!" He turned and opened his arms, and Kelly stepped in again. "No. That's not why I came here. I just…." He half laughed. "Did you know my dad saw us?"

Kelly let out a bark of laughter and buried his face against Seth's chest. "No!"

"Yeah. That's how he knew about us."

"Well, that and the place probably smelled like come."

Seth chuckled. "Well, yeah. But you can pretend that's something else if you don't see your kid naked on the couch, you know?"

Kelly nodded again. "He never said anything."

Seth just kept holding him, thinking that he needed to eat more, but that Seth had been drained dry by their absence too. This moment, here, was like drinking a big glass of water after he'd been practicing for hours.

"Why'd you come?" Kelly murmured after another moment.

"You needed me."

"The investigation's not over." Kelly let out a big sigh. "Castor Durant's dad is all over the news still, yelling about who killed his little boy." He pulled back and feathered a touch over Seth's jaw. "Why didn't you tell me? All those emails and texts. You didn't mention it once."

Seth shrugged. "I wanted you to get better. Had to make sure you weren't scared. That's all."

Kelly gave a short bark of laughter, but it wasn't a joyous sound. "That's all? Seth, you can't go outside while you're here. You can't let my parents see you, or my brother. Dad lied to the policeman who came to my room—and he was the nice one. But he got shot, and this other guy is all hard and shit, and he comes pounding on my dad's door and starts yelling at him to get with the program!"

"What's the program?" Seth asked, thinking about music. Was he supposed to play something?

"Telling them what we know about Castor Durant's death!"

Seth blinked at him. *A big bag full of slimy wet cement.* "What do you know?" Did Kelly know he was a killer? Oh God. He had to go. He couldn't be here if Kelly thought he was—

"I know you got beat up," Kelly said, touching his face. "I know someone else was there—"

"All I know is that I got beat up," Seth told him, pulling reluctantly out of his arms. "And that Castor Durant was dead. I don't know anything about someone else, though. Do you need me to go now? I... if you think—"

"Don't you fuckin' dare!" Kelly said thickly, holding on to him so tight he couldn't breathe.

For a moment Seth was soaring, flying so high in an attempt to get away from this conversation, from what it would do to him if Kelly told him to go away.

"Seth, *mijo*, stay with me."

From far away, Seth said, "What did your dad say?"

"Dad didn't say anything to the second cop, like he didn't say anything to the first cop. But if Matty had been there—"

Seth frowned. "Matty?"

"He'd have told on you."

Seth nodded, unsurprised, coming back to earth again a little. "Well, then, I'll just stay in here until it's time to catch my train."

Kelly shook his head, and his red puffy eyes filled up again. "That's it? That's all you got?"

"You needed me," he said again, his throat aching. He wiped away one of Kelly's tears with his thumb. "I can't be here all the time, but as long as you want me, I can be here when you need me."

Kelly closed his eyes and nodded. "Okay. It was a hard day. Not gonna lie."

Seth dropped all his stuff at his practice corner, thinking sadly that it was probably lonely without him, and then kicked off his shoes. "C'mon. Can we snuggle? I want to sit on the couch with you, and you can tell me all about it."

Kelly nodded and wiped his face with the back of his hand. "Yeah. Yeah. Let's do that. Your dad'll be here in a while. You want pizza? I'll text him. He told me to do that—let him know if I was here and wanted anything."

Seth bit his lip, wondering if this was the first time Kelly had really asked. "Yeah. Yeah. Tell him to bring pizza."

After fumbling with his phone a little, Kelly stuck it back in his pocket, and they settled themselves on the couch.

"What?" Kelly asked. "What was that grunt?"

"This couch is… broke. I never noticed that before."

Kelly grunted too. "Yeah, well, don't expect new furniture anytime soon. Your dad made like it was no big deal to buy me that tablet and the phone, but that shit's expensive."

"I'm trying not to spend much," Seth confessed. "I… extra food's pricey."

Kelly cocked his head. "You keep sending me stuffies!" he protested.

"But Amara showed me how to do that so it doesn't cost a zillion dollars." Seth grinned. "You like them?" Kelly told him so, often, but Seth wasn't above needing praise.

"Oh yeah. I keep most of them upstairs, and the girls play with them. Mom got me a shoebox, right? And they decorated it super cute, and it's the Seth's Friends Home. It's got glitter and rainbows and shit. And Matty glares at it, but he can't yell about it because Mom threatened to send him to her mom's house to finish school if he did that. It's all the way in West Sac—he'd have to go to a way worse school than ours, and he wouldn't see his skinny-assed girlfriend there. So he's mostly just taken to glaring at stuffed animals. It's sort of funny."

They both sighed because it wasn't funny at all. Seth had lost his friend. Kelly had lost a brother. It was like Matty was dead to them and this angry stranger had taken his place.

"You need to take pictures," Seth told him, ignoring the pain in the ass that was Matty for the moment. "Like, with the girls and stuff. I can print them out and put them on my wall."

Kelly stroked his chin again, and then laughed. "*Mijo*! Your chin grew fuzz! When did that happen?"

"I have no idea what you're talking about," Seth mumbled, although he'd mostly been ignoring the phenomenon because he was pretty sure once he started shaving, that would be it. He'd be stuck on that hamster wheel forever.

"Yeah, well, I wish I didn't. I've got to shave every day now. It's bogus. Dad bought me an electric thingie so I don't have to spend as much time in the bathroom with puke face."

"Mm." Seth was so done with Matty. He was tired from the trip and from worrying and just so happy to have Kelly in his arms, chest to chest. It was funny that Kelly thought he'd start going at the sex thing as soon as he shut the curtains. He wanted the joy of getting used to having Kelly in his arms again. "Why'd today suck?"

Kelly let out a sigh. "Do I have to say?"

Seth rolled his eyes. "No, but if you tell me now, you don't have to talk about it for the rest of the weekend, and we can just pretend, you know? That it's… it's last year. And I don't have to go anywhere Sunday afternoon."

Kelly sighed and sagged against him. "Okay. That's a good offer. I can pretend that. I'm all about pretending it's last year. And I can do this with you every day."

Seth's own eyes burned. "I'd love to do this with you every day. Now talk."

Kelly rambled—that was a given—but this ramble was worse than the others, ranging from Jimmy Durreson touching his shoulder in second period and Kelly freaking out, to how he hadn't had anyone to eat lunch with because Seth and Amara were gone, to how the rape counselor would not shut up about the rape, to about how his sisters were just so loud and just so shrill, to how the things he used to love, like his sisters and like school and art, all had scary sharp edges to… to….

Seth had no words at first, but as Kelly came to a halt, panting on his chest, Seth realized he was humming.

"What's that?" Kelly asked after a moment.

"It's the theme from that movie—you know, the one about people's dreams?"

Kelly laughed softly, some of his manic emotion seemingly drained just by telling Seth about it live, in person, where they could touch. "Seth? That's about most of the movies out there."

Seth smiled, but he kept humming, changing the song.

"*The Little Mermaid*? Are you kidding me?" But Kelly was relaxing even more. The skin under his eyes was dark and bruised, and he seemed to melt against Seth's chest like he hadn't slept in months.

Three months. More.

He hadn't slept in three and a half months.

Oh God. They hadn't touched like this in almost four months.

Seth changed the song, and if his voice wobbled a little, Kelly was too relaxed to hear it.

"*Shrek*," Kelly murmured. "I know that song too. This is nice. It's like my little sister's music, and they make me happy."

Another few bars and Seth changed it again.

"*El Dorado*. Mm. I liked that movie. Like you and me without the girl. Except I'd be one of the people in the village, and you'd be an explorer who had to leave and break my heart."

Seth took a breath, ready to change the song.

"No. No. That one. It's pretty. Do the funny song about being a god."

So Seth did that one, from beginning to end, only stopping when he realized Kelly was fast asleep on his chest.

When would his dad be there? An hour? Half an hour? Seth remembered that he didn't have to worry anymore because his dad knew, and they weren't doing anything bad, just sleeping, with all their clothes on, Kelly's mouth slightly open like it had been the day Seth realized they were in love.

TWENTY MINUTES later the door to the apartment flew open and his dad rushed in, a giant pizza in his arms.

"Kelly! Did he call you! Did Seth call you and tell you where he was going?"

"Shh!" Seth hushed violently, waking up and trying not to startle Kelly. "Hush. He's asleep."

His dad stared at him, his angular jaw so much like Seth's that it was like looking into a pale mirror. He fumbled for a moment and almost dropped the pizza.

"*Seth*?"

"Yeah?"

"The school called! You left and didn't check out. Your roommate got worried and told them you'd disappeared!"

Oh crap. Amara hadn't put *Tell Vince you're going home* on the list, so Seth hadn't said anything. He'd just packed his shit and left.

"Oh." Seth blinked slowly. "I'm here."

His dad took a really deep breath, slowly, and again, and again, walking to the table with measured steps and setting the pizza down.

"I can see you're here," his dad said, like he was holding on to something tightly with his teeth. "*Why* are you here?"

"Because Kelly needed me."

Some of the tension leaked from his father's back. "Ah. Yeah. Well, can't argue th—"

"And you did too."

Dad turned around, the skin around his eyes fighting itself to decide if he was going to smile or cry. "Can't argue there either. Could you, I don't know, maybe call the next time you do this?"

Seth smiled. "Sure. I can do this again, right? I mean—" He bit his lip. "I guess it's not a real good idea to be seen here for a while."

His dad shrugged. "Nobody's said anything directly, but no."

"Well, still." His mouth wobbled. "Did you think I wouldn't miss you, Daddy?" And now his eyes were burning again, dammit.

His dad saved him, kneeling by the couch and kissing his brow, like he had when Seth had been a *really* little kid, before Mom died, before the dark time when Seth hadn't had a daddy but a violent shadow looming over his life. "I know I missed the hell out of you," he said, and they leaned their heads together over Kelly's sleeping form.

Some breaths. Some heartbeats. Seth's dad stood creakily to his feet. "Here. I'll go change and shower. Maybe you can wake Kelly up and we can eat. Watch a movie." His dad's mouth twisted. "I... Kelly's been sleeping in your bed. I... I'm at a loss here, Seth. It's not appropriate but—"

"Clothes on, Dad," Seth promised. "He...." His voice cracked. "He's so tired."

Dad nodded. "I'll take your word for it."

"Thanks, Dad."

And it was funny. For the rest of the weekend, his dad did that. Maybe because they weren't fighting over Bridgford anymore, or because his dad knew about Kelly. Maybe the having no secrets was the thing, or the moving out. But even when his dad and Kelly took turns trying to teach him how to shave the next morning, laughing uproariously as Seth managed to leave five perfect scraggly hairs in different places on his chin, he didn't feel like an angry kid anymore.

His father had given him that, maybe.

His dad had given him his adulthood, so Seth could come home and be his boy.

And most of the weekend was quiet—by necessity. Kelly woke up to eat pizza and then fell asleep on Seth again as they sat on the couch. Seth woke him up to go strip to T-shirts and boxers, and then Kelly fell asleep almost instantly, Seth snugged up behind him.

It was as if he was making up for not sleeping for a really long time.

In the morning, Kelly went upstairs to play with his sisters, say hi to his parents, maybe convince them everything was normal, and Seth stayed downstairs to play chess with his dad. At one point, he looked longingly at the violin, and his father shook his head.

"The whole world knows when you're practicing," he said gravely. "You may just want to practice fretwork or run through it in your head."

Oh.

Seth hung his head. "No music here?"

"Well, maybe just for now. I… I'll be honest. A young guy—Rivers—kept coming by, talking about how he'd make sure the guy who took out Castor got a fair hearing. I was…." His father shrugged. "I was thinking about it, Seth. I hate that you're… you're afraid while you're here."

Seth thought about it. "Not afraid," he said, moving his rook. He was really good at chess. "Just limited."

Craig Arnold sighed. "Well, I'm not sure what to do about it until the case goes cold. Rivers got shot. He's still in the hospital, from what I hear. I guess…." He grimaced. "Kelly's dad didn't like his partner—at all. It turns out, Rivers was wearing a wire because his partner was dirty. So we actually *had* a good cop on the case, but now we don't. The guy that's taken his place is, well, not a good guy. Nobody's telling him shit, but then you aren't here. So maybe you're right not to be afraid. Just… limited. But what are you going to do about Kelly with these limits?"

Seth didn't look up from his rook, which he was about to sacrifice for his knight. "Come when I can. And when Kelly turns eighteen, I'll take him with me."

"Oh."

Seth finally glanced at his father's expression. "Oh what?"

"That's actually a good plan, Seth. But… but that's a long time away."

Seth shrugged. "I can practice a piece a thousand times. The night of the performance, the flute section can rush the tempo, the cymbal can crash a half a beat late, and my strings can fray at the worst time in the world. All I can do is practice, Daddy. I'll talk to Kelly. All we can do is plan."

His dad snorted softly. "Wow, you're really getting wise."

Seth flashed him a grin. "Well, you know. I try."

Dad just shook his head and moved into checkmate. Then they cleared the board and started again.

KELLY CAME back down in the afternoon while Seth was working on homework, and for a moment, his pacing almost drove them both crazy.

"Why don't you *draw*?" Seth asked the third time Kelly bumped his chair in a pass around the living room. "I'm sorry we can't leave the apartment, but it didn't used to be so hard for us to be quiet together."

"I *can't*!" Kelly exclaimed, his voice aching with frustration. "You don't understand! People are like 'Art is therapy, Kelly,' but the things I draw, they're ugly! And horrible! And I don't want people to look at them and think I'm ugly and horrible too!"

Seth regarded him for a moment, trying to put that into context in his head. "But your therapy art isn't *for* them. You know that song I was humming to you? That's *your* song. I play that every night. I don't care if it drives my roommate batshit crazy. That song is *yours.* You do whatever you want with art that's just for you. You draw a picture of your sister, you make it pretty. You draw a picture of how shitty you feel? You do whatever the fuck you want."

Kelly flopped dispiritedly on the couch. "It's so awful," he mumbled. "What if… what if you see it? What if Mommy sees it? And you think that inside of me is so awful, you don't want me near you on the outside either?"

"You're so dumb! What makes you think either of us wouldn't love you for that? God, Kelly, draw what you feel! Burn it if that feels better, but don't worry about me or your mom or your dad or your shitty fucking brother. *We* weren't in that fucking room!"

Kelly stared at him, his pinched misery lightening to something… soft. Almost awestruck. "You're… you were," he said after a moment. "And later… you… you were someplace worse."

Seth looked away. "Not worse," he muttered, although he dreamed of Castor Durant's red smile, the way his neck bone could be seen as his head tilted back at a 90-degree angle. "Just… just as ugly. And I got songs for that too." He threw a furious look at Kelly. "But nobody bitches about those songs being ugly. Nobody's got room to bitch because they've got their own shit to sort out." He sighed, his anger fading. "Just… just don't let him steal this from you. It's been yours from the very beginning. I had the violin. Your stupid fucking brother had soccer. You picked up a crayon and said, 'This is my thing.' Why does he get to destroy that? What did he do to deserve to take away this thing that makes you happy? It pisses me off."

Kelly chuffed a little bit of air and walked near so he could kiss Seth's temple. "I can see that," he said after a moment. "I'll…. You promise not to look over my shoulder?"

"Yeah. You promise to show me anyway? I…." Seth stared at Kelly, so damned happy to see him, see his face, even tired and not smiling and sad. "I'll probably hate it, but only because it's your pain. So let me see it. We'll both hate your pain. And maybe you'll find something sweet that doesn't hurt after a while."

Kelly shook his head in wonder. "Your brain. It's sort of a wonderful place, Seth. Have I ever told you that?"

Seth's eyebrows knit together. "No. Nobody has ever told me that. Please don't. It's weird." He had a small sheaf of printer paper in his writing folder, and he pulled it out and handed Kelly a spare pencil. "There's better stuff in the pen drawer in the kitchen," he said. "And I think we have printer paper—"

"You do," Kelly said with confidence. "Your dad lets me use your printer, since I keep my tablet here."

Seth smiled at him shyly. "Thank you," he said. "You take care of my dad real good."

Kelly let loose with a tearful laugh and grazed Seth's cheek with his knuckles. "Yeah. That's what happens here. I take care of your dad. If you need me, I'll be on the couch, bleeding through a number two pencil."

"Fabric cleaner's in the kitchen," Seth said, hoping Kelly was ready for a smartass comeback. "In case, you know, you get blood on the couch."

"Asshole," Kelly muttered, but he was smirking as he said it, so maybe he was healing after all.

Seth went back to work, but for once, he kept his brain in his kitchen instead of in outer space. He heard the pencil start tentative scratching on the paper, and for a moment, he kept his back ramrod stiff in case the scratching stopped. But it didn't.

It kept going and going, hard and intense, like Kelly couldn't draw fast enough.

And more.

A piece of paper was pulled off the top and replaced by another one. And another one. And another one.

Kelly's breaths became labored.

Suspect.

Shuddery.

Seth held his own breath, his fingers hovering over his laptop keyboard. *Does he need me? Should I wait? What does he need?*

"Seth?"

Seth was squatting by the couch before the syllable was out. Kelly had taken his drawings and folded them in half, and Seth had promised he wouldn't look over his shoulder.

"Yeah?"

"I was raped."

"Yeah."

"It really sucked."

"I know, baby."

"But… but… it's not all that's ever happened to me."

Seth pushed Kelly's curly, coarse hair back from his forehead. "No."

"Some shit has been really good."

Oh. Kelly. "I really hope so."

A smile flickered across his mouth. "I want to live for that stuff. I… that thing that happened in that tiny room. There's so much more to my life than that."

"Yeah."

"Okay. I'm done drawing for right now." He actually looked at Seth instead of at the papers in front of him, and held his hand out and stretched it. "Hand cramp."

"You did really good," Seth praised him. "Really good. You're brave. You know that, right?"

"I didn't fake out a bunch of gangbangers by yelling 'It's the cops!'" Kelly told him dryly, and Seth grinned.

"I have no idea what you're talking about."

Kelly burst out laughing, the tears that had gathered around his upper lip sputtering onto the folded pages in his lap. "You're such a dork."

"Yeah. But I'm your dork."

And Kelly grinned back. "You hopped on a train and cut school because you heard I was sad through layers of bullshit. You'd better not be anybody else's."

Seth chuckled, and Kelly laughed back, and that's where they were when Seth's dad got back with groceries—holding each other and laughing, like everything in the world was gonna be okay.

THAT NIGHT they lay in his bed again, fully clothed, and for the first time, Seth felt the restriction of that.

He tempered it, though, satisfying himself by splaying his hand on Kelly's bare stomach under his shirt.

They talked this time, quietly, mostly about small things. Then Kelly surprised him.

"It was a good day. I… I just know I'm not gonna be all better from just one good day."

"Maybe… you know. You graduate next year. Maybe you can get some scholarships to one of the schools in San Francisco. We can see each other more. Maybe…." He took a deep breath. "Get an apartment. The older kids can live off campus, but I'd have to get a job. Maybe… you and me…."

And Kelly took off with it. With planning. With who they could be if they held on just right.

It was spun sugar, maybe? Maybe cotton candy dreams, giant castles out of clouds, because they were still kids.

But maybe cotton candy dreams show a person where the bones of real dreams may lie. Maybe if they had steel in their hearts and spines, they could build a skyscraper out of dreams and put that steel in the girders and the clear glass of vision in the windows, and the bedrock of their faith in the foundation.

Maybe they could build something lasting from their cotton candy dreams in the sky.

Seth fell asleep dreaming of a tiny apartment, and Kelly being a famous artist, and falling asleep like this every night.

LEAVING WAS hard.

Seth's dad and Kelly dropped him off at the train station, and Seth kissed Kelly hard, right in front of his dad, and then hugged his dad and kissed his temple as he sat in the driver's seat.

"Take care of each other," he told them, his voice rough.

On the train, with that giant whooshing rumble of the tracks purring in his mind, he found himself pressing his forehead against the glass, looking across the dusty Sacramento farmland as he cried.

He pulled himself together enough to order an Uber back to school, and this time he checked in with the dorm supervisor to apologize and tell them he'd returned.

The man in charge—a roundish college student with earnest brown eyes and horn-framed glasses—was legitimately hurt.

"Seth! I get that you wanted to go home, but we were worried about you. Vince was freaking out."

"Sorry," Seth said, trying to remember how to be human after the weekend when it hadn't been such a stretch. "It… it felt like an emergency."

"Was it?"

"Yes. But not in the way you'd think."

Kent tilted his head. "What kind of emergency was it?"

"The kind where everybody has needed each other since May, but we never got a chance to have that big group hug."

Kent raised his eyebrows. "Okay. Okay. Sometimes emergencies are like that. Next time you have one of those, *let me know.* For one thing, I've got a car, and I can save you an Uber ride."

Seth smiled then. One Uber ride was another stuffed animal for Kelly. "Okay. Thanks, Kent!"

"Not a problem. Now go make up to Vince. You really hurt his feelings."

Oh.

He'd almost forgotten Vince's name—he certainly hadn't mentioned him to Kelly *or* his father.

"Okay. I didn't mean to."

"Yeah, well, sometimes people care about you whether you're paying attention or not."

Oh hell.

Seth grabbed his stuff and made it up the stairs to his dorm room. The boys' rooms and the girls' rooms were identical—two hard cots, side by side, with about five feet in the middle. They had a window by the head of their beds and a desk each at the foot, and a shared closet next to the door.

Vince was sitting at his desk, doing what Seth thought of as "angry math." It was a thing only Vince did, where he pressed the pencil so hard, Seth had once curiously looked at the blotter underneath and could tell what problems Vince was doing.

"Vince?"

Vince barely glanced at him before going back to his work, and Seth guessed angry math was a real thing.

"Vince, I'm sorry I didn't tell you where I was going."

Vince closed his eyes and took a deep breath, still not looking up. He was a handsome boy from Hawaii, whose Polynesian ancestry shone through in his copper-skinned, wide-cheekboned features. Seth had always figured they'd been put in the same room because most of the other students at Bridgford were white. Maybe the counselors, in their misguided way, had thought these two boys would have something in common.

Seth had always wondered what would happen if he told Kent that he really didn't have much in common with anybody there, except Amara.

But now, looking at the hurt on Vince's face, he thought maybe he'd been wrong.

"I didn't mean to worry you," he said helplessly, wondering if this relationship would be broken beyond repair before he ever knew it existed.

"You did," Vince said, scribbling furiously on his paper.

"I… things weren't right at home. My boyfriend and my dad sort of needed me—"

Vince swung around suddenly, fury written on his face. "See? I didn't even know you had a boyfriend. Or a dad instead of a mom, or both. You practice until the rooms close and come in here and do homework and then go to bed. And sometimes, you and me don't even talk. But you're another human goddamned being, Seth, and it's my job to look out for you, and…."

A beat. Another.

"And what?" Seth asked, curious.

"And you don't even know I'm here."

Seth grimaced. "I try really hard to give you time in the bathroom," he said, because this was true.

"I don't even know if you *crap*!" Vince burst out.

"I do. I have a break between second and third. I come back when you're not here."

For a heartbeat Vince just stared at him. "Auuuuughhhhhhh!"

Seth flinched. He wasn't sure how that was failing as a human being, but apparently it was. "I… you know. Didn't want to be a bother."

Vince scrubbed at his face—clean-shaven, because that was something he did every morning too. Seth had actually considered asking him for help in that area, but…. God. How embarrassing. The only person he could tell things like that to was Kelly.

"How about a *friend*! You know, I'm new too! And I'm a *junior*. It would have been *great* this last month to have someone to talk to."

"About what?" Seth asked, thinking that now he could make himself available when he'd apparently failed before.

Vince sighed and tilted back in his chair, apparently giving up on Seth. Well, Seth couldn't blame him.

"I can't think of anything right now." Vince sighed. "What was wrong at home?"

Seth swallowed and looked away, and Vince rolled his eyes and turned back to his homework. Oh. Well, shit. Seth could at least tell him what he'd told Amara, right?

"My boyfriend, he got beat up," Seth said. "Really bad. Right before I was supposed to leave. I… I found him. He was in the hospital. I found the guy who beat him up, and…." Seth shook his head.

"Those bruises? Your eyes?" Vince said, swinging around to face him. "We were all talking about it, that first week in the summer program. Your boyfriend was worse?"

"A week in the hospital worse." Seth swallowed, remembering how sad Kelly had been. "He's still… not okay."

"Oh. Shit. I'm sorry." He looked sorry too.

"I just had to make sure he'd be okay," Seth finished. And then, because Vince had been human to him, he added, "I'm sorry again. I didn't mean to make you worry."

"Mm." Vince just kept looking at him, like there was more to say.

"Do you miss your home?" Seth asked after a silence that felt like an atomic wedgie.

"Horribly," Vince admitted, rubbing the back of his neck. "Everything in Hawaii is either mountains or sea." He gestured around them, the valley before the mountains that guarded San Francisco. "This shit ain't either. And it's not green. Or it's not, at least, past the grounds. I can't stand it here."

Seth smiled wistfully. "Remember when we played at San Francisco State? And we got to go to the ocean for half a day after the performance?" After the first leg of their journey touring Stanislaus State and Fresno State—in June!—the gray July day spent on the coast had seemed like heaven.

"Yeah."

"That was the only time I've ever been to the sea."

Vince gaped at him. "It was cold as fuck!" he burst out.

Seth shrugged. "It wasn't 110."

Vince let out a laugh and then sighed. "I take off my shoes in the practice room," he said, seemingly at random. But Seth didn't mind.

"Yeah? Does it help you play?" Vince played trumpet. Seth didn't understand wind players—it seemed like you might as well talk, but he didn't like to judge.

"Helps me *be*," Vince said passionately. "I wore flip-flips all my life, and I swear, here? They act like you're spreading the plague."

Seth thought about it. "Aren't they called flip-flops?"

"Not in my family. My little brother, Marcus, called them flip-flips. It's like a family tradition."

"Sounds like something Kelly would say."

Dear Kelly—

I got back to the dorms okay, and had to apologize to my dorm mate for scaring him. It was okay, though. We talked. Apparently he's nice. I had no idea. And he promised to keep teaching me how to shave.

But don't worry.

He doesn't like me like you like me.

Did you know that when you lean your head on the train window in the dark, and you're zooming through all the farmland in the valley, it looks like the ocean?

I want to take you to the ocean someday.

I want to play music that sounds like the valley at night on the train.

And the ocean.

And you.

But Vince has a little brother named Marcus, and I told him about Lily and Lulu and Agnes, and he told me about Marcus.

And you know something?

Talking about you to somebody made you feel more real.

I need to remember that.

You're so good with words and pictures. No wonder the whole world is real to you. I'll try to be more like you.

Love you.

Sleep good.

Seth

Making It Through

KELLY HUSTLED toward the bus stop in the chilly February morning, shoulders hunched against the wind.

He wasn't even sure if the bus ran on Saturday, but he had just enough money in his little bank account to pay for the train ticket, and not enough for a cab or an Uber. But God, he *had* to make it to Bridgford.

Before his head exploded.

Those magic hours with Seth hadn't fixed everything, but they'd given Kelly some tools to keep working on it. And Seth hadn't just visited that once. He'd come before Halloween, and for Thanksgiving and Christmas. He'd had to stay inside those times, and even for a space cowboy like Seth, wandering restlessly through the increasingly shrinking apartment wasn't a treat.

But he'd been able to be there for Kelly as Kelly worked shit out in his own head.

Kelly was getting better at working that shit out in his own head.

He drew every day now.

Some days he drew scary things—things he'd done, things he'd seen, in that dank and horrible abandoned store.

Some days he drew his sisters or his mom and dad, or even, on occasion, Seth's dad. He sent pictures of those drawings to Seth, and Seth had shown him a room full of printed-out drawings—they were all over his walls.

Some days he got out his colors and just drew feelings.

He would listen to Seth's practice tapes on those days, and try to draw Seth's music. He wasn't sure what the results were worth, but those days always made his soul feel bright and shiny. He could do that a lot!

Some days, when his heart hurt too much, he would make Seth take selfies, and he would sketch those.

The day before had been one of those days.

HIS MOTHER had been baking sugar cookies, setting aside frosting for his sisters in Valentine's Day colors, along with sprinkles, and Kelly had thought, "I'll have to take a plate down for Seth and his dad."

And then he'd realized what he'd thought. And he remembered that he and Seth wouldn't get Soccer Wednesday on Valentine's Day this year, and that he wouldn't get to give Seth a birthday blowjob like he had the year before.

And that he and Seth hadn't done more than kiss in the last few visits, even when his father had been gone. Kelly's body had been... healing, even though all the cuts and bruises and strains had disappeared long ago.

But he still ached and flinched from touch, except when he was really comfortable.

And Kelly realized—truthfully in his own mind—that he wouldn't be able to do the same things he'd done the year before with Seth, because he wasn't the same person inside. The person who'd been so fearless and joyful at what their bodies could do was afraid now. And Seth knew it and wasn't pushing because Seth just wanted him to be happy.

He'd needed to draw Seth in the worst way.

He had about three sketches done, sitting beside him on the coffee table, when Matty stormed in, his face red from arguing with Dad. Kelly wasn't sure what they were arguing about now—grades, or Isela, or the beer he'd smelled on Matty's breath yesterday after school, or how Matty had mouthed off to his coach during soccer and had almost got kicked off the team.

Kelly didn't really care anymore.

He didn't have a brother anymore. This foul-mouthed, bitter stranger was part of the reason Kelly didn't sleep much at night. He kept dreaming Matty would sneak up behind him and strangle him, or slit his throat as he slept, or suffocate him with a pillow.

Terrible, violent dreams left Kelly soaked in sweat, and left him spending the next two or three nights in Seth's bed, until he could look at his brother again and not imagine Matty's hands around his throat instead of Castor Durant's.

So Matty storming in wasn't anything new, and the way he disrespected Dad wasn't fun either, but as he swept by Kelly's stuff on the coffee table, the pictures of Seth swirled off and Matty stopped mid rant.

"*Him*? You're drawing pictures of *him*?"

"Yeah! So?"

"That fucking faggot—"

"Matty, stop!" Dad snarled. "Or the next thing you hear is going to be the door slamming behind you!"

"You don't know, Dad! All this shit you're giving me, and you don't even know you have a faggot living under your roof, where he can get to the girls! You should have *seen* him and that other fag, kissing on the fucking camping trip, kissing like perverts in the woods—"

Kelly gaped and then pulled himself up and stood. "As opposed to *you*, assfucking your girlfriend over a log? Because *that* was fucking classy, Mateo—*that* was something you should have told Mom and Dad about!"

The back of Matty's hand caught Kelly's mouth just right, and he flew backward into the wall.

He lay there, stunned, sliding onto the couch. When he came to, Matty was in a three-point restraint.

Holy God.

His father had his knee in Matty's back and an elbow between his shoulders as he restrained his son's wrists behind his back.

"Call Craig," Dad said to Mom, his voice choked. "I'm going to need his help getting our son to your mother's house."

"Daddy!" Matty wailed. "No!"

"You want to come back home?" Xavier Cruz grunted. "You *really* want to come back home? Then you come back as my son. *My* son doesn't just beat his little brother in the face for no reason. *My* son doesn't hate his brother for no good reason. *My* son doesn't hate his brother's boyfriend for no other reason than he's your brother's boyfriend. You want to know what I wish? I'll tell you what I wish! I wish you'd been attacked that night. I wish you'd had to learn what being beat up on was like. I wish you'd learned humility and kindness the way your brother seems to always have known. So yes. We're sending you away. Because it's easier for us to love you from far away when you're not being a monster to us here."

"But, Daddy," Matty cried, actual tears on his face. "I… I can't leave. Isela's pregnant, and I don't know what I'm going to do!"

"Holy God," Mom muttered. "You're still not our son. *My* son would have taken the condoms I put in his room every month for a year and *used* them!"

Dad stared at his wife. "You've been giving him condoms? Jesus Christ, so have I!" He let go of Matty's arms and smacked Matty on the head. "What in the fuck, son? Were you *selling* them?"

Matty pulled painfully to a sitting position, looking at his father with wounded defensiveness.

"She said she was on the pill," he mumbled. "And then this week, she said she lied. We have to get married right after graduation."

"*Fuck!*" Xavier Cruz rocked back on his heels. "Jesus fucking Christ. Mateo, you're not even fit to parent a *dog* at this point. I want to take you to your grandmother's because I'm afraid of having you around your *sisters.* What in the hell?"

"I'm sorry, Daddy," Matty said, and Kelly hated him more in that moment than ever, because he sounded sincere. And heartbroken. And confused.

Kelly stood up and headed for his bedroom.

"Wait—Kelly—" his dad called, but fuck it.

"No, no, I get it," Kelly snapped. "You've got to worry about your grandbaby and your number one son. What the hell. I'm just the gay one. I'm gonna be *fine*—"

His mother was the one who caught up to him as he started throwing clothes in his backpack for school. "Going downstairs?" she asked softly.

"Apparently for the rest of my life," he replied, hating Matty for that most of all. He'd been happy, listening to his sisters, smelling sugar cookies, enjoying his home.

"No," she said, stopping his hands as he tried to strangle a pair of socks. "No. Your brother, he's going to live somewhere else, even if we have to wait for graduation to get rid of him. Your dad's right. I don't want that shit in my house." She squeezed his hands. "*You*, I still want. And Seth. And the two of you together."

Kelly grunted. "I… I just wanted to tell you my own way," he muttered.

She laughed softly. "You did. All last year. Every time you looked at each other. Daddy figured it out camping. He came up to me that night you boys were in the lake and said, 'If they don't know they're in love, they're dumb as a box of diapers.'"

Kelly had to laugh. "We knew," he said. "We've known for a while."

She nodded. "He's been visiting, hasn't he? Besides Christmas."

He'd told them about Christmas so they'd understand why he was spending so much time with Seth's dad and why Craig wasn't coming upstairs.

"Then it's good Matty's going. Seth can come upstairs when Matty's gone. It's not the whole neighborhood or the city, but it's not just Craig's apartment either. It must be making him crazy not to practice."

Kelly thought of the longing looks Seth cast at his practice corner, and the way he brought the violin out sometimes and just practiced bow and fretwork without actually running the bow across the strings. "Not so's you'd notice."

She gave him a small smile, and he realized how pinched her full mouth had become this last year. "And the girls miss him. Well, we'll have to get rid of your brother, then." She sighed. "But right now, yeah. Go ask Seth's dad if you can stay for a while, okay?"

Oh God.

"Okay."

Kelly added some more clothes to his backpack. And then some more. And then he took them all out and packed a new one so he could use that backpack for his schoolwork.

His parents were still talking to Matty as Kelly threw a pack over each shoulder and slid out the door.

Seth's dad had gotten used to him just coming in the front door by now, but he must have heard something going down upstairs, because he looked up... and grimaced. "Dammit, Kelly. Sit down, and I'll get you some ice."

He came back with an ice pack and asked Kelly if he wanted to talk about it.

Kelly grunted around the pack he held to his lip. "My brother knocked up his girlfriend. Apparently that means we all gotta suffer."

Craig sighed. "I'm sorry. What're your parents doing?"

"Trying to invent a time machine so they can go back and not have him," Kelly said. "I think the only thing stopping them is that me and the girls would have to go, and they like us."

Craig snickered. "Time travel could be very useful in this situation. So you're here for a little while?"

Kelly sighed. "Yeah. I... I was just starting to like home again too."

"I'm sorry, kiddo." He patted Kelly's shoulder. "I'm doubly sorry that it's this weekend."

"You got a date?" Kelly perked up. He'd started to think that Seth's dad had been alone too long. He wanted to start setting him up with all the divorced women in their neighborhood, but Seth's dad seemed like too much of a catch for those women. It had to be someone special.

"No, I've got overtime." Craig shrugged. "But Sunday we can catch a movie if you like."

They did this sometimes. They both liked comic book movies, it turned out, and Kelly was glad to have a friend.

"We'll see," Kelly said, his mind wandering. All day tomorrow? God. He couldn't do it. He needed to get the hell out.

"You have other plans?" Craig cocked his head expectantly, because he was still a parent, and Kelly appreciated that.

"I'll let you know," he said. In his head he was making plans already. He had an allowance from watching the girls after school, and with Seth's dad paying for shit, he'd saved some up.

While Craig went into the kitchen and started to fix dinner—a salad and some hamburger patties, bless his heart—Kelly pulled out his phone and started to plan.

The next morning he left a note—*Going to see him. K.* He wanted to say when he'd be back, but he couldn't. He couldn't help it. He just didn't ever want to come back.

But the plan was to go spend the rest of his formative years on Seth's floor, and it didn't have a contingency plan for his father pulling up next to him in the family minivan, window rolled down.

"Get in."

Kelly didn't look up. "No habla English." Of course the irony was, he didn't habla Espanol either, because his father didn't speak it in the house, and he'd taken French in school. All he knew was *mijo.*

His dad sputtered. "Look, you little dickhead, I'll pay for your ticket there and back, just get in the damned car!"

Well, shit. On the one hand, it meant he had to come back. On the other, it meant he'd have more money for food if he went with the living-in-Seth's-dorm option.

"Coffee on the way?" he bargained, and his dad laughed.

"Sure."

He got in the car, and Dad threw him a hat—something his grandma had knit for… well, anyone in the family who would wear it. It was made with big chunky yarn and had flecks of something pink in it.

"Really?" Kelly asked, eyeing the hat.

"Did you bring one of your own?" Dad asked pointedly.

"No."

"It's cold outside. You forget your own hat, I provide. Also, are you insane?"

Kelly grunted. "Seth does it sometimes."

"Yes. This is true. But Seth didn't walk out the door one night and almost not come back!"

"He did too," Kelly said. "He did too, and you know it. And this time, I needed to be somewhere with him where we can walk outside for a change. I...." He let out a little grunt. "It's not fair."

"I know."

"I've been looking at JC's, you know, near Northridge or San Francisco. So we can...." This sounded so grown-up. "So we can live together and go to school."

"We'd miss you," his dad said, sighing. "I'm not ready yet. Definitely not ready for Matty to be grown-up. Seriously not ready for you to grow up either. You're only sixteen."

"Well...." Kelly looked out the window into the foggy streets. "I'll be seventeen when I graduate. If we were rich and shit, you'd be sending me away to a college, never to see me again."

"Screw *that*," his dad muttered. "There's, like, no *way*!"

Kelly laughed then, with all his heart, because his dad sounded about sixteen himself.

"Well, you know. Bridgford isn't that far away. Maybe you can visit—isn't the train station over there?" Because his dad had passed up the old brick building in the pocket behind Old Sacramento and was zooming toward the freeway.

"The way I figure, I'll get you there in about two hours," his dad said. "Look around—nobody out. We can stop for coffee in Vacaville."

Kelly swallowed. "Don't you got things to do today? Matty and—" He tried so hard not to say "skanky whoring bitch." "—Isela?"

It was his dad's turn to laugh, and he didn't slow down. "Tell me how you *really* feel, Kelly."

"He's stupid," Kelly muttered. "I mean, I'm not gonna argue he's stupid. And he's mean. And he's an asshole. But... but trapping him? That wasn't right. He was just dumb, being led around by his peter that way."

"Yeah." Dad took a deep breath. "I can't argue. Not today. And I'm pissed at him. He doesn't deserve my time like you do. But we're having a good conversation. Even if all we do the rest of the way down is argue over music and sports, I'd rather spend my morning driving you to Bridgford and coming home than dealing with your brother's bullshit."

Kelly smiled, a thing that had gone cold in his chest the night before warming again. "I mean, she's gonna be pregnant until what? August?"

"That's the plan so far," his dad said.

"Yeah, well, they can frickin' wait. I'll even let you pick the music."

"How about *you* pick the music. I know Seth sends you practice videos. Let's hear what he's doing."

Kelly's chest got tight. He remembered when Seth said just talking about Kelly to his roommate made him feel better. This was his dad's way of making up for the fact that nobody talked about Seth in his house anymore. Everybody was too afraid of Matty or Isela, of somebody telling Seth's terrible secret and getting him into trouble.

Kelly never got to talk about one of the things he was a complete expert on, and Dad was giving him a chance to do that.

He wasn't going to squander it.

"Okay, so this is one of those violin concertos that people do all the time when they want to sound super good at something. It's like the violin is the center of the entire orchestra, and Seth is going to perform it at the end of this year. And it's a big deal. Because he's not even college level yet. It's like his first thing—the thing he did during his summer break at the college where he was supposed to have a buddy telling him how to be a college student when he was still in high school."

His dad nodded, like maybe he was used to not talking when Kelly was on a roll.

"He totally pissed off his buddy because he was way better than she was, and she went and told the professor that he needed more work because he was going too fast, and suddenly he had to learn all this shit, while everybody else was running around the school and going places and stuff. I mean, I guess he got to do some sightseeing, but he was a little depressed. So anyway, he hasn't gotten any worse, and this is him practicing."

He found the file on his phone and hit Play, and then sat, breathless, as Seth's first chords drifted over the sound system.

His dad listened, mouth open, as they changed freeways to 80-West, and then kept going. About the time they hit West Sac and found a gas station area that had coffee, both of them were a little choked up and misty-eyed.

"He's really good," his dad said, pulling off the freeway.

"Wait 'til you hear the special mash-up that's all my favorite stuff," Kelly told him proudly.

"He did that for you?"

"Yeah. We... uh... you know. Talk every day."

His dad took a deep breath and pulled the minivan up to a pump. "I guess he really *is* your boyfriend, isn't he?"

Kelly nodded. That was the word he used at school. He'd been asked out a couple of times—Jimmy Durreson and Tevin Crane knew all the gay people, and they didn't seem to believe that Kelly wasn't single.

"Yeah, Daddy. I'm gay. I've got a boyfriend." And that was Seth, who was still dreamy and out there, but who would probably come down from outer space for him.

"Your mom and I mean it, son. It's not that you're gay. We worry about you because the world is hard. And because you're young. But not because you're gay."

Kelly grinned. "That's good. It's not going away."

His dad laughed, and they both got out to use the bathroom and get some coffee. In spite of the cold, Kelly liked his iced and sweet, and while he was waiting for the in-store barista to get her shit together, he pulled out his phone.

You gonna be around today?

Yeah. Amara and I are going shopping in ten, but we should be back in a couple hours. Why?

Be at your dorm by eleven. Trust me.

Okay. Why?

But Kelly put his phone back in his pocket and laughed.

THE TRIP down to Bridgford went fast, because he and his dad didn't let any silences fill it. His dad pulled him up to the front of this big *Gone with the Wind* kind of building and parked. Then he took Kelly in to check him in as a visitor.

"He's here to see a friend," his dad said. "He'll be taking a train back tomorrow, and he can sleep on the floor tonight. Is that okay?"

The young man at the desk—his name badge said Kent—nodded. "Yeah, no problem. As long as he's not seeing a *girl.* That's the rule."

Kelly controlled a smirk, and his dad rolled his eyes. But Seth had a roommate. And besides, that's not the reason Kelly was there, and they both knew it.

His dad turned around and gave him a hug. "Okay. I'll text you to let you know when your train leaves and order you an Uber—"

"I can take him," Kent said quietly. "It's supposed to be part of my job."

Kelly grinned. "That would be great! Thanks!" Then he went back to hugging his dad. "Thanks, Daddy. This makes you the best, you know that, right?"

"Well, you know. I can't compare to Seth's dad and pizza Friday."

Kelly just held his dad closer, feeling lucky, damned lucky, and then his dad kissed his brow and headed home.

HE WAS actually there a half an hour early. He followed Kent's directions up the stairs and down the hallway, and found the door. Then he threw his bag of clothes on the ground, making sure the one school book he'd brought was flat to the floor, and slid down on top of it, leaning his back against the wall.

Kicking back, he closed his eyes and prepared to wait for Seth to get home. He'd been there for maybe five minutes, arms crossed, catching some z's, when the door opened and he found himself looking into the face of one of the prettiest boys he'd ever seen.

"Hello?"

"Hi. I'm just waiting for Seth Arnold. He's coming back in half an hour, right?"

The boy rolled his eyes. "If you say so. I mentioned missing root beer, since the school went soda free, and he and that girl just sort of took off. It was weird."

Kelly pushed himself up, using the wall as a brace. "He's going to get you root beer. You know that, right?"

The boy just stared at him. "How would you think that?"

Because I went for root beer in May and almost didn't come back. "Superstition. Leave it at that. Anyway, I'm just waiting. You can go back to doing what you were doing."

"You could come in?" Vince asked, opening the door and gesturing.

Kelly cocked his head and regarded the tiny room, and an absurd part of his brain had a giant flameout.

Seth wasn't in that room.

Kelly didn't want to be in that room without Seth.

"I'll just sit here," he said, ignoring the way his body burned with cold sweat.

Vince cocked his head back. "I'll bring you a chair," he said.

And then he brought two and sat out with Kelly and talked.

Mostly they talked about Seth, and Kelly was surprised to find that *his* dreamy boy was not the same boy everybody else saw.

"Yeah," Vince sighed, handing Kelly a water after they got their chairs situated. "At first, I thought he was deliberately being an asshole, you know? Not talking, practicing until the last possible moment, spending every available minute doing homework. It actually surprised me that Amara liked him, because she's so sweet, right? Everybody loves her, and I couldn't figure out what she was doing hanging out with this silent, brooding prick. I was like, 'abusive boyfriend'?"

Kelly burst out laughing. "Seth? No!"

"Seth, yes!" Vince protested.

"He's shy," Kelly said. "And… and not here all the time."

"You think?"

Kelly had to appreciate Vince—he was beautiful, yes, but he was also a smartass. "I know," he said mildly. "He'd…." Kelly shrugged. "He'd go to fetch you root beer because you wanted some and he didn't want you to get lost if you went yourself."

Vince shook his head. "What is it you two have against root beer?"

Fuck. "I went to get root beer in May and almost didn't come back," he said bluntly, and Vince clapped his hand over his forehead.

"Oh! He said you got beat up—that's what happened?"

And then because Kelly had spent months talking about it to the counselor and drawing it in pictures and dealing with how real it was and how it wasn't all he was, he said, "A group of… well, they like to think they're a gang, but they were just druggie shitheads mostly. They all beat me, and one of them sexually assaulted me. It sucked all around. Seth—he blames himself a little, because he was arguing with his dad, and I was gonna go get us root beer floats, and they'd be done arguing when I got back."

Vince had gasped when he said "sexually assaulted," but now he nodded a little.

"What was he arguing about? Because he seems okay with his dad now."

Kelly rolled his eyes. "About coming here. He didn't want to leave either of us, mostly."

"Bummer. So he talked more before?"

"No. I'm the one who talks. I've got, like, this big family—"

"Wait, wait, don't tell me—Lily, Lulu, Agnes, and your older brother, Dickhead!"

Kelly snickered. "Yeah, those people. Anyway, Dickhead was super good at sports, so I had to be super good at talking, and I guess it worked, 'cause Dickhead is home getting bitched at for knocking up his girlfriend, and I got a ride down here so I can sleep on my boyfriend's floor." He punctuated this with a yawn, and Vince laughed.

"So, you want to come in and nap on his cot? They were taking the local bus, and sometimes that takes forever."

Kelly yawned and thought about the room again. He knew Vince now. It didn't seem quite so small.

"Sure."

By the time Seth got back—with root beer and Vince's favorite cookies and a bag of cheddar potato chips for himself—Kelly was sleeping on his cot, happy just to smell him on the sheets.

ALL TOLD, the weekend wasn't a big deal.

They had a quiet junk food party in Seth and Vince's dorm room, smuggling Amara in because they all liked her and because she also brought marshmallow chocolate graham cracker cookies and she'd share.

They watched scary movies on Vince's computer—because it had the biggest screen—and Amara slept on the floor with Vince's pillow, and Kelly slept on Seth's bed, mashing him back against the wall.

The next morning, Seth and Kelly got up super early and went for coffee, and for once Seth talked, pointing out the landmarks of the little town of Almond Falls, which appeared to be not much more than a wealthy commuter community into San Francisco.

"If you had more time, we could take a bus to the city," Seth told him as they sipped coffee in a charming little shop that was *not* Starbucks. "I haven't done it yet. I want you to come."

Kelly looked at him. Seth was still wearing a sweatshirt that had been rotting off his body in high school, and his hair was too long because nobody was nagging him to go to the barber shop two blocks down and get it cut close to his head. "You need to not save everything for me," he said after a moment. "You... you need to go have life without me and then show me what it looks like later."

Seth frowned unhappily. "But—"

Kelly looked around—comfy chairs, some very rich food in the glass case, some indie art on the walls. "This is a good place," he said. "You knew to take me here. Go to the city with your friends, Seth. Show me the best parts when I come visit."

Seth gave a tremendous sigh. "I hate this."

"Well, you know the only difference between how we're living our lives now and how we'd be living our lives if all that shit didn't go down?"

He shook his head, because unlike Kelly, who could draw things that weren't there, Seth could only play things that were. "You can't come home," Kelly told him baldly. "That's it. That's the only thing. Because you and me, if we were gonna make it, we were gonna have to figure out how to make it while you were out in the world being special. Big question is, can we still do that?"

"You're special," Seth told him soberly.

"But I'm homegrown special."

"Until you graduate," Seth said with some authority. "Then you can be out-in-the-world special too."

Kelly nodded. That was doable. "Deal."

SO *THAT* was the plan. *That* was the conversation that got Kelly back on the train and didn't let him cry too much. *That* was the promise that got him through the next few months of Matty this and Matty that and we gotta cut down on everything so Matty can have an apartment when he marries his girlfriend right outta high school in what was probably the most doomed relationship of all fucking time.

But the one thing that never got cut down was that somebody's dad, once a month, took Kelly down to see Seth.

Once a month. It wasn't so bad, right?

Once a month, they could touch each other and pretend everything was normal. Pretend all the bad shit never happened. Pretend that they had a future waiting as soon as Kelly graduated.

They just didn't know it was pretend.

Matty got married the weekend after graduation. Seth's dad was invited, and Kelly begged him to come, so he did.

Seth was not—but not because Mom and Dad didn't want him to be there.

Matty said it. "His dad can come, but that little psycho's not invited. He's bad for the kids."

Which was probably Kelly's first inkling of something larger, but Kelly was too pissed off to deal.

"Well, no, Seth, get another best man. And for that matter, get ready to fork out some money from your own pocket for the chair rental, 'cause Seth's dad was doing that from work. And if you're feeling *really* rich, by all means pay for the cake, 'cause that's a friend of his receptionist, and he's paying her for you."

Matty stared at him, his mouth opening and closing, and Kelly stared back, jaw thrust out just like their dad when he was mad.

He knew this.

His mother had told him so.

"Isela…," Matty whined, and Kelly flipped him off.

"Get a new best man. I know you're fucking broke and trying to afford an apartment and shit, but God, Matty, who died and made you king of everything?"

So while Kelly was *at* the wedding, Matty's other forward from his soccer team was his best man.

And Kelly didn't want to burst Matty's bubble, but Randall had hit on him twice.

So the wedding happened in Isela's church, and Isela wore white over her baby bump, and Kelly told Seth it was incredibly boring, but that wasn't entirely true.

Kelly cried a little, not for his dickheaded brother, but because he wanted one of these someday, and the boy he wanted it with hadn't even been invited to this one.

But finally—*finally*—Matty was out of the house.

Kelly spent less time with Seth's dad over his senior year, which was too bad, but he had a license now, and once school started, it was his job to drop Lily and Lulu off at the good junior high, where Seth had gone, because they were both super geniuses or something. Agnes was still in grade school; she only had one more year.

Kelly *wished* he'd gotten the room to himself, but they moved Agnes out of Lily and Lulu's room, put a little silk screen in the corner so she could change, and everybody breathed just a little easier.

Kelly figured it was really only fair.

He told Seth almost everything—leaving out stuff like Matty's groomsman grabbing his ass whenever they met or scholarships he was applying for in San Francisco. He figured if it came true, he could surprise Seth, and if it didn't, well, they were still planning.

How to move out.

How much money they'd have to make.

Where they'd go to school.

Dreams. So many dreams.

"Mm…." Kelly was lying on top of Seth in his bunk, in one of their rare moments alone. Vince and Amara had opted for the fast-food run this time, and Kelly had discovered—much to his surprise—that he felt like making out.

He'd pounced on Seth, mouth open, hands busy and everywhere, and his shock when he wanted to stick his hand down Seth's nylon shorts and stroke him off was nowhere near his excitement when he welcomed Seth's touch to do the same.

Ah! Oh God, oh God, oh God….

Damn.

It had taken about two minutes, and after they'd changed and washed off, Kelly made Seth lie down so he could lie on top of him.

"What are we gonna do for the next hour?" He laughed, and Seth chuckled and wrapped his arms tighter around Kelly's shoulders.

"Plan for your graduation," Seth murmured. "I can come, right?"

"Absolutely." He hadn't invited Matty.

"Good. I… I really want to be there. Next week, right?"

"Thursday afternoon."

"Good. I have my train ticket all ready, and I'm set for time out of school." Seth hugged him super tight. "I know it's just for your graduation and dinner, but I'm so happy to be going home for you."

"I'll be happier when I know where I'm going to school next year," Kelly said glumly. He'd been accepted by all sorts of state colleges, but Matty wasn't making enough to keep the apartment without help, and Isela wouldn't get a job. She kept saying she had to be home with her baby, but *Kelly* spent more time taking care of baby Chloe than Isela did. Isela dropped her off at least four times a week to go have a church meeting or something with her girlfriends.

Kelly's mom—who had been looking forward to working *outside* the house and actually doing the books for the restaurant *in* the restaurant and seeing other people besides her family once in a while—actually cried last Saturday. Kelly was all set to take the girls to a movie, leave their mom and dad alone, and boom! There's Isela with Chloe, who was dressed the same way she'd been dressed two days ago, but stinkier, and with diaper rash that Kelly could see from across the room.

Kelly had taken the baby, told his mom that he and the girls would go play with her at the gym—it had water games and those pipes that made rain and stuff—and gone to change her and put on some ointment.

The girls had been disappointed, but even Agnes had told him that Mom needed a frickin' break.

Agnes had also told him that Isela was the worst mother since Grendel's mother, because apparently his baby sister was also a genius and getting *Beowulf* in the fifth grade. Kelly could have been jealous that his sisters were such geniuses, but they seemed to think he walked on water and Matty was the suck, so he could forgive them for being way smarter than he was and getting twin 4.0s or the "you're so smart you're smarter than the teacher" awards in grade school.

Kelly liked baby Chloe, but he'd noticed, and so had his mom and dad, that she seemed, well, *needier* than his sisters had. When Lily and Lulu were born, Matty and Kelly had spent as much time as they could holding the girls. They'd gotten home and vied for the one who'd been awake or not nursing. When they'd started playing, they always had a Matty or a Kelly to lie on the floor with them and show them the bright colors or the squeaky sound. Agnes had a Matty and a Kelly and a Seth *and* a Lulu and a Lily to play with.

There'd been times when Agnes had been like, "No, fuck off, go away!" His parents said they'd never seen a baby roll into a corner before so she could coo at the wall, but it was probably just too many people up in her grill watching her being cute and all.

But not Chloe.

Chloe needed someone—anyone—all the time. She cried if they so much as set the car seat down.

She cried like she was used to crying, because nobody heard her.

Kelly wanted to live with Seth—they'd been waiting, waiting to see if they could be grown-ups together. Waiting to see if they could make love in their own apartment, free from watching eyes and fear of discovery and the stomach-cramping terror that a policeman would knock on their door the minute Seth arrived at his dad's apartment and ask Seth what he'd been doing two nights after Kelly had been attacked.

Not even Kelly wanted to know the answer to that question.

He hadn't asked either.

Two things going on at that crime scene.

But he couldn't think about that, couldn't think about if the pretty policeman who'd barely survived his own hell had been wrong, and the only thing that had been going on had been Seth getting blood on his hands.

But he still wanted them to be together.

That didn't mean he didn't worry about his mom, dealing without him, or the girls, who wouldn't have Kelly to help with their homework so they could keep being super geniuses, or Chloe, whose father seemed to have forgotten how to make babies happy and whose mother had probably never known.

He tried hard not to burden Seth with this, but Seth wouldn't let him be quiet about family. He asked about the girls, made him show pictures, and even cooed over the baby. Here, in his arms, as Seth searched through his phone and talked about how he wished Lily and Lulu could come visit, and asked if he could send Agnes her own stuffies from Amara's seemingly inexhaustible supply, it hit Kelly hard that even though Seth hadn't lived downstairs for almost two years, his family was still Seth's.

Seth didn't talk about why he didn't go upstairs often and visit, even when he was home, and Kelly didn't talk about why Seth couldn't go home that often.

When Castor Durant's name came up, it came up in context with Kelly's assault, and not with Seth showing up with choke marks around his neck and an eye the color of blood and the pathetic body found in a field with the head almost cut off.

As Kelly grew older, assumed the responsibilities of his sisters, of his niece, acutely aware of how his brother had failed his family and determined not to do the same thing, he realized that loving his dreamy boy could be the ultimate of foolish recklessness.

He was planning to move in with a *murderer.*

But every time that word hit his brain, his brain zigged and zagged the other way.

Not *his* boy. Not *his* Seth. It wasn't murder if it was self-defense, was it? Seth hadn't walked away from whatever had happened unscathed. He'd been held down, beaten, just like Kelly had.

Two things going on at that crime scene.

And more than that.

Kelly found he possessed a singular selfishness about Seth.

Didn't Kelly get anything that was *his*?

This boy, this *young man*, took care of him. In almost two years of cuddling, kissing, walks on the beach—yes, they had made it to the beach—Seth had only touched him intimately *once*, because Kelly had initiated it and invited it and was comfortable.

Two years, and Seth had marched at Kelly's speed—slower than a glacier. Slower than history. Slower than a constipated dinosaur—and hadn't complained once.

"Seth?" Kelly asked now, rolling over and splaying his hand over Seth's stomach under his shirt.

"Yeah?"

"Are we ever gonna—" He couldn't say *have sex*. It didn't sound right. Not after the last two years. "—make love again?"

To his surprise, Seth looked away, biting his lip in a way that made Kelly think of the dorky little laughs he let out sometimes, when he wasn't expecting to be amused.

"I... I had this plan, see?" Seth said. "And it's dumb. Because... because you haven't said anything, but... but I think... see, I think you want to stay and do junior college for two more years."

Kelly gasped, sitting up in bed. "How did...?" He swallowed, suddenly tearful. "You wanted to move out—"

"I do," Seth told him, and his eyes were red and shiny. "I do. But... but, Kelly, you're not ready. I... I get it. I mean, it hurts." He grimaced. "I can't pretend. Anyway. So I've got this dream, you know? Like, you turn eighteen, and I know it's dumb, but for some reason eighteen is a big age. It's like you're free to consent, you know? I'm sorry. I'm saying this wrong. But... but I want to take you somewhere. Somewhere nice. Like... like remember when me and Vince and Amara went to Monterey last summer?"

Kelly nodded. Seth hadn't wanted to go, but Amara's parents had rented a house for a week, and she'd invited her best friends—which were apparently both boys—and Seth had sent Kelly pictures every day.

Kelly, who had only made it to the beach at San Francisco, had looked at the bright clear expanses of Monterey Bay and fallen in love.

"I wanted to do that. With you. I wanted to rent a house. Like, I've started saving money for it. And, like, my dad could come for the last couple of days, but before that, it would be, like, just you and me. Just... just us. And we could... we could have space. And privacy. It wouldn't have to be rushed. And you'd never have to feel trapped. If it didn't work out, we could go running on the beach and maybe swimming because sometimes it's warm enough and nobody would know or care, and we could try again."

Kelly gaped at him, unaware that he was crying until he wiped his mouth and his hand came away briny. "This? This is what goes running through your head when I think it's only music?"

Seth looked away. "Yeah."

"Wow."

"Yeah."

"We could do that?"

"Yeah."

"That's a real pretty picture," he said, before he started to sob in earnest. "I want that. Can we do that?"

Seth's arms, warm and kind, were all he'd ever wanted. That word, that terrible word that went with Castor Durant and that terrible time, that word could go to hell.

"Yeah."

"Let's do that. You're right. I... I can't leave my family, not right now. But let's do that."

"Okay. Let's do that."

And Kelly couldn't talk after that. He was too busy crying, and he couldn't even say why.

HE'D PULLED himself together by the time Amara and Vince got back, and the weekend, well, it didn't get much better than that. Sunday morning, his dad texted and said he'd be there around six o'clock to pick him up, so they braved the hour on the bus to the beach and got back, breathless and happy, at six thirty.

Kelly was surprised his dad wasn't there yet. He and Seth sat on the steps leading up to the boys' dorms, looking out at the grounds—pretty, green, parklike—and talked after their return.

Darkness fell, and Kelly looked at his phone uncomfortably.

"Do you think he got held up in traffic?" he asked. He didn't even want to try calling. His dad had never mastered the art of Bluetooth phones in the minivan.

"Here," Seth said, pulling out his own phone. "Let me call my...."

At that moment, Craig Arnold pulled up in the Cadillac, the often refurbished, constantly cosseted red Cadillac that he swore he'd never part with.

He came to a slow stop and got out of the car, looking at both boys unhappily.

"Dad?"

Seth's dad came around to them and held out his arms, and as they both went in for the hug, Kelly saw his face, rumpled and swollen, eyes red like blood.

"Mr. Arnold?"

"Seth?" he said quietly. "I need you to go pack for at least two weeks. I'll come in and sign you out in a few. Can you do that?"

And Seth—he didn't say, "But I have a performance in a week." He didn't say, "No! Tell me now!" He just went, squeezing Kelly's shoulder like he knew what was coming.

Kelly couldn't fathom what was coming. "Mr. Arnold?"

"Kelly, your dad and brother were in an accident this morning. They weren't coming here. I thought you should know that. I guess... I guess they got in a fight, and Matty was driving, and he wrecked the car."

"My brother—"

"Matty's okay," Mr. Arnold said, and Kelly heard it then. The terrible pause.

"No." *Oh God. No.*

"I'm sorry, son."

"No."

"I'm so sorry. It happened on impact."

"No no no no no...."

And Seth's dad held him forever and ever after that. Even after Seth came out, his few possessions in his arms, and took over, Kelly could hear his own wail in his ears, in his head, in his heart, for years and years.

"*Daddy, no!*"

Songs from Outer Space

THERE WAS nothing Seth could do.

Nothing.

He held Kelly in the back of the car all the way to Sacramento, while Kelly whimpered because he couldn't sob anymore.

When they got to the hospital, Kelly's mom was in one of the many family rooms in the ICU unit at Kaiser, and so were his little sisters. Lulu was asleep, iron-straight black hair in stunning disarray, Chloe cradled in her arms.

Oh. Yes. Seth could see it—the thinness in the baby's limbs, the convulsive way she clutched at Lulu's shirt.

Kelly was right to worry about this baby.

But now was not the time.

Linda pulled her son into a long, intense hug, and while she was doing that, Seth and his father had a short conference.

"I'll take the girls home," he said. "Do you want to stay here with Kelly or come help with the girls?"

"Wherever he needs me," Seth said on automatic, but that got to be trickier as the week went on.

That night he stayed in the hospital, sometimes holding Kelly's hand and sometimes holding Chloe because Linda kept expecting Isela to show up to take care of her daughter.

"I don't know what she's doing," Linda muttered. "I—your husband is in the ICU, how do you not show up?" She shook her head. "I...." And for the first time, Seth saw her broken. "I can't. I can't go see him. I'm so damned mad. Oh God, Kelly, I'm so mad at him. He took your daddy from me, and I...."

And she and Kelly were clutching each other, crying, and Seth was standing, helpless, Matty's daughter in his arms.

After a moment, an attendant stepped into the room. "Family of Mateo Cruz?"

Linda gave a bitter nod, not letting go of Kelly's hand. "We're moving him from ICU to recovery. He's been asking for family. Did somebody want to go see him?"

Watching Linda and Kelly stand up, hand in hand, faces grim as they struggled with themselves not to reject Matty completely, Seth got a glimpse into the alien world of true family.

Not even Matty would get denied now.

That was forgiveness.

It was a lesson Seth took to heart.

They started toward the recovery unit, and Seth gathered all of Chloe's stuff, the baby still asleep on his shoulder. The attendant—Nurse Osborne—stopped him. "Are you family?"

"Friend," he said. "This is his daughter."

"Do you know where the mother is?"

Seth shook his head. "No. I guess Matty's mom tried to reach her, but no dice."

Nurse Osborne was an older woman, with close-cropped gray ringlets and skin a weathered oak. "What do you know about that child's home life?"

Uh-oh. "I... I'm not around," he said, feeling like a heel. "Kelly comes to visit me, and he... you know. Tells me about his sisters and Chloe. I guess he and his mom watch her a lot."

Nurse Osborne nodded. "Mm-hm. Are they a good home?"

Seth frowned. "They're the best," he said staunchly. "They kept *me* safe when I wasn't at home. His parents are...." *Oh God. He couldn't help it.* "His mom is the best," he said, voice breaking. "His dad was.... Oh God. I'm gonna miss him." He started wiping his face with the back of his hand, baby still rocking against his shoulder, but Nurse Osborne pulled out a tissue.

"I can't get any better recommendation than that. Okay, sweetheart. I'll let you go visit your friend in a minute—"

"He's not my friend," Seth felt compelled to say. "Not anymore. Not after his brother and I started dating."

Her eyebrows went up. "Well, I'm not surprised. That one—he's got an attitude. And that's not his only problem."

Seth stared at her, and she just nodded him toward the thick metal unit doors, which were standing open from when Linda and Kelly had gone.

Seth made it through, car seat dangling, baby bag over one shoulder, Chloe drooling on the other. And unlike when Kelly had been in recovery, his stomach ached with wrongness.

I shouldn't be here.

He could hear Matty before he even got to the room.

"I just want some fucking painkillers! Is that so wrong! I've been in an accident, dammit!"

"Yeah, Matty," Linda snarled. "We know. You know why you got in an accident? Because you were fucking *high*, you asshole! You let your father get into the passenger seat with you—nice father-son chat, he thought, right? And you were *high*. That's why no painkillers. *That's* what the nurse told me. They're not sure they can give you anything because you might overdose. Do you get that? *You are that fucked-up.*"

His mother's voice hit high C, and Chloe choked and woke up.

"Is that my baby?" Not screaming, Seth could hear the slur in Matty's voice. "Bring my baby here! Chloe, baby—"

Seth froze in the doorway, paralyzed.

"Oh my God—*Mom.* You let *him* hold my baby? Him? Jesus, that guy's a fucking psycho—he should be in a fucking *cage*!"

And there, in the white-tiled corridor of the hospital, Seth felt as exposed as a fly pinned to a cork board.

"You shut up," Kelly hissed. "You shut up. The only one who believes that is you. Dad *loved* him. Dad wanted him to be part of our family. He'd rather drive me down to fucking Bridgford any day of the week than listen to your drugged-out bullshit, so not another fucking word—"

"Yeah, you keep lecturing me, little brother. That psycho's got you by the cock—"

Kelly and Linda both exited the room, slamming the sliding glass door behind them with unnecessary force.

"I'm sorry," Seth muttered, under Chloe's crying. "Here. I'll take her to the waiting room. I'm sorry. I should never have come. I'm sorry."

Chloe, who had fallen in love with Seth at first sight—Seth thought it was his deep voice—gave a tiny hiccup and settled, whimpering, clutching his sweatshirt in her tiny fists.

She was eight months old?

"Agnes was bigger than this," Seth said into the sudden silence. "And not as scared. Poor baby. What's so scary about the world?"

"Matty!"

Linda and Kelly both straightened when they heard the voice, and Linda grabbed Kelly by the hand and ushered Seth to the other end of the unit. "Come on," she told them. "There's doors at the other end. Hurry!"

By the time they rounded the corner out of sight, they could hear Isela, a full panicked cry, her father trying to calm her down.

She screamed at Matty like he was getting sucked down in a flood.

As Seth and Linda and Kelly made their exit—closely pursued by Nurse Osborne, Seth noticed—he had a moment to think that both of them had already been swept away.

NURSE OSBORNE led them back down a couple of corridors to a quiet waiting room that was hard to spot from the main corridor and told them to stay. She came back shortly with a harried-looking white woman in her early thirties, wearing jeans and a T-shirt and a fuzzy brown ponytail, and a rather severe-looking doctor, his East Indian features lean and narrow, his eyes flinty with condemnation.

"Your son is a drug addict," the man—Doctor Takeri, his name badge proclaimed—said. "His blood work came back with high concentrations of opioids. We told you this."

Linda nodded.

"We notified the police, but the fact is, your son went off the road and hit a tree. There was minimal property damage, and only the car's occupants were injured. He'll be charged with driving while impaired at the very least, and you will need to get a lawyer in order to keep him out of jail."

Linda gasped. "Police? Why has nobody—"

"Because we were waiting for the blood work, you understand? Now about the child—"

"The child lives with her parents right now, is that correct?" The social worker stepped forward. Trisha Alford. She probably had a lovely family, but Seth clutched Chloe closer to his chest.

"Yes," Linda said, sounding dazed. "Her mother leaves her with us a lot."

"Does she work outside the home?"

Linda and Kelly exchanged looks, and they both shook their heads.

"She says Matty should provide." Linda's weariness was palpable.

"Mrs. Cruz, I know this is hard to hear, but that child can't go home until we've checked the home out for drugs and drug use. And I've got to tell you, hearing that girl screeching away, I'm not really hopeful that we won't find it in both parents. Are you prepared to take care of that little girl?"

Linda nodded. Without hesitation, she nodded. Seth swallowed and clutched Chloe a little tighter. This baby needed Kelly's mom right now. Kelly needed his mom right now.

Nobody needed him.

In fact, he might be the biggest danger to the Cruz family, next to Matty's drug use.

Ms. Alford's next words confirmed it.

"We'll need to check out your house," she said. "She'll need a space for a crib, even if it's in an adult's room—"

"Will my son Kelly's room be okay?"

And for the first time in forever, Kelly and Seth met eyes. "Poor Agnes," Seth mouthed, and Kelly smiled.

It was small and strained, but Seth could do that much, at least.

"There's room for a crib and a changing table?"

"Yes," Kelly said decisively, his eyes never leaving Seth's. Seth knew. They both knew what this meant. It meant that Kelly wasn't just staying home for junior college. It meant he was staying home until Lily and Lulu got old enough to help in the same way Kelly could. It meant he was home until Agnes left for college, and that he'd be helping his mother with the rent for years to come.

It meant that their amorphous time in the future, that had seemed so close, had just become a world away. It had dropped off the horizon. The curve of the earth obstructed its existence entirely.

And it also meant that Seth was going to have to make himself scarce. Chloe was being taken from her parents. One word—one *breath*—about Seth being involved with Castor Durant's death, and she'd be taken from Kelly's family as well.

Seth's eyes burned, and he clutched Chloe a little closer, even as she threatened to rip them both apart.

Kelly's lips moved, a message meant just for Seth. *I'm sorry.*

Seth returned with a small watery smile. *I still love you.*

Kelly nodded and wiped his eyes with the inside of his shirt. Seth almost missed it then, but Kelly shook his head and pulled Seth's attention back to his face. *Forever. I promise.*

And then everybody was listening to the doctor who'd seen too much and the social worker who felt like she could do too little. Chloe fell completely asleep, and Seth set her inside her car carrier and buckled her up.

He pulled Kelly aside for a moment as the doctor was explaining the hospital's policy on admitting patients into their rehabilitation center and how Matty would be eligible for fifty-six days on his insurance from work, but after that, he would be asked to pay for it or be transferred to a state-run facility.

Seth wasn't sure how Linda and Kelly could keep all the details straight.

"I'll take a Lyft back to the apartment," he said quietly. "Do you want me to take her with me, or should you and your mom keep her from here on out?"

Kelly slumped forward. "You have to go?" he asked plaintively.

"What if Matty sees me again?" Seth explained, hating that he had to. "Chloe needs you guys, Kelly. They'll take her away if he starts screaming about… things."

"And you could be locked in a cage," Kelly muttered. "Don't forget that!"

"I'd do it," Seth said frankly. "I'd give up everything and serve my time if it meant we could be together—"

Kelly shook his head. "It would just mean we could *never* be together," he said. "Go. I'll take her."

Seth gave a little whimper. "We just met," he said wistfully, looking at her sleeping face. "Maybe we can meet again."

"Don't give up on me—"

"Never," Seth said. "I'll be here for you as long as you need to be here for them. I swear, Kelly. I'm not… not always here in the present—"

"That's not true, *mijo.* For me, you are always here."

Seth kissed his forehead and handed him the baby carrier. "You know where I'll be."

Linda had broken away from the officials by then. "You'll have to leave her here—"

"He knows, Mom," Kelly said patiently, and Seth took this moment to look her in the eye.

"I'm so sorry, Mrs. Cruz. I'm so…." He couldn't. "Very sorry," he croaked, and then she hugged him, just for a second, and he'd never forget that, because her world was crumbling around her ears, the foundations of her heart ground to powder by the last twelve hours, and she still had a moment for him.

"We're grateful for your help," she said softly. "But you're right. You should go."

Seth nodded and turned to leave, pausing for one more look at the baby. "You have a good home," he said. "It's good that you're keeping her. She needs you like I did."

And then he was gone.

The buses weren't running anymore. He had to call a car. The Lyft driver didn't seem to expect a lot of chitchat, which was fine, because Seth's throat was too swollen and his ears hurt too bad to even think of talking.

WHEN HE got to the apartments, he went straight upstairs to knock softly. The picture of the Cruz family—taken right after baby Agnes was born—that sat on the far wall hit him like a slap in the face as his dad opened the door.

Xavier Cruz had been a good man. The best. *Fuck.*

"Kelly didn't come with you?" his dad asked, his voice pitched low enough for Seth to figure out the girls were asleep already.

Seth just shook his head. Later he would brief his father on the whole thing. On Matty's monstrous decline, on the things he'd say if he saw Seth again, of how Seth couldn't be seen with the Cruz children for their own good.

Of how the future he'd envisioned, of him and Kelly being grown-ups together, having a life, being lovers—all of it—had suffered a terrible blow tonight, when it had been so very fragile in the first place.

Later he'd tell his father these things.

Later.

At that moment, all he could do was look at his father mutely, inexpressibly glad that he was there.

He fell into his father's arms and cried.

SETH DID a lot of work behind the scenes over the next few days. He took a car and went grocery shopping for the Cruzes while his father watched the girls. He helped keep their house clean and cooked, when only Kelly was home, exhausted and needing to spend time with his sisters in grief. He looked through closets and found funeral clothes for everybody—including Linda, whose outfit had needed dry-cleaning and mending, but she was too busy getting Matty enrolled in rehab to even mourn her own husband.

Vacuuming the rug, dry-cleaning, casseroles—Seth made sure all of that was done.

And then he disappeared down the stairs to his apartment when the whole family was there, or when the social worker visited.

Fortunately he wasn't able to make it downstairs when Isela's father came to try to pray with the family and get them to admit that the children picked up drugs from Linda and Xavier.

He was the one who held Kelly back as Kelly launched himself at Mr. Cortez's throat, screaming about how his stupid church fucked up his brother and now it was like he was dead too.

Mr. Cortez took off right quick after that, and Seth just stood there, his arms wrapped around Kelly's shoulders, until the fight went out of him and he sagged against Seth helplessly.

Linda looked at him then, as though seeing Seth and her son for the first time.

"Seth?"

"Mrs. Cruz?"

"You've been wonderful. Could you take my son the hell out of here for an hour or two? The funeral is tomorrow and… and you've done so much. God. Go downstairs. Practice. You must be itching for it. Play us something beautiful, okay? Javi—he used to wait by the heater to see when your music would seep out. Just… both of you, go pretend to be boys for a little while. It will make me happy."

It was such a kind thing to say.

He'd never tell her, or Kelly, but one of the hardest things he ever had to do with his music was play something beautiful that didn't sound like mourning.

He found Irish sea shanties. Sometimes they were remarkably complex, and playful, and dancing, like waves. And sometimes they were plaintive laments. The arrangement he had veered from one to another, just like his own emotions, and he found he could share that from his heart.

It was all he could do.

He played each one fast, then slow, adagio, adante, forte, pianissimo, playing with interpretation, with mood. Kelly sat on the couch, his arms wrapped around his knees, eyes feasting thirstily on Seth's face.

Drinking him in like he was preparing for a drought.

Seth finally put the violin down, arms aching a little from the weight, and realized that Kelly had moved next to him, sitting on the back of the couch. His face was tight and wet, like he'd gone swimming and not wiped it off.

"Where's your dad, *mijo*?" Kelly asked into the heavy quiet.

"Work. He'll be home at—"

"Seven thirty." Kelly's mouth twisted. "We have two hours. Set your alarm, Seth."

Seth did, his skin prickling with knowledge of what this meant.

"Now come."

Kelly grabbed his hand and led him to the bedroom, where they both stripped down awkwardly. The memory of where they'd been two years ago versus where they were now made their fingers stiff, and the action of being alone, naked, with each other, a painful rediscovery.

"Your chest grew," Kelly said softly, coming to put his hands on Seth's shoulders.

"I had to work out," Seth admitted. "So I could hold the violin longer." He grimaced. "And because my arms were developing differently, and it was weird."

Kelly laughed, and some of the newness faded.

Seth traced fingertips along Kelly's jaw. "Stubble."

Kelly rolled his eyes. "Pita."

And then, because Seth had realized he found these things fascinating—and had been to the beach enough times to be fascinated by them in other bodies, even though he hadn't said anything—he skimmed his hands along Kelly's ribs to the V cut of his stomach muscles.

"You work on this," he said softly, and a sudden pulse of heat told him Kelly was pleased.

"Jimmy Durreson told me I'd never keep a boyfriend if I got fat," he confessed, and Seth grinned.

"I'd love you fat," he said, his fingertips pushing gently against the muscle to see how—ooh!—hard it was.

"But you like me now!" Kelly laughed, and Seth saw him then, the laughing boy, as though the pain had fallen away like an empty shell and what remained was the soft bubble of *now* that would protect them until his alarm buzzed.

"I love you now," Seth corrected, and then lowered his lips to Kelly's clavicle, teasing with his teeth.

Kelly gasped, and Seth kept going, the ache in his groin blooming with the suddenness of a blow.

Kelly's nipples. Ah! He could have stayed there forever, teasing, pulling, the sweetness of Kelly's skin on his tongue. But Kelly tugged at his hair—growing long, the ringlets hardly tamed by oil right now—and Seth fell to his knees and looked up, asking permission. Kelly feathered a touch along his cheekbone, then skated his fingertips along Seth's lips.

"Yeah," he said.

Seth remembered how to do this.

He licked first, and tasted, and stroked. He squeezed slow, long, and hard. He hollowed his mouth and took Kelly in, pushing his head down as far as he could.

This time—this time, it went all the way.

Kelly gasped and started to shake, and Seth cupped the backs of his thighs so he could help support his weight.

"I'm gonna—ah! Seth!"

And Seth tasted, bitter, he'd forgotten how bitter, and earthy. And salty. And good.

Kelly sank to his knees on the patterned rug of Seth's room, resting his face against Seth's throat and laughing shakily.

"Augh! Oh my God, *mijo*. I'm not sure I can stand."

Seth's next sound was a whimper, because he was still hard and aching, his cock jutting from his lap like a jousting lance. He dropped his hand to it, and Kelly stopped him.

"I may not be able to stand," he said, his voice a low, gruff rumble. When had that happened? When had Kelly's voice sunk to gravel? "But I am going to taste you. I am going to take you apart."

Seth shivered. Helpless. He could be helpless in front of Kelly. Kelly would guard him when his mind flew to the stars and his body shattered into glitter and twinkle-dust.

Kelly started at his throat, and bypassed the nipples so he could concentrate on Seth's arms.

"I have a confession to make," he whispered, licking a line down Seth's bicep.

"Yeah?"

"I really love guys with guns."

Seth chuckled. "Lucky me."

Kelly propped up on his chest, looking suddenly concerned. "No. Not lucky you. Lucky *me*. I… in a thousand years, Seth, I could never doubt you love me."

"Don't." Seth bit his lip. It would feel like a thousand years, wouldn't it? "Ever. Don't ever doubt I love you."

Kelly nodded and kissed his chest, and *finally* took in a nipple.

He sucked until Seth bucked his hips up and back, shaking with desire, *aching* with need.

And then he moved, spreading Seth's knees, propping his thighs up, and grabbing Seth's own hands to put on his backside.

"Spread 'em," he demanded tersely, and for a moment Seth wanted to roll over, because… because… but Kelly put his mouth on Seth's cock and shame went out the window, or slid down the floorboards.

Kelly's mouth was magic, and the spit and precum sliding down between his cheeks tantalized, and then… oh my God, Kelly *touched him*, right there.

Seth spurted a little and then whimpered when Kelly pulled away. "Getting excited?" he teased.

Seth opened his mouth to say yes, but Kelly's finger *kept touching him*, sliding softly, teasing, *penetrating*. Oh my God, was he doing what Seth thought he was doing? And what came out of Seth's mouth was fractured, gasps and groans, little grunts and whimpers, and Seth gripped his bottom and spread it, begging.

"More?" Kelly taunted.

"Nungh!"

Another finger, two of them, spit-slickened, stretching. Seth's brain was exploding, his body shaking with sweat, and he wanted more.

"Kelly!" He was lost, adrift, pleasured without an endgame, drowning in sensation without a tether to hold him to earth.

Kelly sucked him in hard and then released him. "Stay right there," he muttered, and then pushed up and disappeared. Seth wanted him back, but he was shaking too hard, too dazed and empty to think about what he was doing.

Kelly came back with a pillow, a box of tissues, and a jar of cocoa butter that Seth used for his skin. Seth went to prop himself on his elbows, but Kelly's hand in the middle of his chest stopped him.

"Let me do this," he whispered. "I'll make it good. I know I'm young, but—"

Seth stroked his hand and settled back down, trustingly. Kelly was the oldest of the two of them. He always had been. Seth knew that.

"I'll be careful," Kelly promised, and then nudged his hips up, and the pillow under them was a welcome relief.

Some of Seth's brain function was returning, and as he sank onto the pillow and reached down to hold his cheeks open again, he said, "Hey, we could have moved this to the *oh my God bed. Fuck don't stop!*"

Kelly's throaty chuckle was as earthy a sound as he'd ever heard, and his fingers, slick with the cocoa butter, stretching, spreading. Seth floated, his body shaking, until Kelly pulled out again.

"Mm...."

"You need me," Kelly told him, positioning his body carefully.

Seth stared at him, suddenly frightened. "So much."

"You work so hard," Kelly whispered, "taking care of us. You need me to take care of you."

Seth swallowed, naked and spread out, vulnerable on the floor of his childhood bedroom. "Yes."

"Remember me inside you when you're gone."

And Kelly slid inside him, the pinch and ache and burn of him delicious.

"Deeper."

Ah! Kelly thrust a little harder, a little deeper. Seth tightened, fighting to relax around the invasion, and he froze.

Kelly fell forward, slicking his sweaty hair back from his forehead. "It's okay, baby. I'll take care of you. Just let me in."

Seth bit his lip, closing his eyes so he could concentrate, like when he was playing. He sank into the music of his own flesh and began to fly.

"Oh...." Kelly's low moan echoed through his body, and he nodded.

"Faster," he begged.

Kelly would do anything for him—here, now, flesh to flesh, Kelly would do anything.

He pulled back and surged forward, and again, and again. Slowly at first, then building as they both got used to the mechanics. Back and forth, until their bodies oiled each other, adapted, learned the pathways of pleasure and trust.

And faster.

Seth kept rising, past the ceiling, past the sky, up into the stratosphere, where he could see Sacramento, then California, then the continent and the sea. Higher, higher, his breath laboring, the oxygen thin, until the earth spun beneath him, blue and lovely, all problems too small to see.

His chest ached, his body pulled tight, and he exploded, pulled back to earth, back to himself in a heartbeat as his physical self exploded into orgasm, and he pitched off the shelf of climax in time to hear Kelly groan.

Seth opened his eyes and caught his lover, his heart, as Kelly came undone.

Here, anchored to reality, he felt the pulse and throb of Kelly inside his body, the heat and wetness as it flooded him. His own cock lay flat against his abdomen in a cooling puddle, and Kelly fell on top of him, trembling and lost.

"You need me," Kelly whispered.

"Forever and ever," Seth told him. "I love you."

"Forever and ever."

That's all they could say for a while.

THEY WASHED up. Kelly showered while Seth cleaned the carpet, and when he was done he stepped into the shower and let Kelly take care of him.

Washrag, everywhere. Kelly's touches, gentle, reverent, in all the places he'd been.

"Sorry," Kelly murmured, standing behind him, arms around his waist.

"For what?"

"You had plans for my birthday, all pretty."

"I still do."

Kelly shoved at his hip and turned him around. "Yeah?"

Seth nodded. "That's how we'll do this," he said. "We won't miss a day, even if it's just a text. We won't miss a week, even if we just Skype. And you will come visit, whenever you can. You will come see me, and we will… we will shove all the things we want to be to each other into that week, that month, whatever. That's how we'll do this. That's how we have to."

Oh no. He'd been so strong, all week. Kelly was the one grieving. Kelly was the one making the sacrifice. Seth didn't get to do this. This wasn't his time to mourn. This wasn't his—

"We have to," he repeated, voice creaking. "We have to, because I need you, and we have to make this work."

"Shh...." Kelly kissed him, water and brine running into their mouths. He pulled away, his eyes as red-rimmed as Seth's felt. "It's a good plan," he said, his voice rusty. "We can make this work."

Seth closed his eyes and nodded, knowing the odds were against it. Knowing they were too young to promise forever. Knowing all the reasons he should just say goodbye now.

But he couldn't. It would be like amputating a limb.

The water ran cold, and they got out, toweled off, changed back into their clothes. By the time Seth's alarm went off, they were dozing in front of the television on the couch, lost in stupid TV.

Seth picked up his phone to turn it off just in time to get a text from his dad.

I'll stop for takeout. How many?

"Dinner with my dad?" Seth asked, and Kelly nodded.

"Yeah. Let me text Mom."

Seth's phone buzzed again.

I'll bring some for upstairs.

Seth laughed a little. "Tell her Dad's bringing dinner."

Kelly laughed too and texted, and the rest of the evening went like that. Quiet. Like normal. Like tomorrow they couldn't be saying goodbye to Xavier Cruz, one of the best men Seth had ever known.

Like tomorrow, Seth wouldn't be walking away from the boy he loved and leaving him to grow up alone. Like they wouldn't be breaking all the promises of hope they'd made to each other's hearts since the day Seth had looked at him sleeping and fallen in love.

It had to be normal, Seth figured. Anything bigger than normal would destroy them, pound them into dust, break them into a thousand pieces.

They couldn't do this in a thousand pieces. Someday, Kelly would be free. Someday, Seth would be able to take him away to whatever world awaited.

Someday they would be together.

If they were going to make it to someday, they had to be whole today.

It was the only way this would work.

May to November

SETH'S DAD gave the eulogy, and when Kelly's uncle Beto from El Paso asked, "Who the hell is that guy?" under his breath, Kelly realized he *could* be an asshole to family.

"That guy held us together these last two years, you prick! He was my dad's best friend, and he's the one who fucking stepped up and helped us plan, so shut your fucking piehole."

Uncle Beto had the nerve to look affronted, but Kelly remembered his mother killing herself to make big batches of cookies to send to Beto and his family for Christmas every year and getting bupkiss in return, not even a Christmas card of his perfect kids all going to Ivy League schools and shit.

Jesus, his mom, at least, deserved a gift certificate to Starbucks or something.

Kelly gave zero shits about Beto and Cherise Cruz.

His useless fucking brother was standing in his goddamned wedding suit, looking wrecked and sobbing constantly through the service. He'd gotten rehab and probation, with a day off for the service, because apparently the legal system was that fucking random, but Kelly gave zero fucks about him or his absent wife either.

Seth stood quietly next to him, his hair buzzed super short, thanks to his dad's clippers that morning. He was watching his father say goodbye with features made older by grief.

Kelly should let him go.

He should.

God, he wasn't eighteen yet, and he'd been broken twice, and twice Seth had been there to pick up the pieces and to tell him he'd be there, whenever Kelly needed.

Kelly should tell him to go out into the world and forget about him, and forget about Sacramento, and get a big job and take his father with him into the wide world, because if anybody deserved a vacation at the beach, it was Craig Arnold.

But he wouldn't.

He wouldn't and he knew it.

He'd been all talk the day before, about Seth needing him. Seth had bought it, eyes huge, pupils blown from orgasm, body offered up like a sacrament, a blessing to all of Kelly's brokenness, and Kelly had taken Seth into his being like wine and bread.

Kelly knew the truth.

Seth's father was comfort.

Seth was hope.

He couldn't let Seth go. Not now. Not when he needed hope the most.

Kelly was a bastard, a user like Matty, because he'd grab hold of that lifeline Seth was offering and drag him down.

His mother had asked Seth to play.

Seth was leaving right after the service. His packed bags were in his father's car; his violin was next to him. He would play Leonard Cohen's "Hallelujah" at the end of the service, and his father would walk him out before the priest said the blessing.

It was such a huge fucking imposition. Mom hadn't realized what she was doing until it was too late and they'd made the plans, but Kelly had.

And because his mother had asked it, had wanted Seth to be a part of Xavier Cruz's goodbye, Kelly hadn't been able to tell his mother Seth couldn't do that.

So Kelly sat, his hand in Seth's, and silently willed his uncle Beto to piss off, because anybody who questioned what Seth's family was to Kelly's family could jump off a fucking cliff.

And then the eulogy was done. And the priest was reading about the book of Timothy and zombies, and Kelly could do nothing but clutch Seth's hand and hate the world.

Now it was people telling their Xavier stories, and Kelly wanted to howl. He felt Seth's squeeze of his hand and waited for the story of how his father had kept a coworker from leaving his wife, because apparently the man was that dumb and he should learn to cook himself if he didn't like her cooking. As soon as *that* asshole wound down, Kelly stood.

"When I was fifteen," he said, not even sure where he was going here, but suddenly needing to say this so badly, he couldn't stop. "I... I fell in love with my friend, and he fell in love with me. And we thought we were so subtle. But my family knew. And my friend moved away, and I missed him and needed him. So I took off one day, to spend all my money on a train ticket for twenty-four hours on his dorm room floor.

And Daddy stopped me, and gave me a ride, and gave me food money, and told me he'd be back to pick me up, because he'd rather spend two hours in the car talking to me than doing anything else in the world. That was my father. The only man close to being as good as he was is my boyfriend's father, but that's another story. My father loved us. He wanted us to be happy. He'd teach us the best things about us so we could be. That's what all these stories are—they're Xavier Cruz, helping the people in his life be happy. We're not going to be happy for a long time, now that he's gone, but someday, someday we will be. Because that's what he'd want. And I'd do anything to make my daddy proud."

The church was silent for a moment, and the priest asked everybody to stand for the hymn.

Seth stood with his instrument and kissed Kelly's hand before walking to the podium and morphing, like a caterpillar into a butterfly, into the magic music man that Kelly had seen since they were boys.

He had more presence now, looking around the church with intense green eyes to make sure everyone was silent for him, and then launching into the plaintive song—not a hymn, really, but a lament, that people could not be their better selves.

That was the moment Kelly saw people cry. Even dumbass Uncle Beto let the music touch him, let it say goodbye to the brother he must have loved at some point. Kelly couldn't. He was all cried out. He wasn't going to bleed for all these people, most of them strangers, when he'd bled in front of the people he loved the most already.

But he loved Seth for his music, for this gift he could give the grieving, for this moment of mourning and solace.

This was why his boy was perfect. This was why he was hope.

When he was done, Craig and Kelly were behind the pews, waiting for him, moving swiftly as the priest gave the blessing.

Isela might have been absent, but her father was there, and Kelly hadn't missed him giving Seth the stink eye either. Of course, he'd probably been stewing in his own piss the minute Kelly opened his mouth. Kelly hoped Mr. Cortez got pleasure from that, because as far as Kelly could tell, not much else would make him happy.

The heat of an angry June sun beat down on them, and Kelly cursed the damned suit and slick shoes that came with weddings and funerals. Girls got to wear dresses for this sort of day, even if they were black. Seth allowed himself to be steered toward his father's car, while his father summoned a Lyft on Seth's phone to take him to the train station. But when they got there, he put a hand on Kelly's arm.

"Dad, did you bring it?" Seth said, turning to his father.

Craig smiled slightly, his face still bearing traces of grief. "Of course. Kelly, if you give me the keys to your mom's car, I'll take this there after you open it, okay?"

"Open what?" Kelly asked numbly.

"Your graduation present," Seth said, handing Kelly a midsized, heavy package. "We… you know. We'd been planning to give it to you when you graduated."

"Today," Kelly realized with a shock. Another year his teachers got to give him pity grades, but this one… this one should have been a celebration.

"Yeah. Anyway, open it."

The only reason Kelly's fingers functioned was that he knew Seth was there on borrowed time. He ripped through the incongruously bright paper, at a loss.

"Oh," he said when he saw it. On any other day, he would have cried. "Oh. You guys. This—this is… oh my God!"

It was an electronic drawing table, artist quality, that was compatible with the tablet Seth's dad had bought him two years earlier. Expensive— so expensive—but something they had clearly saved for.

Something they'd wanted to share with him in joy.

"I know it got lost," Seth told him. "But we're proud of you. Graduating. Going to junior college. Being an artist. Don't forget to draw. Send me pictures. I'll keep printing them out, okay?"

And Kelly found he *could* cry.

"Thank you," he murmured. "Thank you. I won't forget. Every day. Every week. Every break we get. You're my hope, Seth. Someday."

The car pulled up then, and people started milling out of the church. Kelly had to step back and let Seth's dad hug him before they both started throwing bags in the Lyft. One last kiss—full-mouthed, adult, promising all of the things they'd been together on that quiet afternoon—and Seth was gone, leaving Kelly alone to greet the crowds and take care of his sisters and Chloe and comfort his mother and—

"Here," Craig said. "Come bring it to the car with me. Your mom has help in there. You look like—"

"Like going in there and dealing with those people would get on my last fucking nerve?" Kelly sniffled. "Yeah. Something like that."

Seth's dad threw an arm around Kelly's shoulder and steered him down the parking lot. Kelly could take comfort after all.

SUMMER WAS interminable. The only thing that kept Kelly sane was that his dad had gotten the family a gym membership for Christmas the year before, so he took the girls swimming three times a week. Between that and free science day camp, he and his mother managed not to lose their minds with a baby in the house—and no Javi to help.

Thursday, Friday, and Saturday nights, without fail, Seth's dad knocked on the door when he got home. Thursdays, he warmed up leftovers. Fridays, he brought pizza. Saturday, he spent the morning shopping and cooked—mostly Italian and pot roast and meatloaf, but he made a lot, for the entire family, including some for himself.

They started calling Seth on Saturday nights on Kelly's tablet and propping it in the corner so they could Skype. It was almost like he was in the room.

Almost.

Seth spent grave amounts of time listening to Lily and Lulu talk about how they were both completely different and totally individuals, because Lily's hair was straight, like an arrow, and glossy, like her father's had been, and Lulu's was in tight ringlets, like Seth's and her mother's *before* she went to the beauty parlor every six weeks.

They frequently put Chloe up in her car seat and let Seth talk to her. He would sing Disney songs in a voice that was its own instrument, while she squealed and laughed, as happy as any of them saw her over the rest of the week.

At the end of the conversation, when everybody was gathered around the table about to dig in, he'd say goodbye.

"Love you all! Bye! Call me next week!"

And then he'd be gone.

He texted Kelly every morning, and Kelly—as time went on—started to appreciate how a boy who never spoke started to talk about more and more things on the little shining box in Kelly's hand.

Vince has a girlfriend named Stacy. She thinks Vince walks on water, and she tries hard not to be like her parents, who I think are not particularly nice about brown people. I think Vince might change their minds, though. He's nice to everybody, right?

Or,

There is a first-year violin here who is really good, but nobody seems to notice. I feel bad because I had all this help and this kid is drowning. I tried to do what you'd do—I asked him if he needed anything. He told me he could do it himself, and I had a big lightbulb. Aha! This is why he's drowning. I'll ask him next week if it looks like he can't breathe.

Seth had also taken to sending Kelly "The Daily Amara." She was frequently playing the flute, concentrating with a solid line of "fuck off and let me do this" between her eyes, but sometimes she was eating or laughing at the computer or throwing stuff at Seth. She did that a lot, and since she was laughing, it made Kelly laugh too.

Then there were emails, several times a week. Phone calls, late at night when the girls were asleep and it was just Kelly in the living room, drawing whatever he wanted while the TV played in the background.

Kelly had to admit that if Seth hadn't worked so hard at keeping in touch those first six months, he would have given up.

Waking up every morning without his father was a pain he wasn't sure he'd ever get over. Waking up and knowing Seth wasn't anywhere nearby felt like a fresh wound every day.

He kept his phone under his pillow, so when it buzzed, he'd have Seth right there.

But he wasn't stupid, and he knew that he lived in a human, fallible body.

Taking the girls to the gym was an exercise in "Look, asshole, but don't touch. Don't smile. Don't think about flirting."

There were days when he wanted a hug so damned bad.

But still, Seth would be there, on his phone that evening. Could he tell Seth about the hug he wanted? About the guy at the drive-thru with the really nice eyes? About the body on that blond guy who kept checking Kelly out in the mirror as he trooped the girls across the gym floor to the pool entrance?

He wasn't sure.

Where were they?

Whenever he thought of sex, he thought of Seth, on his bedroom floor, staring at Kelly trustingly, needing him so badly, but never admitting to it, not once, because he knew Kelly had more than he could bear.

Until Kelly promised him he'd never let him down.

That's where they were.

Oh.

School started—Kelly enrolled in American River, because it was a little bit farther away than Sac City and he'd see fewer of the assholes he'd gone to high school with. Kelly's mom made him take a full schedule, but Kelly got creative and took four classes, back to back, on Tuesday and Thursday, plus a night class on Monday when nobody had anything special after school, so he could find a part-time job.

He applied in retail—Arden Fair, K-Street, even Sunrise—but didn't hit pay dirt until he found a vintage clothing store in Old Sac, right across from his sisters' favorite store, Candy Heaven.

It wasn't glamorous, but it wasn't food service either, and Kelly counted his blessings.

Besides, they let him do his homework when the store was slow and everything had been picked up. Score!

The only setback was, well, the other gay guys, who had apparently decided Kelly was chum and they were sharks.

As. If.

But it did make shit uncomfortable sometimes.

"Marco, you grab my ass one more time, I am walking out that door," Kelly snarled one morning in late October. The place had been hopping all day. Vintage clothing stores were great places for Halloween shoppers looking for the weird and wonderful. Besides being cleaned out of most of their 80's fashions and their faux 20's fashions and hospital scrubs, lab coats, and their cheap ball gowns and such, they'd also been raided for all the ugly Christmas sweaters under the sun. Kelly's boss, Vashti, had shown Kelly where the secret stash was. They'd go up the day after Halloween.

Kelly loved some of his coworkers—Julia, who was prickly and shy and biromantic but demisexual, Raven, who was every bit as much of a woman before the surgery as she would be afterward, Callum, who was square and plain and gruff, but who could tell when a customer was having a bad day and point them to the complimentary M&M's in a heartbeat.

Good people here; Kelly approved.

But Marco and Clifton he could fucking do without.

"What's the matter, Kelly? You afraid a little ass grabbing's gonna break your hymen?" Marco teased, a lewd smile under his dark brown Tom of Finland mustache. It really wasn't his fault. He was just being a crude asshole, but lots of guys were. But Matty had gotten out of rehab and spent the entire last week knocking on the door in the evenings, trying to see Chloe and screaming Kelly's sexual history across the apartment complex, and Kelly was a wee bit sensitive.

Kelly whirled around and pinned Marco's skinny body against the shoe shelves, a hand at his throat.

"You. Do. Not. Have. My. Consent." He bit out each word, specifically, like chewing leather bullets.

Marco's eyes widened, and he struggled against Kelly's hand. "Okay… okay. Sorry. Just playing. Jesus, Kelly. I was just flirting with you!"

Kelly let go of him, and he sagged against the shelves, knocking the women's boot section into pink vinyl disarray. It was telling how shaken he was that he didn't raise a hand to his styled hair, and pale blond Clifton came running back to make sure he was okay.

"You two pick that shit up," Kelly snarled and stalked down to the register, where Vashti was looking at him in surprise. "What?"

Vashti shook his head and gestured with his chin to the back of the store. "Sorting dock," he said quietly. "We'll talk." Then, louder, he said, "And Marco, not another word. Consider this your first and second warning. Hands to yourself."

Kelly got out to the sorting dock and moved automatically to a pile of donations. Ugh. The garbage bags they'd been packed in reeked of cat pee. He shredded the bag and started carting the clothes to the industrial-sized washer to sort. He managed to put together a load of jeans from that bag alone and dropped it in the washer, silently forgiving the people who'd bagged them. Indigo attracted animals—ammonia was part of the fixative in the dye, and it got pissed on a lot.

He added an extra helping of fabric freshener to the tray and started the load, and then leaned back, catching his breath. His pocket buzzed, and seeing that Vashti wasn't there yet, he checked it.

Seth had sent him a video—something he'd had to do for a project— and Kelly's heart swelled a little. He lived for these.

He hit Play and saw Seth standing in a blackened room with only his instrument and his music. He was wearing a bright neon blue T-shirt over his jeans, and Kelly blinked. That wasn't usually his style. For one thing, the shirt looked new.

Then he started to play, something simple and bouncy, and just as Kelly got into the melody, the screen split, and there was Seth again, but this time wearing neon yellow. He was in the middle of playing the same song, but a different part, the harmony, and Kelly gasped. Oh, this was fun! Then Seth appeared again, this time wearing neon green and playing a… a sort of bigger violin—a viola? Was that the word?—and it was playing the alto line of the song. Kelly laughed delightedly and clapped his hand over his mouth. Oh! Seth had not told them he was learning other instruments. Was that part of his coursework? And just as Kelly was amazed at what his boy could do, the screen split a final time, and there Seth was, playing the bass line on a cello.

He kept it simple, none of the flourishes or complex finger work he did on the violin, but Kelly could still hear it—that pure, sweet instinctual knowledge of how to make that instrument sing.

The song, which started out simple, grew complex and powerful, swelling into a final amazing, moving crescendo that literally left Kelly breathless.

After the final flourish, one by one the screens disappeared, leaving Seth smiling shyly into the camera.

"That was my original composition," he said, as though prompted. "Oh. It's titled *Kelly's Concerto.*" Someone off camera said something, and he blinked, looking even more self-conscious. "Number Three," he added. "*Kelly's Concerto Number Three.*"

Kelly clapped his hand over his mouth and ignored the burning in his eyes.

Okay.

There you go.

That's why he ignored the guys in the gym and put up with Marco, the hands-grabby asshole.

Because who would do that for you? Yeah, sure—it was for school. But that was his third try, and it was gorgeous.

"Pretty music," Vashti said, closer than Kelly had expected.

He startled and almost dropped the phone. "Goddammit!" He glared at Vashti, his heart hammering in his throat, and Vashti grimaced and took a step back.

"I'm sorry, Kelly. I got sucked into the music and forgot the whole thing we were out here to talk about."

Kelly jerked back, suddenly wary. "Am I fired?"

"No! God no. Marco's lucky he isn't. How long's he been doing that?"

"How long have I been working here?" Kelly countered.

"Clifton too?"

Kelly shrugged. Clifton was a follower. "Whatever. Some days, I'm just over it."

Vashti shook his head. "Well, yeah, Kelly. You should be over it all the time. Nobody should have to work with that going on. We wouldn't ask Julia to do it, or Raven. And we won't ask you."

Oh God. Using the system. Kelly needed to remember that sometimes it was the system because it worked. "Yeah. Thanks, Vashti. I'm sorry."

Vashti sighed and pulled a hand through his own slightly shaggy black hair. His skin was a rich copper color, and he had cheekbones to die for, but Kelly had always been struck by the compassion in his unapologetically kohl-rimmed earth-brown eyes.

He was a pretty boy, and he knew it, but he never abused it.

"Can I ask?" he said after a moment.

"About what? The music?" The video had stopped playing, reverting back to Seth in the original frame, playing in the blue shirt. He'd been hinting at something big for Kelly's birthday, and Kelly still remembered his sort of romantic idea of taking Kelly away for the big eighteen.

Of course, the more Kelly kept trudging along—work, school, taking care of his family—the more he became painfully aware that a milestone like eighteen didn't mean much more than another day.

But Seth and his dad had been so kind about celebrating his graduation when the day might have gone completely unnoticed by anybody, even his mother, that Kelly was determined to celebrate it anyway.

Seth wanted to treat him special because he was glad Kelly had been born. Kelly could get on board with that.

"Well, yeah," Vashti said, laughing. "But also...." He bit his lip. "The way you got mad at Marco, and the way you jumped when I got too close. Kelly, is there something we should know about making you more comfortable here—"

Fuck. This?

"Yes, I'm a sexual assault survivor," Kelly recited, bored. "No, I'm not made of glass. Yes, I got pissed when Marco grabbed my ass for the thousandth time, and no, I don't want to talk about it now."

Vashti grimaced. "Sorry. Just…." And then, suddenly, he looked super embarrassed. "I… you know. Keep asking you out after work, and you always have family stuff. My bad. I shouldn't assume that's why you wouldn't want to date me." He bit his lip. "Ego."

Kelly's jaw actually dropped, and then he started to laugh.

Oh.

"I *do* have family stuff," he said kindly, when the laughter had faded. "My dad…." Fuck. "He died this summer, and we're taking care of my stupid brother's little girl, who needs all the grown-ups she can get. And I've got three sisters, and they miss Dad so fuckin' bad. And my mom is trying to keep it together, and she needs me. She just does. It's not a good time for Kelly to be dating."

Vashti perked up, and Kelly could almost hear the offer—*I could be part of that*—because he was a good guy, and Kelly couldn't put his ego through the grinder again.

"And that music?" Kelly said. "C'mere. Watch."

They stood there, shoulder to shoulder, and Kelly could smell the richness of the patchouli Vashti used in his hair and feel the heat he let off on this brisk October day. A part of him poked at his brain about needing that hug, but a sudden, more grown-up part told him how cruel that would be to everybody involved, including Seth.

On Kelly's little screen, Seth finished and said the name—*Kelly's Concerto Number Three*—and Vashti clapped his hand over his eyes.

"Oh!"

Kelly chuckled a little and leaned just a smidge away. "Yeah."

"That guy really loves you."

"Yeah. That super talented really adorable guy really frickin' loves me."

"So, no dating Vashti." He grimaced and looked sad, but not wrecked, and Kelly was happy.

"No. I'm sorry. No." And suddenly Kelly knew he had to tell Seth about this. "Here. Let me take your picture. I can tell him about you, that you're a friend."

Vashti smiled crookedly for the camera. "Why would you do that?"

Kelly shrugged and checked the shot. Good. Seth would know that Kelly had options, but only chose Seth. "So I'm not ever tempted for it to be anything else. You're a good guy. A good boss. And you're hella cute. But… but before I even knew I was gay, I knew I was in love with him."

"Can't compete with that," Vashti agreed, and Kelly nodded.

"Not so far."

"Thanks for being honest." Vashti sighed. "Well, they need us in there. Clifton and Marco are still weeping over the shoes, and Raven's about to beat them both to death with a pair of pink vinyl boots. This place doesn't run on love, right?"

Kelly laughed. "Nope. Sadly not."

THAT EVENING—MONDAY—AS he sat on a bench in his night class and waited for the professor, he sent Seth a text. The night was perfectly cool. The briskness of October hadn't really set in this year.

This is Vashti—he's my boss, and he's super cool, and he was crushing on me hard. I showed him your video, and he said, "That guy really loves you."

And I told him, "That super talented super cute guy really frickin' loves me."

I thought you should know, is all. I missed touching you today. I needed a hug so bad. But he wasn't you.

He sent the texts, one after the other, and the photo, and looked at his phone for a moment, wondering if Seth would pop on like he did sometimes.

It didn't happen this time, and once the teacher came in, Kelly turned his attention to his work. It was a basic drawing class, and he loved it because it taught him all sorts of things he hadn't known to teach himself, things he'd overlooked by trying to learn from art books alone.

He spent the evening lost in sketching the teacher's cat—and wishing he could have one of his own for the twenty-thousandth time—and walked out into the night feeling somehow calmer and better about things.

When he got to his car, his pocket buzzed.

Check your email when you get home.

But thank you for telling me about Vashti.

I wish I could hug you.

I wish I could let you go.

But I can't do either of them. So I planned. You'll love it. I promise.

Kelly was so excited he opened his email in the car.

It was a rental agreement for the day after Christmas through the first week of January, with a typically brief note: *My dad will bring you down, and we'll spend the week together, all three of us. Your family's welcome—it's his present to your mom and sisters. Then they'll all go home, and you and I will be there for the second week.*

And you'll know my touch again by then.

And we can fly.

Kelly hugged the phone to his chest, not feeling silly or sappy or anything bad. That super sweet, super cute, super talented boy really fuckin' loved him. And life was not all drudgery from school to home to work.

And Seth Arnold wrote him music and gave him dreams when he was too tired to find his own. And in a couple of months, they would hold hands together and fly.

Dangerous Hobbies

SETH LOOKED around the dive bar with narrowed eyes and tried to stay in the present.

When he'd auditioned, in the daylight, the black paint on the walls had been chipped, the red paint on the concrete floors had been stained, and the stage had been a splintered death trap. At night, the curtains, the dark lighting, the loud music—all of it managed to look seedy instead of disintegrating, but Seth knew the risks.

He did not belong here.

The clientele of this little shit show west of Vacaville was mostly poor, an awful lot of white, and favored big boots and big hair. They hadn't ID'd Seth when he'd come in to audition as a fiddler for the house band, and they hadn't asked any questions either.

Seth had played "Devil Went Down to Georgia" straight up, although he'd been practicing country music rhythms since he'd seen the ad.

The thing was, he needed money.

The good news about Bridgford was that he had free room and board—and education, for which he was more grateful every day.

The staff was great about steering him toward financial aid, and although he hadn't mentioned it to Kelly, the times he'd traveled with the orchestra during the summer had been funded by a grant.

But he'd graduated from buying Kelly stuffed animals with his lunch money to rashly renting a house with his FAFSA money, and he'd been desperate when he started looking up ads on the internet.

Everything classical insisted on daytime practices.

But he was nineteen now, and he could go off-campus without permission or notification. The ads for bar bands had all talked about rehearsals at night. Country and rock music were often much simpler than classical music—he felt like this doubled as practicing without doubling his practice load, which was already extensive.

But most of all, he needed the fucking money.

It wasn't that he was trying to buy his way into Kelly's affections. It was that he was trying to keep Kelly afloat! Seth knew, because his dad told him, that Matty's hospital bills and Xavier's funeral expenses had wiped out the Cruz savings. Dad said that Linda hadn't told Kelly, but Kelly had gotten a job anyway because he wasn't stupid.

None of the baby's furniture had been usable. All of it had been secondhand and out of code, because they'd sold the new stuff Isela had gotten at the baby shower to fund their opioid habit. Seth's dad, who had offered to go get Chloe's things, had hauled it to the trash and gotten new furniture on credit. He'd bought other items too—clothes for Chloe and clothes and school supplies for the girls. He'd privately told Lily, Lulu, and Agnes to come to him when they needed things, and not to bother their mother.

But he couldn't keep doing it forever. Even *with* Seth's room and board paid.

So Seth had resolved to get a job, which was a laugh riot, since he didn't even have a driver's license and his job skills were for shit.

He could do one thing—play the fucking violin—so when he'd seen the ad for the fiddle player in a country-western band, he'd borrowed a hat from the drama department and a flannel shirt from Vince, who hated the cold with a passion.

He'd worn tennis shoes with frayed laces because that's all he had.

The pay wasn't a lot. He couldn't have survived on it, but it was enough to rent the house in Monterey. It was enough to send money home to his dad to help pay the Cruz's expenses.

It was enough to help.

And all he had to do was haul his gay black ass to this place, where neither of those things was particularly welcome, and play as well as he had in the tenth grade.

The playing was easy. Butch, the fifty-something paunchy, graying, red-faced guy who played the lead guitar, said he was the best fiddle player he'd ever met, and Seth had smiled and politely thanked him. His son, Guthrie, played the drums, and he'd given Seth a sideways look, speculative. Guthrie was stringy, in his twenties, with shoulder-length surfer-blond hair and slightly crooked front teeth a little like Seth's own.

For the most part, Guthrie listened to his father's instruction, and his uncle Jock's—who played bass—and hung out until it was time for him to play.

Seth could deal with him as a musician, but he made Seth nervous.

It wasn't that he was unfriendly or threatening. He just stared at Seth from the corner of his eye, like he expected Seth to do something super excessively interesting or something.

But he played. Together they played three nights a week, and oh, thank you God, this was their last gig until after Monterey.

"You looking almost happy there, Fiddler," Guthrie said as they were setting up. "All excited about Christmas?"

Christmas? Christmas was three days away, and Seth would be alone in the dorms, mostly. Everybody else got to go home.

But the day after….

"I see my family the twenty-sixth." Big breath. Kelly. But he didn't talk about Kelly at the Stomp, because why would he?

"Mom, Dad, kid sister?" Guthrie prodded.

"Dad. Family friends. Going to the ocean."

Guthrie blinked slowly. "Girlfriend?" he implied slyly. "*Boy*friend?"

Seth could feel the blush rising to the surface of his skin and couldn't fight it. But it was dim in the bar, and he was pretty sure he could hide it. "Friend," he replied, his voice as mild as soap.

Guthrie let out a frustrated sigh. "Fiddler, I'm trying to get to know you. Do you mind?"

Seth shrugged. "I'm very average," he said with no irony at all.

Guthrie burst out laughing, so hard he dropped the power cord he'd been hooking up. Seth ignored him and Butch's irritated, "Goddammit, boy, get your ass in gear!" and continued to work doggedly at his tasks.

He played well that night. He knew it in his bones, and even though he didn't care for the music or the venue—too loud, too much shouting— and he hated the now-familiar smell of beer, the thought gave him pride.

When they were done—"The Devil Went Down to Georgia" being their finale—the crowd was silent for a moment and then rose to their feet. Someone in a sentimental mood called out, "Christmas! Christmas music! Christmas!"

Butch grimaced because they hadn't worked up any Christmas music—they'd had a tough time putting together the forty-five-minute set they had, given everybody had a day job—and Seth spoke up quietly.

"I know some," he said, because he'd pretty much cut his teeth on the school Christmas program. Nobody here would mind that it was simple. They wanted… sentimental.

Butch nodded at him. "Go ahead, boy."

Seth played "I'll Be Home for Christmas" and "Carol of the Bells" and, in the end, "Hallelujah."

The crowd held their breath through three songs—not moving, not twitching, not even breathing—and Seth closed his eyes and thought of Kelly. Thought of home.

When he was done, there was an awestruck silence, a lovely, peaceful blanket of quiet, like snow, and then sincere and heartfelt applause.

Seth bowed deeply once and smiled shyly, before turning around and inviting the band for their final bow too.

Someone passed a Santa hat around, where it ended up full on the corner of the stage.

It was a luminous moment, transcendent, and Seth was lost in the haze of it as they packed up and people emptied out of the bar.

He found himself alone in the parking lot, in the thinning traffic, circling around behind the bar toward the bus station.

"Hey! Fiddler!"

Seth pulled his windbreaker up to his ears, cold because he didn't really have a cold-weather coat, and turned toward Guthrie as he came out with his last drum case.

"Don't take off so fast. We've got some money for you. I can give you a ride if you want one."

"It's an hour away," Seth said, eyebrows raised, and Guthrie half laughed.

"I did not know that. This way to my truck, okay?"

Seth followed him, their long legs falling into easy strides, and Seth was lulled into complacency.

The heavy fist seemed to come out of nowhere.

"Fuckin' faggots! Give us your fucking money!"

For a moment, Seth lay sprawled out, clutching his violin and watching as two shadows threw Guthrie against the truck, raining blows on his head.

He wasn't sure when he moved.

Like he had with Castor, he started with a kick, this time to behind one assailant's knee. That guy went down, and Seth used his elbow to catch the other guy in the middle. The first one came back, and Seth kicked him again, high on his upper thigh, and then cracked the other guy—shorter—in the jaw, hard with his elbow again.

And again. Both men were down, and Seth was kicking them, hard in the ribs as they whimpered. One of them voided his bladder, and Guthrie wrapped his arms around Seth's waist and lifted.

"Easy there, boy. Easy! You're going to kill them!"

"Fuckers!" Seth growled. "Fuckers! No! Just fucking no! Not again! Not ever fucking again!"

Guthrie carried him to the truck door, opened it, and shoved him in, and Seth came to his senses. "My violin!"

"Yeah, boy, fuck!"

The violin came sailing in next as Seth scooted to the passenger seat, and Guthrie jumped in and gunned the engine. The truck pealed out of there in a spatter of mud, and Seth tried to wrap his brain around what had just happened.

"You okay?" Guthrie asked after a few terror-fraught moments. "You... you sort of came unglued."

Seth took a couple more shaky breaths. "Did they hurt you?" he asked.

"No, sir, but they were gonna. How about you?" Guthrie pulled off in front of a gas station and took stock. "Oh boy, they got you. Your face is swollen. Your lip is bleeding. How's your hands?"

Seth flexed them. They were practically untouched. "Elbows," he said. "Have to play."

Guthrie laughed, the sound hysterical and jarring. "Man, you are something else. But brother, you can play something special. I did not believe that shit you did tonight. I almost cried myself."

"It's all I know how to do," Seth said apologetically.

"Yeah, that and fight."

Seth shifted uncomfortably. "Think they're okay?" he asked, not wanting to think about Castor Durant and what he might have done, but unable to think about anything else.

"Who in the fuck cares!"

Seth let out a choked laugh. "I... I don't want to kill anybody," he said. *No. Not again.*

"Those boys? They took you out first because they thought you were the weakest, right? And then it was goddamned two to one. You didn't kill 'em, but I'm pretty sure they're gonna be pissing blood for a week."

Seth grunted. "Should I... should I go back to the bar?" he asked hesitantly. "They'll.... Will they press charges?"

Guthrie shook his head. "Seth, they jumped you!"

"But I'm black," Seth said, like maybe Guthrie hadn't noticed. "And gay." Which he probably wouldn't have said if he wasn't so damned rattled. "And the cops hate me just for… for… being me!"

Guthrie took a breath. "Sounds like you've got experience," he said after a moment, the truck idling noisily.

"Some."

"That sucks." Guthrie grimaced, and in the light from the gas station, Seth could see his face was sort of appealing. He had a big nose—Roman, he guessed they called it—but a strong chin to balance it out, and brown eyes, which were as big a shock in his pale face as Seth's green eyes were in his.

"Mostly."

Guthrie let out a laugh and turned to him, eyes soft. "I guess you let your instrument do the talking," he said.

"Yeah."

"That's 'cause you got talent for real. I just took up the drums because they helped me get laid."

Seth gaped, and the question pushed at him, because Guthrie was looking at him like he was special, and he knew his face was swelling, and he probably looked like shit.

"You're not gonna ask?" Guthrie needled.

"Girls or boys," Seth said, mesmerized by his eyes.

"Both," Guthrie said with a wink.

The wink did it. Not the both—because whatever flipped his switch—but the wink.

It was flirty and playful, and Seth didn't *do* flirty or playful.

Unless he was with Kelly.

He pulled back a little. "I have a boyfriend," he admitted. "He…." Oh, Kelly—sending him pictures of his cute boss, thinking Seth wouldn't understand temptation. "He was going to move in with me next year, but… but his dad died, and he has to take care of his sisters and his niece. I got this gig so I could rent a house somewhere, for him and his family, and they could be somewhere different. Somewhere they didn't have to see their father in every corner when the whole world was happy. And so I could—" He took a deep, shuddering breath. "—see him. And see my dad."

Guthrie was still staring at him, but his eyes were shiny, and he bit his lip, like this hadn't been a possibility. "You can't go home?"

And Seth almost told the lie. Of course he could go home, but this was for Kelly, right?

"No. I...."

"Not your first fight," Guthrie deduced, and Seth waited for the condemnation or disgust.

"No." He only wished he knew exactly what he'd done that night. Like tonight, he'd sort of lost it. He would have done anything back then, with Kelly in the hospital and fury shining off him under the low-hanging moon.

Guthrie nodded and pulled the truck into a parking space and turned it off. "Here, you go into the bathroom and wash up, and I'll go get us some coffees." He paused and pulled out a wad of cash from his pocket. "Dad and Butch took a third total, and they told me to give the rest to you."

"What about you?" Seth asked.

Guthrie shoved the cash into his hands. "Merry Christmas, Fiddler. Go wash up."

Seth half expected the truck to roar away while he was splashing water on his face and checking the damage.

Ugh. Extensive. His eye was brick-red again, and his jaw was swollen and his lip split open. Thank God he didn't have to sing or anything. But his knuckles were unscathed, and he had a righteous wad of cash in his pocket.

And maybe a new friend.

Seth left the bathroom and climbed back into the truck, shivering a little. When Guthrie got in and thrust a hot coffee into his hands, he was supremely grateful.

Guthrie started the truck and took Seth's direction to the freeway. "So, Fiddler, can I ask you a question?"

"Yeah?"

"You, your boyfriend, your dad, your boyfriend's family. What's that like?"

"What do you mean?"

"Being out? Having everyone in your life know."

Seth blinked, and it occurred to him that Butch and Jock probably did *not* know Guthrie "liked both."

"We, uh, wanted to hide it. Because, you know…." He gave a brief smile. "Making out. Nobody tried to keep us apart to make out."

Guthrie burst out laughing. "That's… uh… frank."

"Everybody knew. Nobody was surprised. I wasn't going to go away to school so we could be together. Dad said he'd help us be together as best he could. That's all."

Guthrie expelled a slow, even breath. "I… I had a guy I liked a lot. But I couldn't make myself introduce him to Pop. Pop can be pretty brutal. The guy left."

"That sucks," Seth told him. "Sorry."

Another laugh, and Seth realized he could like Guthrie because he was like Kelly—there wasn't pain that he couldn't laugh at.

"Well, keep playing for us, okay?" Another slow, even breath. "You're like the only person I can talk to who's not trying to get a piece of ass."

"It's a decent ass," Seth said, and Guthrie cracked up.

Seth was proud of himself for that, and settled down to let Guthrie ramble all the way back to Bridgford. When they pulled up, Seth pulled out his phone. "Can I take a picture?"

"Sure. Why?"

"So I can show Kelly. He thinks he's the only one who gets tempted."

Guthrie grinned, the expression making his own bruises rakish and devil-may-care. "So I'm a temptation?" he needled.

"No," Seth told him. "But you could be."

Guthrie laughed again. "You're all right, Fiddler. But I better get out of here before these blue bloods rip apart my weenie white-trash ass."

Seth got out of the truck and waved to him as he drove away.

I can't wait to see you in three days. This is Guthrie—we performed together.

He sent the text and went inside, surprised when his phone buzzed, because Kelly was usually asleep this time of night.

Doing WHAT?

Playing music off-campus—why?

He looks beat up!

Rough crowd.

Ha ha. Are you okay?

Seth shrugged and texted, *Yeah, fine. You'll let me see everybody open their presents in two days, right?*

Yeah, Seth. Your dad is coming too.

Good. Thanks for taking care of him for me.

He's not exactly decrepit.

Yeah, but he's lonely. Make sure he doesn't go to bars. They're terrible places.

Understood. He checks in every night—I think so we know he's not.

Good. Seth yawned. *Why aren't you asleep?*

Because I was thinking about you and wishing I had a room without a baby in it.

Oh. Yikes. Yeah, Seth didn't get any private time with Vince around either.

Well, a couple of days.

Matty wants to spend Christmas Day with us.

Don't mention the day after, okay? Seth felt cold in his stomach at the thought.

No shit. We already talked to the girls about it. Even Agnes knows he doesn't get to come.

Okay—make sure I'm off the phone when he's there.

God, I love you. Just take care for the next couple of days, okay? I don't want to do anything to jinx it. It's like I'm shaking I need to see you so bad.

Yearning. Seth knew the taste of it now, the bitterness of want, the cramping in his stomach that came with unfulfilled need. *I promise.*

Me too. I love you. Good night.

I love you too. Good night.

"You asshole."

Seth didn't let his death grip around Kelly's shoulders relax one bit. Kelly wasn't pushing him away, but he was still pissed.

"I have no idea what you mean." Seth stuck his face in the hollow of Kelly's shoulder and breathed deeply.

"I almost hung up on you Christmas morning, you realize that, don't you?"

Seth had asked for Amara's help before she left to visit her family, and had spent some of his "Christmas bonus" on makeup to hide the bruising. There was no hiding the swelling in his lip or his nose or his eye, though.

He'd ignored Kelly's surprised gasp and powered through Christmas morning, oohing and ahhing over each of the girl's presents as they held it up for the phone. His dad had outdone himself—with Seth and Amara's help, actually. Amara knew where to shop on the cheap, mail order, and Seth had money his dad didn't know about. Between the two of them, they'd sent his dad clothes and school supplies and toys for the girls, and art supplies for Kelly.

And, on Amara's prompting, a gift certificate at a day spa for Linda, whom Amara regarded with fear and awe. "My mom had no job and two kids, and every time she drove me to flute lessons, it was like I owed her my life."

Seth had been on his own for his dad, and in the end, he'd sent him something… odd. And whimsical. A model kit of his beloved car so his dad would have something to do in the evenings while hanging out with the Cruz family that would give him a reason to come home.

His dad had looked at it and then looked at the camera and grinned. Like a little kid.

"I loved these when I was in school," he said. "I had over a hundred of them before I moved out. They were, like, my best thing."

Seth had wanted to dance.

He'd been about to do the closest thing to that—play Christmas songs for the family—when Matty had pounded on the door.

Obviously drunk.

Seth watched the joy in the family dissipate, and his father bent his head and sighed. "We'll go deal with this, son. Merry Christmas. We love you."

Kelly's expression told him everything as the girls all cried, "We love you! Goodbye! Goodbye!" and he had to hit End Call.

Later that night, Kelly had written him a long, rambling email about calling the cops on his brother because Seth's dad had gone outside and offered to take Matty to a meeting, and Matty had swung on him.

Craig Arnold was no fool. He'd ducked and gone inside and called the police.

And Matty had been put in a drunk tank and asked to sleep it off.

And Craig had bailed him out the next morning and taken him back to rehab—on his dime.

Seth had wanted to cry, and he was pretty sure Kelly *did* cry, but they weren't going to talk about that now.

Now, the Cruz family minivan was on its way to Monterey to get the house ready—and hopefully warm it up in the chill of December—and Kelly had Craig's Caddy and was there to take Seth to see his family.

Except first, Kelly had to yell at Seth.

"You—I asked Mom, you know that? After Matty was all sorted out, I said, 'What did he look like to you?' and she said, 'Like he put makeup on to hide his bruises,' and I said, 'Yeah, me too, but no, he'd have *told me if something happened*!'"

Seth shrugged. "Was a robbery. Me and Guthrie fought back, that was all."

Kelly pulled away and regarded him with flat, unfriendly eyes. "Guthrie."

"I showed you his picture. He's the drummer in the band." Seth couldn't stop smiling at him. Kelly was so beautiful. His hair had grown—long enough to put up on the back of his head with an elastic—and his chin had squared up. He was still working out, his neck and pecs were looking *very* grown-up, and he'd shaved, maybe just for Seth because he'd had stubble Christmas morning, when he'd looked delicious and mussed.

God, he got better every time Seth got to touch him.

Kelly cocked his head. "And I haven't heard of this band before now because...?"

Seth chewed his lip. "We needed money," he said, matter-of-fact.

"Seth—"

Seth turned around and grabbed his bag. He'd been waiting out on the steps of the dorm building in the foggy morning. "We should go," he said, picking up his violin case and walking determinedly to the Cadillac. "By the way, can I tell you how much my dad must love you to let you drive this car? He won't even *teach* me to drive."

"Seth—"

Seth threw his stuff in the back and then got into the passenger seat, looking at Kelly and smiling. "Come *on*. I know it's going to be cold and stuff, but tomorrow we're gonna take the girls to see the aquarium, and it's gonna get super foggy tonight!"

"None of that is a reason for us not to talk about this," Kelly grumbled, slamming the car door. Seth waited until he turned to put the keys in the ignition to ambush him with a kiss, and to his surprise, Kelly melted into his arms like Seth had hoped he would from the beginning.

It was like being shot through with sunshine, that kiss. And when Kelly took over, pressing him into the car seat, ravaging his bruised mouth, plundering Seth's chest with greedy hands, Seth actually whined with need and with happiness and with pure rollicking lust.

The kiss went on and on until Seth was hard and aching under Kelly's insistent hand, and Kelly's groin pushed temptingly against his thigh. With a gasp, Kelly pulled away and turned to rest his head on the steering wheel.

"You make me stupid," he complained. "God, I want to yell at you for keeping secrets and making money and spoiling us, but I'm just so fucking grateful, and…*augh*! I just need to kiss you some more!"

"Yeah. That." Seth couldn't catch his breath. "You know, we could go up to my dorm right now and—"

Kelly turned toward him with a glare. "Oh no. No, no, no. You've been working toward us, in a house, by ourselves, with a bed and a view and everything. I'm not going in for a quickie in the dorms when I've got… perfection a couple of hours away."

"But our family is going to be there for a week!" Seth complained.

"They're going to the aquarium tomorrow—you told me yourself. And this is all very clever and all, but I need to hear more about this fight or we're going nowhere."

Seth sighed. "I've been playing for a country-western band—they call me the Fiddler—"

"That's original."

Seth booped him on the upturned wrinkled nose, and his grin back was so infectiously Kelly that Seth felt sunshine in his heart, just like when they were kissing.

"Hush. Anyway, we play this dive bar called the Stomp, and two nights ago, I did a Christmas set, and they passed the hat…."

Apparently reassured that Seth would keep talking, Kelly turned the car ignition and set them on their way toward Monterey. By the time they arrived a few hours later, Kelly had asked him dozens of questions— and answered Seth's questions about his job.

"Vashti's a good guy," Kelly said for the umpteenth time. "But…." His smile went crooked as they negotiated through the tricky tunnel that was part of downtown. "He's not you. He knows it. He's dating someone else now, anyway."

"Yeah. Guthrie was just glad to have a friend to talk to about it. Like, the only people who know he's bi are the guys he's hooked up with. It's sort of sad."

"That sucks. Left or right?"

"Straight along the coast road past this curvy part. Then there's going to be a road inland."

"Name?"

"Yarrow."

"Pretty name. I like it. We should name a baby that."

Seth chuckled. "Sure. Chloe is looking good. She still remembers my voice—that's sort of cool."

"Yeah, but she's still behind in a bunch of milestones, Mom calls 'em. Like she's sixteen months old, and she should be walking already, and her speech is way delayed, and she doesn't... doesn't change from thing to thing, you know? Like we used to be able to distract Agnes from someone leaving by giving her a toy. Chloe doesn't do that. It's frustrating. She cries a lot. But Mom thinks it's because Isela did drugs when she was still pregnant and then ignored her after she was born. It's like we used to get so tired because she was over at our house half the time. We didn't realize we were her parents, you know?"

"Yeah. That's not your fault. Your brother...." Seth sighed. He'd heard Matty's voice on Christmas day. "I... I don't understand what broke him so badly. He's not... I mean, the hating *us* is one thing. But all the other shit—that's not your family. How does he not know better?"

"I got nothing." Kelly sighed. "Or maybe a little. I think...." He gave Seth a sideways glance. "Never mind."

"No." Seth felt suddenly older. "Don't do that. Tell me."

"I think Castor Durant was at Isela's church a lot when we were all in high school. So Castor, he gets Isela started, and Isela, she hooks Matty. And Matty, he's been getting high with the guys who attacked me. And I think that... that fucked him up. Like... like once upon a time he loved his brother. And then he said stupid hateful shit, and his brother got hurt. And now he does drugs to forget what he did to his brother. And then Dad happened, and now he does them to forget what happened to Dad. And it's just making his life worse. You know?"

Oh, it made so much sense.

"I think you're really smart," Seth said helplessly. "Turn left here." He hated to go left—the waves were crashing just yards away, giant and wild and fierce. But they only had to go a block, up a hill, and the house loomed, a modern structure with a wraparound porch and two stories. If Seth was not mistaken, you could stand out on the second story porch from the bedroom he'd told his dad he and Kelly would be sleeping in. You could look out over the hill and to the sea.

The minivan was already there, and Kelly whistled lowly.

"This... this looks like something special," he said. "You doing that band at night—that was to pay for this?"

"Yeah." Seth couldn't stop smiling at it. It was beautiful and romantic and... and *big.* Like what squeezed out from his chest every night. "It's...." He bit his lip, embarrassed. "I could never have afforded it in the summer. It's... you know. Off-season. It's gonna be cold, but at least there's no snow. Kids can't swim—"

"You don't know these kids." Kelly laughed. "And they can play in the sand and go to the aquarium—"

"And go shopping and go to the pier and see the seals." Seth had done all these things with Amara's family. "It's... I mean, it's only a little colder here in the winter. I...." He knew his entire heart was in his face, radiating from his eyes right now, but he couldn't help it. "I wanted to make your life beautiful," he said simply.

Kelly's eyes darkened. "You always have." He pulled Seth into a kiss that was... warmer and less horny than their last one. Seth responded, letting it fill him, and they pulled away from this one with some control.

"Want to go see how they like it?"

Kelly nodded and rubbed his thumb on Seth's bruised lip. "What'll we tell them about this?" he asked.

Seth shrugged. He really hadn't thought that far. "How about I ran into a pole?"

"How about you got jumped by two rednecks because you were playing at a dive bar," Kelly said, brooking no bullshit. "Please, *mijo.* My family has been hurt by so many lies right now. The truth is a much better story."

Seth nodded soberly. "I understand. I just didn't want anyone to worry, you know?"

"Yeah, well, the one thing I've learned this past year? It's that worry means love."

SETH SPENT the entire rest of the day surrounded by women. There was Linda, who was still as much a mom as ever, and Lily and Lulu—who still insisted on wearing the same clothes, even though it got easier to tell them apart every day—but they were partway to grown, because they were in junior high. Agnes, in the sixth grade, was just as sassy as her older sisters, and tiny Chloe seemed to light up when Seth was close enough to actually touch.

It was nice, having girls around. He'd forgotten how much he'd loved to play with them. Lily and Lulu seemed to be having a competition, telling him about school and how they were both in science and math classes, and everybody expected them to like poetry, but Agnes liked poetry so they didn't see why they had to. Agnes kept trying to hang on his arm—the one not carrying the baby—because she was impressed by how strong he looked.

Linda kept throwing him frustrated looks that spoke dire things about the conversation that would happen after dinner was ready while Chloe just clung, whimpering, because her favorite human was finally under her hands.

For about an hour, the happy chaos was enough to keep the questions at bay.

Then they all sat down to spaghetti and meat sauce and salad— something Linda could make special that Seth and his father had managed to screw up on a regular basis—and Linda surprised him by reaching out to either side of her and making the kids take hands. Seth grabbed Kelly's, but he had Chloe on his knee, so Lily took her hand on one side and Seth's dad's on the other.

"Are we *praying*?" Kelly asked.

"I'm giving thanks," she said simply. "The last two years—they've been rough." Her voice grew thick. "Really rough. And sometimes in the rough times, you think you're all alone."

Kelly grunted. "Yeah."

"We're not alone," she said, looking Kelly in the eyes.

He smiled crookedly. "I got your back, Mommy."

"And we've got yours," Craig said softly.

She swallowed and nodded. "And that's why we're holding hands. I'm as pissed at God as anybody, but I've got to give thanks for everyone at this table."

Seth squeezed Kelly's hand and was relieved to feel the squeeze back.

"Thank you," Craig said softly.

"Good." Linda released everybody's hand. "So, Seth, now that we're thankful for this lovely gift, what in the hell happened to your face?"

Seth tried to contain a smirk. "I was born," he said. "Dad, can you dish up some spaghetti for Chloe? Chop it into little bites. I'll eat when she's done."

"I will beat you!" Kelly muttered. "Jesus!"

Seth glared. "I was walking across a parking lot with a friend, and we got jumped," he said. "They were trying to rob us, but we fought back."

Kelly snorted softly.

"What? I told the truth!"

"And I saw his face. It wasn't as bad as yours!"

"You can fight?" Lulu asked, fascinated. "How do you fight? Your hands aren't beat up at all!"

"Elbows," Seth said. "Feet. I still run."

"Cool," Agnes breathed. Her mother glared at her, and her grin back, through a round face so much like Kelly's, took Seth's breath away.

"Was this at Bridgford?" Craig asked, pulling his attention away.

Kelly sent him a meaningful look.

"No. I, uh, sort of got a playing gig at, uh, a place."

Linda and Craig were looking at each other with twin expressions of exasperation on their faces.

"A place," Linda said, raising her eyebrow at Seth's father.

"A place," Craig repeated. "He very clearly said a place. He said 'a gig,' and he said 'a place.'"

"A place can mean many things." She nodded as though pondering.

"A place can be a planetarium," Craig agreed.

"It can be a small stage at a riverfront café," she mused.

Craig looked directly at Seth until Seth started to squirm. "It could be a strip club."

Seth swallowed. "It could be a country-western bar?" He smiled ingratiatingly, but his father's grimace told him that this option wasn't any better than strip club. "I made…." He resisted the impulse to look at Linda and Kelly and whisper. "I made some money," he finally said. "It, uh… you know. Money is good."

Linda blinked slowly and then looked from Seth to Craig.

Seth was sort of relieved when his father looked away from her, his ears turning red.

She didn't yell, though. Her eyes got bright and shiny, and she looked around at her daughters, her granddaughter, her son, and chewed her full lower lip. "I don't suppose you'd stop doing this if I asked," she said after a moment.

"I just started to talk to my drummer," he said plaintively, and Kelly snorted.

"Is it interfering with your classes?" Craig asked. "I can work more overtime—"

"Please?" Until that moment, that word, Seth hadn't realized how much this meant to him. "Everybody...." He looked at Kelly, and his throat grew tight. He had to look away. "This is my way to help. Please?" There was more. Everybody telling him he had to go out and play. That his music was his way out, his way up. All the work people had done, going to his concerts, giving up time to see him. When did he give back? When did they get something out of it?

This was his turn.

His father looked at him helplessly.

"He said please," Linda said, amused and impressed at once.

"He did." Craig twisted his mouth. "You're nineteen, you know. It's not like I could stop you."

Seth let out a humorless little chuff of air. Of course they could stop him. All they had to do was beg him not to. Tell him why he shouldn't. But he was helping. This once. He was giving back.

"That's it?" Kelly asked, like he'd been holding his breath and this was his chance to breathe. "You're going to let him?"

"You object?" Craig asked, and Seth kicked Kelly under the table.

Kelly gave him a look that said he kicked like a noodle and he'd have to do better. "Of course I object. He got *beat up.* They tried to rob him—"

"Only because we made extra that night." Seth nodded. "It was Christmas. People wanted Christmas songs. Can we eat now?"

"Seth! Your face—"

"I thought you liked my face?" He kept his eyes wide as he said it, and he saw Kelly's own eyes narrow in suspicion.

"You are doing that on purpose."

"Doing what?" He only knew a little bit what Kelly was talking about, but if it let him keep playing gigs and making money, he would cheerfully pretend he had no idea for longer.

"Just...." Kelly suddenly deflated. "You could get hurt," he muttered. "I have to know you're out there—you know that? Like... like the stars. Like if they go out, I couldn't wake up in the morning."

"But I'm not a star," Seth said reasonably. "I'm a real person. I need to have a place to meet you."

"In fucking Sacramento?" Kelly cried out, and Seth knew what he was thinking, about their little apartments, about his job selling used clothes, about his brother, pounding the door drunk.

"Everyone I love is there," he said simply. "Chloe, sweetheart, are you going to eat that or wear it?"

Chloe smeared some more pasta over her face and chewed on her fist to get the rest of the flavor out. "Mmf!"

Seth kissed the back of her head. "Agnes, are you getting your name on a plaque at the school this year?" The graduates from the grade school got awards like the Socrates Award and the Aristotle Award and the Hercules Award. The Cruz children had monopolized the plaques— Kelly had gotten the Socrates Award for thinking outside the box, and so had Lily. Lulu had gotten the Aristotle Award for being the best all-around student, and Matty... Matty had gotten the Hercules Award for citizenship.

"We don't know until the end of the year," Agnes said smugly. "But since I challenged the teacher on the reading assignment because I felt like it represented people of color badly and as cruel stereotypes, I think I might have a shot at the Socrates award."

Everybody at the table stared, and Agnes grinned back. Once again, Seth was forcibly reminded of Kelly at this age—but Seth missed the bubbles. Looking sideways at Kelly, Seth wondered if Kelly would ever bubble over like that again.

"You really said that?" Kelly asked, as though shaking himself out of a dream.

"Yes. The textbook is old, but you know much of that industry is controlled by a small group of people in Texas anyway, right?"

A slow smile crept over Kelly's face.

"Really?"

"Oh yes." Agnes reached for another piece of sourdough bread and spread some butter on it. "Lulu did that report on it last year."

"You remembered!" Lulu crowed. "I'm only a little good at English," she said soberly. "I was really proud of that."

The smile grew, like the creeping part had only been distance—like a whale seemed to get bigger slowly because it was coming from a long way away.

"Think we might see whales?" Lily asked suddenly, and it was like Kelly's freaky genius sisters suddenly became little kids again.

"Oh my God!" "That would be great!" "I'd love to!"

And all three of them turned shiny eyes to Seth, who didn't want to break their hearts. "You should ask the people at the aquarium tomorrow," he said. "They would know."

"You guys are coming, right?" Agnes asked, and Seth opened his mouth to say "Yes! Of course! I'd crawl through broken glass for you guys, just to prove to your brother I love you!"

"The next day, *mija*," Linda said gently. She fixed Seth and Kelly with a kind glance. "The boys need to talk."

They groaned, but in a way that told him they'd get over the disappointment. And to Seth's immediate confusion, he felt Kelly's hand, warm like the sun, spreading over the knee that wasn't bobbing under Chloe.

"That's right," Kelly said, his voice so very earnest. "Talk."

THAT NIGHT, they all played Monopoly until the girls started falling asleep between their turns. Seth had given Chloe her bath in the kitchen sink after dinner, blowing bubbles at her like he used to do for Agnes and playing in the water. She laughed and splashed and giggled, and when she was clean and dry, she fell asleep in his arms as he rolled the dice to move his game piece—the shoe—around.

Craig took her with him as he went to bed.

"No," Linda said softly. "She's—"

"I put the porta crib in my room," he told her. "You and Kelly get a full night's sleep tonight." His eyes darted to Kelly and Seth and back again, and his face flushed. "If they want one."

Linda's eyes grew bright and shiny, and before she shuttled the girls off to their room, she bent and kissed the boys on the cheek, Kelly first.

When she got to Seth, she flicked his bruised cheek lightly. "If this happens again," she said softly, "you and me, we're going to have a different conversation."

Seth nodded soberly. "About manatees instead of whales," he said.

Her eyes narrowed, just like Kelly's. "Sure, Seth. That's what we'll talk about."

"Good. I like manatees."

She muttered to herself and walked away, and Seth shook out his arms and stretched. He'd been holding the baby for hours.

"Night, boys," Craig said over his shoulder.

"Night, Dad!"

"Night, Mr. Arnold!"

And then they were alone.

"You *are* infuriating," Kelly told him. "You know that, right?"

Seth just smiled and stood up before holding out his hand. "C'mere. I want to show you something."

"You don't need a come-on, you know *that,* right?"

Seth just chuckled and pulled him through the house to the sliding glass door that led out to the porch. They were both wearing T-shirts and no shoes, and Seth knew they couldn't stay out long, but as he tugged Kelly outside and shut the door behind him, he heard Kelly gasp.

This was worth it.

A fog had rolled up while they were eating, blanketing the whole world in mystery. It had rolled out since, blown away to the sea, and all that was left before them was…

Everything.

Stars burned cold overhead, shifting in time to the music of the universe, and the sea roiled beneath them in an endless hush.

"Wow," Kelly whispered.

Seth pulled him tight, his back to Seth's front, and held on.

"The world is so big." Kelly's voice—troubled, worried—pinged in Seth's chest, a plaintive note that wouldn't stop ringing.

"See those two stars?" Seth had taken astronomy this year—his first college science class, actually.

"Yeah?"

"They only *look* like stars from here."

"What are they really?"

"Suns. Twin suns. They revolve around each other, each one carrying their own planets that revolve around them. But they're tied together. Like gravity. And there may *seem* to be all this space around them, but they're really the beating heart of their own solar system. Only they know. *They* know that their other half is out there."

"But… do they ever get to be the same sun?"

Seth tightened his grip. "Not in astronomy. But humans aren't stars, baby. Because we're here. And I'm touching you. And that's not going away."

Kelly turned in his arms then and raised his briny face to Seth's and his shaking hands to Seth's cheeks. He didn't say anything. He didn't have to.

Seth lowered his head and took Kelly's mouth, his kisses, as Seth's own, starting their own thermal detonation. Body heat boiled between them, and Kelly moaned, kissing harder. Seth wrapped his arms around his shoulders, bending so he could slide his hands down the back of Kelly's jeans.

Kelly stiffened and pulled away.

"I'm sorry. I'm sorry. Kelly—"

Kelly shook his head and placed his fingers over Seth's mouth. "Bed." His smile was jagged and bright and dark, like stars. "I want to touch you when I'm warm."

Seth nodded and allowed himself to be pulled back to the house, into the warmth.

They undressed in the dark, both of them leaving their clothes in careful piles on their luggage, and then slid into the bed in their underwear, their chilled hands and feet making giggly contact with their warm places. Finally, Seth took Kelly's hands and tucked them under his arms, shuddering as the cold threatened to overwhelm him.

Kelly shuddered too, and as they warmed up together, he scooched closer, until he was firmly in Seth's arms.

Then Seth could talk.

"Did you… you know…?"

"No." Kelly kissed his chest. "I didn't get afraid. I just… I wanted this. You wanted beautiful for me. I just wanted you."

"We got both," Seth said happily.

Kelly's low chuckle warmed him. "You are feeling very smug, aren't you?"

"Mm…."

Kelly found his mouth in the dark, and it was like those moments on his father's couch again. Long and slow, slow and deep. Mouth, lips, tongue, teeth, every stroke, every thrust, every foray a new and exciting combination. Seth's nerves lit up, crackling with energy, with wanting, and Kelly whined, pulling away.

"This was not well thought out," he panted.

"How thin are the—"

And in answer, they heard Chloe crying downstairs and Craig's warm voice, vibrating through the floorboards.

Seth groaned softly, burying his head in Kelly's shoulder. His erection—oh God. In the last six months, he'd been *made* of erections, but at the sound of his father's voice, it throbbed quietly into flaccidity. "This isn't *fair!*"

Kelly's strained laugh just emphasized the point. "*Mijo*, I don't know if I can let my mother hear me—"

"I *know!*" They giggled some more, their hands growing familiar and languid on each other's skin.

When they finally settled down, Kelly curled up next to him, settling like a cat—still for the moment but twitching, ready to chase mice should he hear one.

"What now?" Seth asked sleepily.

"Tell me about your astronomy class," Kelly commanded.

"Sure. If you tell me about sketching a nude model."

Kelly snorted. "His penis was *very* oddly shaped."

"So's the universe."

They started giggling again.

And then they talked and talked and fell asleep when the air in the house was so still, they could smell the foggy cold of dawn.

They woke up to the smell of eggs and bacon, and the feel of the other body in bed.

Before Kelly could roll away, Seth pulled him close, and Kelly went, both of them grunting with exhaustion and excitement.

"Seth?"

"Yeah?"

"This sex thing—we'll get to it."

"God, I hope so. Today. Definitely today."

"But here's the thing."

"You keep talking, I'm gonna sleep through bacon."

Kelly pinched him. "Stop it. Anyway, the thing is, waking up with you next to me is about the most awesome thing ever. Can we remember that?"

"Yeah."

"Let's go get us some bacon."

"And some sausage." Seth laughed, that high-pitched "dee-erp!" that had haunted him from high school, and Kelly kissed him, quick and hard, before rolling out of his arms.

They dressed in sweats, and both of them put socks on, because the chill outside seemed to be seeping in through their toes, and then ran downstairs, the muffled thump of their feet on the hard blond wood sounding through the house.

Craig was actually doing the cooking, forking bacon onto a plate covered with paper towels to sop up the grease. An egg casserole sat on hot pads on the table, and Linda was setting down a platter of fruit.

Lily, Lulu, and Agnes were already starting on the egg casserole, their hair back in ponytails, their faces freshly scrubbed. Chloe banged on the table from her portable high chair that affixed to the table with clamps.

"You hungry?" Seth took a piece of cantaloupe and cut it up into little pieces for her and then grabbed the little plastic bowl and put some egg casserole in it with her dull fork.

She looked at the egg casserole skeptically, poking it with a slender finger.

"She doesn't eat eggs?" Seth asked.

"She doesn't eat much," Kelly said with a sigh. "We keep taking her to the doctor, and they don't know what to tell us. She's just... I don't know. Behind. On everything."

Seth handed her a piece of cantaloupe and smiled at her, and she giggled back. "But still awesome," he said loyally. Matty's daughter. It was still hard to believe.

Breakfast was as lively as dinner had been, and Seth and Kelly promised the girls that they'd go to the aquarium and sightsee with them the next day. But sitting next to Kelly, feeling the thrum of blood under his skin, remembering the night before, both of them flesh to flesh, Seth knew he and Kelly wouldn't be any good at all to them if they didn't get some time to themselves.

He needed, in a way that precluded food and air and even music.

He needed Kelly to be a part of him.

They showered after breakfast, while everybody was gathering together to leave, like they were getting ready for a normal day. Seth used the bathroom in his dad's room so they could get done faster, in time to hug everybody on their way out.

As he was shutting the door, Craig said, "We'll call on our way home." He gave them both a look that spoke of that long-ago day when he'd seen more than he'd cared to through a two-inch strip of curtain. "We'll give you an ETA, so remember to keep your phones on!"

And then they were gone.

Seth eyed Kelly with a certain grim awkwardness. "Should it bother us that they know what we're gonna do?"

"Who *cares*!" Kelly gasped back, grabbing his hand. "I'm just so excited we're gonna do it!"

They ran upstairs together, shedding their clothes as they went—but leaving their socks on.

"It's cold," Kelly muttered, crawling into bed. "I don't care how dumb it looks. I'm not sucking on your feet."

Seth pulled the covers over their shoulders and giggled. "I hope not. My thing is about three feet north."

Kelly rolled his eyes and reached under the pillow, producing a bottle of lubricant and a washcloth from the bathroom. "You're taller than that. I'd say three and a half."

Seth snickered. "Wouldn't that make me seven feet tall?"

"I don't even know what you're talking about!" Kelly pulled down the covers, mindless of the chill. "You have a bruise on your chest—and oh my God. Your chest!"

Seth grinned a little. "Still working out." The grin faded as he traced Kelly's collarbone with his fingertips. "You're still too thin. I...." He shrugged and brushed Kelly's chin. "I miss when this was rounder."

Kelly captured his fingertips and kissed them. "Not my fault," he said. "I grew two inches."

Seth knew his eyes widened. "Nuh-nuh—serious?"

"Yeah. Mom measured me on my birthday. I'm actually taller than Matty." Some of his glee faded. "As tall as he was the last time we measured."

Seth rubbed his full lower lip with a careful thumb. Neither of them wanted to talk about Matty—he knew that. But Seth had fed his daughter that morning, held her sleeping weight in his arms.

Chloe was the little burden that would keep Kelly home after Agnes had left, would keep them apart if Seth couldn't find a way to go home.

"You were always bigger than Matty," he said soberly. "Always kinder. You ever wonder why I didn't crush on him?"

Kelly shrugged. "'Cause I would have committed fratricide?"

Seth laughed softly. "Sure." His thumb found the silky hairs of Kelly's upper lip. "Are you growing this out? Like a chia-stash or a goatee?"

"Naw. I just really wanted to rim you, and I figured I'd give you less razor burn this way."

"Uhm… uh… so…." The warmth, the intimacy that had formed around them as they took their familiar inventory of the changes time had wrought boiled and steamed around them. Seth's head sank into the pillow, and he dropped his shoulder back, spreading his body out for Kelly's plunder, inviting him to live up to that reckless promise.

Kelly's laugh had a raw edge to it, a fully adult sound that said he knew what he'd just done, and he was unrepentant. He thrust his tongue into Seth's mouth and took and took, leaving Seth breathless.

Kelly's hands weren't idle.

He tormented Seth's nipples without mercy, stroked Seth's upper arms, his stomach, his hips. One hand, rough from doing laundry and dishes, slid along his thigh and around his groin, and Seth actually found some words.

"Don't tell me you forgot where it is!"

Kelly's chuckle made him, if anything, harder.

"I know. Just wanted to make sure you remembered who it belongs to."

Seth scowled, then reached down Kelly's body, groping him roughly. For a moment he froze. So much effort. So much mental and physical effort to be nothing but gentle when they were in bed and naked.

But Kelly grunted and bucked into Seth's hand, and Seth couldn't stop for the world. Kelly's cock filled his palm, wider, maybe even longer than it had been when they'd started doing this, was it already three years ago?

God, they'd been young.

They were supposed to still be young, but Seth would be turning twenty, and Kelly was eighteen. They were real adults now, not kids screwing around.

And Kelly's cock, thrumming in his grip, felt serious, like this thing they were doing, it had consequences and echoes.

Seth closed his grip, squeezing some, and stroked again while Kelly kissed him, kissed him until the thoughts, the hesitation, stopped swirling around his brain, kissed him stupid, until he moaned and spread his legs, inviting any exploration, any possession Kelly would take.

"Me." Kelly pulled Seth's nipple into his mouth and sucked hard, and Seth let go of his cock to bury his hands in Kelly's coarse straight hair. "You belong to me."

"I know," Seth gasped. "Won't ever forget."

Kelly gave a whimper and moved to the other nipple, his hand skating around Seth's cock again to fondle Seth's sac, his tightened, aching testicles.

"Nnung…."

"Hurt?" Kelly let go.

"No. Yes. Everything aches." Seth felt like he was whining, but he was lost. "Kelly… man, I…." He was shaking hard, like he was on the edge of coming but couldn't.

"Shhh…." Kelly kissed down his body, took Seth's cock into his mouth, and sucked.

Seth exploded, hard and completely, like he'd never been touched before, and Kelly kept sucking, kept nibbling, his fingers doing their dance again, until he grew hard all over again.

The shaking eased a little but didn't quit, and Seth moaned. "I still want you."

Kelly shoved at his legs again, and at first he thought Kelly wanted him to hold them up. But Kelly sat back on his haunches and eyed him with complete practicality.

"Hands and knees," he said, all but crossing his arms and getting out a diagram. "I think that's how I want you."

Seth could hardly put two words together. "Because…?"

"Because." Kelly gave that smile where his nose wrinkled and his eyes got small, and Seth couldn't ever deny him what he wanted when he did that.

He rolled over to his stomach, pulling his knees underneath him, crouching like a kid playing leapfrog.

Kelly leaned over, tracing soft lips down Seth's spine, breathing into his ears, on the back of his neck, using his palms and fingertips to mark Seth with his heat.

Seth crouched there and moaned, letting Kelly call the shots, letting his desire build and his erection throb with renewed life.

"When'd you get to be such a tease?" he breathed, shuddering as Kelly's tongue flicked toward the back of his cheek.

"When you sent me a picture of a redneck with a black eye," Kelly said, his breath disturbing the fine hairs on Seth's backside. He rasped his teeth in the same place, and Seth's brain—never very reliable on planet Earth—began to fuzz out, leaving only Kelly's touches in place of words and rational thought.

"Yeah, well, you sent me a picture of your super-hot boss. Oh my God! *Kelly*!"

Kelly was apparently done with banter. He was right at the part where his tongue did intimate, probing things into his sensitive places. Seth tried to say the words, tried to tell him that he liked this—this was good, this was *great*, Kelly should maybe penetrate him, maybe, oh my God, *fuck him* right now and forget about extraneous humans who had nothing to do with this place, right here, where, oh dear Lord! Kelly was thrusting a finger deep inside him, deep, and now two, stretching, and oh… God, there were no words… no words….

Seth buried his face in the sheets and screamed, his entire body shaking, sweat breaking out from his shoulders to his lower back.

He didn't come, but that was due to a supreme act of will.

Kelly's filthy chuckle behind him didn't make him sweat any less. "Good?"

"I want…."

"What?" Kelly scissored his fingers then, stretching more, and Seth sobbed.

"Fuck me," he said clearly, the shame of the obscenity burned away by pleasure and need. "Fuck me. Stick your cock up my asshole and *fuck. Me.*"

Kelly made a sound behind him, a grunting, helpless sound, and then he shifted on the bed. Seth felt the shock of cold lube dribbling down his crease before Kelly thrust in, muttering *"Damn you, Seth!"* before shoving all the way in to the hilt.

Not gentle. Not slow. Not like last time. Seth fought the urge to tense up, which would make the pain more, and relaxed instead, welcoming. He'd begged for this. He *needed* it. Pain didn't bother him.

Emptiness did.

Kelly paused, breathing harshly, his cock throbbing deep inside Seth's body, and Seth sighed and melted, every muscle relaxing in submission.

"Move," he urged, not sure if Kelly could even hear him.

Kelly must have, because he pulled back slowly, and Seth whimpered. Going. He was going. Then Kelly thrust again and he almost sobbed.

"*Yes!*"

Ah! Again! And again! Every thrust forward was a victory that lit up his nerve endings, filled him, made him whole. Every pull back was a tease, a torment, a fear of being left alone.

Again!

"*Harder!*" Seth begged, shaking. Sweat prickled his forehead, his lower back, and Kelly's hands on his hips slid around as he tried to get a better grip.

"You're killing me!" Kelly gasped. "I'm gonna... oh God, Seth, I'm gonna—"

"Oh please." Seth's stomach contorted as the first sob rocked him. "Please, Kelly. Come."

Kelly groaned and fell forward, rutting hard, so hard Seth lost traction and his legs spread behind him as Kelly pumped come into his ass. Seth's cock ground between his abdomen and the bed, and that was it, that was all he needed, and he lost hold of his orgasm, spasming so hard his stomach muscles hurt.

Oh God. Oh God, oh God! Kelly was twitching behind him, and he was lost, facedown in the bed, bereft because Kelly was pulling out now, and he had nothing to ground him, no framework for....

"What are... what are you...?"

Kelly's tongue, plied again, hungrily and... so carnal. So forbidden.

Seth screamed and lurched forward, oversensitized, twitching on the bed.

Kelly pulled back, then lay next to him and took his mouth. Seth tasted heat, desire, the earthiness of Kelly's come, and his body wouldn't stop shaking.

"Sh... sh... *mijo*.... Oh wow. What's the matter?"

For a moment, Seth was afraid. His body was replete, but he needed more. His heart was happy but afraid. With a roar that was almost orgasm, the void of the last six months rushed Seth's chest, and he started a slow, hard sob.

"I miss you," he gasped into Kelly's chest. "Oh God. I miss you so much."

Kelly moaned—not a sexy moan, a sad one—and they were both crying, kissing, tasting salt and sex on each other's skin as the final, more painful crest hit them both.

THEY DIDN'T move for a long time, even after they calmed down. They just lay there, arms around each other's shoulders, breath shuddering, bodies trembling in aftermath.

"That was…." Kelly's chest rose and fell.

"I don't let myself," Seth said, by way of apology. "I don't let myself miss you. I miss you, and… and I want you too bad. Everybody starts looking good to me, and I don't want everybody."

"I just want you," Kelly mumbled, nibbling his ear. "I hear you. I… I get home at night, and Mom's with Chloe, and the girls need me, and your dad's making dinner or doing something nice, and I just… I keep thinking how much easier it would be if you were there."

Seth rolled so he could rest his head on Kelly's chest. "I'd be there," he said eagerly. "I could leave Bridgford and go to Sac State, and we could be—"

"Arrested," Kelly said, the word falling like a brutal sword.

"I was going to say happy," Seth mumbled, the truth no easier to hear in Kelly's arms than it had been in the back of his head for the past three years. "When can I come home?"

"Not this year," Kelly said wearily. "The local station just did one of those unsub shows—Castor Durant was one of the cold cases." He grunted. "They left out my name, thank fucking God, but they mentioned 'a young African American person who may be a person of interest.'"

Seth was horrified. "Like… like when? When did this happen?"

"Right before Thanksgiving." Kelly let out a breath. "Not even a mention that there were two people at the crime scene that night—"

"I can't verify that," Seth said, because he couldn't. "But… maybe I can visit? Like Easter? Or summer vacation?"

"Just wait," Kelly begged. "Wait. I'll come with you some day. You know it, right? I'll come with you. I'll…. We can go to…."

"Italy," Seth said, voice falling glumly.

"I beg your pardon?"

Ugh. Seth hadn't wanted to broach this, but fuck. Fuck all the things.

"There's a symphony in Italy, and they want me to come play in the fall. I've been trying to tell them no—"

"Don't you dare!" Kelly fought to sit up, pretty much dumping Seth next to him. "Italy? You have a chance to go play in *Italy* for a semester—"

Shit. "A year."

"A year!" And at first, Kelly sounded excited, like Seth had when he'd heard that. And then it hit him. "A year?" His voice trailed off.

"I told them no," Seth explained patiently. "See, San Francisco has been offering me a place, and they'd let me finish my education at San Francisco State, and—"

"And they're not going to have any more of a hard-on for you *after* Italy? Seth!"

"I don't want to leave you!" Seth argued, the tears threatening again. "Is that so fucking wrong?"

Kelly shook his head and wiped his own eyes with his palm. "No. Baby. No. It's not wrong. But…." He bit his lip and smiled, crooked, like a broken stick. "I mean, they got rentals in Italy, don't they?"

"Every weekend in San Francisco," Seth begged.

"Italy. Seth. This is everything your father ever wanted for you and was afraid to ask. This is everything *I* ever wanted for you and was afraid to dream about. And here you are, *Italy* on a platter, and you're going to throw it away—"

"For you? You bet."

"Well, I'm not gonna let you! Have you even told your father about this?"

Ugh. "No. Because it'll be just like Bridgford all over again. And look how good *that* turned out!"

"Yeah, Seth." Kelly's voice fell flatly, reminding Seth of every blessing he'd had in the last three years. "Look."

Seth's lower lip wobbled. "Don't you want to be with me?" he asked, empty again. Suddenly, viciously, he wanted Kelly's cock back in his ass, wanted to be joined, because then it felt like this chasm between them—the chasm between Italy and California—couldn't ever open up.

"Well, yeah." Kelly's broken smile reappeared. "I want to see you in Italy."

Seth shook his head and made to get off the bed. He could go walking on the beach. Into the water. And never come back.

But Kelly grabbed his hand and tugged. "I'm not ready for you to go yet," he said, and it sounded like it had more than one meaning.

"I'm not either." Seth searched his eyes, waiting for the moment of sad rejection, the moment where Kelly would say they should just end it, because he wanted Seth to go away for a year and Kelly couldn't wait that long.

"We'll talk about it," Kelly told him, running his knuckles gently over Seth's cheekbones. "We'll think. Baby, someday, I'll be able to leave. Or you'll be able to come home. Or we can meet in the middle of the world or something and it will all be okay. But until then, you have to—you have *got* to take the things your talent earns you. Don't you get that?"

Seth shook his head. "I didn't want it," he whispered. Young. How was Kelly so old and he was so young? Especially right now, when Seth's insides, his cock, all of him was still pulsing with come?

"But you must have. Because unless you were with me, your head was with your music. And you'd come down from that place to be with me, but that was because you loved me. It's a gift."

"That's not fair," Seth whispered. "It's not fair to call it a gift when I have to choose between it and you."

Kelly sighed. "But you have to be gone right now anyway. Because people are still talking and Matty is still… well, he's in rehab again, and maybe it will stick. But he could come back any minute and shoot off his big mouth and Chloe will get taken away—"

Seth closed his eyes. "That can't happen." He knew this.

"No. No, it can't. So if you've got to be gone—why not be somewhere awesome?"

Seth shook his head, not ready to concede, and helpless tears slid between his eyelids. "This was so not the conversation I thought we'd be having right now," he confessed.

Kelly let out a chuff of air. "Well, if you want to talk about doing that again, I'm good for it. But maybe…."

He was biting his lip shyly.

"What?"

"Maybe we can walk on the beach first? I… you know. I really love the ocean too."

Seth smiled—God, he was ready to smile. "Yeah. Okay. That's good."

They walked on the foggy, chilly beach, and Seth let the roar of it fill him, let the heat of Kelly's hand in his and the beauty of the wave foam crashing near their feet, consume him.

And the loneliness of being far away from Kelly, too far to touch, was kept at bay for the rest of the afternoon.

Footsteps in the Sand

KELLY HATED running. His bare feet fell unevenly on the damp portion of the beach, his calves, his thighs, his arches working overtime to bounce back up and take the next step.

He couldn't go fast enough.

Step, step, step, shush, shush, shush… God, he couldn't go fast enough.

"Kelly!"

Augh! Dammit! Seth didn't even sound winded. "Kelly! It's not your fault! Dammit—wait!"

A wave washed up, and Kelly swerved, trying to pull up, but the dry sand sucked at his feet, and the incoming tide kept coming and coming. Brine froze his ankles, his shins, his knees, and *fuck,* he went down, tumbling, coming up sputtering and shaking and unable to run anywhere, anywhere at all.

"Baby…."

Seth's arm, warm and kind, wrapped around his shoulders, and before Kelly could even chatter, "Go away," Seth had taken off his own sweatshirt, ripped Kelly's sodden one off, and replaced it.

It was old and soft—Seth's first Bridgford sweatshirt—and warmed by their mad dash along the beach.

"I'm sorry," Kelly mumbled. "God, I'm sorry."

"All you ever have to say is stop," Seth whispered, his lips by Kelly's ear. "Ever. You don't have to be sorry. You don't have to explain. I know."

"I thought I wanted it."

"I know."

"I wasn't ready." *A body, hot, behind his, invading. Flesh where he didn't want it. Friction. Burning. Pain.*

They'd tried in the daylight, after the family had gone back to Sacramento, playful, intense—the way sex had always been for them— and this time… this time, oh God, Kelly had wanted it.

Seth seemed to love it so much, and he was so trusting, opening up his body like that.

And Jesus, Kelly owed him.

Kelly had told Seth's dad about Italy on the third day of their stay—and Seth was right.

It was Bridgford all over again, without the actual fighting.

"Italy?"

"Dad, drop it."

"But, Seth—"

"I've got to decide on my own."

"But… you know. Italy."

"Please, Dad. This might not be the last time I get to do this—"

"But it might! That's why it's called opportunity!"

"But I have opportunities right here." He'd glared at Kelly and then looked helplessly at Linda, who'd shrugged, clearly on the fence about it.

And Kelly'd winced at every exchange, because Seth had been right—this was his decision. Adulthood—Seth had it.

But they'd woken up that morning, naked, laughing, hands warm on each other's skin, and Kelly thought about how Seth hadn't complained, not once, hadn't blamed Kelly for sticking his little pug nose in where it didn't belong, and Kelly'd thought, "Hey, I should give it up for this guy, 'cause he's really awesome."

And then his brain had exploded into that fetid room of his nightmares, and he'd rolled off the bed and barely managed to fumble into his clothes, a bewildered Seth scrambling after him.

But Seth was wrapping him tight in his sweatshirt now, murmuring soft things in his ear, and there was nothing scary about him, nothing at all, just comfort, just kindness, and Kelly wanted so badly to be everything for him that he burst into tears.

Seth just held him tighter, the two of them on the beach, the frigid tide surging around their ankles, until Kelly could hear his own teeth chattering.

They were both wearing sleep shorts still, because they'd had them on the night before, before they'd slid out of them to make love.

"You're cold." Seth rubbed his arms underneath the sweatshirt. "C'mon. Let's go back to the house. We can go shopping."

The hell? "Sh-sh-sh-o-p-p-ing?" Seth had to guide him, he was so damned cold.

"Yeah. Carmel, remember? We were gonna go look in the art galleries? And then we decided to do that other thing, which was fine, but it's not the only thing. I thought you wanted to see art."

Kelly cried harder. By the time they got to the house, up the stairs, and into the shower, Seth had to hold him up because he could barely breathe.

The warm water worked its way through his muscles, and then Seth—all that surprising strength, that purpose that seemed to come from nowhere—manhandled him tenderly until he was wearing sweats again, wrapped in a blanket, a cup of hot chocolate folded in his hands as Seth stood next to his bed and practiced.

Kelly couldn't remember him saying anything about the music, but it was like that time he'd come home from school because he'd heard Kelly's need from a hundred miles away. He'd just sung Kelly to sleep, because that's what Kelly needed.

This was the same. Kelly was warm, the heat of the mug seeping through his hands, the softness of the comforter relaxing his body, and Seth's music—ah. Ah, God. Seth's beautiful music.... He liked pop music as much as anybody, but the spin the violin could put on it wrapped around Kelly's soul like the comforter around his shoulders.

After about twenty minutes, Seth set the instrument down in its case, and the bow with it, and sat on the edge of the bed, his hand on Kelly's thigh.

He didn't say anything, just waited patiently, with pale green eyes that could have been looking for life on Mars or looking for the sense in Kelly's heart.

"I...." Kelly closed his eyes. "Why would you want to stay with me when you're in Italy and a thousand hot Italian boys are throwing themselves at you? I can let you go.... I just.... I don't want you to walk away from me in your heart."

Seth's hand tightened on his thigh. "Sex is good," he said simply. "But only because it's you. We don't have to do that one thing unless you want to. I'm fine the other way around." He bit one side of his lip, and his eyes grew wicked and danced. "I'm *great* the other way around. I'm... when I miss you, it's not because I miss you in bed." He let out a breath. "Although I do get horny for you, I won't lie. I just...." He closed his eyes and gripped Kelly's thigh a little harder. "This. Touching. Talking. The things we don't say in text. The things that are too small on the telephone but that we'd say if we had each other around all the time. The way your eyes look when you say something, so I know if you're being funny or sarcastic or not."

"You don't know?" Kelly asked, surprised.

Seth shook his head. "I'm really bad with sarcasm, Kelly. It took me a while to figure out how much Matty despised me because I wasn't sure if he was being sarcastic or not."

Kelly captured his hand and brought his palm to his mouth. "My mom is sarcastic as fuck," he said after a moment. "The girls are stunning at it. I, like, learn at their feet."

Seth's chuckle went a few degrees further to bringing his body back to normal. "I noticed. But see? That's what I miss. Not… you know… what you do for me in bed."

"I just want to be everything for you." That was simple enough, but it left Kelly feeling naked.

"You are." And talk about simple. Seth slid off the chair, his knees on the ground, and rested his head in Kelly's lap. "You see?" he asked hoarsely. "You see what I mean? Italy—maybe next year. Maybe I could ask them if I can do it next year. For my senior year in college and not my junior year. Maybe I could ask them if I can do the graduate program. And for another year or two, I'm at the San Francisco Conservatory of the Arts—"

"It's not the best music program," Kelly said, because he'd looked it up on his phone. "What, USC too fucking lazy to bang down your door?"

"I told them no," Seth said mildly. "And CSU Northridge too."

Kelly wasn't sure whether to laugh or howl. "Anybody else we should know about?"

"No."

"Which means, of course, that yes, you've gotten offers from all over the country, but the only one that really twisted your nipple was the one in Italy." *Holy Jesus.* While Kelly had been slogging through work/school/birth/death, the world had been prostrating itself at his lover's feet, and Seth had been too involved in Kelly to so much as smile and wave.

"New York was fourth chair," Seth said without conceit. "I'm… well, I've been learning first chair since, you know, my junior year in high school. Italy would be first chair. So, you know, New York—"

"Can kiss your skinny brown ass. I get the picture." Kelly took a stress gulp of hot chocolate, grateful it had cooled slightly. He tilted his head back then and tried not to take out his frustration on Seth, who had been nothing but patient.

"I just like challenges." The serenity in Seth's voice actually got through, and Kelly managed a smile.

"Like your neurotic boyfriend."

Seth muttered something and buried his face against Kelly's thigh, and Kelly pulled out of his guilt spiral long enough to push gently on his forehead so he could see Seth's expression.

His green eyes were shiny, and his cheeks were flushed, and it hit Kelly that the last hour—that had been rough on him too.

"*Mijo*—"

"It's scary," Seth whispered. "Remembering being alone, where nobody can help you. Don't ever be ashamed of remembering that. I'm ashamed I made you."

Kelly scraped at the dampness on his cheek with the pad of his thumb. "No shame. Please. I just went too fast, you know? I thought, 'Hey, Seth seems to like it! I'll just bend over. It'll be *great.*'" He let out a sigh and realized he was a shitty boyfriend on a lot of levels. "Thanks for... you know. Backing off when I started to freak."

Seth shook his head. "Don't thank me for that. Not acting like a scumbag is, like, the least you can expect from your boyfriend, right? People don't get a thanks from the universe for not being rapists. It's, like, the lowest bar for being a decent person is stopping when someone says no."

Kelly chuckled, cupping his cheek again. "God. I love you so much." He leaned down and Seth pushed up, and they shared a chaste kiss. "I just... if I'm gonna send you out to Italy, I... I want to be whole inside. Someone to come back to."

Seth squinted at him. "So you're not whole inside because you won't *bottom*? Jesus, you're stupid. I mean, I still love you, but that's really dumb."

Kelly shook his head. "Come here. Come here and set my chocolate down and kiss me some more. I wanna make out, okay?"

Seth grinned. "*That's* what I'm talking about. Then Carmel? The art galleries—"

"Yeah, yeah. I get it. You want me to see art. Whatever. Kiss me now, here, because we can."

Seth's mouth was heavenly. They stopped just before stripping down and making love again, but they did manage to pack a lunch and make it to the art galleries.

Seth got Kelly to pick a sculpture he really loved, an abstract pottery piece with a metallic shimmery glaze that reminded Kelly of infinity.

"You're buying this for me, why?" Kelly asked, aware he was being spoiled, and that every grand gesture Seth made was another night of him working in a honky-tonk dive bar where he could possibly get his face beat in again.

"Because it made you think of forever," Seth told him. "That's what I want you to think of when you think of me."

God, for someone who was only on planet Earth maybe 10 percent of the time, he sure did know what to say when he was down there.

DROPPING SETH back at Bridgford and driving home was like ripping out his soul. Seth's eyes were bright and shiny and red-rimmed as he got out of the car and warned Kelly soberly about driving safely. His voice—surprisingly husky anyway—was deep enough to rub on the ground. Maybe it was that look on his face, the quiet devastation there, that changed Kelly's mind, made his determination waver.

Maybe it was the way Seth didn't tell him again when he and Guthrie got into another fight at the Stomp in February, right before Valentine's Day, his birthday, when Seth surprised him by taking the train to Sacramento and meeting him at his job with flowers.

Maybe it was how Seth had been working another gig—a chamber music gig with three women who had come to a performance and begged Seth to help them get their quartet off the ground by being a guest player—just so he could send money home to his dad, which ended up sending Lily and Lulu on their eighth-grade trip to Fort Bragg.

It didn't matter, really, what it was. Kelly ended up giving in.

Seth graduated from Bridgford that June with Kelly and Craig in the audience. His graduation present from Craig and Kelly's mom was a trip to Disneyland for the two of them—three days and three nights in Disneyland. Seth had known it was coming. He'd saved enough money to spoil the shit out of Kelly's family, which was nice, and they got busy every night after the fireworks, which was *great*.

But it couldn't last, of course. After their vacation, Kelly helped him move straight to the dorms at the conservatory.

The trip to Italy was still on the table. The offer was a year of graduate school, playing with a symphony in Florence, and Kelly would be damned if Seth passed it up. But in the meantime, Seth had two years. Kelly had two years. They had two years to pray their life wouldn't go to shit if Kelly went down to visit three weekends a month, staying in Seth's single occupancy dorm room, learning to make love like it could happen regularly and not like it was Christmas for the body that only came along once every six months.

Maybe two years would do it. Maybe it would be enough. Maybe it would sate that hunger Kelly had inside for Seth's touch, his smell—like bow rosin and the sweating wood of the instrument.

Maybe.

Maybe they could fill up on each other with regular visits so Seth wouldn't be drained dry of Kelly and need somebody else by the time he was done with Italy.

Kelly would pray for that. He'd live for that. He'd hope for that. Because he wasn't ready to walk away yet. Not in January, as he drove back from the best two weeks of his life, and not in June after Seth walked the stage.

And not that summer, when they found excuses, any excuses, to take the car or the train from the Bay and back and spend a night, or two, stretched out at Seth's dorm, or on Seth's bed at home, bodies touching, breath mingling, pretending they'd never have to part.

Matty got out of rehab in February.

In March, he got a job.

By the time Seth graduated from Bridgford and on to the conservatory, Matty was living in his own apartment—tiny, with a newly rehabbed Isela, and they were high on fucking religion again.

And neither of them was making any attempt to parent their daughter. They'd come see her, yes, hold her, coo over how big she was getting. They'd stay for dinner—which Linda cooked—and talk to the girls about religion and make sure Kelly knew he was still going to hell if he hadn't renounced his homosexual ways. And then they'd leave without helping to clean up.

Chloe didn't really know either of them. She'd rather talk to Seth on the phone, actually. In fact, Seth had taken to calling before her bedtime and playing children's lullabies for her as she fell asleep.

When Matty held her on his lap, she frequently asked for "Set."

Lily was the one who said, "Don't mind her—it's a cartoon character. It's based on Egyptian mythology so, you know. Mummies. Egyptian gods. Sethmet, Osiris, Set—it's fun."

Kelly and Linda, who had been casually ignoring how she kept reaching for Kelly's phone and saying, "Set! Set! Set!" had smiled and nodded, and Matty?

They weren't sure whether he bought it or not.

Isela had stared at them with the simple gaze of a kitten and said that was nice, she'd have to watch it with her sometime. Lulu told her that Dora the Explorer was on instead, and conversation moved on.

But Matty—Matty looked at his daughter, puzzled, a sad little smile on his face, and Kelly actually felt a moment of sympathy for his brother.

This hadn't been how they'd thought of having kids.

Kelly knew that when he and Seth talked about family, they talked about one like Kelly had—or even like Seth and his dad. They talked about laughter and warmth and knowing what your kid watched on television.

But as Matty held out his arms for Chloe to toddle into, he had the realization in his eyes—this wasn't how he'd wanted his life to be.

Kelly could almost forgive him.

Almost.

One Friday night in early September, after Kelly and Linda had, with Craig's help, dealt with back-to-school nights and soccer practices and, oh my God, the girls' homework, Kelly threw his backpack over his shoulder, kissed his mom on the cheek, and shook Craig's hand as he sat on the couch with Chloe in his lap and Agnes asleep against his shoulder. Craig had given Kelly a book to bring to Seth over the weekend—some science fiction thing that they both liked—and Kelly was glad to do it.

He hit the landing and rattled down the stairs, pulling in a sharp breath when he almost ran into Matty, leaning against the wall of the fourplex, finishing off a cigarette.

Well, they didn't teach you how not to smoke in rehab. Kelly guessed it was a habit his brother was going to keep.

"Where you off to?" Matty asked, but not like he cared.

"Hanging with friends." The lie came so easily. Not talking about Seth had become like breathing. Even in the apartment, they all talked about Kelly's boyfriend, or about "how things were in San Francisco" or about "next time you guys go to Disneyland." Unless Craig was there, the hunger to hear about his son written so plainly on his face that it made Kelly ache, they didn't actually say his name.

"Friends in Egyptian mythology?" Matty asked snidely, grinding the butt out under his shoe.

"Sure. Osiris, Ra—you'd like them. They're righteous dudes."

Matty advanced, breathing nicotine right up into Kelly's face. "You can't expose my daughter to that psycho pervert, you know that, right?"

Kelly kept his eyes guileless. "But we *can* expose her to a guy who committed manslaughter, right?"

"It was driving while impaired!"

"That's because of random fucking chance and a broken legal system. Go ahead, tell me why you're better. I changed her diapers, remember? She had diaper rash that could burn through ointment. We had to take her to the doctor, remember? Tell me why you're so much better than I am. Tell me why you got any right to judge."

"Because I know things you don't!" Matty snapped. "And you, wiggling your ass for him because we grew up together, like that makes any fucking difference—"

"Matty, at this point, anything you could tell me on this subject is a fucking lie."

"He killed Castor Durant!" Matty said the words, but his eyes darted to the left, and Kelly sucked in a breath. "You knew?" And Kelly ignored the little bit of triumph in Matty's voice to focus on that look.

"I thought I did," Kelly said, blinking hard. "I thought... I thought I knew, and I was okay with that. Because he got the shit beat out of him, and it was self-defense."

"It was *murder*!" Matty hissed, and Kelly shook his head.

"No. Because you're lying. I'm not sure what about, but... but you're lying. What are you lying about, Matty? What is it you know that you think I don't?"

"Don't let that psycho near my baby!" Matty snarled, breaking free and heading for the stairs.

"He's in Italy," Kelly lied. "You got no worries."

"Talk about lying!" The contempt practically dripped through the concrete. "If he was in Italy, he'd take you with him!"

Kelly shook his head. "I can't go," he said, and for once, he didn't try to hide it—the anger, the bitterness, the hurt. "Some motherfucker left his daughter on my mother's doorstep and then killed her husband. Some motherfucker asks our mother for money twice a month when welfare can't make ends meet. Some motherfucker comes here and eats all her good food every Sunday and makes us all pretend we're happy to see him. I'm too busy helping Mom pay rent to go to Italy, and I'm sure you're damned proud of that, so don't even fucking bother to say it. Now if you'll excuse me, I've got friends to see."

He clattered across the parking lot then to Craig's car, since Craig could drive his safer Toyota with the girls in it all weekend.

Once there, he stopped at a gas station before blowing through the night traffic to the Bay, his heart beating with righteous anger the whole time.

Fucker.

Mother*fucker.*

Thinking he knew something about Seth that Kelly didn't.

Thinking he was going to shock Kelly about who killed Castor Durant.

Kelly knew.

Kelly had known since day one.

Two things going on at that crime scene.

But Matty had been lying when he said it, and now Kelly knew that. And he'd be wondering, fucking bothered by that until somebody broke and told.

But Seth acted like he couldn't even hear the words, "What happened that night." And Kelly—Kelly had tried to bottom a couple more times, and each time, Seth had calmed him down when it didn't work, and talked about feeling helpless, being afraid, with so much passion, Kelly knew he'd been there.

Whatever had happened that night, Seth had almost died.

So as pissed as Kelly was, he was going to take something away from that meeting. Maybe—just maybe—Seth *hadn't* killed Castor Durant. Maybe—just *maybe*—Matty knew who had.

Two things going on at that crime scene.

Fuck.

Kelly was going to have to be nicer to his brother, wasn't he?

SETH AND Amara were playing chess when Kelly got there, and Kelly had a chance to sympathize with their friend, who never seemed to have a date on Friday nights.

"When are you going to get a boyfriend?" Kelly asked, barging in and throwing his stuff in its customary corner.

"How do you know I'm not gay?" she asked, without looking up. "I could be in need of a girlfriend. Check, Seth."

"You like boys," Seth said quietly. "You're still in love with Vince. Checkmate."

Amara looked up from the chess board to stare at him. "How in the fuck would you know that? Vince is at USC and—"

"And you've lost twenty pounds," Seth said, grimacing sadly at her. "And I knew in the middle of our first year at Bridgford. Vince got a girlfriend, and you... well, for one thing you almost lost a challenge to Christopher Cramer, who was a shitty flute player and a total dog. You kept your seat, but only because you, I don't know, started practicing in your sleep, like a nun. You never told him. Are you going to set up the board again?"

Amara wiped her eyes with the back of her hand. "Don't you and Kelly want to stink the place up with loud and obnoxious boy sex?"

Kelly plopped next to her with a sigh. Actually, that had been on his agenda all the way down the fucking freeway. But Seth was looking at her with such compassion, and Kelly realized that right now, she needed both of them.

"We can do loud and obnoxious boy sex after we watch *Paranormal Activity*. Seth, tell me you've got snacks."

Seth started to put away the chess pieces and smiled slightly. "Actually, Guthrie is coming with pizza. Don't get mad. He's fighting with his dad right now, and I guess I'm his gbf."

"His what?" Seth could just do that, knock around slang like he'd been using it all his life.

"Gay best friend," Amara said, helping put the chess pieces away. "Except, since we're just dropping Bibles full of truth on people's heads,

I'd like to point out that Guthrie's been in love with you since I met him in March, Seth. I don't know how you don't know that."

Seth wrinkled his nose. "That's highly unlikely. I told him in December I had a boyfriend. Smart man's money is to go crush on someone else."

Together, using the same weird synchronicity that they seemed to have developed while at Bridgford, Seth and Amara moved about the dorm, setting chairs up to surround the end table where they put the computer so they could all watch the movie.

But they didn't stop talking about each other's love lives, and Kelly had to admit, even the idea that Guthrie was in love with Seth—and Kelly thought it was obvious—was less uncomfortable than his conversation with Matty.

It was like his lie to Matty really was the truth. He was hanging with friends.

Such a small thing on a Friday night.

Too bad Kelly had to drive two hours to do it.

Guthrie arrived with pizza, and because Amara had said something, Kelly was looking carefully at his face.

Oh yeah.

He smiled at Kelly, was polite, warm and friendly even.

That's what made it love. His eyes were sad. Not angry or resentful or secretly hoping Kelly got an incurable disease.

They were *sad*, like he knew Kelly was better for Seth and Kelly was what Seth wanted, but it hurt him because *he* wanted to be that person.

Of course, that didn't stop Kelly from draping himself shamelessly over Seth's body as they watched the movie.

When the movie ended and the pizza was mostly eaten, Seth hugged Amara and sent her to her dorm and then told Guthrie to text him when he got home. Everybody left, the party in Seth's dorm room was over, and it was just the two of them.

Well, first there was sex.

Kelly had needed Seth's body all week. He'd started to dream about things—about the way his hip bones stood out and the super-pale shade of brown on his abdomen, below his belt line, or the almost purple color his cock turned when he was just about to nut.

They'd gotten good at sex in the past months since Seth had gotten his own room, and Kelly had him naked, on his hands and knees and begging, within five minutes of Guthrie's awkward goodbye.

He wanted to fuck all thoughts of the pretty white country boy with the blond ponytail right out of Seth's head—and to shoot all his worries about what his stupid asshole brother was up to out his balls. Sweat dripped into his eyes and his hips bounced off Seth's backside with a resounding *thwack* while Seth gasped beneath him. He clenched at Seth's waist convulsively, his fingers biting into the soft flesh of his hip bones, his stomach, his thighs.

Seth gave a faint moan, and Kelly's orgasm was just… just within fingertip's reach. His hand moved on its own, cracking across Seth's ass with a sound like a gunshot.

Seth convulsed, clamping tight around Kelly's cock, and he fell facedown on the bed, twitching, probably shooting onto the sheets beneath him. Kelly fell with him, his face buried against Seth's back, hips still rutting, trapped in the heaven of his rippling muscles, his slick entrance, the heat of his heart.

They were lying there, panting, when Seth shifted and moved his hand, rubbing the spot on his backside that Kelly had smacked.

"Ow…."

Kelly rolled to his side so quickly, he actually spattered come onto Seth's thighs and examined the red mark he'd left on Seth's ass.

The darkening red mark. The soon-to-be bruise that he'd left on Seth's ass.

The *oh my God, bruise!* that he'd left on his kind, patient lover who had spent a year of his childhood walking on eggshells *in fear of being hit.*

Kelly buried his face against Seth's arm. "Oh God. Oh God. I'm so sorry."

"Little rough, Kel."

As rebukes went, it was pretty gentle, but Kelly wasn't being nearly so kind. "I didn't mean to—oh God, Seth. I'm so sorry. That was too hard. I'm so sorry. You're so patient with me, and oh my God, I didn't mean to. I thought it was… you know, sexy smacking, and I didn't mean for it to be so hard. It just got out of hand." Oh God. He sounded like an abuser. Probably like Seth's dad, that terrible drinking year that Craig couldn't seem to let go of.

Now Kelly knew why.

Kelly tried to roll out of bed. "Fuck. I'm sorry. I'll go. I'll just walk away. You don't need me or my baggage—fucking Guthrie could probably manage not to *bruise your fucking ass*, and I'm sorry. I'm so sorry."

Seth rolled to his side, wincing a little. That didn't stop him from reaching up and grabbing Kelly's hand. "What in the hell? No. You do not get to just fuck me and leave me. Get back in bed and cuddle, dammit. Jesus. It wasn't intentional. I get it."

Kelly allowed himself to be reluctantly cajoled back into bed, but once he got there, he pulled Seth up so his head was on Kelly's chest and squeezed him so tight, it probably hurt to breathe.

Seth didn't complain, just let it happen, and when Kelly finally relaxed his hold, he mumbled, "So, uh, anything you want to talk about?"

Kelly let out a strangled laugh. "Only everything. I'm so sorry, baby… I… God. I won't do that again."

"Just, you know. Control." Seth shrugged. "I mean, it made me come. I must have thought it was sexy. It just… really stung afterward." And he sounded so surprised, so befuddled and dear he was just so completely Kelly's dreamy boy, that Kelly's throat grew tight.

"I missed you," he admitted. "Was a fuckin' busy week. Matty was, like, lurking in the bushes as I left tonight. Saying shit, lying mostly, but saying shit. Some lady coughed up your picture this week—like, Isela's dad and Castor Durant's family have been stalking the neighborhood since that piece on TV. What's it been, like almost four years later? All his gang buddies are either dead or in prison. They *all* fingered him as a predator, but no, he's clean as God's fingers.

"Anyway, after that thing on TV, some old lady admitted she saw you out—*maybe* that night. But maybe not that night, because she said it was the night of all the police at the gas station, which was *my* night in hell, not yours, and she lives by those apartments by that big vacant lot. Anyway, she could have seen you either one of those nights. She doesn't remember which night, but she remembered the white curly hair and the brown skin and a white T-shirt falling off your neck, which is half the shit you own, so even if she was looking at some other blond-haired black kid, it's not like the cops are going to be searching our neighborhood, which is too damned bad because you're not the only one there who looks like that."

He wasn't. Kelly could think of two kids their age right at that moment who lived in their neighborhood that fit Seth's description.

Seth grunted. "Shit. So much for coming home Thanksgiving." He sighed. "But the good news is, we got the house in Monterey again, same two weeks, if you can get it off."

Part of Kelly wanted to cry in relief, and the other part just wanted to cry because dammit, he was so… so not *there* for the bad shit. Was it just Kelly who knew how bad this could be?

"Seth, man, don't you realize what this could mean?"

Seth turned his head. "It could mean I'm the first chair violinist in Folsom Prison. Do you think I don't know that?"

Kelly had bruised his ass. He couldn't even threaten violence, not even in jest or supreme frustration.

Dammit.

"But Seth, what are you going to—"

Seth's look alone stopped him. "Well, if the police show up at my door, I'm going to answer their questions. They may believe me, they may not believe me. I may go to jail, I may not. If I *do* go to jail, I'll get out, live my life, and hope my boyfriend waited for me. If I *don't*, I'll finish the trial and hope my boyfriend waited for me. Either way, I'll be able to see you and your family and my dad and Chloe, which is something I can't do right now. And I won't have this shit hanging over my head anymore. Did I cover it?"

Kelly sagged into his double bed. "Yeah. Yeah, you covered it. You know, if you get busted, maybe we can hire a super-spiffy lawyer and you can get a book deal out of it."

Seth half laughed. "Yeah. That's my priority. Fame." He sagged into the mattress, suddenly looking as tired as Kelly felt, and it hit Kelly, not for the first time, that Seth was carrying more than a full college load. His classes were performance classes, and in spite of Seth's dreaminess—or maybe because of it—he spent more time in practice for a performance than Kelly knew he spent on homework for regular academic work.

"Sorry." Seth yawned. "Had two performances at the Stomp this week—Fiddler and the Crabs is our name now, and I guess it's caught on. Anyway, the quartet had a couple of gigs and a practice and…." He yawned again. "A gig tomorrow. I hope you don't mind. You can hang out with Amara if you want. Guthrie can take me—"

"Guthrie?" Kelly's palm still stung from that smack, and now he wanted to smack Guthrie's blond surfer face. "Why's he—" Oh yeah. There was no way in hell Kelly wasn't going to *that* performance.

"They wanted someone who can play triangle and xylophone. He's trying to earn money for school, and the ladies in the group seemed to like him." Seth frowned, his eyes small and puffy in the darkness. Kelly was keeping a very tired man up. Seth sagged into the bed. "You like him, right?"

And Kelly had to be honest. "I'd like him more if he loved you less."

Seth grunted. "Don't mind Amara. I think she wanted to crush on Guthrie a little, but I'll tell you something—I don't think he likes women as much as he said he did. I've met some bi guys and girls here at school, and they date or crush on both. But I really think Guthrie's not... you know...."

"Bi?" Kelly couldn't stop his eye roll. "Yeah, I know. And I think Amara's right too." That look on Guthrie's face—the one that said he wanted what was best for Seth, even if it wasn't him. "I think he's been in love with you since Christmas."

Seth whined. "Oh shit. Do you need me to walk away from him? You know, stop seeing him? That would sort of suck—that's both my jobs—"

"No." Kelly wished they were having sex again. "No. Vashti broke up with his boyfriend, and he's been looking at me hopefully again, but I don't want to quit. You don't need to." He sighed and kissed Seth's shoulder with all the tenderness in his heart. "You'd tell me, though, right? You'd tell me if I needed to walk away? You'd say, 'Kelly, I love you, but it's just too hard. Can you walk away?'"

Suddenly Seth's eyes were very wide and very focused. "I will *never* tell you to walk away," he said, and Kelly heard the ring of a vow in his voice. "You will *never* hear me say that."

Kelly felt his lips tilt up, and for a moment, he tried to contain his expression. But he couldn't. It should have been old. They'd been telling each other they were in love for getting close to four years now, but the joy, the pride of it, it hadn't gotten dim or sad or easy.

It had only gotten more intense, more real, with every stolen moment.

"Good," he whispered. "Good."

He fell asleep holding Seth close, his palm still tingling, his heart still raw.

But Seth's vow rang in his ears. "I will *never* tell you to walk away."

It sustained him. It sustained him through the next morning, watching Seth perform in a cheap tuxedo that nobody saw, because he played like an angel—while Guthrie tried not to watch him with limpid, tragic eyes. It fed him through Sunday evening, when he'd had to drive home alone, heart aching, already exhausted by the week ahead.

It sustained him through the next few months, when Seth kept sending him pictures of Fiddler and the Crabs as they played a little holiday tour with Seth as their headliner—Seth said they made a ton.

It was food for Thanksgiving, when Seth couldn't come visit because, sure enough, his picture was on every telephone pole for a mile, but nobody could recognize him because it had been three years, and even Kelly hadn't realized how much softness he'd had around the chin.

Kelly's birthday night was rough. Vashti and the people from work took him out to Gatsby's Nick, and he was too young to be served alcohol, but he went out onto the dance floor and let the music take him over, bopping up and down and losing himself in the press of bodies. When he came off the floor, Vashti insisted on a selfie, him in the middle, Marcos and Clifton in front of him, Vashti kissing his cheek.

He sent it to Seth, not thinking, really, about how Seth must be missing him, but Seth's text to him was a sober reminder.

Do you need me to walk away?

NO! But I wouldn't mind a birthday call tomorrow morning.

Deal.

Seth had called—and flowers had arrived, which had apparently been delayed the day before—and they were okay until the trip to Monterey, but Kelly knew now how they would handle the end if it ever came.

Do you need me to walk away?

Kelly was pretty sure he never could.

The View from Mars

TWO WEEKS before Seth graduated from the conservatory, he walked out of a modest recording studio in San Rafael with Guthrie by his side.

"You boys want to come out and celebrate?" Butch asked, smiling mightily. "It's not every day you cut a record, you know."

"Thanks, Dad, but no," Guthrie said before Seth could accept. It was their last time playing together, and Seth had agreed to cut the record because Butch got a contract. It wasn't forever money—but it was enough to help supplement the Cruz family while Seth was in Italy, with a little leftover for Seth's surprise for Kelly, and a small apartment in Walnut Creek in the three months before Seth's plane took off. Seth had wanted to go closer to Sacramento, but his string quartet had a number of paying gigs then too, and Seth wasn't sure if he'd be able to make money in Italy.

He was supposed to be a headliner, but he also thought he was in a graduate program, so what did he know?

"Well, okay, boy. We'll see you at your graduation, that okay?"

Seth smiled, grateful. "You can meet my dad," he said happily. "And Kelly." They would be coming down too. He was embarrassed at all the attention people were paying, but apparently graduating from college was a big deal.

Since Bridgford had been a little deal, and he hadn't done a high school graduation per se, he was taking people's word for it. He personally was looking forward to seeing Kelly graduate from junior college. *That* was happening the week after Seth's walk across the stage, and he couldn't wait.

They were going to take a trip up the coast, to Mendocino, and see if the ocean close to Oregon was more or less magical than the ocean in Monterey or San Francisco.

They would be together—Seth was voting on more.

"Of course," Butch said, grimacing. "Kelly." Eventually everybody had figured out that Seth was gay. And eventually, Butch and Jock could say Kelly's name without looking at each other like Seth having a boyfriend wasn't out of the fucking park. Every time Seth talked to them about it, he got a little more hopeful that someday, Guthrie would be able to bring a boy home and they wouldn't lose their shit.

Vince had come back from USC his senior year and applied for the San Francisco Conservatory. At first Seth had been baffled—he'd been so adamant that USC was the place he'd be happy.

Apparently, any place Amara wasn't couldn't make Vince happy.

So Amara and Vince had paired off, and Seth had always had Kelly. But Guthrie hadn't dated, really—not girls, not boys—since Christmas, two and a half years before, when he and Seth had gotten beat up and had become friends.

Seth wanted his friend to be happy.

Which meant that what Guthrie wanted right now was important.

"He'll be happy to meet you," Seth said guilelessly. "I've told him so much about you guys."

Jock and Butch nodded uncomfortably, and Guthrie snorted. "You're gonna make their heads explode, Seth. Hop in the truck. I actually made reservations."

Seth wrinkled his nose and looked down at himself. "I'm not dressed," he said, even as he swung into Guthrie's now familiar ancient Chevy pickup. He waved at Jock and Butch, who were looking... well, concerned, and Seth had a moment of doubt. Had Guthrie come out and not told him yet?

"I've got something behind the seat," Guthrie said calmly. *He* was wearing nice slacks and a tie and a jacket. Nobody had told Seth there was a dress code for recording songs you'd been playing for two and a half years. He'd *barely* committed to buying the used tuxedo so he could play with the string quartet.

Seth turned in his seat as Guthrie got on 280, and pulled out a department store garment bag with, oh my God....

"This is new," he mumbled, not sure if that meant what he thought it did.

"It's a present," Guthrie said firmly. "You dress like shit, Seth. If you're going to walk the stage, you need a suit at least, and not the shitty tuxedo you wear for gigs."

"But I'm wearing it to dinner?"

Guthrie sighed. "Yeah. I'm taking you to dinner. At a really fancy place. No, it's not a date unless you want it to be." He kept his eyes on the road and his hands on the wheel, but Seth could see a smile try to climb up the corner of his mouth. "You're going great places, Fiddler. To Italy—and someone's paying you, which is like fucking amazing. And as far as I can tell, every spare penny you make goes to your boyfriend's family, which is super sweet and all, but…." He shook his head. "Just once, just tonight, I'd like to see you dressed pretty and not worried about spending money. This is a gift to myself as well as you. Please accept it."

Seth hung the suit back up behind the truck seat. "Where should I change?"

"We're swinging by my apartment—don't get any ideas. You've got about fifteen minutes to spare."

Seth snorted. "No ideas gotten."

Guthrie's apartment wasn't bad. When they'd first met, Seth had assumed he lived in a double-wide with a Formica table and a sink full of dirty dishes, but it wasn't that at all. A basic suburban apartment, yes, but he had curtains and the leather couches were clean and the TV modest but well placed. He'd put posters on the walls—Kenny Chesney and Blake Shelton and Miranda Lambert—but given how much he loved country music, Seth thought it fit.

Speaking of fit, so did the suit. Very well. Seth buttoned the collar of the beige shirt and tied the bronze-colored tie in surprise. The suit itself was a warm blue, and the contrasting colors looked… well, sort of amazing with Seth's darker skin and his pale hair.

Feeling self-conscious, Seth availed himself of Guthrie's electric razor by the sink and used a little bit of toothpaste on his finger, and hell, some more deodorant, in case what he was wearing decided to quit. It wasn't like Guthrie hadn't slept on the floor of his dorm room enough times. They were buddies, right?

He looked himself in the mirror.

Buddies?

Oh God. He needed to explain the buddies thing.

"Seth—I swear, we're gonna be late!"

Later.

DINNER WAS really good—a steakhouse in San Francisco, overlooking the bay. Guthrie ordered for both of them, even a glass of wine each, which Seth had never done before.

"Seriously?" Guthrie stared at him. "You've never even had wine?"

"I, uh, just turned twenty-two in February," Seth mumbled. "I've been at Bridgford or the conservatory for the past five years. You've seen what I do on the weekends."

Guthrie took a sip of wine. "Yeah, but Seth! Not even beer?"

Seth shrugged, uncomfortable. "My dad was—is an, uh, recovering alcoholic," he muttered. "I didn't like what it did to him."

Guthrie's eyes went wide. "I did not know that. When did he stop drinking?"

Another shrug. "I was in fourth grade. Right after I started playing. He, uh… you know. Got rough with me. Kelly's dad heard and came downstairs and, well, I stayed at Kelly's place for a month, and my dad went to rehab. It was… uh… you know."

"Scary," Guthrie said, setting his wineglass down. "Getting close to three years we've known each other—I never knew this. Is there anything else I should know?"

Seth couldn't even smile or laugh about this. "Lots of things," he said. "But… you know."

"Not gonna tell me."

"You wouldn't like me if you knew," Seth consoled.

Guthrie waved off the waitress, who was asking him if he wanted more wine. "I'm not sure about that. Kelly seems to know all your secrets."

Seth gave a wistful smile. "He's been there longer."

"Yeah." Guthrie gnawed his lower lip. "I… any chance you'd let another guy try to figure you out, Seth?"

Oh. Oh no. Seth looked away and took a quick swallow of wine. "I, uh, Kelly—"

"You can still be part of his family if you two aren't going out. I mean, you guys, you'd still be friends, right?"

Seth frowned. "But what I have… in my chest. When I look at him." Nobody had ever made him articulate this before. "It's like he's a perfect chord. You know, when you hear a perfect chord, you get goose bumps? And your heart gets tight in your chest? And the sun starts leaving halos around people, and you can almost close your eyes and see the whole world spread out beneath your feet?"

"No," Guthrie said, his voice subdued. "I love music, but not like that."

"That's how I love music," Seth explained, in case Guthrie had missed it, right? "That's what looking at Kelly makes me feel."

Guthrie let out a laugh that sounded more like a sob, and he almost pulled his hand through his queued hair, dislodging the rather handsome ponytail at the back of his crown. "Oh, it fucking figures," he said, his voice raw. "The way you love Kelly is just one more thing about you that I'll never understand."

Seth knew his eyes were burning. "I'm sorry," he whispered. "I... I knew you loved me a long time ago. I just... you were just such a good friend. I loved playing with you so much. I should have just—"

Guthrie shook his head. "Don't say it." He rubbed his own eyes with his palm. "Playing with you the last few years—it's been... it's been the *best*. Going back to school, picking up something else besides my day job waiting tables? Playing music with someone as good as you? I... I wouldn't trade our friendship for another heart three times as broken." His voice cracked on the word *broken*, and he didn't say anything else for a couple of moments.

Seth's head buzzed, and he wasn't sure if it was the wine or the emotion.

He dedicated himself to his steak, just in case it was the wine, and after a few awful bites, he tried to wipe his blurry eyes on his shoulder.

"Stop," Guthrie said, humor lacing his voice. Seth looked up in time to see him pull a handkerchief from his pocket, like someone who'd practiced wearing a suit. "Here." He reached across the table and mopped up Seth's face, pausing at his nose so he could blow if he needed to. When he was done, he folded the handkerchief carefully and put it back in his pocket. "There. You can plow through that steak some more if you want to. Or we can go back to before you broke my heart and we can enjoy ourselves some more."

"Yes, please," Seth said weakly.

"Good. What's Amara going to do after graduation?"

"Well, she and Vince both got offered jobs down in LA," Seth said. "I think they're moving down there. I'm going to Italy, and I guess they promised they'd put out my portfolio recording when I was done and submit it around. Hopefully I'll end up in San Francisco again."

"Why not Sacramento?" Guthrie asked, taking a casual bite of steak, as if this wasn't the goddamned $64,000 question.

"I, uh, can't really go back right now," Seth mumbled. Guthrie had never asked. Never once, after that first night. Why Kelly came down to see Seth way more than Seth ever went to see Kelly.

Guthrie's eyes narrowed. "This have anything to do with how worried you get when we beat assholes in a fight?" Twice more, for a total of four times, they'd been jumped at the Stomp. The last time had been in front of Butch and Jock. Seth had used kicking and elbows on his guy, Guthrie used fists and fury, but it had been quick work to get rid of the hecklers who'd yelled obscenities at Seth during their entire set.

Word had gotten around, apparently, after that last time. Nobody had heckled Seth since.

"I... uh...," Seth stammered, and Guthrie shook his head.

"Never mind. You already told me it wasn't your first fight. I just... all this time later and there's a lot of shit I don't know about you, Fiddler. But the one thing I'm pretty sure I do know is that you couldn't have done anything so bad you can't go home."

"It doesn't matter if I did it or not," Seth blurted, apparently weakened by emotional honesty like any other human. "What matters is Kelly's brother can use... use the *threat* of what they think I did to take back custody of his daughter." Chloe—ah, God love her. She'd be four this August, and she was gradually creeping up through those milestones, mostly because the girls and Kelly worked with her every chance they got.

Something in her precious little brain had been broken when she was a baby, or even before, in the womb. Her hands didn't work the way they should. Her balance and coordination were off. Her language skills were two years behind. Kelly's mom had gotten her enrolled in special preschool programs to help—she'd be getting on a bus that August to go to school, which terrified the entire family, because she was so damned tiny. Craig and Linda and Kelly were scrambling to find a way to drive her to and from preschool that wouldn't interfere with Kelly's school schedule. Lily and Lulu were almost ready to drive—if Seth could get enough money together to buy them a car, *they* could help transport Chloe and Agnes, and that would help immeasurably, but it couldn't happen until Seth got back from Italy at the earliest.

"That would be bad?" Guthrie asked, pulling Seth from the incessant worry of the Cruz family and how to help keep them afloat.

"Matty isn't...." Seth closed his eyes. "We used to be close," he said, and he and Kelly knew this story so much, that pain was rawer than it should have been. "We used to be friends. And then... I mean, I know what we *think* happened, but I don't know what *really* happened. What we *think* happened was bad enough. Anyway, got really awful. About me and Kelly together. About me in particular. He's in and out of rehab. The last one seems to have stuck for the drugs, but he's drinking too. Just… he and his wife, they just… they go to church and then act… not godly," he finished, feeling weak. "We don't want her to go with them."

Guthrie nodded and pinched the bridge of his nose. "Seth, you… you have the problems of an old man. Do you realize that?"

"So does Kelly."

Guthrie nodded, and then grimaced. For the first time Seth heard the unspoken thing, the thing that had never occurred to him.

If he broke up with Kelly, he wouldn't have any of Kelly's problems.

He actually pondered that for a moment, and then remembered Chloe, as she'd been when he'd snuck up to Sacramento that spring break. She'd spent as much time as possible on Seth's lap, making him read her cardboard books, making him play violin for her, making him sing. The stuffed animal collection that had started out as Kelly's and then, piece by piece, had become the girls', had been passed down to Chloe, and he'd brought her a new set of them, complete with a backpack to carry them. She'd worn the backpack every day, and Seth had played with her until she'd fallen asleep.

The rest of the family had assured him that they needed the break—and he could believe it. Chloe needed. Constantly needed. He only had to fill her void for a week at a time.

But he'd loved that week. Besides seeing Kelly and his father, he loved being her person, the grown person she loved more than anything.

The thought of Italy was killing him.

"They're my problems too," he said softly. "I… I can't—"

Guthrie actually touched his hand. "I hear you. I'm sorry I even brought it up. Here. Let's finish. We can have dessert."

The trip home was easier. They talked about what Guthrie's dad's band would do without Seth, and how Seth had put in a word at the conservatory to see if they could find themselves another "fiddler." There were lots of kids who liked country music, Seth told him. He was pretty sure they'd have a replacement before Seth's plane took off.

"For the band, maybe," Guthrie said as they pulled up to the gates of the conservatory. It wasn't actually in the city proper—it was situated on the peninsula, another big campus like Bridgford but so much closer to the sea. "Not for me."

Seth opened his mouth, and Guthrie held up a hand.

"Look, I'm going to ask something huge," he said. "And you can say no, and either way I'll still be in the audience when you graduate because you're my friend. But I'm going to ask anyway, okay?"

"Sure."

"I'm going to get you to your dorm and then you're going to look at me like this was an ordinary date. But before you grab your violin from behind the seat, and your bundle of clothes, just close your eyes and let me kiss you. Like we might have another one. Like…." Seth could hear it, how hard it was to ask. "Like you might love me someday, like I might have a chance. I know I don't. I know you can't. But… but maybe, just maybe, one kiss and I can go on with my life, okay?"

"Guthrie—" He was going to say no.

"Because you're right. I do love you. And I don't love you any less after tonight. And I won't love you any less when you leave. It's going to take time, you understand? And maybe when you're in Italy and not… not in my truck four times a week, saying things that don't make any sense to anybody but the people who know you, maybe *then* I can fall in love with someone else. But right now, I just want one kiss, so when I kiss someone else, I know what it's like to kiss someone I love."

"Okay."

Guthrie swallowed quickly, like he hadn't expected that. "Okay?"

Seth gave a wobbly smile and grabbed his stuff first, because he could see the exit was going to be everything here. "Good night, Guthrie," he said, his lips quirking just a little. "I had a really nice time. The meal was wonderful. And I really enjoyed your company." His voice hitched at this next part. Maybe because it was a little true. "It would be nice to do it again sometime."

Guthrie nodded, like he understood this game. "Good night, Seth. I had a great time too. I loved getting to know you some more. I'd love to do it again sometime too."

He lowered his head then, and Seth closed his eyes, accepting the warmth of Guthrie's mouth on his. He didn't expect the attraction or the urge to respond, but he opened his mouth and let the kiss deepen, giving back some, letting Guthrie cup his cheek and tangle tongues together.

Guthrie pulled back then, his eyes bright and shiny. "That was real good," he whispered.

Seth nodded. He knew now—knew it didn't have to be Kelly to make his body feel good. But he also knew kissing anybody else but Kelly only made his heart lonelier than the moon.

"You're a really good kisser," he said, lips twisting. "Drive safe, Guthrie. Text me when you get home. I don't have many friends I care about like I care about you. I need you to keep safe."

"Will do."

Seth slid out of the truck with his clothes and his violin case in hand, and waved as Guthrie pulled away.

He got back to his dorm room and pulled out his phone, unsurprised to see a text from Kelly.

So, how'd recording go?

Good. Butch thinks we'll make some money there.

How's Guthrie?

Seth swallowed. He never could hide things from Kelly.

He decided to walk away. I gave him a kiss goodbye—I hope that's okay.

The phone buzzed in his hand.

"Are *you* okay?" God, his voice sounded so good. So warm. Seth's eyes spilled over again.

"Not really. I mean, we're still going to be friends but… but it hurt. I hurt him. I didn't ever want to hurt him."

"Yeah, baby. I know."

"He asked me how I knew I loved you."

He heard Kelly's gasp on the other end. "What did you say?"

"I said you were a perfect chord. You were so beautiful you made light and sound better. Looking at you, I heard the best music, the kind not even angels can play."

Kelly let out what sounded to be a half-broken laugh. "Wow. That's how you feel about me?"

"Yeah. I'll be honest, Kelly. If I didn't know what I feel about you, I'd be tempted to say what I felt for him was love."

"But it's not, right?"

Seth's heart constricted. "No, baby. Just as a friend. Like I love Amara. You're… you're Kelly. It's like comparing Folsom Lake to the ocean."

"It's a good thing you've got game, Seth, or I'd be worried."

Seth couldn't laugh. "It's not a game," he said roughly. "This thing in my chest, for you. I mean… it's been there so long, right? We were kids. It's been… what? Five years? And you'd think it would get weaker. Like, we see each other maybe twice a month. But it's not. It's getting worse. It's getting more painful to be gone. It's getting harder every time we have to walk away. And most days, I can put a damper on it, I can muffle the sound of my heart screaming. But… but tonight my nerves are all raw, and I can't… I can't make it silent tonight. I'm sorry—"

He cried then, helplessly, like he did sometimes when they were in bed and Kelly had to leave, or like Kelly did, usually their first day alone for a long week. His body had to purge, the loneliness, the anger, the things it held back when the other half of his heart was far away, connected by the fragile string of love.

SOMETHING ABOUT their trip to Mendocino was different.

Maybe it was the hotel room—small and close, with the roar of the sea right outside. They ran on the beach together in the morning, did something in the nearby town in the afternoon, and then….

There was nothing but them and the king-sized bed.

All Seth knew was that the evening they arrived—Kelly driving, of course, because it was something he'd still never had time to learn—they had checked in and set the bags on the ground, and Kelly had suddenly been… hot.

His skin had been heated from the car, of course, but Seth couldn't look at him without his heart hammering in his chest and his breath catching. He'd dropped his suitcase in the middle of the floor and stared.

"What?" Kelly rubbed irritably at his nose. "Cliffhanger?"

Seth squinted at him. "No."

"What?"

Seth's skin prickled—everywhere. His scalp, his neck, his shoulders, his buttocks… his *cock.*

He opened his mouth and closed it, and finally managed to croak, "I want."

"You want what?" But Kelly was smirking, his eyes lighting up from within, and he removed the baseball hat he'd worn to shade his face.

"I want." Seth licked his lips, and his palms broke into a sweat. He could hardly breathe.

They'd gone out for dinner after his graduation, and then everybody had gone home, leaving Seth in his dorm room again.

Alone.

He'd shown up for Kelly's graduation from junior college and slid in through the crowd, ignoring anybody who looked like they knew him. They didn't know him, even if he'd had classes with them in high school, in junior high, in grade school.

The only people who knew him were sitting in the middle, saving a seat for him.

He took it, and Chloe clambered over Lily and Lulu's laps to come coo on his. It was just that easy. Every damned time.

After the morning graduation, they'd gone out to eat again, mostly, Seth suspected, so he could talk to the girls and hold Chloe. Lily and Lulu were finishing up their first year of high school, and they wanted Seth to know that they were tied for third in their class, right behind Sheila Thompson and Alex Crawford, and that they *would* overtake their foes on the field of academic battle if they had to leave blood on the ground.

Agnes had rolled her eyes and whispered, "I get to be in *plays* next year. Eighth grade is gonna *rock.*"

And Chloe—Chloe had clung to him, humming her favorite lullaby, saying his name occasionally and showing him the new stuffie he'd sent her the week before.

They'd had to pry her out of his arms when he'd gotten into Kelly's Toyota to leave.

And that had been it. So familiar. Seth comes, Seth throws everybody into an uproar, Seth leaves. He'd chatted with Kelly, catching up as human beings, listening to him destress about finals, filling in with details about Italy they hadn't discussed yet, and it had all been very… normal.

Very… everyday. Happy, but with that undercurrent of not enough that had tempered every heartbeat of his life for the last five years.

Until this moment here, when Seth couldn't fucking breathe, and his cock felt like it was going to split at the seams, and Kelly was all he could see.

"You want?" Kelly asked, his voice suddenly gruff, low.

A man's voice.

Seth's mouth was so dry. "I want."

He took two strides across the room. Kelly met him halfway, and they were on each other, devouring, voracious. Seth couldn't taste him enough, couldn't touch his skin enough. Their clothes fell where they stood, Kelly's capable hands splitting Seth's old T-shirt from the neck down where it fluttered to his feet.

"Lube," Kelly muttered, shoving Seth's pants down around his ankles while Seth kicked off his shoes. "Now. Not joking. Fucking now."

"Cocoa butter in my pocket." Seth always kept a small tube, because his hands got chapped on the strings.

"Bend over."

For a moment, he was exposed, his ass thrust out behind him as he leaned over the bed. Kelly's fingers shoved lube roughly around his entrance, and just the rasp of his skin, in and out, was enough to make Seth spurt precome over the comforter.

"Good enough?"

"Now," Seth gasped. "Fuck me right now."

His body was shaking, needing—it was beyond want. It had become air and water, sun and rain, how he needed Kelly inside him.

Kelly wasn't gentle, but they'd worked up to this, to roughness, to every touch not being spun glass and cotton batting. They were human, made of flesh, and their flesh had its demands.

Kelly's cock *demanded* entrance to his asshole, and his asshole *demanded* Kelly be inside him. Kelly battered his way in and both of them groaned, but Seth's arms still shook as they supported him, and he felt a droplet of Kelly's sweat spatter in the small of his back.

"Yes," Seth growled. "Yes. *Yes. Yes. Yes. Yes. Yes. Now!*"

Kelly held nothing back. His hips shot forward, bounced away, and shot forward again. He mauled Seth's exposed body—his flanks, his thighs, his ass—with greedy hands, and he fucked and fucked, hard and without apology, while Seth saw fireworks behind his eyes at every stroke.

For a wild moment, there was nothing in that room but the sound of their flesh slapping, their grunts, growls tearing from both throats.

Seth was close, so close, driven to climax brutally fast, and Kelly was panting like a runner behind him. "Harder!" he begged, and Kelly squeezed his backside hard, his hand stuttering, rubbing sweetly when Seth needed the bite of pain.

"Do it," he begged. "Harder!"

"Baby—"

"*Harder!*"

Kelly's hand came whistling out of nowhere, cracking across his ass in a stinging slap.

Seth convulsed, squeezing Kelly's cock unmercifully, groaning from his toes as he came. Kelly cried out behind him, rutting in a frenzy as he poured himself into Seth's body, rocking them both with aftershocks.

Kelly toppled over his back and Seth sank to his knees, his chest sliding through the semen puddle on the comforter.

"We're here," Kelly said weakly.

"Go us." Seth blinked against the spots in front of his eyes. "I'll get on the bed if you get off me."

"Sure. In a minute."

Seth chuckled as Kelly draped over his shoulders. "Don't want to get up yet?"

"I don't want to stop touching you."

Seth sighed, his face mashed up against the bed, knees aching. "Then don't. I'm good right here."

Eventually they did get up. Seth pulled down the covers and got in bed while Kelly ran to the bathroom and came back with a warm washcloth that he used to wipe himself off.

"I'll take that." Seth extended a hand, but Kelly waved him off.

"Nope. Gonna do it."

Seth grunted, uncertain, and rolled to his side.

"You're embarrassed *now*?" Kelly shoved playfully at his shoulder. "Sorry, *mijo*. That boat has sailed." He started rubbing the cloth along Seth's stomach and groin, making observations as he went.

"And who gave you permission, that's what I want to know."

"What did I do now?"

"Hair. You've got hair on your chest, you've got hair on your upper thighs, hair on your balls—" Seth moved to cover said balls, and Kelly batted his hands away and washed him tenderly. "Gonna have to stop calling you *mijo* and start calling you *papi.*"

"Doesn't that mean daddy? I mean, isn't that icky?"

Kelly shrugged. "Vote's still out. As far as I can tell, it's pretty evenly divided among Latino gay guys. Some of them go 'Ick!' and some of them go 'Hel*lo* Daddy!'"

Seth snickered. "Let's not."

"Well, I *could* call you *papacito,* but, uh…." He ran the washcloth lovingly up and down Seth's shaft, which was starting to fill again with his touch.

"Not small?" Rulers had never been Seth's thing, but he was pretty sure he'd grown in the past few years.

"No, Seth. It wasn't small when we started, and it isn't small now."

Seth smiled slowly. "Natural ability—not gonna knock it."

Kelly snickered and rubbed the washcloth along Seth's stomach. "It would be a totally sexy washboard, but you don't eat enough."

Seth grunted. "Always too many things to do," he said plaintively. "It's so weird, when we take vacations. There's nothing to do but eat and practice."

Kelly pinned him with a hard glare. "You had better be talking about practicing sex," he ordered, and then his hot mouth engulfed Seth's rapidly cooling prick.

"Yeah, sure," Seth gasped, rolling over to his back. "We should totally practice that some more."

Kelly chuckled around his head and then reached around to rub Seth's backside. Seth hummed, because he could still feel the sting, but it had been a slap, not a blow, and he knew Kelly had flattened his hand for maximum sound, minimum force.

"It's fine," he murmured, massaging Kelly's scalp through his longish hair. "You did it just perfectly."

Kelly pulled Seth in to the root and then sucked backward, releasing his head with a pop.

"Don't want to hurt you again," he said gruffly before plying his tongue.

"Won't—ahh!"

Kelly was relentless, sucking hard, and harder, then using the cocoa butter again to relube Seth's entrance and play with strong fingers. Seth braced both feet against the bed and spread his knees, hands flailing on the comforter.

Kelly pulled back and said, "Play with your nipples, dumbass. You know what you like."

Seth propped himself up on his elbows and wrinkled his nose. "While you watch?"

Kelly's eyes—pupil's blown with passion—went to half-mast. "I could watch you do things to yourself and come all over your face without touching my cock," he threatened. "Do *not* underestimate how sexy I think you are."

Seth groaned and fell backward, fingers plucking at his nipples, thighs already trembling, Kelly's fingers lodged solidly in his ass.

His body hit a high, a plane of existence where pleasure was the only goal, and he sailed there, shaking, until he couldn't have stopped himself from begging if he'd been gagged with Kelly's cock.

Kelly shoved his thighs up to his shoulders and thrust inside again. Round two.

When they were done, they *finally* went out to eat, and when they came back, they took a walk under the stars.

Seth turned Kelly in his arms and kissed him, their blood heating to a boil at the first touch of their lips.

Kelly took him a final time that night, bent over a picnic table under cover of fog on the deserted beach.

Round three.

They were just getting started.

By the end of their first week, they were both deeply grateful for Seth's cocoa butter—and Seth was starting to feel like he sloshed when he walked.

The morning of their sixth day, Kelly started kissing his way down Seth's chest and Seth stopped him, kissing Kelly's shoulder, his bicep, his nipple, all the way down to Kelly's cock, which had gotten thicker since they were younger, if not longer.

"Mm… this is a good plan too," Kelly mumbled, and Seth fumbled for the cocoa butter, which was never very far away. He played with Kelly's cockhead for a few moments, teasing, letting his breath, his lips, the gentle edge of his teeth do things for Kelly that plain suction couldn't, and just when Kelly started getting squirmy, he took him in completely, sucking hard and thoroughly, from root to tip.

When he got to the end, he let Kelly flop out, hitting his abdomen with a solid thwack, and fumbled with Kelly's fingers, opening the cocoa butter and scooping a generous portion onto them.

Then he spread Kelly's legs and guided his hand to his own hole, pushing slightly, making Kelly thrust, rubbing the cocoa butter into his own tight orifice, letting him set his own speed.

Kelly grunted, shifting his hips for better access. "This is… this isn't bad, *mijo*. This… this is sort of good…. Ooh… that stretches. That…

I keep thinking it's gonna hurt, but it's my own fingers, right? No pain. Just… mmm…. That's nice. I like that. I'll do that again."

Seth smiled, then shifted to Kelly's other side and resumed his blowjob, making sure that Kelly's penetration with his own fingers took the center stage.

His cock stayed hard—got harder, in fact—and Seth kept playing, kept teasing, kept stroking. Kelly's movements got stronger, more assured, and then, as things got awkward, more frantic.

"I… I can't…. Seth, I want more. I want more and harder. I can't go fast enough…. *Seth, please!*"

There was enough cocoa butter for Seth to pull Kelly's hand away and slide two fingers in easily, and Kelly moaned in welcome as he thrust them in to the hilt and sucked him down until his cock bottomed out in Seth's throat.

"More," Kelly gasped, and Seth added another finger, stretching and pumping, sucking and stroking, keeping things firm and hard—but not rough.

"Ah!" Kelly bucked against his throat. "Please… please give me one more chance," he begged. "C'mon, Seth. I need to be fucked so bad!"

They'd never gotten this far before.

Seth took a leap of faith and moved between Kelly's knees, pulling his thighs up so they were on his shoulders, finding his asshole with the head of his cock and pausing, poised at the entrance. "Sure you're ready?"

"*Fuck me!*"

Seth thrust in.

"*Yes!*" Kelly's back arched off the bed as he sought to drive himself farther down on Seth's cock. There was no hesitation. No pain. No fear.

Seth pulled out so he could fuck forward again. Oh God. Kelly was so tight. So willing. Abandoned, sprawled out on the bed, all of the fears and worries he harbored—every fucking day—scattered as he lost himself to Seth's invasion.

His face had fallen slack, ecstatic and dreamy, even as Seth picked up the pace.

"Mm…. Seth, this is so good. Man, if I'd known it was this good, you would have been fucking me for *years!*"

Seth just kept thrusting, not stating the obvious—Kelly had needed to relax enough for this to feel good, and he hadn't been ready until just this minute.

But they would have time to talk about that later.

Right now, Seth was losing himself in the warmth and safety of his lover's body, and his skin started to prickle as he approached a mighty crest.

"Kelly!" he cried out, not wanting it to end so soon. "Let me see you stroke—"

Kelly grabbed his own prick, hand squeezing tightly, like he loved it most, and with that, just that, a convulsion rippled through his body as he came.

Seth exploded into his ass.

Together they shuddered, coming without stop, as though they hadn't been banging each other silly for the last seven days.

It was Seth's turn to fall forward over Kelly's body. Seth's turn to feel the richness of the heat where his cock remained, sliding in come. Seth's job to kiss Kelly's temples, nuzzling his cheeks and peppering his shoulders and collarbone with tiny kisses of praise.

"So good," he whispered. "God, you feel so good. You were so tight. I hope that felt as good to you as it did to me—"

"Amazing," Kelly mumbled. "Amazing. But God, I think I'm useless for the whole rest of the day. I'm all high now, floaty from that. How do you even function after sex like that?"

Seth took his mouth and didn't bother to answer.

He was thinking that music put him under, just like submission did. He was thinking that sex always felt like the next step on the staircase to heaven.

If that was true, then they must have gotten to heaven while they were in Mendocino that year. So many things they had planned—more driving up the coast, hiking through the redwoods, trips to lighthouses.

They spent most of their time in that tiny hotel room, naked and wanting, panting and lunging, sated and wearing each other's come on their skin.

They would return and spend the rest of the summer getting together every weekend, sometimes with the family, sometimes not. But always, always, they spent Saturday night at the very least in Seth's apartment, getting so good at sex it was like they were training for a medal.

But they both knew what they were really training for.

Seth came home the three days before he left for Italy. He spent the time in the apartments, playing with Chloe mostly, but also keeping company with his dad, Kelly's mom, Kelly's sisters.

His family.

He must have said, "I'll Skype every Saturday, I promise!" about fifteen hundred times.

The night before he left, he and Kelly spent all night in his room, talking about everything and nothing at all. Kelly and his father were taking him to the airport the next morning—he was flying out of Sacramento to LAX at 6:00 a.m.

At 3:00 a.m., Seth's alarm went off, and he pulled Kelly closer, smelling his hair, his neck, the sweat that the warm August night had left on his body.

And Seth said the one fear he'd kept back since the trip to Italy had come up two years before. "You won't forget about me, will you? Even if you... if you walk away, you won't forget?"

Kelly shook his head. "You're so dumb, sometimes. No. No, Seth. I will never forget you. And I will never walk away."

Seth should have told him it was okay. Seth was going to be all the way across the world—Kelly had a right to live his life.

But he didn't.

He couldn't.

"Neither will I," he whispered.

They dropped him off in the still darkness, with a child's checklist for getting on the plane—including keeping track of the passport that Kelly had needed to help him acquire. He'd never been on a plane before.

As he stepped through the doors to the terminal, he looked back and saw his father holding on to Kelly like he was still a kid, both of them waving even though Seth should have been inside long before. Seth waved back madly and then turned away, wiping his face on his shoulder.

A year, right?

What was a year after two weeks of Mendocino and a lifetime of being in love?

Dancing Alone

"No, YOU can't come in." Kelly folded his arms in front of him and glared at his brother.

"Where's Mom?" Matty looked like shit. His hair, always cut close in high school, had grown out, but it didn't fall straight like Kelly's and then curl—instead it stood up in a thousand cowlicks. His face was lined already, at twenty-three, and his beard was past the stubble stage and into full grown Astroturf. He was wearing cargo shorts in late November and a dress shirt with a thousand stains on it, including one that looked like vomit.

And he smelled like a brewery.

And vomit.

"Mom is at the movies," Kelly said, proud of this, because he'd managed to shove Linda out and into Craig's car again this month.

Apparently this habit had started during the summer. The girls were all old enough to babysit, and God, if anybody deserved a break it was Mom. And she seemed to enjoy Craig Arnold's undemanding company, which Kelly didn't mind at all.

More than once in the past months, she'd gone downstairs carrying his dinner and had ended up staying and watching TV.

Kelly had thought he should go down and see if the drapes were drawn or if there was a two-inch gap in the front that showed him enough to be scarred for life.

At first the thought had made him chuckle, but then he'd think about his father and about those moments with Seth and about how badly his mother deserved something, anything at all that made her happy, and he decided he wouldn't go look after all.

"She left the kids home alone?" Matty asked, frowning, and Kelly rolled his eyes.

"I'm about to turn twenty-one, dickhead. The twins are fifteen. Hell, Agnes is twelve and can stay here by herself if she wanted to. You got four people here who can watch your daughter for you—don't fuckin' worry."

Behind him, he heard Chloe getting excited. "Set? Set? Set, where are 'oo?"

Seth talked to her at least once a week over Skype, and Kelly was pretty sure his sisters called him up when Kelly was at night school too. Not that Kelly didn't have his own ways and times to talk to Seth, but he had to admit, he always felt a little jealous when he got home and his niece was asleep in her crib, hugging the latest stuffed animal Seth had sent her, humming to herself.

It wasn't a warm pair of arms—no. But Seth's face, his voice, his smile, on that little screen, had started to take on an enormous role in Kelly's dreams. Sometimes after Seth signed off, he'd stroke the screen with his fingertips and remember the summer when even for a short time, they'd been able to sate themselves on skin.

But Matty heard his daughter's voice, and his face closed down like a thundercloud. "Is he here?" he asked, trying to shoulder his way into the apartment. Kelly stood his ground, blocking with his shoulders. Sure, back in high school Matty had the advantage—he had been muscular and quick. But Kelly was horny and lonely, and he had access to the gym and a sand bag, and he could beat Matty on his worst day in his sleep right now.

"No, he's not here!" Kelly had to laugh at that one. "Oh my God, if *only* he was here."

"My own daughter barely even talks to me, and you let her be in the company of that psychopath? And you think that's funny?"

"He's in Italy right now," Lulu said, coming up over Kelly's shoulder. "I dare you to find him. And she doesn't talk to you because you show up once a week and try to get in her face. She's got to know you before she likes you." Lulu wrinkled her nose. "But not now. God, Matty, take a shower."

Lulu disappeared, and Matty was left, bewildered.

"Isela wouldn't let me hold her. She said she was the mom, it was her job. I don't know how… I don't know how to hold her. Italy? Did you say Italy?"

"You can't hold her when you're like this." Against his better judgment, Kelly felt his sympathies stirring. God, Matty. They'd grown up loved. They'd grown up *loved.* He wasn't sure what had made Isela, her circle of friends, her church, so attractive, but the puzzlement in Matty's eyes right now was killing him. "Think about Dad, Matty. He left for a month to go to rehab because he didn't want to be around us drunk. Remember that? That was his own free will, you know? He only wanted to be his best self for us." Kelly used his shoulder to gesture. "Is this really how you want your kid to see you?"

"I… I don't know what to do," he rasped, scrubbing his mouth with a hand that looked like he'd been chain smoking his whole life. "Isela… just disappeared. I hear about her, this guy, that guy, and I'm all alone in the apartment. I got nobody. Nobody, Kelly. Remember us, growing up? All the noise, Mom and Dad talking, us kids raising hell, and I thought, 'God, I just want some quiet in my own fucking head.' But it got quiet, and it's awful. It's fuckin' awful. And I'm all… I'm all alone."

Fuck. Oh fuck. Kelly took a deep breath and held up his hand. "Wait there."

He closed the door behind him and saw his sisters looking at him with varying degrees of skepticism.

"Thoughts?" Like they wouldn't tell him what they were thinking.

"Hell no." That was his Lulu, but Lily grimaced.

"He's all alone, Lu. I mean… he used to be a real person and everything."

"Yes," Agnes said, but then her shoulders slumped. "I just don't want to be here when he's here. And he's so weird with Chloe. And now he's just gonna be weirder. Never mind. No. Yes. Darn."

Kelly half laughed and reached into his pocket to pull out the key to downstairs. He'd never given it back—still, in fact, used it two or three times a week. If things got too loud, if his sisters were making him crazy, if he needed a quiet place to study, there was always Seth's apartment, where Seth's room held more of Kelly's clothes and books than Seth's things, and where Seth's dad was always happy to see his son's boyfriend, and not just because of the connection to his son.

"I want this back," he said soberly, and the girls nodded back. Even Chloe, who had ceased to wiggle in Agnes's arms. "Pack a bag for Chloe. Lulu, bring the porta crib—set it up in Seth's room. Craig's got groceries and cable. I'll get him showered, get him sober, kick him out in the morning. Deal?"

The girls all nodded, and Kelly turned back and opened the door, prepared to give Matty sanctuary and a little bit of home.

But Matty was gone. Kelly could hear his feet clattering on the bottom stair even as he called out his brother's name.

"Never mind," he said softly, closing the door. He expected his sisters to all look relieved, but they didn't. Lily wiped her eyes on the inside of her flowered shirt, and Agnes's lower lip wobbled.

And to Kelly's horror, his own eyes burned.

With a terrible little sound in his throat that was *not* a whimper, he opened his arms and they all rushed in, hugging hard and deep, not one of them talking about the cut in their hearts that kept bleeding, the death that recurred daily, the loss they couldn't lose.

THREE DAYS later, Kelly's phone buzzed as he walked down L Street on Saturday night. He checked it, thinking Vashti and Edgar weren't usually so impatient, and saw Seth's name instead.

Are you having a good birthday?

Seth had sent him flowers.

Fucking flowers. Kelly had opened the box in shock. The card read, *I always wanted to do this at school,* and Kelly had looked at the arrangement—red roses and white carnations, classic!—and smiled, hoping he could manage not to sob like a big sap, because he'd expected his twenty-first birthday to be crap from beginning to end.

He had texted Seth a picture, then one of each of the girls tucking a rose or carnation into her ponytail so they could look pretty at school and then one of himself with the rest of the arrangement behind him.

He'd put on a smile—he hoped—because the gesture was lovely, but inside....

He couldn't shake the sadness, the need.

He hadn't told Seth about his encounter with Matty on the landing three nights ago. Hadn't told him that Vashti had broken up with his last boyfriend and was going with Edgar, who was a douchewaffle. Had stopped telling him about how Chloe had days when she ran around the apartment chanting, "Set? Set where a' oo?" and then crying when it turned out that he really *wasn't* there, and she had to listen to the recording of *For Kelly #6,* his latest, that Seth had recorded with an entire orchestra behind him—and apparently, had sold and was touring to promote, for money, because Seth kept sending that too.

Just voicing these things hurt him.

Kelly wasn't sure he could say them to Seth without losing his shit.

But God, he had to lose something. Anything. So when Vashti had asked him to go out dancing at Gatsby's Nick with him and Edgar the Douchewaffle, Kelly had said yes.

It didn't matter that Edgar was one of those flirty assholes who tried to touch him too much, or that sometimes the club scene freaked him out.

What mattered was that, as of that morning, drinking was legal, Vashti had promised to have his back, and he'd taken a Lyft to the club.

God, something needed to give.

Yeah! He lied to Seth. *Going dancing!*

Have fun. Call me when you're done. I need to tell you something.

Kelly frowned at the phone. *Something bad?*

No. Something great! But later. Have fun. I love you!

And Kelly wanted to call him *right then*, but the music from the club was already clouding the air, and Vashti was probably already inside, but Edgar was standing in front, waving him in, his blond hair spectacularly coiffed and that weird dorky predatory grin on his pale face.

It didn't matter. Edgar was incidental.

I love you back, he texted, and he shoved his phone into his jeans with his wallet. A part of him gave a huge sigh of relief. No talking. No baring his soul. He gave his coat to the coat-check girl, made sure everything was secure in his back pocket, and hit the dance floor like a demon screaming from God.

Two hours later—and three vodka shots down—he was still dancing, but not even the sweat and the movement and the screaming calf muscles could drive the devil out of him.

Suddenly he was just really lonely, even in the middle of all those people.

Suddenly he needed to talk to Seth more than he needed to breathe.

He turned to leave, making his way to Vashti to bail, when he felt an unmistakable hand on his ass.

He whirled, unleashing a quick punch, before he even knew who it was. "Back off!"

Edgar was clutching his chest and looking indignant. "Dude, I was just wondering where you were going!"

"Taking off!" Kelly yelled over the crowd. Hell, he didn't want to get into this. All the rubbing, the grinding—yeah, it had made him horny, and the only place he had to go was to his room, which he shared with the world's loneliest four-year-old. God, even if he took the easy way out and slept at Seth's apartment, he couldn't fap off in Seth's bed with his father in the next room. But that's what his body was screaming for, dying for Seth's voice, at the very least, and a dark room, and his own hands on his skin if he couldn't have Seth's.

"Are you sure?" Edgar's smile turned skeezy. "You know, we're pretty good on the dance floor." He took two steps right up into Kelly's personal space and put his hands on Kelly's hips. "You, me—we could go out back and take a breather."

Kelly turned around fast enough to catch Edgar with his elbow. "No. Now fuck off. I'm gonna go say night to Vashti."

Vashti, who'd been buying the drinks, at least deserved Kelly's respect. "Vashti! Man, I gotta go!"

Vashti turned around and then shoved Kelly out of the way. Edgar stumbled by, his fist coming down, because apparently he'd been swinging at Kelly while his back was turned.

"Classy," Kelly muttered, tripping him so he'd go sprawling.

Edgar hit the floor on his hands and knees, and Kelly turned back to his boss and friend. "Man, I gotta get out of here," he begged. "Like… like now. Thanks for the drinks, but…." He was almost crying. Even Edgar's warmth had felt inviting—and it hadn't been invited in the least.

His body was crying out for a lover's touch, and here it was, for free in every corner of the dance floor. Only he couldn't afford to take it.

"Yeah." Vashti scowled at Edgar and grabbed Kelly by the elbow, hauling him toward the door. "No worries. You want to go somewhere else?"

Kelly shook his head. He did, but he didn't want to tell Vashti where. "I'm gonna go home," he said, his voice still projecting above the crowd. "Thanks for the drinks, man. So much. You're a good friend."

Vashti gave him a crooked smile. "That's nice of you to say, given my boyfriend just groped you without consent." His smile faded. "Text me tomorrow. You can commiserate with me on being newly single."

Kelly closed his eyes and hugged his friend, hard.

Hard enough for Vashti to feel what was going on in his tight jeans. Vashti pulled away with raised eyebrows and too much hope. "You, uh, sure you don't want to, uh, commiserate with me?"

Kelly shook his head and backed away. "Tomorrow!" he promised, and then ran from the club the same way he'd run into it.

Like he was running from his problems and couldn't go fast enough.

Ever.

The wait for the Uber gave him a chance to cool down, and he was almost coherent when the driver got to him.

"A cheap hotel," he said. "Someplace not gross. Just not home."

"Know a place," the guy said. "Five-dollar ride, ninety-nine a night."

A chain hotel, near the airport—it was all Kelly needed. He checked in and practically ran for the room and slammed the door behind him as he stripped off his club clothes and jumped in the shower.

His cock stayed hard in the shower, and he barely dried off. Just stripped down the bed and grabbed his phone, still naked, throwing himself on top of the sheets with the little bottle of complimentary lotion in his other hand.

He didn't even have time to open the lotion.

He just closed his eyes, thought of Seth, grabbed his cock, and stroked.

One, two, three, *fuck*! The first jets of come hit his chin, and he rolled to his side, still twitching, still *hard*, but now maybe a little bit more able to think.

He took enough time for a couple of sobbing breaths, still shaking with the aftermath, with the need that had not stopped thrumming under his skin. Then he wiped his hands on the sheets, moved so his head was on the pillow at least, and texted Seth.

What are you doing right now?

Composing in my room. Seth was living in a boarding house of sorts with other musicians—and suddenly the time difference hit Kelly.

You were up at four in the morning! Because that's when he'd texted, right?

Yeah. Woke up horny. Was thinking of you.

Kelly's strangled laugh rattled in the darkened hotel room.

I'm naked and alone in a hotel room right now for the exact same reason.

His phone buzzed in his hand—Skype.

Kelly hit the picture with one hand and reached for the lamp by the side of the bed with the other. When the light came on, he looked into Seth's sleepy-eyed gaze and smiled for the first time in three days. The tension bled out of his body in a rush, but the arousal remained.

"Oh God," Seth rasped. "Instant boner. Gimme a sec."

He set the phone down on his desk—Kelly could see the computer screen—and there was some rustling.

When he came back, he was naked, and not just from the waist up. Kelly had caught a glimpse of his fattening cock before he'd picked up the phone.

Kelly watched as Seth made himself comfortable on sheets that looked slept in but not soiled, and a part of him—the part that was forever cold when Seth had to leave—warmed again. Not up to core temperature, but enough that Kelly could breathe.

Seth held the phone back so Kelly could get a look at him, and the look was good, but it was also a little less of him than Kelly liked seeing.

"Getting skinny," Kelly said softly.

"Which is funny, 'cause I feel like all I do is eat." Seth lowered the phone enough for Kelly to get a good look at his dear, dorky little grin. "You're…." He bit his lip then, and a look of sorrow crossed his face.

"What?" But Kelly knew. His mother never said it, but the portrait was still up in the living room.

"You look more like your dad every day. I hope that's okay. I… I mean, he's the best guy I've ever known, so it's like a huge compliment, right? I just… I can still see the parts of you that are just you. It's weird."

Kelly's smile had a bitterness he knew his father's never had. "I think maybe you're the only one who can see the just-Kelly parts. I think maybe everyone else sees who they want to see, but you see me. The parts that were Daddy's, the parts that are Mom's. And me."

Seth's grin grew wolfish, and the sentiment of their conversation evaporated like steam. "Gonna show me all the parts that're just you now?"

Kelly chuckled, feeling dirty and gleeful. "Lots of me, covered in me right now," he said, panning the phone across his body where spunk cooled in glossy puddles.

"Started without me? 'Cause, uh, if I was there, I could lick that up for you."

The image behind Kelly's eyes was drawn from those two weeks in Mendocino—when Seth had done that exact thing. He moaned breathily and stretched, bending his knees and exposing his whole body to the air.

"You could, uh, move around while you did it. So you're licking my abs, and I'm licking your dick, right?"

Seth remembered too. "Wasn't my dick that one time."

Oh God. They'd been on round two, and Seth's backside had been gaping, dripping in come. It was one of the most erotic things Kelly could remember thinking, much less seeing… and tasting.

"I'd do that to you right now," Kelly told him. "I'd fuck you and fuck you and eat you out until you came again."

Just saying these things—filthy, forbidden—was enough to make Kelly's cock flex, then splat again on his stomach.

"And I'd take you to the back of my throat and lube you up with my fingers and—"

"Nungh…."

Kelly had bottomed—several times. The panic and the fear and the pain had been replaced with hunger, as long as it was Seth's smell, Seth's touch, Seth's voice.

That wonder, that discovery, arched his back, thrust his cock into his palm, made him grunt as he stroked.

Made him need.

"Put the phone down," Seth ordered, and Kelly did it because Seth knew what he liked. "Suck on your fingers. Get them wet."

And then, while Kelly's fingers were getting sucked and slobbered on, Seth detailed what he'd do to Kelly's body the next time they were together, how he'd touch, what he'd lick, how he'd devour Kelly whole.

His voice, smoky and aching and hungry in the dark, was as dominating as his presence on stage, as his presence in Kelly's life, in his mind, in his heart every time else. He drove Kelly to thrust his fingers into his backside, to fuck his fist with the other hand, to scream out loud, every detail, every moment of what he was doing, what he wanted to be doing, how he craved Seth's hands, his ass, his mouth, his cock—

His cock.

This explosion was bigger than the first one, starting from his toes and rolling to his taint, his asshole, his balls, his gut… his heart.

He didn't just cry out, he howled, shuddering, twitching, flailing.

Needing.

Finally, *finally*, the wave receded, and Seth was whispering into the phone.

"You back with me?"

"Barely," Kelly whispered, bringing his hand up to his mouth. He couldn't taste Seth—he wanted to taste himself.

"Gonna show me?"

Kelly chuckled. So dirty. Like twelve-year-olds. Well, maybe not Seth. Seth hadn't known sex until he'd looked at Kelly and seen him.

Kelly showed his hand, covered in white cream, and deliberately licked it off. Seth gave a grunt, then a moan, and as Kelly watched his face avidly in the phone, a shot of clear liquid hit his chin and spattered across his cheek.

Oh.

"Show me," Kelly whispered, sucking on the webbing between his thumb and forefinger.

Seth did, looking him gravely in the eyes through fiber optics and thousands of miles.

Oh Lord.

His eyes....

Kelly shuddered again, in letdown, and sank into the bed, not even bothering to wipe away the decadence of the last half hour.

Even the smell of his come permeating the air felt like a release.

"Happy birthday to me," he said, feeling comfortable in his skin for the first time in weeks.

"That wasn't even the real present," Seth told him, breathless and happy.

"Wasn't that the flowers?" Kelly frowned, puzzled, and Seth's shy, dorky smile made its appearance again.

Derp. There went Kelly's heart, dropping down the tunnel, in love with him as he always was. It was like every time he could see the landscape of the world without Seth, he'd actually *talk to Seth*, and the world would shake him into wonderland, where love existed, all over again.

"Naw. I told you I wanted to tell you something. You still have your passport?"

Kelly had gotten it when he'd helped Seth get his. Poor Seth—all the things he'd needed. He might have space-cadeted himself right out of Italy if Craig and Kelly hadn't stepped in and helped him get his paperwork done.

"Yeah."

"Well, like, I've got this conductor, right? And he's super rich, like, 'a different house on three continents' rich. And he's going to New York for three months and...."

And Seth explained what he wanted to do, and Kelly's heart—which had felt cramped and claustrophobic and small and angry since watching Seth disappear on a plane in August—took a great big deep breath and began to soar.

HE SHOWERED again and caught another Uber after that. For a moment, he thought about calling Vashti but decided against it.

Vashti had been a good friend, but not a great one.

Kelly thought they needed a little talk.

His mom was up watching television when he got home. Something dark and noir with lots of bodies and a cynical hero—the girls hated detective shows, and this was her chance to watch what she liked.

"Hey, sweetheart." She smiled tiredly as he walked in. "Good night dancing?"

"Mm. Best part of the night was talking to Seth afterward."

"Seth?"

"I, uh, called him. Missed him." He spent a lot of time not talking about Seth, but the family knew.

"Yeah? How is he?"

"He's great. He's got… well, he's sort of wondering if we can, you know, all…."

She had some tweaks to add to the plan—some of them surprising, some of them thoughtful.

But while they talked, Kelly sat on the couch and leaned his head against her, grateful for the soft woman smell of his mommy, the acceptance, and now, hearing her plan about an opportunity she'd never have thought of, the joy.

He wanted to ask about her and Seth's dad and tell her it was okay, but he was just so grateful, this night. It could have ended disastrously. There were so many bad choices he could have made. But the ones he did make were leading him where he wanted to go.

"This sounds so good." He let out a sigh. "So good. I can't believe Seth put all this together."

"I can, baby. That boy loves you."

"Yeah, but for how long?" *Oh. Oh no.* He hadn't meant to make his voice that bitter. "I mean, you know, I don't know how long I'll be—"

"Lily and Lulu graduate in two and a half years," she said, her voice as level as he'd ever heard it. "Tell him until then. Tell yourself until then."

"But Mommy—school, rent, Agnes, Chloe—"

She gave a short laugh. "Don't you think Seth will want to take Chloe with him, if it's possible?" she asked gently. "And the girls are already working toward scholarships. They'll have jobs. They can help me pay rent after you move out." He saw the flush under her dusky skin. "And you know, I might not be alone forever." Her smile—warm and weary and so welcome—came back, and she started to play with his hair, like she had when he'd been a child. "You've been my brave little man for a long time, Kelly. So much longer than you should have. But I need you to have a life and a future. Seth? He's everything you deserve in life, *mijo.* If you can care for Chloe, give her a home where she's her daddy's shining star, you will have given everything I could ask for, you think?"

Kelly bit his lip and let his mother offer him this. An end. A light at the end of the tunnel. A ready-made family in a faraway place, wherever Seth landed. A chance to be with the man he loved.

"KELLY! I thought you weren't coming in today! I was going to call you after my shift."

Kelly looked at his boss and friend grimly. "Vashti, you and me need to talk." He kept walking, past Raven, who was putting together a very pretty Christmas display, and past Julia and Callum, who were both being absurdly gentle with an aging queen who had trouble sitting down, much less trying on the boots she'd made up her mind to wear.

Vashti didn't even ask him where he was going. They blew through the store and didn't stop until they hit the washer and drier, where Kelly crossed his arms and scowled.

"What?" But Vashti looked away. "This isn't about Edgar, is it? Because I broke up with him last night."

"And I appreciate that," Kelly conceded. "I also appreciate the trip to the club, and the drinks, and the way you had my back."

"But why—"

"I appreciated everything *except* the come-on."

Vashti froze, a guilty grimace on his face. "Yeah. That was in… poor taste."

"I thought we were over this. I mean technically, you hadn't even broken up with Edgar by then!"

"I...." Vashti let out a sigh. "Look, Edgar was a... a trophy, you understand? A prop. Sure, he was an asshole, but I just wanted someone to prove to you that I moved on after Andre! You... you let me talk to you when I'm dating someone. You go out with me. You relax and be my friend—"

"But it's pretty shitty to just pretend to be my friend when you want to get in my pants!"

"I'm not *pretending* to be anything!" Vashti retorted. "You are just... prickly. You don't let anybody in. You just hide behind your fake boyfriend—"

"My fake boyfriend?" Kelly tilted his head. "Who was it whining about all the time I took off this summer to see my fake goddamned boyfriend!"

"You know what I mean!" Vashti yelled, pushing away from the washer where he'd been leaning and pacing.

"No, I don't. Enlighten me."

"You've been having a long-distance relationship since I've known you, Kelly. What's it been? Three and a half years? Who does that? Who does long distance for their prime sex-life years? What kind of bullshit—"

"*He can't come home!*" The words were ripped out of Kelly's chest, because Vashti didn't know what he was dealing with—the sudden PR push about Castor Durant's cold case, the social movement against the evils of the "liberal lifestyle," the five-year anniversary of Castor's death—all together in the same pot. Kelly had to smell that shit simmering every day. "He can't! Don't you get it? He can't. My brother will use his presence to take his daughter back, and that's bad fucking news. My brother's stupid father-in-law is a god-awful human being, and he's got connections that will fuck up Seth's life for good if shows his face. He visits, and he's got to stay in his apartment the whole time, because our entire neighborhood knows what he looks like, and we don't want word to get out. So I can't fucking leave, Vashti, and he can't fucking come home."

"So *what*? You're stuck in limbo? You don't get a life? You go stepping and fetching whenever this guy calls your name? I don't get it! You're... you're so *vital*, Kelly! So alive! So fierce! Don't you deserve more than to date a ghost?"

"A ghost?" Kelly could still hear Seth's voice, smoky with passion, in the darkness of the hotel room. "Seth is more there for me halfway across the world than you are right here in this room. Do you know he's been sending my family money? This whole time! He's getting recording contracts and performance gigs, and he dresses like a homeless person and eats peanut butter and jelly so my little sisters can go on science field trips and trips to Ashland to see plays!"

"That's great, but what's he doing for—"

"*And he's paying for my entire family to go to Tuscany*!" Kelly belted it, not even because he was angry but because he couldn't contain his joy. "Five weeks in Italy, Vashti—and you can give me the time off in two months or you can fire me, but you're not fucking stopping me."

Vashti dropped his chin to his chest and rubbed the back of his neck. "God*dammit*, Kelly. How is a guy going to compete with that?"

"You weren't supposed to compete with that!" Kelly's shoulders drooped. "You were supposed to be my friend and be happy for me. That's what you were supposed to do."

"I'll have to hire someone to take your place!" Vashti whined, and Kelly shrugged. The store was notorious for turnover. He wasn't particularly worried. He knew every vendor for a three-block radius— and most of them would be happy to have him on board.

"If they're still working here when I get back, I'll have to find somewhere else to work until I graduate." He was on track for two and a half more years, actually, because some of the classes needed for his computer graphics degree only rolled around once every year or so. His degree. His freedom. All of it. All at the same time. Him and Seth together—he could almost taste it.

Tuscany would be a sampling of that freedom.

The next two years would be appetizers and wine.

But the rest of his life with Seth was about to be their breakfast, lunch, and dinner, and he could hardly wait.

Vashti let out a sigh. "I… I don't know if I can be your friend and your boss with how I feel about you," he said at last. "I mean… I won't be a douchebag at work, but, Kelly, I can't keep being your dance bae either."

It hurt. Kelly wouldn't lie. "I was never gonna be yours," he said plainly. "I'm sorry that hurts too much. I really liked having you as a friend."

And he walked toward the connecting door to the store, just like that.

"Kelly… wait!"

Kelly turned around, and Vashti shrugged. "Movies Sunday? Forget all that shit I just said. I broke up with Edgar, and I really fucking need a friend."

Kelly nodded. "I can do that."

Vashti's lean, pretty face lightened in a smile. "So you'll get me something in Tuscany, right?"

"A T-shirt in the airport?"

"Aw, man, fuck you!"

Kelly grinned. "Nope. You'll be lucky if you get the T-shirt."

"I'll keep hoping for a snow globe. I mean, a guy can dream."

And Kelly hoped that was all he'd dream about, because Kelly *had* hope now. So much hope. His life was just beginning. He knew it.

TWO AND a half months later, Kelly stood naked on a porch in Tuscany.

Seth's conductor friend wasn't just nice—he was stinking rich too. His "house" was a villa along a private beach. A crisp breeze blew off the water, only to be heated by the sun on the white sand beneath the landing. Succulents and yarrow dotted the beach, and the smell was different here—richer with grapes and flowers that were different from the yarrow in Monterey or the redwoods and ferns in Mendocino.

Italian salt air, he and Seth called it, but God, the ocean still roared beneath his feet and the sense of freedom here—it wasn't going away.

His mom had been the one to suggest Kelly go first and spend three weeks there alone with Seth. They'd spent five weeks total—two touring Florence, Venice, and Rome and three at the villa. Seth had performances during those first two weeks. Kelly had been alone, blissfully alone, taking walking tours of the Coliseum, Pompeii, museum after museum after castle.

He'd sketched everything for the first couple of days, but after looking at his hand work, after three years on the computer, he'd started to realize that about the only thing he drew well by hand was his family.

And Seth.

But he didn't care. He drew it anyway, just to prove that he, Kelly Cruz, had gotten on a plane by himself and journeyed to a place so far beyond Sacramento that people at home didn't believe it existed.

He took every pamphlet in English that he could manage, and he looked up every story he could find on his phone.

And for three nights in those weeks, he made it back in time to put on a tuxedo and sit in Seth's little-used box seat and listen to his man make the music of the gods.

Seth wasn't "on tour" or "on a graduate program" in Italy—whatever they'd said to him to get him to come, he'd either misunderstood or blatantly lied.

Seth was a *headliner* in Italy. He was their star attraction. His name was on the motherfucking marquee.

Apparently his conductor had bought him three tuxedos and had them dry cleaned—for all Kelly knew it had been part of his contract once the poor man realized Seth could barely dress himself.

But no wonder Seth had the money to send for the entire family.

And seriously, leave it to Seth to eat PB&J for breakfast, lunch, and dinner, and save up enough money to fly Kelly's whole damned family in and out.

Kelly had already started on a letter to thank the conductor. Seth said that was probably a good idea since he'd had to convince the guy he couldn't sleep with him because he had a boyfriend.

"I thought he was married! With a family!"

"Yeah, but he's bi, and apparently his wife and lovers are fine with it," Seth said, shrugging. "I'm not sure if it's Italy that's weird or just music people in Italy or maybe these particular music people in Italy. Whatever. He was disappointed, but then I told him about you guys, and he asked if I wanted to invite you over. I offered to rent the place, but he said just to pay the maid, since she was doing groceries and laundry and stuff. So, you know, if you could help remind me to give Rosa a fuckton of money, that would be *great*, because she's a really nice lady, and I don't want to screw her over."

Kelly had gaped at him when he'd explained the sitch—as Seth was showing him around, after the last of his performances. The place itself was a marvel of cherry wood and giant wraparound windows, and for a moment, Kelly was sort of depressed.

"It's pretty and all," he said, looking out over the ocean. "But, you know, how're we gonna…?" He didn't make the time-honored finger-in-the-hole gesture, but he might as well have.

Seth had come up behind him, draping his warm body along Kelly's back. "Nobody can see us," he murmured. "See that path down to the ocean?"

"Yeah?"

"It's private. The only people who should be on that beach are attached to this villa. So, yeah. When your family gets here, we need to be done, but until then...."

Kelly had turned in his arms. "We can fuck like... like...."

"Like Seth and Kelly on holiday, I hope!"

And so they had.

It was Mendocino all over again, with swimming, even though it wasn't summer yet. They sat on the beach and rubbed lotion all over and ran up to the villa to have sex. Sex actually *on* the beach sounded great, but they'd learned their lesson in Mendocino. Sand. Everywhere.

They would walk into town and shop and hold hands and then go back for lunch.

And hey—more sex.

Voracious and naked and free.

And talking. No moment was too small. No irritation, no joy. The whole story of Kelly's birthday came out, and Seth just held him and listened. Seth showed him pictures that he'd held back—a group of friends, male and female.

Another Guthrie stared at him with limpid green eyes and a sort of frustrated sadness.

Kelly looked at Seth's phone over the dinner table as they sat side by side wearing nothing but robes, and tapped the face, making it bigger. "Do I need to walk away?" he asked, completely serious.

Seth understood what he was asking. "No. He's kind, but I've kept my distance." The pain he'd worn when talking about Guthrie—who had come out, and written Seth immediately because his father had stopped talking to him—crossed his face. "I... can't do that again. It hurts."

Kelly stroked his hand, the bronze-toned skin supple and smooth, because he might forget to eat but he always remembered his cocoa butter. "The stupid thing about living our lives like this is that... that it becomes Kelly's life and Seth's life—and it's only *our* lives for a little while." Seth turned his palm up, and Kelly laced their fingers together. "Mommy said it would be just until the girls graduate. She said...." He swallowed and smiled hopefully, because he loved his niece too. "She said we could take Chloe with us if we wanted. If you want."

Seth's slow smile was all he could ask for. "There's schools," he said unexpectedly. "I... you know. Talk about Chloe a lot. Amara said there's schools back in the Bay Area. So, you and me, we could move there and get her enrolled and...." He bit his lip. "Live together. Do you think we could live together? I mean, it wouldn't be all sex and vacation like now."

Kelly smiled through blurry vision. "I would love to be boring on a Friday night with you," he said. "I would love to work a job, any job, and come home and get Chloe from her special school and take her to see you perform. I would... every way I think of us together, it makes me happy."

"You'd have to nag me," Seth said seriously. "I keep ending up living in places where people take care of me. Remember my apartment in Vacaville? I used to forget to take out the garbage and clean the toilet."

Kelly laughed softly. "Seth, how much money do you make?"

Seth shrugged. "I got no idea. I have sort of an agent. Gianni found her for me. She puts the money in the bank, and Dad tells me when he takes something out. There's always enough for what I need, you know?"

Kelly rolled his eyes so far back in his head, it almost hurt. "You know, I'm pretty sure we could hire a maid. Just saying. You're a world-class soloist—you get that, right? What little kids want to be when they pick up a bow, you're that!"

Seth cocked his head, wrinkling an entire side of his face. "No," he said, absolutely positive. "'Cause when I started at Bridgford, they told me that a good musician doesn't get that good until they hit their thirties, at the very least. So I haven't even peaked. We'll have to wait another ten years to hire a maid."

He was totally and completely serious, and Kelly wasn't sure whether to cry or to bang his head against the table or to kiss him, through ice cream and coffee, and possess him, completely, over the kitchen table.

He did the kitchen table thing—it was a sturdy piece of furniture, and it held up terrifically.

And he didn't have to explain to his lover that Seth *was* the giant who walked with his feet among the stars and his head in the clouds and that Kelly was the mortal who climbed the money-stalk every so often just to visit his world.

Kelly loved him. God, sometimes it just had to be that simple.

Today, with the family arriving in three more days, and the clock ticking in the back of their minds—always, always the clock—Kelly was going to let it be that simple.

He stared out at the sea with the cocoa butter next to him, grabbed a fingerful and reached behind him, allowing the breeze and the sun to play on his skin as he let his fingers play around his orifice, burning, stretching, filling.

Knowing Seth was behind him, sitting at his desk for a moment to do some composing, where he would look up and see Kelly, pleasuring himself.

And if he didn't look up?

That was okay too, because Kelly was *truly* pleasuring *himself.* He was celebrating how wonderful this felt, the freedom from the fear this act might have brought him once, how much his body felt like *his*, so much like his that he would give it to Seth without inhibition.

He heard a sudden intake of breath. A gasp. An "Ooooooooooooh...." on the exhalation, and turned his face to the dazzling sky.

Three… two… one….

Seth's hands were shaking too hard to be gentle, but Kelly didn't need that, not now. He was bent roughly over, his hands gripping the wooden railing, his ass thrust out, as Seth breached him and surged inside, his breadth stretching, his length stuffing, his body the most welcome of invaders.

Kelly let out a cry—happiness, triumph, pure sex—and begged.

"God, Seth, took you long—*enough!*"

Hard. Seth liked to fuck hard, and Kelly liked it too. They liked it all, hard and fast, soft and slow, the heavy-duty power fuck.

His body would *never* tire of having Seth's inside him, and Seth would bend over and plead for Kelly as often as he could.

But not now.

Now Seth was taking over, fucking him from the inside out, and Kelly was disintegrating, flying outward, soaring over the ocean under the sun. His body was life and sex and hope—and Seth, human music, playing his soul like the violin.

Frayed and Broken

Two and a half years later…

LATE. SETH was late.

Kelly frowned at his phone in annoyance. Seth had needed to attend an out-of-town engagement right before Agnes's appearance in the high school play. It wasn't a big deal, really, but Seth had such a stellar record of sneaking into these things, holding Chloe, taking them out to dinner, and then sneaking away—often with Kelly to his apartment in San Francisco—that the lateness seemed out of character.

But then, so had Seth's excessive workload, until Kelly had gotten shitty with him the night before.

So you're in New York again but you'll be here?

Yes.

Do you need me to walk away? Kelly had been kidding, mostly. It was their code, every time they saw somebody in the photo record who showed up a lot, or who seemed… interested in the other person. It was a way to ask, politely, if there was anything to be worried about without getting stupid and mad and jealous, and as codes went, it wasn't bad.

Kelly's sentence was almost up, and he wanted Seth more than ever. Every text, every Skype, every cheap hotel for privacy and phone sex—all of it had been worth it. Kelly was almost free, and Seth had been saving for a house, browsing the property outside of San Francisco with an idle eye.

But New York kept calling.

Kelly figured Seth wouldn't know he knew, but Craig was over at their house almost every night, and the semisecret affair he carried on with Kelly's mother was becoming less and less semisecret every day. He'd been the one to tell Kelly—on a note of frustration—that the opportunity to play first chair in David Geffen Hall didn't come along more than once in a lifetime and he wished Seth would listen to reason.

Kelly had swallowed, biting his lower lip, for once—oh God, just this once—unable to put Seth's career first.

Craig had rolled his eyes. "Do you think he wouldn't bring you and Chloe with him? You can get a job as a graphic designer in New York as easy as you can get one in San Francisco."

Kelly had gasped then. "But... but family...." Because being farther away had not once—not once—occurred to him, not in the last interminable years.

"Jesus, Kelly, you and Seth have managed a perfectly functional relationship for the last eight years. Do you think we're going to just go away if you move to New York?"

But Seth hadn't mentioned anything, in spite of an increasing number of short trips to appear there as a soloist.

So the question—*Do you need me to walk away*—had been facetious, but he'd pulled it out because he wanted the truth. Sometimes Seth really *was* that flaky. Sometimes he just depended on everybody's acceptance of his silence to not talk about the stuff that made him uncomfortable. It was the same tactic he pulled when money came up and Linda and Kelly looked at their taxable income versus what they spent and realized that Seth had been funneling the equivalent of Kelly's entire income into the Cruz family coffers, with his father's silent, capable help.

They still hadn't had that conversation, and Kelly wasn't sure they ever would.

Seth's answer had been typical Seth.

Because why? Who am I dating besides you?

Kelly had sent back a picture of Seth with his violin. It was the only new thing Seth owned besides his tuxedos. He'd gotten it from a master craftsman in Italy, and he'd confessed, red-faced, that it had its own seat when he flew.

He'd named it Chloe.

Seth's answer was satisfyingly fervent. *No! I'm sorry! I'm just trying to put by some money so we can look at houses after your graduation!*

Oh!

Well, that would have been good to know before I got all butthurt, wouldn't it!

Sorry! I didn't want you to worry.

Of course he didn't.

Well, relax a little. I don't need a house. Just you.

But he knew it did no good. Seth felt... guilty. Not about Castor Durant so much as about not being there. It didn't help to tell him that he needed to go out into the world. It didn't help to remind him of his gift—his glorious gift—that would be languishing, unnourished, unappreciated, if he'd stayed in his father's apartment and lived the life Kelly had. He had an obsession with having left the Cruz family when they'd needed somebody, and Kelly hadn't been able to convince him that the world needed him too.

But they were going to be together soon, and they'd be raising Chloe, and Kelly had jobs lined up in San Francisco, and their world—their world was going to be bright as the sun.

And as much as he loved his sisters, his mother, even his friends and his hometown, every breath until then felt like he was trapped in a white stucco cube.

They were so close—so damned close.

And this was closing night of Agnes's play, and Seth was late, and Kelly was twitchy. Damned twitchy.

He just kept waiting for his world to explode again.

Craig was sitting on his left, and he looked at Kelly's phone and frowned. "Anything?" he whispered, and Kelly shook his head.

Nope.

Nothing yet.

On his other side, Chloe tried hard not to squirm in her pretty dress. "Seth?"

"He should be here," Kelly told her, thinking this was stupid. One delayed flight did not a disaster make. But the whole family was looking around, eyes darting, twitchy as hell.

Unbidden, Kelly's mind was brought back to that long-ago night when he and Matty had been peering outside the curtain, looking for their father, and Seth had been hoping his wouldn't show up.

The world was a funny, twisted place, he thought bitterly. Matty had come and gone. Sometimes he'd show up with small gifts for Chloe, always looking like a hundred miles of bad road. They'd learned just to ask him in, to feed him, to take what he could give.

And not to expect him to return.

He'd visited the month before, and Agnes had remarked that she could see the track marks on his arms, and they were getting infected. Linda had been doing accounts at the time, and she'd made a little gasp in her throat. Craig—who'd been over cooking dinner, which he did a lot—had left everything to simmer and taken her away from her desk in the corner of the living room and outside for a walk. Kelly had finished dinner, and that had been that.

They all knew.

Matty was an addict, and Isela was nowhere to be found.

Kelly had heard Lily and Lulu talking about his yellow eyes and the red patches on his face.

He wasn't stupid—he knew what it could add up to.

But he'd been telling himself his brother was dead to him for a long time now. He was too pissed off to grieve.

The lights went down, the curtain opened, and the play began—Agnes in the leading role. For an hour and a half, Kelly was able to bury his worry about Seth under his pride for his sister, but when the lights went up and she took a bow with her cast, he and Craig looked at each other again.

Fuck.

They managed to contain themselves, though, to congratulate Agnes, who was over the moon—and upset because Seth had promised her flowers. Lily and Lulu told her they'd take her out with her friends to get ice cream after set breakdown, and Kelly hugged them all before he tailed Craig and Linda out of the school auditorium, Chloe clutching his hand.

Once they got her unhappily situated in her car seat in the back of the minivan, Kelly sat in the middle and leaned forward between his mom and Seth's dad, looking for answers.

"Did his plane get in?" Craig asked, looking at Kelly.

Kelly nodded. "Right on time. He texted me as soon as they landed, and he had a good hour. Here—I'm looking for traffic conditions—"

"I've got them," Craig muttered. "Hell. Oh hell. Linda, here. You take Chloe inside once we get home."

"What's wrong?" she asked, not taking her eyes off the road but not losing the conversation either.

"There…." Craig took a deep breath. "There was a pileup. Multicar. On 5. Several big rigs involved. You go inside with Chloe. Kelly and I will call hospitals. I'll let you know if we hear anything."

"Oh God." Linda covered her mouth with her hand. "Craig, he's got to be—"

And Craig Arnold grabbed her hand and laced their fingers together, bringing them to his lips. "Have faith, honey. Have faith just this once. He's Seth." His voice cracked. "We just need to find out."

She nodded, and Kelly got out so she could carry a sleeping Chloe upstairs. He was on his second phone call when he saw a movement from the shadows.

"Son of a bitch," he muttered.

"I beg your pardon?" came the harried clerk on the other end of the line.

"Shit! I'm sorry. I was looking to see if you had a patient from the car wreck—the big one on Highway 5?" Poor woman. Kelly watched his no-account brother walk out from the shadows behind the Arnold's apartment, something dangling from his far hand. Kelly kept his eyes on Matty but his brain on his task.

"What is your relationship to the patient, sir?"

"He's my boyfriend—Seth Arnold."

"The violinist? The one on YouTube?"

Kelly blinked. Seth's videos—the ones he made where he played the different parts—had gotten enough hits for Seth to hire someone to monetize his own YouTube station. He made a decent amount of money from it, but not once had Kelly ever heard anybody but his own family talk about watching.

"Yeah—"

"So you would be Kelly?"

Oh Jesus. "Kelly Cruz," he said, feeling shell-shocked. Seth and Lindsey Stirling—both YouTube phenomena. Now he knew why people knew about him.

"Oh! Well, I'll have to tell my son. He's out too. He was very excited to see Seth's stuff online—"

"Is he there?" Kelly asked, the fine edge of panic in his voice. Matty had spotted him and Craig in the car and was coming their way.

Oh Jesus. That thing in his hand—Kelly knew those things well. Lily, Lulu, Agnes, Chloe—at one time or another, he'd carried all of them in one.

There was a baby in that carrier, and Matty looked like hell.

"Yes," came the answer. "Yes, he was admitted with the first wave of the injured. He's in ICU in stable condition, but they're awaiting his tests to see if he has internal injuries or any significant head injury. Are you planning to come visit him?"

Oh Jesus. "Yes," Kelly said. "Where is he?"

While the clerk relayed the department and the room number, Kelly repeated it, catching Craig's eyes so he could type the info into his phone. He thanked the clerk and hung up, and then he and Craig looked at each other grimly.

"I'll get Seth," Craig said. "You get your brother."

No. "I want to get Seth!" Kelly snapped. "He's mine. When does he get to be mine!"

Craig dropped his chin against his chest. "He's always been yours, Kelly. But I'm nobody to Matty. Whatever brought him here, whoever that is in the baby carrier, you are the person he needs to see."

"Just...." Kelly looked at this kind man—plain, graying, his amazing green eyes and delicate cheekbones the only testament that his son was the boy Kelly loved. "Just wait for a minute. Let me talk to Matty. Maybe I can come with you, okay?"

Craig nodded. "Okay. Here—I'll park the van. We can take my car instead."

Good idea. Kelly got out and walked toward his brother, his heart panic-beating in every step.

"Matty?"

Matty turned to him blearily, and Kelly saw that Lily and Lulu had been right. His eyes were yellow and the skin under them was gray. His face was blotched. And he hadn't showered in too long a time.

"Kel?" He smiled.

Kelly's throat grew tight. How long, Jesus, how long had it been since his brother had smiled when he saw him?

"Yeah. What's doin' man? Who's that in the car seat?"

Matty let out a harsh, hoarse bark of laughter. "My son?"

Kelly looked at him sideways and then crouched, taking in the baby's appearance. He was tiny—maybe two weeks old? His skin was pink, and even under the soda lights, Kelly could see the hair haloing around his head was a blondish brown.

Chloe's hair and skin and eyes were all brown. There was no doubt she was Matty's child—none.

"Uh, Matty?"

Matty shook his head. "Isela showed up three days ago," he said with a shrug. "She had him with her. I was like, 'Uh... babe?' She said he was mine. Could be. She was around for a while last year. But it doesn't matter. Doesn't matter if he's mine. She took off, and I can't... I just can't. He's a baby, Kel. He's a baby, and he needs someone. And he doesn't have a chance with her. I know I'm a shitty father, but I'm a good enough one to know that my family is raising my daughter decent." He unshouldered the bag on his other side. "I got nowhere else to take him, and I'm almost out of formula and down to my last two diapers."

Kelly stared at him, mouth gaping, as Matty thrust the baby carrier into his hands, followed by the bag.

"Dude, come up and talk to Mom at least! Man, she deserves that much."

Matty shook his head, and then to Kelly's horror, he started coughing. A deep, wet, chest-sucking cough that he covered with his shoulder.

He wiped his mouth, and Kelly saw the blood spots he'd left behind. "Jesus, *Matty*!"

Matty shrugged, like Seth would have, if he'd known. "Vasculitis," he said. "I've got two kinds of hepatitis, Kelly. He can't stay with me. My body's falling to shit. I'll be lucky if I make it 'til Christmas."

Kelly stared at him, his brain shorting out. His brother was dying. His *brother was dying.* And Seth was in the hospital. And there was a baby in the carrier in his hand.

"Craig!" he called as Seth's father rounded the corner from the carport. "Craig, stay right here and make sure my useless fucking brother doesn't go anywhere." He glared at Matty. "We are *not* through with you!"

And then he ran up the stairs to give the baby to his mom. He stopped, halfway up, and called out to Matty. "Hey, asshole! What's this blond baby's name?"

And Matty, the fucker, completely sealed his goddamned fate. "Xavier," he said. "Javi, after Dad."

"I fucking hate you."

And he finished the run before Matty could reply.

Linda opened the door to Kelly and the car carrier and the bag of diapers with the same expression on her face that Kelly knew he must have had.

They knew.

They both knew what this meant.

He told her that Matty needed a doctor, and since he and Craig were on their way anyway, could he please have a towel or a sheet or something so his useless fucking brother didn't bleed or piss all over Craig's car?

She handed him the items fairly quickly, finishing up just when the baby started to cry. She sighed and bent down to free him from the car carrier, her entire body going limp as she picked him up.

"Oh, baby… this is not your fucking fault."

Kelly swallowed. "Mom…." Freedom. He'd been so close to freedom.

"Don't worry. I'll call your sisters to bring home some formula and some diapers. Go. Take care of Matty. Make sure Seth's okay."

"Mom?"

She shook her head and looked away. "Later, *mijo.* We'll have this discussion later. When I can think and my heart isn't breaking. Later."

Kelly tried not to slam the door as he trotted back out into the balmy spring night.

It didn't matter. Every clatter of his feet on the steps sounded like a prison door, slamming shut on all of Kelly's dreams.

Broken Hearts and Broken Strings

ONE MINUTE, Seth's life was golden.

He'd landed on time, the Lyft was speeding along toward Sacramento, and dammit, he was going to make Agnes's play on time.

In half an hour, he'd be sitting on an uncomfortable metal chair in a shitty school cafeteria with cracked tile and a splintering wooden stage, watching Kelly's sister be the star of the show. He'd have Chloe on his lap and Kelly to his side, and they'd be touching, together, and the money from his last film soundtrack recording session with New York would be hitting the bank.

Sure, Gianni Pesci, the conductor from Italy, was in New York now, and he wanted Seth back to play for him again, but Seth had told him, repeatedly, that San Francisco was his home.

Or Sacramento.

Or a shitty high school, where he could give young people the same gift he'd been given.

He didn't care.

Kelly was waiting for him. His family was waiting for him. He wanted to go home.

He didn't see the semi until it was almost on top of them. The Lyft driver swerved hard, saving both their lives, and dove off the road toward the vacant field. He couldn't see the metal fence posts in his hurry, and Seth certainly didn't expect one of them to rip through the front of the car like butter, but suddenly the car was flipping and the world went to hell.

HE WASN'T sure how long he was in or out, but he knew his leg was on fire, and then he was drugged, and his leg and hip still hurt like a motherfucker, but the drugs at least kept him from caring. His head didn't feel so awesome either.

His father was sitting next to his bed, looking older than Seth had seen him look since, well, since he'd started sleeping with Kelly's mom.

Yeah, his dad had confessed. It had been sort of cute, actually. He wasn't even sure if Kelly had caught it, but the two of them had shared a bed in Tuscany. Sure, Craig had *said* he was sleeping on the couch, and every morning, the blanket and pillow would be crisp and pretty on the end of the couch in the living room. Seth had said guilelessly that Rosa was really super-efficient, and his father had seized on that and clung.

But Seth had given his father an arched eyebrow, and Craig had shrugged guiltily. That evening, as Seth was trailing Kelly up to the bedroom to cling tightly to his body as they snuggled and slept chastely, their time together almost at an end, his dad had stopped him.

"You… uh… do you mind?"

"Mind what?"

"Uh… the sheets. I'm not, uh… using the sheets."

Seth had raised his eyebrows. "You're using *someone's* sheets."

And his father had glared, defensively, like a kid. "You know what I mean."

Yeah, Seth had known.

He was happy about it.

His father wasn't alone. The Cruz family really *was* Seth's family. Those years of being alone, by himself, waiting for his father to get home had nearly faded from memory.

But you didn't say to your boyfriend—your boyfriend who talked all the time, rambled on subjects from movies to the shit they put in fabric softener, and yet kept some things so close, so tight to his own heart that they festered in the soul—"Hey, babe, my dad's banging your mom. You good with that?" So Seth wasn't sure, actually, how Kelly felt about it.

He was prepared for any eventuality.

Or he had been, until that semi had come out of its lane and attempted to squash him like a bug.

"How's the driver?" he mumbled. An older man, Indian, with a picture of Jesus hanging from the rearview mirror and a photo of his family stuck in the overhead visor—he had driven like he had something to lose if he died.

Since Seth felt the same way, he was grateful.

"Fine," his father said, holding his hand. "He actually walked away. You got pinned behind the passenger's seat. They had to cut you out."

"How's my violin?"

His dad let out a strangled chuckle. "Good too. You had it strapped in the seat next to you, Seth. I think that Prius would have needed to blow up to hurt your instrument."

"Mm. No blowing up. Head's doing that."

"Yeah. Concussions will do that. You've probably got some soft tissue damage in your neck and back, so they're going to get you an MRI in a bit. I think they'll probably put you under for that, because right now, everything probably hurts."

"Got that shit right." Seth tried to take a deep breath but couldn't. "Bruised ribs."

"Yeah. Not going to lie there, son. You... you were on the fine edge of being not all right."

"Fuuuuuck...." He kept his eyes closed. "Where's Kelly?"

His father's silence was the most terrifying thing he'd ever heard.

"He's okay, right?"

"He is. But...." Again, that terrible silence. "Matty came by tonight. He's... well, Isela had another baby, for one thing."

Oh. Oh no. Nothing good... nothing good came with Matty. "And for two?"

"Kelly took him to be evaluated. He was coughing blood. Matty said it was a side effect of hepatitis, but...."

"Dad?"

"I work in a warehouse, Seth. It's a shitty neighborhood. People who look like Matty generally don't... don't get better."

"The goalpost," Seth muttered. "The goalpost got moved again. The...." He couldn't find words. "Brain's all fuzzy."

"Yeah. The painkillers are setting in. They said you had about ten minutes before you blanked out again."

"Kelly... Kelly needs to...." What? Kelly needed to what? Needed to stay home again? Raise another child? Watch his brother die? Kelly needed.... Seth didn't know. Couldn't think. He was always trying to figure out what Kelly needed, but he couldn't... not now. Seth just needed sleep.

MORE IN and out. More moments with his dad and no Kelly.

Finally he opened his eyes and Kelly was there, in his peripheral vision. Seth realized he had a neck brace on—probably that soft tissue damage his dad had been talking about—and he could see Kelly but couldn't look him in the eyes.

But he could still tell Kelly was crying.

"Don't cry, baby," he mumbled, and tried to come more fully awake. Breathing was easier, and he felt the stiffness on his ribs, which meant they'd been taped. His head felt better—yay!—and his leg was heavy. So heavy. He frowned and wiggled his toes. "Am I in a cast?"

"Yeah." Kelly's voice sounded… odd. Like it came from a swollen throat. "You got a cast. God. Seth—I… you have to not get hurt again."

Ooh… that was good to hear. "I'll make it a priority." He tried to smile, but couldn't. "You… can't move out again, can you?"

Kelly let out a wounded sound. "He's dying, Seth. Doctor confirmed it. Cirrhosis and carcinoma. The hept… heptsomething carcinoma is gonna make it go quick. Except quick isn't quick. You'd think it was a guillotine or something, but he can be around next month or next year or five years. He's just… just dying. I'm…. He's going to stay at my mother's, and she's got his… God, it's not even his baby. Do you know that? He's like, 'Here's the baby I named after our father, but he's got blond hair and blue eyes,' and this kid cries all the time, just like Chloe, and… and we can't leave the baby either, because… oh my God. Seth! My life is a sinkhole! You're lying there, hurt, and *my* life is what we're talking about!"

"Kelly…," he rasped. "Baby, calm down. We'll see through this. We always—"

"No. No, we won't. Because it won't stop. It won't stop, my life. God, Seth…." He choked on a sob. "Your agent called. Your agent called, and she was crying—not because you'd been hurt, because she didn't even know about that, but because you were turning down New York. You didn't even tell me New York was on the table!"

Mm… Seth's head hurt more than he thought it did. "It wasn't. Too far away from your family."

"But that's you, fucking up your life for me again!" He pulled in a sob, but it didn't work, and Seth couldn't keep up with him. "Don't you get it? You will do that again and again for me. You're here, in this fucking hospital, because you were trying to see my sister in a play. Do you get how fucked-up that is?"

"How'd she do?"

"She's brilliant. All my sisters are brilliant. I'm the dumbshit who's just plugging along in mediocrity here, Seth, and you're… you're willing to settle for that!"

Seth couldn't sit up. He couldn't sit up, and he couldn't yell, and it wasn't fair. "Stop it," he rasped. "Stop it. Dammit, Kelly, I'm not settling for anything. This mediocre thing you're freaking out about? That's all I ever wanted."

"Well, you need to find it somewhere else, because I'm not willing to let you throw yourself away on me and my fucking sinkhole of a life. You need to walk away."

Seth pulled in a gasp and then coughed and then swore. "No," he rasped. "And fuck you for doing this when I…." He caught his breath again and realized that even though he'd spent his whole life working on using as few words as possible, they were going to have to do it for him now.

"I. Will. Never. Walk. Away."

Kelly was still crying. All Seth wanted to do was soothe him when he was crying, but he couldn't.

"Please, baby. For me. Maybe… maybe someday, my brother will be dead, and I can just walk out of this fucking town, and maybe you'll still be single. But maybe you won't. And if you're not, that'll… that'll be what was best for you. Because right now, I'm not what's best for you. I'm pissed off, Seth. I'm pissed off, and I'm… I'm… God. I hate. I have so much hatred in my heart right now. I'm afraid it will just poison everything I've ever felt for you, and I…." His voice cracked in a sob, and he kept on going. "I can't let that happen. You're my good thing. You're the one good thing in my life. And if I let the rest of this shit touch you, I wouldn't even have that anymore. So you gotta… you gotta stay away. Please. If you love me, you'll stay away. Because I love you, and I'm not in a place where I can be there for you. And you deserve so much more, baby. God, Seth. You deserve so much more. You gotta walk away."

Seth shook his head—as much as he could—and said it again. "I. Will. Never. Walk. Away."

And before Kelly could say the final thing, the irrevocable thing, he managed to go on. "But I get you need space. 'Cause, baby, you're not sounding… not sounding sane. And I can't hold you. I can't hold you, and your family is all up in the air, and you're afraid. You're so afraid. I can see it from here." He took two more breaths, and Kelly let him. "You tell me when you want me. You tell me when you need me back. I'll keep in contact with the girls. I'll keep contact with Chloe." God. Chloe. He wanted to hold her so bad. "And if you need me to walk away, you say it. You say it, and I'll be out of your family's life for good. But if you can't say it—you can't tell me you're walking away—then I'm gonna fucking be there."

"Fine!" Kelly was shouting. "Fine! I'll say it!"

"You look me in the eyes!" Because Seth couldn't even tilt his head. God. Helpless. He was so fucking helpless. "Look me in the eyes and tell me you can't love me anymore. Tell me, after all of this, you never loved me enough to share a life. Look me in the eyes and tell me that, and I'll let you go."

Kelly's face appeared above his line of vision, distorted and swollen through tears. "Seth—"

"Do you love me?" he asked, and instead of strong and mad, his voice sounded broken to his own ears. "Did you ever?"

And for a horrible moment, Kelly's face froze, like he was trying to do something with it that hurt. "Yes," he rasped finally. "Goddammit. You know I love you. That's not—"

"Then you take your time. You take whatever time you need. I didn't know what sex was before you. I'm not gonna need someone else now. You might. I don't know. Maybe it's that. I don't care. You take your time, and you call me when you're ready." Seth's chest hurt, and he couldn't stop the tears. Dammit. They had seen daylight. It had been shining on the calendar, the day Lily and Lulu graduated, and the day they could walk away, free. And now the world was sunk in darkness, and Seth couldn't breathe.

"You go to New York," Kelly told him, steel in his voice.

"No—"

"No, that's my condition. That's… I'll…." His indrawn breath was ugly, jagged, not even human. "I'll say it. I'll walk away if you don't. Go to New York, Seth. Go and fly."

A sob racked him, and it hurt. "No—"

"I swear to God, I'll do it!"

"Fine," he managed to say. "Fine. Whatever. You think that's gonna keep me away from you? You think that's gonna make me want you any less? You listen to me, Kelly Cruz. You keep talking about me walking around in the stars—you *are* my star. You are my true star. And I will *never* walk away from you."

Kelly leaned over the railing then and buried his face against Seth's throat. "I'm sorry," he whispered. "I was supposed to… it was supposed to be over. I'm sorry I'm not strong enough to do that now."

His mouth fell on Seth's, briny, desperate, so damned sad, and Seth responded. Kelly was the one who ripped himself away, hardly able to breathe.

"I love you, *mijo*. Goodbye."

And then he was gone, and Seth was sobbing so hard, the nurse had to come in and sedate him. They were afraid he'd crack a rib.

HIS FATHER came in the next day to help pick up the pieces, and Seth could tell by the way he spoke, by his care when talking about Linda, when talking about Kelly, when talking about the whole family, that he… he was on Kelly's side.

"This isn't fair," he rasped. "Dad, I want to be there—"

"How much help are you going to be if you end up in jail because Matty can't keep his mouth shut," his dad said bluntly, raking his hand through his graying blond hair. "C'mon, Seth. You and Kelly, you've endured separations before—"

"But he wants me to walk way, Dad." Seth wasn't sure if he could convey how bad this was. "He… he wants me to go to New York."

Craig smiled tiredly. "Then go to New York. Come back for Christmas. Come back earlier. Come back for his birthday. Just… just give him some space now."

Seth nodded, but his dad wasn't fooled. He bent over the bed and used a tissue to wipe his face. "You're hurt," he said softly. "And your heart is hurt. And so is Kelly's. This…. Have some faith. I've watched you both grow up, you know? You're both such good men, Seth. I can't… I can't emphasize that enough. You both have such good hearts. Go to New York. Give your lover some space. He'll come back."

Seth rolled his eyes, because they both knew there were two options to that statement.

"Or he won't. But if he doesn't, you'll be somewhere you can start fresh. Okay?"

Seth grunted. Fine. Whatever. He didn't care.

"Good. I'll call Amara and what's her name? Your agent? The really pushy one?"

"Susan," Seth said reluctantly. "Susan Sargent." She represented Amara too. He wasn't sure how that had happened, but she seemed to be making him money, so he guessed he was okay with that.

"Good. I'll have her set you up."

"Dad, she's not supposed to—"

"Sure, she is. That's what you pay her for. Besides, she's been so pushy about the New York thing, I bet she'd let you live in her basement for free if you agreed to go for a year—"

"A *year*!"

And Craig's lighthearted air of adventure bled away, leaving in its place what this really was. "Matty's threatened to out you before, Seth. And he's not going to be rational now. He's going to be feeling like shit and in a lot of pain. I love Kelly—don't get me wrong. But I'll be damned if I see you go to jail because Matty can hold a grudge."

Matty just had to go to the police and talk about Kelly's boyfriend, who looked like hell the morning after Castor Durant was killed. Seth would be in jail, Chloe would be in foster care, and everything Seth knew would be over.

Oh God. Maybe—just maybe—Seth should have talked about this earlier.

Maybe even eight years earlier, before the weight of the things he'd never said threatened to weigh him and Kelly down to the bottom of their own personal rivers.

"Dad, about Castor Durant, I don't think—"

Craig shook his head, his face growing gaunt. "Don't," he begged. "This has been a rough week for all of us, Seth."

"I could go to jail," he offered softly. "I could call the police and tell them everything. I could not have this hanging over my head anymore. Whatever happens, Matty, Isela's dad, Castor's father—they wouldn't have this to hurt our family anymore."

Craig shook his head and wiped his face with the back of his hand. "No." That was all. "Just… please. No."

And Seth couldn't, not against his father. Not against Kelly. Not now when everything hurt, from his broken leg to his pulverized heart.

"Someday I'm going to have to—"

"Please."

Seth sighed, and felt his eyes closing, and wished that maybe they'd stay shut forever. There just didn't seem to be any point to waking up right now.

AMARA AND Susan checked him out of the hospital—his dad was there to say goodbye, and so was Kelly's mother.

But not Kelly.

Seth wondered bitterly if Kelly thought that would make it hurt any less.

Susan had already sublet his apartment—to Vince, because Amara had been offered New York too, but Vince was still in San Francisco.

"I'll come with you," Amara said brightly, shouldering Seth's carry-on and his violin as his father wheeled him out. "We figured we'd do the bicoastal thing for a year, because their trumpet player is retiring, and Vince is on the shortlist for auditions."

"But what if—" Seth had never been the one to ask that before, but Amara just shrugged.

"Then I come back here and teach and find gigs, and Vince keeps his job. Or the other way around." She touched his shoulder then, so softly he realized, all in a heartbeat, this was for him. Entirely for him. They were sacrificing a year of their lives so Seth wouldn't have to move to New York alone. "We'll find a way, sweetheart. We'll all find a way."

"We'll get him a gig in New York," Susan said, exhaling vape fumes even though she hadn't puffed in the hospital even once. "I'm no kind of agent if I can't get *that* kid a job." She dropped her head and spoke in a fake whisper loud enough to make everybody in their party laugh. "Just looking at him blowing on a trumpet makes my panties wet. If I didn't like Amara so much, I would have eaten that boy up in a gulp. Me-*owr.*" She made the time-honored cougar gesture, and Seth managed a small smile. She wouldn't—he knew that. She didn't sleep with clients. In fact, she was known for her ethics on an international scale. Gianni had told him that when he'd given Seth her number out of sheer frustration.

Rail thin, in her forties, Susan was brazenly redheaded, brazenly single, and had the voice of a three-pack-a-day smoker—but now she apparently vaped stuff like bubblegum and pink strawberry lemonade surprise. Her entire life was seeing her "kids," as she called them, into comfortable livings, and given that symphony musician wasn't exactly like computer tech in the growing industry department, Seth was pretty sure she earned every penny of her commission.

Together, Susan and Amara got Seth into a waiting town car, but they didn't leave before Seth hugged his dad and Linda with all his might.

"You're getting right on the plane?" Linda asked, to make sure.

"Yeah. Won't have me in your hair anymore." He was trying to joke, but his heart hurt.

"You listen to me," she told him, bending down to make sure he saw her eyes. "My son loves you, and so does my family. You are not a bother. You are not in our hair."

Seth gave her a small smile. Except he was.

She sighed and kissed his temple, and his father was next.

And then Susan had circled around and made sure his leg was inside and stretched out in front of him before she shut the door.

They drove straight to the airport, and Susan dosed him with painkillers before getting an airport people-mover to haul him to the plane. By the time they took off for New York, he'd passed out, his head leaning on the glass, leg stretched out in front of the seat next to him, because he got two first-class seats.

Someday, he thought as he went under, he really would sleep forever. Waking up was just too damned much trouble. Without Kelly, everything was.

When Your Head is in the Stars, You're Everywhere

"KELLY, HE'S crying."

Kelly looked up from his tablet and frowned. He'd taken a job that let him work from home four days a week, and that suited him. He dropped X-man at daycare while Chloe was in school and then picked them both up and worked a little in the afternoon if he could. The situation was… well, perfect, actually, considering how bad it could be.

The restaurant his mom had once done the books for had gone belly up, but that turned out okay. She'd gotten a job as a receptionist at Craig's warehouse—they got to go to work together, which was great, because she was practically living downstairs anyway, so Matty could use her room. It was a situation that benefited everybody… as long as Kelly didn't have to talk to his brother ever again for the rest of their lives.

But Chloe was so good. She'd play quietly or watch television when he was busy—but he tried not to be busy too much. She really loved to sit on his lap and show him small things, like her ever-increasing stuffed animal collection—or watch Seth's videos on the tablet, which was a special form of agony.

Seth's YouTube channel had seen a big influx of new music over the summer and fall. Gorgeous new songs—complicated, all of the instruments he was proficient in, plus the violin, which was his baby and soared over them all.

Sad.

Heartrendingly sad.

The first time Kelly heard Seth's new work, he'd wondered if he was still breathing. His chest hurt so bad he wasn't sure he could.

And Chloe listened to all of them and told Seth about them in the weekly family Skype call. The one that happened upstairs, that Kelly always worked super hard to miss, because if he had to hear Seth's voice across the fucking phone, he'd drop everything and *drive* to New York just to hold him again.

"Who's crying, *mija*?" He heard his father in his voice and silently apologized. He didn't feel much like he lived up to Xavier Cruz's memory these days.

"The man in Nana Linda's room."

Chloe didn't like Matty. It wasn't Matty's imagination—she regarded him distrustfully, even after the past five months. He'd smile when she wandered in there, and although Kelly knew he was in pain, knew walking made his edema ache, knew his joints hurt and he could barely eat, he'd stand up from the recliner they'd moved there and hold out his arms.

"Wanna see Daddy, Chloe?"

"Wanna see Seth."

And then she'd walk away.

"What happened?" Kelly asked now, steeling his heart. Even though Matty had earned this life through hard living and being a dick, Kelly was starting to feel sorry for his brother. Chloe meant everything to Kelly—to Seth too, for that matter. If she ever turned her back on him, he wasn't sure if there'd be enough pieces left for even Seth to pick up.

"I was sitting in his lap, showing him Seth music." She smiled. "There's new Seth music, Kelly. Wanna hear?"

Oh, Kelly had heard. It was stunning. The dying song of a swan prince, the lament of a saint for his demon lover—Kelly had listened to it the night Seth released it, and had cried for an hour, unable to even muffle the sobs.

"Heard it, angel. That's why Matty's crying?"

"Yeah. I got him tissues."

Kelly ruffled her hair, which they kept short because his mother was, in her words, done with ponytails for good.

"I'll go talk with him and—"

And at that moment, X-man woke up in his crib in Kelly's room. Chloe was sleeping in Agnes's room now, but Kelly? If Kelly wanted a private life, he was going to have to rent another hotel room.

It wasn't worth it without Seth's voice in the dark.

By the time Kelly got in to see if Matty would live—for the day, at least—he'd settled X-man with a bottle and was burping him over his shoulder.

Matty was sitting up, his head leaning back against the headboard, tears tracking over his sallow face.

Damn him. While Kelly felt like an old man with no life and no hope, his brother looked achingly young.

X let out an enormous belch, spitting all over the diaper on Kelly's shoulder and startling Matty enough to wake him up.

"Wow," he murmured. "Just… damn, baby. That was impressive."

Matty wasn't getting high these days, or when he did, it was on prescription pain-relief pot that he vaped when the kids couldn't see him. He'd told Kelly bitterly that there wasn't a lot of THC in the prescription stuff. No pain? Sure. Good dreams? Fuck it. You were stuck in your own head until you died.

But no pain and some lucid thinking meant—oh God—sometimes he sounded just like Kelly's brother.

"He ate pretty good," Kelly admitted, shifting him so he was in the crook of Kelly's arm. He was five months old and pretty big. Not quite sitting up, and he had a sort of soggy body tone that spoke of more delays, like Chloe. But boy, did he like being held. Didn't matter who, either—Agnes, the twins, Chloe, Seth's father.

Matty.

"Can I hold him?" Matty asked softly. "He's pretty cute. I missed Chloe at this age."

Five months ago, when this arrangement had first started, Kelly might have retorted that he'd *had* Chloe at this age, so he must have been pretty high to forget his own daughter.

But not now.

Death was chasing Matty down on a freight train. His hair was gone from chemo, he could barely walk himself to the bathroom, and about the only happiness he had was talking Chloe into letting him a little bit closer, and holding X.

Matty had all the regrets he needed right now. Kelly didn't want to make anybody unhappier by giving him extra.

"Sure." Kelly gave him the barf rag automatically and let Matty take him upright, because even though X had trouble with soggy muscles, he did love to look at people's faces.

"Hey, guy. Giving your uncle Kelly trouble? That's no good. You gotta suck up to him now, so when you get to the part where you can run around, he thinks you're cute enough to chase."

Damn. Matty was charming when he wanted to be. "Don't listen to him, X-man. You guys are *always* cute enough to chase, right, Chloe?"

Kelly made himself comfy at the foot of the bed, partly because Matty couldn't always stay awake and Kelly needed to be there for the baby, but partly, he had to admit, because his brother was actually being… *his brother.* Kelly had missed him.

So fucking bad.

"Chloe said you were crying," he said softly, and Matty grimaced.

He held out the tablet, and Chloe took it and hit rewind on Seth's video again. Kelly's stomach cramped with grief.

"Turn it down a little, angel. Okay?"

Chloe sighed and took it into the corner of the room, where she could hear it alone—she thought. Every note that hit Kelly's ear sounded like Kelly's desertion.

"It's gorgeous," Matty said into the sudden silence. "He must really love you."

Kelly wanted to shrug and say, "He'll get over it," like he didn't care, because he didn't want his brother to see him bleed.

But he'd been bleeding for five months. God, maybe a *sober* Matty could see what kind of damage he'd done and give a shit.

"He'll get over it," he said, but his voice broke and his throat ached. He looked his brother in the eyes and showed him the extent of his grief.

Matty looked away. "No," he admitted, turning his gaze to Xavier. "I… I don't think he'll ever get over you."

Kelly grunted. "What do you want me to say to that?"

And Matty lifted his chin and caught Kelly's eyes again. "I want you to say you'll call him. You'll bring him back. Mom said he was just waiting for you to say so."

"I'm not going to say so while you're still here!" Kelly wondered if he was insane, or if his brother was just that stupid. In the front room, they could both hear the door open. "That must be Agnes," Kelly said into the silence. "She was practicing today, but sometimes she can catch the earlier bus."

Lily was at class tonight, and Lulu was working at a nearby restaurant. Tomorrow they'd switch, except Lily would be working retail.

"Chloe," Matty said, keeping his voice soft. "Baby, why don't you go show Seth to your Aunt Agnes."

Chloe stood and smiled, then ran into the other room with glee. From the living room they both heard Agnes, on a whoosh of breath, like she was picking Chloe up. "Heya, Chloe-monster. How's things?"

"Seth made the man cry!"

"Yikes! Here—let's start dinner so we don't have to listen to that go down!"

Matty chuckled at the ensuing clatter from the kitchen and then cleared his throat. "Why won't you call him?"

"How many times have you threatened him?" Kelly asked evenly. "Called him a psycho. Told me he was a murderer and you were going to call the cops? Threatened to get your daughter taken away? Just offhand. General. Ballpark. C'mon, Matty, tell me. Because he's been offering to turn himself in to the police for years, just so it's not hanging over the family's head. Think about that. He's got... he's got *this gift* and *the world at his feet*, and he's offering to go to jail so *we're okay.* So ask the question again!" Maybe his words hadn't come out so evenly. Maybe his voice was rising and some of the anger he'd been trying to let go of was threatening to cave in his chest.

Maybe he was wondering if he was strong enough to smother his useless fucking brother with a pillow and say, "Hey, he just fucking up and died!"

Matty wasn't looking away from him, though. Wasn't lowering his head in shame. Wasn't glowering defiantly.

He was crying.

But he was looking Kelly in the eyes. "Remember when we were kids?" he rasped. "Seth would come over and play whatever we wanted. I'd want to play Hot Wheels, and he'd say something like Monopoly, and we'd end up playing Hot Wheels. And he'd just be so happy."

"I hate you so much right now." Kelly could hardly get the words out.

"And he'd just... I don't know... you'd be talking and think he wasn't listening, and then he'd just turn around and say something—something so important. Like I'd be complaining about grades or a teacher or something, and he'd say, 'Mr. Bradshaw gave three kids Pop-Tarts this morning. Did you see that?' And suddenly my B didn't matter, because this teacher was a person and Seth saw it."

Kelly was dying. Kelly *wished* he was dead. "Matty—"

"And he was... he was just such a good friend." Matty wiped his eyes with the back of his hand. "Castor Durant—he was so good at the blackmail. Take a hit, church boy, or I'll hurt your brother and his friend. Take another, or I'll tell your girlfriend's father you took the first. It just went on and on and on...."

"You outed us to him," Kelly snarled. "You made our lives hell—"

"Do you think Castor Durant hadn't been threatening you all year?" Matty asked, his voice tangling. "And every day, I was getting deeper and deeper. And one day, I was high, and it just slipped out—you and Seth. I... I was hurt, you see? Because I was a dumb kid, and I was high half the time, and I thought you and him meant I lost my brother and my friend. And... and that was it. I couldn't protect you. I couldn't protect Isela—their fathers were friends, you see? And then... that night when you were attacked, I was so mad at you. You put me in that position. It's all I could think. You *made* me have to give you up to Castor. If you and Seth hadn't... hadn't been—"

"In love?" Kelly asked bitterly.

Matty squeezed his eyes shut. "Here, now? With no drugs in my body—I regret it. It... it was so innocent, you two. I don't know why I couldn't see it that way then."

Kelly pulled in a breath, and another, not sure if there was enough oxygen in the world. But his brother wasn't finished with him. Not yet.

"And then you were attacked. And... and I was part of it. I hated so much—and part of it was hating you because I'd been in hell for months. Every time I went to Isela's church, Castor was there, and he was giving me drugs, and he was threatening my family, threatening Isela. And I couldn't tell anybody, and I was so scared. And you... you went through fifteen minutes of hell and the world ground to a halt."

"Fifteen minutes? Is that all you think it was?" Like it was yesterday. Foul hands, worse smells, violating his skin, his senses, *his body*—

"No." Matty was staring into the void, lines of sorrow etched so deeply in his face they might have gone straight to the bone. "No. That's one of the things you know when you're looking at the end of things. You know how much hell other people went through, when you were making your own."

"Matty, I gotta go. I can't—"

"Call him," Matty whispered, relentless. "Blame it on me if you want. Get him here. Tell him you're sorry. Take my daughter, my son...." He looked at Xavier, his father's namesake, with a look of tenderness that Kelly would have said he wasn't capable of. "Isela was a victim too, Kelly. I was supposed to take her away from Castor, from the church, from all those things that hurt her. I got sucked into it just like she did. She never had a chance. Take my son and daughter and raise them. Be happy with our—" Finally his voice broke. "—with our friend. Our dreamy, stupid friend, who was always so much smarter than either of us but who loved us anyway."

Kelly had to breathe. He had spots in front of his eyes, and he had to… he had to….

With a sob he sank to his knees by his brother's bed, face pressed against the faded flowered comforter, Matty's hand in his hair.

"I'm so sorry, little brother. So sorry. Be happy. Please? For me?"

But Kelly couldn't answer. He couldn't think. He had his brother back, but he was dying, and Kelly was lost in the pain of being reborn.

AGNES CAME in not long after that and took Xavier into the other room, quietly, probably expecting not to be noticed. Kelly hadn't moved, and Matty's hand hadn't moved in his hair either. Matty finally broke the silence.

"Man, this was sweet and all, but I need to pee, and believe me, that's super exciting for both of us."

Kelly stood and stretched and wiped his face on his shoulder. His brother's organs were shutting down—his kidneys were at 50 percent. "You had to be fucking dying?" he asked, shifting his brother's swollen legs and ankles over the side of the bed.

"Yeah. I know. What an asshole."

"I'm saying." It took an effort—Kelly had to help Matty to his mother's toilet and back, even had to help wash his hands. They got him back in bed, and Matty sighed.

"So. You gonna call him?"

Kelly sighed. "I left him in the hospital, Matty. He could barely turn his head. Talk about dick moves."

"Sorry. My timing was pretty shitty. I know that now."

There was something facetious in his voice, something of the brother Kelly had loved, that made Kelly smile. "*Now* you know that? You couldn't have figured that out when Seth was kissing me in the woods?"

Matty reached across the bed and grabbed his hand. "Call him."

"He's still in danger from the police. I don't know if you've noticed, but every year, Carlton Durant puts that police sketch all over the local news, makes Castor a celebrity cold case and all this shit. I can't call him. Even if…." He trailed off. There was no if. There never had been.

Matty nodded, looking troubled. "Yeah." He sighed. "Yeah." He leaned his head back against the bed. "Do *you* think he did it?"

"I don't care," Kelly said, adamant. He'd had eight years to think about this. "I used to think that made me a bad person, but now I don't care about that either. Did you see him before he left for Bridgford?"

"No," Matty said, his expression dark and faraway. "Or if I did, I was too high to care."

"I did. He'd been beat the fuck up. He had choke marks around his throat, same as me. His eye was brick red, his face swollen. Whatever happened that night, it didn't come easy. He didn't walk up to Castor Durant and shoot him in the back. I mean... I love him. I love him more than anyone on the planet, but I helped him get his passport. I know he *still* can't plan far enough to plan a murder. If he did it, it was self-defense. If he didn't, someone did the world a favor." Kelly hadn't forgotten his brother's broken confession of being dragged into addiction, into pain. "I'm just sorry it didn't happen sooner."

Matty let out a fractured laugh. "Me too. Hey, could you lend me your laptop? It's connected to the printer, right?"

"Yeah, sure."

"And lend me Agnes too."

Kelly couldn't help the hurt. "I finally don't hate you, and you're kicking me out of the room?"

To his surprise, Matty's eyes darkened with more pain. "You don't know what that means," he rasped. "That you don't hate me right now. This is me, paying you back. Trust me, little brother. I've got some shit to sort."

Kelly stood, and found himself leaning over the bed to kiss Matty on the forehead. "Sleep soon," he murmured, knowing Matty was in constant pain, every moment of every day.

"I'll be sleeping forever soon enough," he said. "Sleep is overrated."

Well, he hadn't been missing Seth like Kelly had. Sleep was Kelly's only refuge these days.

"In that case, don't sleep yet," Kelly told him. "Let me not hate you for a week. That would be fucking awesome."

Matty smiled, and some peace stole across his battered features. "I won't die until you send for him. That's the deal, Kelly. I gotta make that shit right."

"I'll think about it," Kelly said. In his heart he knew—he had to. God. Seth deserved to not hate Matty too.

"Good. Now send Agnes in, okay?"

Kelly left, taking over dinner and childcare. Linda came up, Craig at her heels, both of them with groceries, which meant fresh salad for dinner and ice cream for dessert, and Kelly felt a measure of contentment steal into his soul.

Craig put away groceries while Kelly's mom went into the front room and started talking to Chloe and playing with Xavier. Kelly looked at Craig, his chest swelling with the memory of the day Seth had left.

Kelly had been downstairs, sitting on Craig's worn and broken denim couch, not even pretending not to cry. Seth's father had walked in, surprising him. So soon? Seth was gone so soon? Kelly scrambled off the couch, wiping his face with his arm.

"Sorry. Sorry. Habit. You probably don't even want to see me anymore. Just, you know, this was my safe place for so long and—"

"Kelly—Kelly, wait." Craig closed the door behind him and held out his arms. "Kelly, what makes you think that's how love works?"

They'd cried together.

And now, seeing Seth's father looking tired, a little sad, Kelly felt like… what? Like it was time? His brother said it was time, so it just—

Who was he kidding.

"Is he coming back for the holidays?" Kelly asked, voice squeaking on the first two words.

"Christmas—the week before," Craig said, giving him an overcasual look. "Why?"

Kelly took a deep breath. "How's… how's he doing?"

"Shitty."

Kelly let out a bark of laughter. "He sounds okay when he calls." Of course, Kelly fled the room—hell, fled the apartment—when that happened.

"Yeah. He forgets to eat. Amara texted me last month and asked if there was some sort of religious vow he'd taken to wear crappy T-shirts. I bought him a fuckton of clothes on Amazon and had them delivered. She says he got them, but she was the one who put them in his drawers."

Kelly let out a little moan. "I… he was supposed to do okay," he said, his throat raw.

"Well, she came home this week, and she said she's been texting him daily to remind him to eat. They've got some other roommate there periodically. *She* thinks he's got a crush on Seth, but she told him to sleep on the couch as often as he could just to make sure Seth did human things. He's not… not here on Earth, Kelly. His music is gorgeous—I know you've heard it. But that's the only part of him that's working."

Fuck. Fuck fuck fuck fuck. "He… it's been six months. He was supposed to do okay."

"Well, yeah. But you guys are supposed to be together."

Kelly shook his head. "My brother's…." And he couldn't say it. Matty had maybe a week, maybe a month. But Kelly couldn't say the word now. Not after how Matty was today, being human, being sorry.

Being real.

"Yeah. Do you really want to wait until then?" Craig's smile—his face was lined, maybe a little more than a man's should be at forty-five, and his hair was silvering. But his smile was Seth's. There was so much hope, so much gratitude in that smile, for the things he had, the things that had not yet been taken away.

Kelly was suddenly exhausted. "I…." Well, he needed to work, but Matty had his computer. *Goddammit.*

"Your mom's calling the hospice nurse," Craig said softly. "We decided on the way home. It's time to get help with him. You can sleep downstairs tonight. I think she wants to be here."

Kelly nodded, suddenly just fucking done. "Can I use your computer?" At least to check email. His tablet had stuff in the cloud, but Craig's laptop didn't have Kelly's art programs.

"Yeah. Sure. Who's got your computer?"

At that moment the shared printer started spitting stuff out in the home office corner of the tiny living room. Agnes hurried out and grabbed a bubble mailer and the pages, turned them away, and folded them like she was resisting the impulse to look.

"You can have your tablet back in a minute, Kelly," she said over her shoulder as she hurried back into the sickroom.

"Sure." Kelly looked at Craig and nodded. It was seven o'clock, and he needed some peace and some quiet and a chance to get his heart clear. And he needed to get his computer back from Matty. And he needed a change of clothes for tomorrow, and a drawing pad, and his phone.

And he needed Seth.

He'd always needed Seth.

It had been madness to try to live his life without him.

He was sitting on Craig's couch, the television muted in front of him, when he finally texted.

He's got maybe a week. Please, Seth, for Matty. Please come home.

It took Seth less than a minute to reply.

Not for Matty. For you, Kelly. All you had to do was ask.

Good.

The TV droned on, performing a marionette dance for all Kelly knew. He had his tablet back—what he *should* be doing was work. The firm that had hired him and agreed to let him work from home was generous, but he still had deadlines.

Only he couldn't think. Not now. Couldn't concentrate, not on his tablet, not on TV.

And his brain was a fucking hamster wheel, like his life had been, the whole of it, running as fast as he could to be with the boy he loved and always ending up right back here, in the same exact place.

In desperation, he grabbed a pad of paper from Craig's office and a pencil, and then pulled up Seth's YouTube channel and set it to play.

And then he pretended that they were kids again, and Seth was standing behind the couch, practicing with that weird intensity that he brought to his music, brought to his lovemaking, and to nothing else in the world.

And Kelly was drawing random pictures that weren't random at all.

Seth's hands, long and supple, his eyes, like green lasers, seeing to the heart of the things he loved best. His mouth, wide and generous, and his white teeth, nibbling at his lower lip as he concentrated on something particularly difficult.

His instrument, singing the songs of the gods, just because Seth asked nicely.

Craig came downstairs in the morning, early, and found Kelly asleep on the couch surrounded by sheets of computer paper, each one specially marked like a snowflake. Kelly woke up and tried to sit up without crumpling them, only to find Seth's dad pulling random pictures out from under his behind and his hips.

"Something on your mind?" Craig asked dryly, setting the sheaf of rumpled pictures on the coffee table.

Kelly gave him a watery smile. "He's coming home."

And this morning, Craig Arnold's smile looked just like his son's. Slow and dreamy like a sunrise.

"Good."

Reckoning

SETH HAD his carry-on and his violin, and a splitting headache and blurry vision that came from spending three days on standby in Newark and three different flights after that with eight hours of layovers.

He wasn't sure of the last time he'd eaten, and he was positive he didn't smell so good.

He knocked tentatively on his father's door, hoping his dad was home. Was the Cadillac there? Who was driving the Caddy these days? Wasn't it Lulu's car? Was Agnes driving? He couldn't remember.

God, let his dad be home.

Agnes opened the door instead, and he stared at her, surprised. She was short, topping out at five three, but she looked so grown-up since…. God. Had it been a year since he'd seen her? 'Cause he was going to see her at her play, but that hadn't turned out so well, and after that, Skype was always so chaotic.

"Agnes, are you driving yet?"

"No, I'm still fifteen. Jeez, Seth, you look like shit! Kelly said you were coming, but we would have had someone come get you from the airport—"

"I had to take a Lyft from San Francisco," he told her, and that still boggled him. So had the price. Yikes.

"That's horrible. Come in—God, come in."

Seth wandered into the apartment he'd always known. Same denim furniture, same brown drapes, beige carpet, same dust.

But Agnes was apparently sleeping on the couch because there was a shit-ton of pink sheets and a comforter folded up on it, as well as a small suitcase with her clothes and a porta crib in the corner with baby supplies—formula, diapers, a bag with what looked like all the baby's clothes.

And a baby in the middle.

Seth smiled a little. "X-man?" He'd heard about the baby and seen the baby on Skype, but he hadn't yet held the baby, and he yearned to. This was part of the family he hadn't had a chance to get to know.

"Yeah. He's asleep. You can hold him in the morning."

"Where's—"

"My stupid brother is upstairs, talking to the hospice nurse because my other stupider brother is…." Her rant, so much like one of Kelly's, trailed off. "Dying," she said with a sigh. "Whatever. You're here, and I'm glad. Come here. I need a hug."

Mm. He needed to hold her, but she peeled out of his arms way too soon.

"You need a shower," she said bluntly. "Oh my God, Seth, what happened?"

"Three days on standby," he said. "Twelve hours in layovers."

"And a Lyft from San Francisco. Jesus, it's like a holy quest!"

"Well," he repeated the thing he'd heard sixty-dozen times in the last four days, "it *is* a week before Thanksgiving."

"Damn. Get in the shower. When's the last time you ate?"

Seth tried to think about it. "There was a noodle place in Newark," he mumbled, "and a Panda Express in Houston, but I had a lot of walking in Houston. And that was just to get to the Sky Tram. Was Houston yesterday or today?"

Kelly's sister had the round face Kelly'd had as a child, but it looked like hers, pleasing and soft, would follow her into adulthood.

Her round eyes looked even more horrified in that delicate little circle.

"Shower," she muttered. "Do you even have any clean clothes?"

"When was Denver?" he asked.

"Holy fucking God. I'll get you some out of your drawers. There's got to be some sweats that won't slide off your bony ass."

Good idea. Well, Kelly's sisters really were all super geniuses, right?

Seth emerged fifteen minutes later feeling a little better—clean, at least, and moisturized. His dad still kept cocoa butter in the bathroom, which sort of hurt a little. Agnes was right—his old sweats were just about perfect, and there were even some old underwear and… oh God.

Kelly's old black shirt.

The one they'd used the first time they made love on his dad's couch.

He almost put it back in the drawer and went through his dad's drawers for a plain white one, but he couldn't.

Kelly.

He was so close.

Agnes had some chicken and veggies ready for him when he was done, and he ate it, almost falling asleep at the table.

"Where's Kelly again?"

"Go lie down, honey," she told him, tousling his hair. He grinned at her, because he'd done the same thing to her as a child.

"You'll wake me up when he's here, right?"

"Sure."

Without quite knowing how it happened, Kelly's little sister, who was the same age Kelly had been when they'd fallen in love, had Seth by the elbow and was taking him through the apartment. She had him lay down in his bed and pulled his old comforter over his shoulders, then kissed his forehead.

"I really love your brother," he told her, because she might not know this. "I fell in love with him when he was your age. And we feel so grown-up now, but a little part of me is still in love with that same boy. And most of me is in love with who he is now. Isn't that weird?"

She kissed his forehead again, and this time something wet fell. She wiped it off with her thumb.

"That's totally amazing," she whispered. "I love you, Seth. Get some sleep."

He was probably asleep before she turned off the light.

He wasn't sure when Kelly crawled into bed with him, turning so his back was to Seth's front. He only knew it felt right.

"Kelly?"

"Anyone else climbing into bed with you?" Kelly asked, and his voice sounded thick.

"No. Caleb sleeps on the couch. Amara and I only have bunk beds, you know."

Kelly's chuckle was strained, and he pulled Seth's arms around his middle. "You'll have to tell me when you wake up."

"I missed you so bad. Any time is forever when you're not at the end of it."

"I missed you too. I thought it would hurt, chasing the dream of you again. And then I didn't even have the dream of you, and it was like I had no heart anymore."

Seth rubbed his chest, his body heat seeping in through Seth's sleep-addled brain like a balm. "Gotta make it better," he said. "You need your heart."

"You're here, *mijo*. Got it back again. Now go to sleep. Agnes said you went through hell to get here. Tomorrow's gonna really suck, okay?"

"What's happening tomorrow?"

Kelly let out a long sigh. "My brother needs to talk to us. He says... he says this is the only gift he can give."

Seth felt an unexpected grief bubbling up. "I'd rather have one of his Hot Wheels."

Kelly started to giggle, but it turned to tears soon enough, and then he rolled over in Seth's arms and they were holding each other, face-to-face, and crying.

That was how they fell asleep.

Children clutching each other in the storm.

WHEN HE woke up in the morning, Kelly was still there.

"Seth, I hate to bother you, but I gotta pee."

Seth relaxed his grip and let him up, then fell back asleep again, for he had no idea how long. He didn't wake up again until Kelly came back into the room, a baby in one arm and a sandwich in his other hand.

"What's the sandwich for?"

"The baby doesn't faze you at all, does it?"

Seth heard the teasing note and let out a little smile. "I like babies. You know that."

Kelly sobered. "Good. Here—you eat and let Mr. X here get a look at you. When you're done, he might even let you hold him."

The baby made that baby sound—a gurgle and a belch or something—and Seth agreed to terms.

"My dad says he's real good," Seth told him, digging into the sandwich. It was the first time he'd been hungry in six months.

"What your dad is leaving out, because he's just as nuts about babies as you are, is that he's soggy."

Seth looked at the baby, who regarded him serenely back through green eyes that definitely weren't Matty's. "Cornstarch," Seth said, smiling slowly to see if maybe this baby would respond. Mr. X chewed on his fist without a lot of enthusiasm and widened his eyes a little. Well, close. "Cornstarch for a soggy baby."

Kelly dropped a kiss on top of Xavier's head. "Not soggy that way. His muscles. Like that smile he's not getting for you. He can barely lift his hands up to his mouth. He's got some problems, Seth—"

"Like Chloe?"

"Well, yeah. But different problems."

Seth smiled at the baby again. This time, he was sure he got a little smile back. "Not problems," he said, completely lost in the baby. "Personality features."

"Oh my God, Seth, you never listen—"

Seth scowled, realizing this could be the finale of the fight they should have had when he'd been in the hospital. "No. I listen. You're trying to tell me that he's a challenge. And that you're going to be responsible for him after your brother dies. And that he'll be my responsibility too, just like Chloe. I hear you, Kelly. Now I need you to hear me."

Kelly gaped. "You don't talk this much ever."

Seth set down his sandwich, not hungry anymore. "The last six months, I didn't have anyone who could hear my heart around me. I had to save it for the week, without talking to you in between times. And that's my point. My whole life, you, my dad, your parents, they moved heaven and earth to know what was in my heart. To give me the things I didn't know how to ask for. To help me in school when paperwork isn't my best thing. And the whole time I was like, 'But, uhm, I'm really not that special.' You all told me I was. So why is taking these children in any different than that. No, they're probably not going to solo in New York at twenty…." He stopped and tried to do the math.

"Five. You're twenty-five, Seth."

"Thank you. I keep thinking it's twenty-two. I have no idea why. But my point is, they're special too. I can move heaven and earth for their specialness, just like you all moved it for me. I got no problem with that. I got no problem being a dad at twenty-six—"

"Five."

"Whatever! I got no problem with that. Yeah, it's young—you think I don't know Amara and Vince aren't gonna wait ten more years? There's people I play with not sure at forty? I get it. But I'm sure *now*. You're sure *now*. Your family's not a sinkhole, Kelly. Your family's a *family*. And I want to be a part of it. I want to be a part of it more than anything in the world, *except* how I want to be a part of *you.*" He swallowed, not sure if that came out right. "I want to be a part of your life more," he clarified. "But the rest of the family is nice too. Agnes looks just like you at fifteen, did you know that? Her face is a little rounder, but it's uncanny."

Kelly was crying, and Seth didn't know what that meant.

"That was a good speech," Kelly said. "That was a life-changing sort of speech."

Seth grabbed some tissues and used them to wipe Kelly's face, since he was holding the really super-placid baby in the crook of his arm.

"Can it change our lives?" he asked after a moment.

"How's that gonna look?"

Planning. Seth had been bad at planning, but good at chess. This was like chess. "How about I go back to New York and find us a house in Pennsylvania or Connecticut or New Jersey or something. It's like this weird little incestuous area made up of three states—"

"The tristate area, Seth. It's an actual thing."

"Oh. Anyway, I get Amara and Susan to help, and we get a place outside the city by good schools for Chloe and X-man, somewhere you can find a job—"

"I work from home." Kelly shrugged. "I need to meet with my bosses once, maybe twice a month."

"See? Then you keep that job, and we find a nanny who can take care of everybody when we're busy, and we… you know. Live our lives. And maybe I move to Italy in two years—"

"This Gianni guy still hitting on you?"

"No. He's sleeping with this girl who plays bassoon. Anyway, he likes me in his orchestra, and he's going back to Italy eventually, and we can go there. And we can bring the kids and do the same thing. And learn Italian. And maybe Germany someday. And we just keep dealing. I mean, it doesn't end just because we're together. Even if it was just us, we'd still have to make decisions and balance your stuff and my stuff. And…." Seth hated to admit this. "Yes. Sometimes my stuff is bigger, but that's because if I don't show up for work, a thousand people who just paid a shit-ton of money to see me are gonna be real depressed. But some days your stuff is gonna be more important, and I can deal with that. But…." And his façade of adulthood slipped away, leaving behind the kid he'd been at the very beginning.

The kid whose world revolved around Kelly Cruz.

"But God, won't it be better to deal with it together? 'Cause...." The last six months came crashing back into his heart, and it almost broke all over again. "'Cause being alone these last months sure did feel like the end of my world."

Kelly nodded, biting his lip, the tears still falling. "Mine too," he confessed. "God, Seth. I'd rather try almost anything than go back to that. Even the dream of you is better than no you at all."

Seth wasn't sure who moved, but they were suddenly kissing, mouths meshed, Seth's whole soul involved in the kiss, even if he could only put one hand chastely on Kelly's waist.

They had to pull back, panting, because there was a baby making sucking sounds on his fist, and Seth smiled and leaned his head against Kelly's.

"Where's Agnes?"

"At school. Same as Chloe."

"That kid go down for a nap? Ever?"

"In about two hours. The good news is he sleeps like a rock and stays that way for another two hours."

"Me and X-man gonna get along just fine."

Kelly laughed softly. "We gotta talk to my brother first." He sobered and pulled back. "He looks sort of… well, like a movie special effect, but worse. Just be prepared. He's all swollen and yellow and bald and shit. It's… you won't be able to see the Matty you knew in all of that."

Seth stared at him in wonder, because he was here and they'd kissed and there would be no more time without the hope of him. "I can still see Chloe and Agnes in *you*," he said. "Is Matty's heart still in there?"

Kelly's eyes—such a soulful brown, and so full of life—didn't quite sparkle, but they did glow, ever so subtly. "First time I've seen it in years."

"I can meet the creature from the black lagoon if I get to talk to real Matty again." The pain of Matty's betrayal, the memory of what they'd been to each other as kids, washed over him. "Your brother was my best friend once."

Kelly's eye roll was almost epic. "That's only because he was older. If I'd been older, I would have been your best friend *and* your boyfriend."

"Yeah. Probably." Seth wanted to kiss his face all over, wanted to devour him whole. Instead he remembered he had to be an adult and pulled back with a sigh. "I need to see if I've got any clothes in my carry-on—"

"You don't," Kelly muttered. "Oh my God, Seth, I pulled that shit out, and half of it was dirty and the other half was falling apart. Your father *just sent* you clothes. What happened?"

"I don't know. You texted me and there was packing and leaving. That's all I remember."

"Well, remember I'm going to Walmart while you're talking to my useless brother, because you can't stay here with one pair of old jeans and three pairs of holey underwear."

Seth met his eyes and smiled slightly. "And a black T-shirt."

Kelly got a good look at what he was wearing and covered his eyes. "And now I'm even more horny. And embarrassed. How do you even have that?"

"I never gave it back." *Because duh!*

Kelly uncovered his eyes and kissed Seth on the cheek again. "Like my heart. Now here. You take the baby. I'll take the dishes, and I'm going to change and shower, because I *have* clothes. I'll take you upstairs before I go get you some shit to wear. Your dad is gonna *crap* when he finds out you left all your new stuff in New York."

He paused and frowned.

"When are you going back?"

"After Christmas. With you."

Kelly raised his eyebrows. "I thought you just said you were gonna go get us a house and—"

"I changed my mind. I'm bringing you with me. We'll sleep in my bunk until we can find a place. I'm not leaving you again. It would kill me."

Kelly traced his cheek with gentle fingertips. "It won't kill you if you know I'm coming soon," he said softly. "I like your plan. Let's follow that. I promise, I'm not letting the dream of us go again."

"I'll think about it." Seth really didn't want to get on another plane without Kelly by his side.

"You do that. And you sound all growly and possessive and weird. I like it, but don't be dumb. We know how to be grown-ups."

"Says you," Seth muttered, but Kelly was giving him the baby and kissing him brusquely on the cheek, and it was time to table this discussion for later.

Xavier Cruz settled into the crook of Seth's arm and looked tranquilly up at him for a minute. Seth tried another smile.

Finally, he got one back.

Yeah, fine. He could wait. He had a family coming to live with him, where he was doing the thing he was best at in the world.

What was another month?

KELLY CLEANED up and walked Seth upstairs, Xavier still in his arms. "The hospice nurse is here," he explained, opening the door. "So I'm going to take X-man—"

Seth grunted and pulled the baby tighter.

"Yes, I'm taking him. We're going shopping at Walmart, and there's X-man things he needs. He's growing out of his one-piece pajamas, and you need to talk to my brother without him as a buffer."

"Damn."

Kelly laughed, and something about the laugh made Seth remember when he'd been fifteen and nothing had hurt him.

"It won't be as bad as you think," Kelly promised softly. He paused in the middle of the living room and looked around. "You know, if you and me and the babies move to New York, and Lily and Lulu take over yours and your dad's apartment and pay rent, and there's only Agnes living here, in her own damned room, do you think we can get them more furniture?"

Seth looked at the tapestry couches and stuffed chairs, the peeling laminate on the bookshelves and TV stand, the curtains that Linda had probably gotten when Kelly was a baby because they were all Seth could remember.

"Maybe they can get a house," he said thoughtfully. "Or move. After Agnes graduates, you know? Maybe our folks can take a trip, get an RV."

He and Kelly met eyes, apparently on the exact same page. "Something, anything, but here," Kelly agreed. And his smile, when it came, was shining. "I should have been patient, Seth. I should have had faith."

Seth shrugged, feeling heat in his face. "It's been almost nine years. Only losing faith for a few months? Coulda been worse."

His heart was still raw and sore. He knew it would take longer than that before he stopped rubbing his chest when he thought of April. But faith—he had it now.

Kelly's mouth on his was sweet but brief.

"Okay. Brace yourself. He doesn't look...."

"Like Matty?"

"Like human. I'm not kidding, Seth. It's bad."

It was and it wasn't. Matty's meat-sack was about finished—Seth wasn't blind. The pathetic fringe of hair around his crown looked mangy and almost infectious, and his yellow pallor and bloating were sickly in the extreme.

But for the first time in years, his eyes weren't full of hate, and he smiled as Seth walked in, gently, like he used to when they were kids.

"Hey, Seth."

"Hey, Matty. What's doin'?"

"Heh heh. Or is that what's *dyin'*?"

Seth groaned and took a seat near the bed. The hospice nurse was sitting in her corner, reading her phone, and she looked up and smiled absently. A middle-aged woman with dyed blonde hair and a formidable bosom, she looked sort of like Seth would expect someone who watched people die for a living looked. Like she could be pleasant and kind on command, but like she saved her deeper involvement for her own family.

"Yeah," Seth said, giving Xavier to Kelly reluctantly. "Sorry about that. Sucks."

Matty paused to look at the way Seth held the baby, bussing him on the top of the little head as he handed him over.

"It does for me," he admitted. "Where you goin', Kel?"

"Walmart." Kelly rolled his eyes fondly at Seth. "He got on a plane with a tiny suitcase full of dirty clothes. And he's so skinny at this point that when they come out of the wash, they'll *still* fall off his ass. Can you believe that?"

Matty nodded, a slow smile on his face. "Some things don't change," he rasped, and then coughed into a bloody wad of tissues in his hand. "Some things do." He grimaced at Kelly. "I'll be done in an hour. Will you be home by then?"

Kelly shrugged. "Hour and a half—gonna get some groceries too. Want something, Seth?"

Seth regarded him blankly, and Kelly and Matty laughed together.

"Good one, Kel!" Matty said, coughing again. "But seriously, bring him some ice cream or something, just for me, would you?"

Then Kelly did something unexpected and tender, something that mended so much in Seth's heart he almost couldn't think or breathe. He bent over and kissed his brother's forehead.

"Don't die until after Thanksgiving. Deal?"

"You want me to die on your birthday? Wow, I must be a real bastard."

Kelly laughed grimly and then kissed Seth's cheek before taking Xavier away with him, still laughing.

Seth was left in the room with Matty and an indifferent nurse, but he was okay. Kelly loved his brother again.

"Thank you," he said quietly, wishing for something to do with his hands.

"For making your life fucking miserable for eight years? Sure."

"No. For coming back and making him okay. He missed you."

Matty looked directly at him, apparently too weak for bullshit or evasion. "I fucking ruined your lives, Seth. And part of it was being high, and part of it was being confused, and a lot of it was being scared of Castor Durant, because he threatened me every fucking day until he died. But after that, it was jealousy, pure and simple. Do you know why?"

Seth shook his head helplessly. "No."

"Because my life was shit, and you and Kelly—you kept that… that innocence from when we were kids. Every time I saw you, I'd expect you to be grown-up Mr. Businessman Musician, like a rock star, using your talent for a buck. But when I did see you, it was through the eyes of my family, where you were a saint and Kelly was living in my father's footsteps, and I'd killed my father and I had nowhere to go but down. You were both still… kind. Still family. And still in love. And I… I mean, I'm an addict. And a drunk. I didn't have many saving graces as it was. But the things I said to you, about being a psycho, a pervert, belonging in a cage—those things… they weren't true. And I knew they weren't true when I said them."

Seth's chest hurt. And his ears and his throat and his head.

And his heart.

"Why did you say them, then?"

"Seth, do you remember what happened the night Castor Durant died?"

Seth shook his head. "Some of it."

Matty nodded. "I didn't think so. I need to tell you a story, Seth. One I won't be taking to my grave—I promise."

Seth swallowed, his mouth suddenly really dry.

"Nurse Cathy?" Matty asked, his voice not getting any smoother. "Is there any way you could get my friend here some water? And me too, if you don't mind. Take about fifteen minutes, I think." His lips thinned, which was what passed for a smile on his ravaged features. "And, you know, maybe don't let him kill me when I'm done here."

"I wouldn't kill you," Seth said automatically.

"I know you wouldn't," Matty told him. "I've always known." He nodded at the nurse again, and she left uncertainly.

And then he told Seth a story about two boys walking outside one night, under a low-hanging moon, rotten as spoiled fruit, both of them searching for vengeance.

And how one almost died and the other escaped.

To die every day thereafter.

Giving Thanks

WHEN KELLY got home that afternoon, Seth was sitting on the couch, just staring into space, his hands dangling loosely between his knees.

"Baby… is everything okay?"

"Yes," he said blankly. Then, "No." Then, "Can we get out of here? Is X-man asleep yet, or can we take him on a walk?"

Xavier was starting to fret in that way that meant he wanted his prenap bottle, and Kelly dropped the mass of Walmart bags on the floor. "Here—take these downstairs and change, and I'll get him a snack and pull the stroller from the back of the car. Meet you in ten, yeah?"

Seth looked at him with such gratitude, Kelly wanted to preen. "That's the best idea."

But Kelly had to ask. "Seth, are you sure? You're… you know. I mean it's been eight and a half years, but the case is still hot. Someone's gonna remember. Sometime."

Seth nodded. "Don't worry about it. Don't ever worry about it again. I'm free."

With that, he left, taking his clothes downstairs, and Kelly couldn't get him to say anything more on the subject.

They walked, such a simple little walk now, as adults.

They didn't walk up to the bus stop, to the laundromat that had been the source of their nightmares, or the minimart that had been razed. The vacant field where Castor Durant had died was now another apartment complex, with a playground in the center.

It looked better that way.

Instead, they walked down to their old grammar school, where not even Agnes went anymore. Chloe's was a couple of miles away because it had her special education program, but this was the school that had all five of the Cruz kids listed on a plaque in the front office. This was the school where Seth and Matty and Kelly had stood up and played the violin and Seth had found his thing, his one true thing, the thing that would set him free and let him fly.

As Kelly looked around, he realized that some things had changed. They'd leveled the kickball field to put in portable buildings, and refurbished the soccer field so it could be used by recreational clubs. They'd repaved the blacktop with the basketball hoops and taken out the tetherball poles. The play structure had changed to something modern and less dangerous than the metal nightmare that Matty had always excelled so much at, and the front office had a new layer of paint.

Mrs. Joyce had retired the year Agnes left. Someone else ruled Three Oaks Elementary School now, and as they walked under the yellow sunlight of November trees, Kelly felt time passing in all his bones.

And it hit him.

They weren't that old.

"Seth?" he said, after Xavier's silence let him know that it really was just him and his lover, alone in the late autumn afternoon.

"Yeah?"

"We have our whole lives ahead of us."

Seth put a possessive hand in the small of Kelly's back, and neither of them was afraid. Whatever Matty had said to him, it must have given him some peace, and Kelly didn't want to shatter it by asking for details.

He'd gone on faith for the past eight and a half years, belief that the man he loved couldn't be a killer. Here, in this serene moment, he knew this for fact. Not belief. Whatever Matty had said, no matter what Matty had known that Seth hadn't, Kelly had that peace in his heart.

"We're free," Seth said simply. "We've always been free. We just didn't know it. But now we do."

"What happened—"

"Later." Seth stopped in a patch of sunshine and turned his face to the sky. "It's beautiful," he said. "But there's no ocean. You know, I'm sure we could find a place back east that's near the sea."

"It's not called the Jersey Shore for nothing," Kelly supplied helpfully, and Seth grinned at him as a reward.

But his eyes were still far away.

"I want to get married," he said softly. "In a church if you want, or in a field if you don't. Or in Monterey on the beach if you don't mind the cold. I want to go back to New York and say my husband's coming, and our adopted children. And this half person I've been, when I'm away from you, he'll get swallowed up by the whole person I am right now." He looked at Kelly directly, the green of his eyes clear as a laser. "Is that okay?"

Kelly remembered his brother's wedding, how he hated Matty for it, and how he'd wanted one of his own. "It's all I've ever wanted," he confessed, locking the stroller and wrapping his arms around Seth. "It's the best birthday and Christmas and Thanksgiving I could ever have."

Seth's arms came around him, warm, so strong, and he knew without a doubt that this man—this man who'd sprung from his dreamy boy—could take care of Kelly like nobody else in the world.

And Kelly would care for him back.

"Ready to go home?" he asked breathily.

"Wherever that may be."

THAT AFTERNOON, they spent time in Seth's father's apartment. X-man went down hard, like always, sleeping quietly in the porta crib while Seth and Kelly disappeared into the bedroom and stripped, looking at each other in awe in their ritual of rediscovery.

"You're skinny," they both said at the same time, and then shared a sad smile.

And then Kelly had to kiss him, to possess him, because Kelly had been the damned fool who'd let him go.

Their bodies remembered.

Their bodies remembered how to move, how to kiss, what to stroke, what to nibble. Their bodies blended together like they'd never been apart, like they'd been primed, these past months, to fit together like lock and key.

This time Kelly was the key and Seth was the lock, and as Kelly thrust inside his lover's trusting body, he felt himself float with Seth. Together they rose up, up, beyond this tiny corner of the earth and into the stratosphere, somewhere they could see the future, somewhere they both existed in place and time.

This time Seth took him for a walk among the stars, before their crest broke, both of them crying out, panting, their noises as hushed as they could make them as they fell back to earth, Kelly still moving inside Seth, their fingers laced together so tightly their knuckles were white.

Their bodies remembered—but they remembered the loss too. They weren't willing to take being locked together for granted.

Kelly collapsed into Seth's arms, and Seth held him as their harsh breathing filled the room.

"Monterey," Kelly said. "The day after Christmas. You find the rental. I'll find the priest."

"Vince," Seth said. "He got ordained in Hawaii three years ago for a cousin. I'll ask him if he can officiate."

"Maybe two rentals," Kelly said. "One for the family and one for us."

"We gotta get super good at this again," Seth agreed. "Fill us up while I go find us a home."

"Our home. You're gonna go find us a house."

"Mm. Yeah."

Promises. Promises they could keep.

Music to Kelly's ears.

MATTY DIDN'T make it until Thanksgiving.

Three days after Seth came back home, the nurse greeted them in the morning after Craig and Linda had left for work, and told them that Matty was unconscious and probably wouldn't wake up again.

An hour later, after sitting next to the bed holding hands, talking to Matty's still form about all the things they should have been doing in the last eight years but couldn't, the heart monitor by his side flatlined, and he was gone.

Kelly called the coroner while Seth called his father. Linda had stayed up half the night, reading Matty his favorite stories, and all the girls had said goodbye that morning, before he'd slipped away.

They'd made their peace. They'd said their goodbyes. It was time for honest grieving.

They spent the week of Thanksgiving practically chanting Matty's name like a prayer, possibly making up for all the years they spat it as a curse.

They had the funeral the Sunday after Thanksgiving. Only the family showed—Isela, her father, their church, all of them noticeably absent, although Linda had tried to let Mr. Cortez, at least, know Matty was gone.

It didn't matter. The family was enough.

Seth played pop songs from their high school, mostly, and then, like at Matty's father's funeral, "Hallelujah."

It did the same thing now that it had then—it let them grieve for someone who was far from perfect, but who had left a dent in their lives just the same.

THE NEXT evening, just as Seth and Kelly were getting dinner on the table, there was a knock at the door.

Three men stood there—one young guy not much older than they were, in a cheap suit, one shark-looking guy with brown hair and a beak of a nose in an expensive pinstripe, and one scrawny, insanely hot tomcat in jeans.

The scrawny one looked oddly familiar.

"Officer Rivers?" Kelly asked, feeling blindsided. "Wait—are you still Officer Rivers?"

Rivers shook his head. "No, Kelly, not anymore. Now I'm a PI for a law firm. But I'm glad to see you doing well. Can we come in?"

"Yes," Seth said unexpectedly from Kelly's elbow. He extended his hand. "Nice to meet you, Mr. Rivers. Kelly, go get my dad and your mom, okay?"

Kelly glared at him. "What in the hell—"

Seth looked at him serenely. "Don't worry, baby. Remember when I said we were free?"

"Yeah."

"This is what's gonna set us free."

"'Scuse me." Kelly looked over his shoulder and slid out the door so Seth could usher their new friends in. "Let me get my folks."

Craig and Linda had no idea what this was about, Kelly could tell. He'd interrupted them in the middle of lounging on the couch, feet up, holding hands and smiling stupidly at the television. And he knew that because nobody had bothered to fix the gap in the curtains in nine goddamned years.

When they got to the upstairs living room, Seth had brought in water for the three strangers on the couch, and the girls—all of them—had gathered, children on their laps as they sat on the floor and looked avidly at this new entertainment.

"So," Seth said as Craig took one of the stuffed chairs, Linda on his lap, and Kelly sat in the other, "this is, uh… well, Detective Kryzinski, and you know Mr. Jackson Rivers. And this is his boyfriend, defense attorney Ellery Cramer." He paused and looked at them all in turn. "I got that right?"

"Yeah." Rivers grinned at him. "You'll have to excuse Ellery. He's a little bit starstruck. He's been following your YouTube channel for the last three years."

"You are so damned young," Cramer said, still shocked. "Holy Jesus—twenty-six?"

"Five," Kelly said dryly, because nobody got that right, not even Seth.

"Do you have any idea what kind of talent you have?"

"No, he doesn't. Why are you here again?"

Jackson grinned. "You haven't changed a bit," he said, sounding happy about it. Then he sobered. "You doing okay?"

And Kelly saw that sincerity now for what it was—real. True. "My brother just passed away," he said softly. "It's been rough."

Rivers nodded. "Yeah. That's sort of why we're here. I'm sorry we're so late. I was, uh, out of commission when your brother's package hit the police station—"

"He almost died," Cramer and Kryzinski said in concert; then Ellery took over. "He'd let you blame him completely, if we didn't say it. He was still in the hospital when your brother's message and evidence arrived. He's not even cleared to go back to work yet. But Kryzinski here came across the paperwork, and we got back from vacation this morning, and Jackson said we had to try tonight."

"Try what?" Kelly asked, bewildered. "Why are *you* here?" He looked apologetically at Jackson. "Besides being your boyfriend, which, let me say, is pretty cool and a mark in your favor."

Kryzinski stood up. "Kid, let me tell the story. Those two talk over each other and get muddled, which is funny because Cramer's one of the best lawyers I've ever seen. He's here to represent you and Mr. Arnold, but I don't think that's going to be necessary. Two weeks ago—when Jackson was still in the hospital—the police department got this. Does anybody recognize it?" He held up an open bubble mailer with Rivers's name written in black sharpie on the front.

To Kelly's surprise, Agnes spoke up. "That's my handwriting. That's the packet Matty had me mail for him before...." Her voice dropped. "Before he died."

Kryzinski nodded. "Did you know what was in it, sweetheart?"

Agnes shook her head. "He typed for a long time, and then he had me go fetch… well, his box. Like a metal box? The kind you keep documents in? It was one of the few things he had when we moved him in, remember, Mom?"

Linda nodded. "Yeah. We just looked through it before the funeral to see if he had any assets to help pay for expenses."

He hadn't, but Seth had covered it. Kelly was starting to wonder exactly how much Seth actually made.

"So," Kryzinski prompted, "he got something from the metal box and…?"

"Well, he had me leave the room, and then he sealed the envelope and asked me to address it. He looked up the address of the police station—homicide division, Jackson Rivers—and then told me to send it in." She frowned. "There was something heavy in it, when he was done. I remember that. It… you could feel it, sliding around."

Kryzinski nodded. "Thanks, sweetheart. That's good to know, all of it. Now…." He grimaced. "Do we have to?" he asked Rivers and Cramer.

"I'll do it," Cramer said softly. "Seth? Seth Arnold?"

Seth nodded soberly.

"I'm going to ask you about a night in May, about eight and a half years ago—do you remember what happened then?"

"I was attacked," Kelly blurted, not wanting that other night to be mentioned. With a defense attorney and a detective in the room, all sorts of things, bad things, could—

"Not that night, baby," Seth said softly. "We may want to ask the girls to leave—"

"No," Lily and Lulu said in concert.

"Are you kidding me?" Agnes asked, nose wrinkled. "You guys, mooncalfing over each other for years, all that tragic, 'Seth can't come home!' shit going on, and you think we're gonna leave the room *now*? The only reason I'd leave the room is to make popcorn, but that's Kelly's spaghetti sauce on the stove, and I'm holding out for that." She waved her hand. "Go on, Seth. Tell the man a story."

Seth smiled at her, slowly. "God, you look so much like Kelly. It's not even fair." His smile died, and he stood up, probably so he could wander.

"See, Kelly had been attacked two days before. And he was so… scared. Those moments in that awful place, with Castor—it had him terrified. And I had to leave, you know? Dad and I, we'd agreed. I had to go to Bridgford. I'd be leaving him alone. So I went out that night, and I was going to find him, and I was going to warn him off."

"Castor Durant?" Rivers clarified.

"Yeah. I just wanted him… to stay away. He'd hurt Kelly. I needed him not to do anything like that again. He was getting high, out in the old field. And I… I was so mad. He laughed at me, and I kicked him, and… we fought. Bad. I didn't know what I was doing."

He came out of his trance for a minute. "I can fight better now, but that night, I was all fury, you know?"

Everybody nodded, and he went on.

"Anyway, he was on top of me, and… and he was winning. He was gonna kill me. He had his hand on my throat, and he was reaching for something on his belt, and my vision went black."

He swallowed, and that eerie self-possession he'd had since the three men arrived on their doorstep disappeared. "When I came to again, he was… dead. His throat had been cut, and he was on top of me, and I was covered in blood."

Kelly stood and grabbed his hand, shaking.

"You didn't kill Castor Durant," he said. And saying it out loud, when he knew it was the truth, did exactly what Seth said it would.

It set him free.

"I thought I did," Seth told him soberly. "For eight and a half years, I thought I did."

"What…?" Craig Arnold's voice was broken. "I thought you did too. Oh God, son. What… what changed your mind?"

"Matty," Seth said, looking at Rivers. "He told me what he wrote you. Do you want me to say it?"

Rivers nodded. "I think everybody here needs to hear it."

"You were right," Seth said to Kelly. "At the ocean, when you said what you thought happened. You were right. Matty didn't mean to sic Durant on us."

"Durant was bullying him," Kelly said. "Every day."

"Yeah. And then Matty got high and let it slip, like you thought. About us. That we were together. And they went after you that night, and Matty—he felt like shit. So I was going to warn Castor Durant to stay away from your family, and so was Matty. But Matty left just a little later. By the time he got to the field, Castor was reaching for his knife, and I was almost dead. Castor didn't even look behind him, and Matty grabbed the knife out of his hand and…."

Seth's face screwed up, tightened.

"And he slit Durant's throat," Kelly finished, thinking, *Of course. Of course. Oh God. Matty. My brother. What did you do?*

"Yeah," Rivers said from the couch. "The thing in the bubble mailer? That your sister sent? That was the murder weapon, the one we couldn't find. It was covered in Durant's blood. Kryzinski here had it tested after he opened the mailer. Matty told the same story you did, but he confessed. To everything. And he sent us the knife, with his prints and his blood—because his hand slipped on the knife—and with Durant's. He said he was dying. He wanted Seth here to not have to worry anymore. Said he'd been unable to come home, not for any length of time, because he'd been afraid he'd be charged with murder."

Kelly framed Seth's face with his trembling hands. "You couldn't kill anybody," he said softly. "I always knew. I always knew—"

Behind them, Craig burst into hard, barking sobs.

"Dad?" Seth said, capturing Kelly's hand but turning toward his father. Linda followed, burying her head in Craig's neck. Seth took an unsteady step toward them, and they were suddenly both up and out of the chair, holding him, making him the center when he'd been the outsider for so long.

"Oh God. Seth… my son. All that you'd been through, and I never knew—"

"Oh, baby," Linda said, kissing his temple hard. "You've been so alone."

They surrounded him, crying, holding him, and Kelly was glad. He'd had counselors and family, telling him he'd be okay.

Seth had Kelly, and the string of their love that they'd clung to so tightly it had sometimes cut their hands.

THE PARENTS eventually calmed down, sinking back onto the chair where Craig held Kelly's mom so hard, Kelly was surprised she could breathe.

"Is that all?" Kelly asked, holding Seth's hand again as Seth sat on the arm of his chair. In the back bedroom, X-man let out a whimper, and

Kelly gave thanks to Lily, who'd given up her seat at the show to give him a bottle and settle him down.

She came back in as he thought about what had just transpired, her arms empty, Xavier in the porta crib near Kelly's old bed, probably. Lulu was feeding Chloe a sandwich at the table, her eyes focused on the people in the living room as if she had to take a test on them in the morning.

"We would like to make an announcement in the press clearing up the case," Kryzinski said. "So Seth is no longer under suspicion. Someone will probably want to interview you, Seth—"

"No," Seth said, looking around. "Can't Isela come back and take the children away?"

"Isela Cruz was killed by Tim Owens, in August," Rivers said, surprising them all badly.

"The Dirty/Pretty killer?" Craig asked. Well, he did love his detective shows, and had a penchant for true crime. When that sort of thing popped up in his hometown, he would pay attention—but victim's names weren't always released immediately.

"Yes." Jackson breathed out slowly, and Kelly remembered him saying he'd been in the hospital. It had been big news—he'd taken out the Dirty/Pretty killer, with Ellery Cramer at his side. Damn.

"She can't ask for the kids back," Cramer said softly, and Kelly wondered that nobody in the room even tried to grieve. Whatever her separate griefs, the Cruz family hadn't known her, and she hadn't been part of them. "And that's another reason I'm here," Cramer continued, and away with Isela, unlamented—not even her father had bothered to tell them she'd died. "I don't do family court, but I have connections who do. Matty said in his letter that he wanted to make sure nobody could take the children away from Kelly and Seth. He seemed to think you'd be together for a while?" He tried to smile hopefully, but he just managed to look skeptical.

"We're getting married," Kelly said defiantly. "After Christmas. Before he goes back to New York to get us a house."

Rivers grinned. "The full-scale happy—I'm impressed."

Cramer rolled his eyes. "Sure, you are." He turned back to Kelly and Seth. "I can hook you up with someone who can make the adoption final before you leave the state. You're both… really damned young. Are you sure you want this?"

Seth gave his dreamy boy smile. "Well, you know. Being a fugitive ages you."

Kelly buried his face against Seth's side and laughed.

THEY EVENTUALLY left, after giving Seth and Kelly a number of cards, including Rivers's personal phone number, in case the press got too rough. But by the time they were gone, the entire family sagged with exhaustion.

The girls brought spaghetti—a little overcooked—out to them as they sat on the couch, on the chairs, and ate, and Agnes got Chloe to bed with minimal fuss.

Somewhere in the drained silence, Linda said, "A wedding after Christmas?"

"Yeah, Mommy. Do you approve?"

"Of course, baby. Isn't tomorrow your birthday?"

"Yeah."

"Happy birthday, son. Is it everything you wanted?" She smiled, almost playfully.

"Best birthday ever," Kelly vowed. "He's all I ever dreamed of. I swear."

Seth looked at him, his eyes crinkling at the corners. "You know, we still need to see France."

Kelly laughed softly.

New dreams.

The world lay at their feet.

Just as soon as they finished their spaghetti.

THAT NIGHT, lying in Seth's old bed where they'd been sleeping, they talked softly, making plans for the future. Sometime, about an hour in, Seth stopped talking and started kissing the back of Kelly's neck, his ears, his shoulders.

Kelly left off talking about the future and concentrated on the now.

Right now, the man of his dreams was making love to him, and they were free as birds, free as sound, ascending the heavens, holding each other close in their hearts.

The song of their love was like Seth's music.

It would forever make the angels cry.

AMY LANE lives in a crumbling crapmansion with a couple of growing children, a passel of furbabies, and a bemused spouse. She's been nominated for a RITA, has won honorable mention for an Indiefab, and has a couple of Rainbow Awards to her name. She also has too damned much yarn, a penchant for action-adventure movies, and a need to know that somewhere in all the pain is a story of Wuv, Twu Wuv, which she continues to believe in to this day! She writes fantasy, urban fantasy, and gay romance—and if you accidentally make eye contact, she'll bore you to tears with why those three genres go together. She'll also tell you that sacrifices, large and small, are worth the urge to write.

Website: www.greenshill.com
Blog: www.writerslane.blogspot.com
Email: amylane@greenshill.com
Facebook: www.facebook.com/amy.lane.167
Twitter: @amymaclane

Choose your Lane to love!

Orange

Amy's Dark Contemporary Romance

Guess who's swimming in the same pond...

FISH
OUT OF
WATER

Amy Lane

Fish Out of Water: Book One

PI Jackson Rivers grew up on the mean streets of Del Paso Heights—and he doesn't trust cops, even though he was one. When the man he thinks of as his brother is accused of killing a police officer in an obviously doctored crime, Jackson will move heaven and earth to keep Kaden and his family safe.

Defense attorney Ellery Cramer grew up with the proverbial silver spoon in his mouth, but that hasn't stopped him from crushing on street-smart, swaggering Jackson Rivers for the past six years. But when Jackson asks for his help defending Kaden Cameron, Ellery is out of his depth—and not just with guarded, prickly Jackson. Kaden wasn't just framed, he was framed by crooked cops, and the conspiracy goes higher than Ellery dares reach—and deep into Jackson's troubled past.

Both men are soon enmeshed in the mystery of who killed the cop in the minimart, and engaged in a race against time to clear Kaden's name. But when the mystery is solved and the bullets stop flying, they'll have to deal with their personal complications… and an attraction that's spiraled out of control.

www.dreamspinnerpress.com

There's blood in the water and death in the air...

RED FISH,
DEAD
FISH

Amy Lane

Fish Out of Water: Book Two

They must work together to stop a psychopath—and save each other.

Two months ago Jackson Rivers got shot while trying to save Ellery Cramer's life. Not only is Jackson still suffering from his wounds, the triggerman remains at large—and the body count is mounting.

Jackson and Ellery have been trying to track down Tim Owens since Jackson got out of the hospital, but Owens's time as a member of the department makes the DA reluctant to turn over any stones. When Owens starts going after people Jackson knows, Ellery's instincts hit red alert. Hurt in a scuffle with drug-dealing squatters and trying damned hard not to grieve for a childhood spent in hell, Jackson is weak and vulnerable when Owens strikes.

Jackson gets away, but the fallout from the encounter might kill him. It's not doing Ellery any favors either. When a police detective is abducted—and Jackson and Ellery hold the key to finding her—Ellery finds out exactly what he's made of. He's not the corporate shark who believes in winning at all costs; he's the frightened lover trying to keep the man he cares for from self-destructing in his own valor.

www.dreamspinnerpress.com

Getting out alive is going to take help from...

A FEW GOOD FISH

Amy Lane

Fish Out of Water: Book Three

A tomcat, a psychopath, and a psychic walk into the desert to rescue the men they love…. Can everybody make it out with their skin intact?

PI Jackson Rivers and Defense Attorney Ellery Cramer have barely recovered from last November, when stopping a serial killer nearly destroyed Jackson in both body and spirit.

But their previous investigation poked a new danger with a stick, forcing Jackson and Ellery to leave town so they can meet the snake in its den.

Jackson Rivers grew up with the mean streets as a classroom and he learned a long time ago not to give a damn about his own life. But he gets a whole new education when the enemy takes Ellery. The man who pulled his shattered pieces from darkness and stitched them back together again is in trouble, and Jackson's only chance to save him rests in the hands of fragile allies he barely knows.

It's going to take a little bit of luck to get these Few Good Fish out alive!

www.dreamspinnerpress.com

Racing
for the
Sun

AMY LANE

"I'll do anything."

Staff Sergeant Jasper "Ace" Atchison takes one look at Private Sonny Daye and knows that every word on paper about him is pure, unadulterated bullshit. But Sonny is desperate, and although Ace isn't going to take him up on his offer of "anything," that doesn't mean he isn't tempted.

Instead, Ace takes Sonny under his wing, protecting him when they're in the service and making plans with him when they get out. Together, they're going to own a garage and build race cars and make their fortune hurtling faster than light across the desert. Together, they're going to rewrite the past, make Sonny Daye a whole and happy person, and put the ghosts in Ace's heart to rest.

But not even Sonny can build a car fast enough to escape the ghosts of the past. When Sonny's ghosts drive them down and run their plans off the road, Ace finds out exactly what he's made of. Maybe Sonny was the one to promise Ace anything, but there is nothing under the sun Ace won't do to keep Sonny safe from harm.

www.dreamspinnerpress.com

Hiding the Moon

AMY LANE

Fish Out of Water: Book Four
A Fish Out of Water/Racing for the Sun Crossover

Can a hitman and a psychic negotiate a relationship while all hell breaks loose?

The world might not know who Lee Burton is, but it needs his black ops division and the work they do to keep it safe. Burton's spent his life following orders—until he sees a kill jacket on Ernie Caulfield. Ernie isn't a typical target, and something is very wrong with Burton's chain of command.

Ernie's life may seem adrift, but his every action helps to shelter his mind from the psychic storm raging within. When Burton shows up to save him from assassins and club bunnies, Ernie seizes his hand and doesn't look back. Burton is Ernie's best bet in a tumultuous world, and after one day together, he's pretty sure Burton knows Ernie is his destiny as well.

But when Burton refused Ernie's contract, he kicked an entire piranha tank of bad guys, and Burton can't rest until he takes down the rogue military unit that would try to kill a spacey psychic. Ernie's in love with Burton and Burton's confused as hell by Ernie—but Ernie's not changing his mind and Burton can't stay away. Psychics, assassins, and bad guys—throw them into the desert with a forbidden love affair and what could possibly go wrong?

www.dreamspinnerpress.com

AMY LANE

CHASE IN

SHADOW

Johnnies: Book One

Chase Summers: Golden boy. Beautiful girlfriend, good friends, and a promising future.

Nobody knows the real Chase.

Chase Summers has a razor blade to his wrist and the smell of his lover's goodbye clinging to his skin. He has a door in his heart so frightening he'd rather die than open it, and the lies he's used to block it shut are thinning with every forbidden touch. Chase has spent his entire life unraveling, and his decision to set his sexuality free in secret has only torn his mind apart faster.

Chase has one chance for true love and salvation. He may have met Tommy Halloran in the world of gay-for-pay—where the number of lovers doesn't matter as long as the come-shot's good—but if he wants the healing that Tommy's love has to offer, he'll need the courage to leave the shadows for the sunlight. That may be too much to ask from a man who's spent his entire life hiding his true self. Chase knows all too well that the only things thriving in a heart's darkness are the bitter personal demons that love to watch us bleed.

www.dreamspinnerpress.com